THRESHOLD

THRESHOLD

BEN MEZRICH

WARNER BOOKS

A Time Warner Company

WARNER BOOKS EDITION

Cover design and illustration by Tony Greco

This Warner Books Edition is published by arrangement with HarperCollins Publishers, Inc., 10 East 53rd Street, New York, NY 10022.

Warner Books, Inc.
1271 Avenue of the Americas
New York, NY 10020

Visit our Web site at
http://pathfinder.com/twep

Ⓦ A Time Warner Company

Printed in the United States of America

First Warner Books Printing: May, 1997

10 9 8 7 6 5 4 3 2 1

To my mother and father,
who believed I could do it

ACKNOWLEDGMENTS

FIRST, I'D LIKE TO EXPRESS MY GREAT SENSE OF LOSS AT THE recent passing of my agent, Jay Garon. His enthusiasm and faith in me kept me writing at a time when it would have been very easy to give up. He will be greatly missed.

I'm deeply indebted to Dr. Jack McConnell, who generously lent his time and brilliance. Dr. McConnell introduced me to the science of genetics, and gave me the basic idea behind the killer gene. Throughout the writing of *Threshold,* he has been an invaluable source of information and inspiration.

I'm likewise immensely grateful to my editor, Rick Horgan, who saw *Threshold* through a number of rewrites and helped turn the raw material of my writing into a real live novel. Simply put, I'm a better writer because of him.

Also, enormous thanks go to Simon Lipskar, an astute reader whose insights and suggestions helped wrest *Threshold* from a primal state of amateurism, turning it into something I could share with pride.

At Harvard Medical School, I owe special thanks to Saumya Das and Or Gozani for providing the scientific background and texture for a number of scenes. Also at Harvard, I'm grateful to Katrin Chua, Manish Shah, Jim Morrill and Erik Finger.

Thanks also to Scott Stossel, and to my brothers, Josh and Jon Mezrich, for their enthusiasm and support. Special thanks to Airié Dekidjiev for her intelligent comments and suggestions. Also, a special thank-you to those at Garon-Brooke who continued my representation after Jay's passing.

I'm especially grateful to Joanne Chang for listening, for putting up with a writer's ego and a writer's hours, and for her enduring belief in me. She's been there from the beginning, and I couldn't have done this without her.

And finally, I'm grateful to my parents for teaching me to chase after my dreams. This novel is as much their accomplishment as it is my own.

Threshold is not meant to disparage, in any way, the importance and benefit of the Human Genome Project. I truly believe that that endeavor overshadows everything else in the history of science, and I have the utmost respect for the men and women who've dedicated their lives to its pursuit.

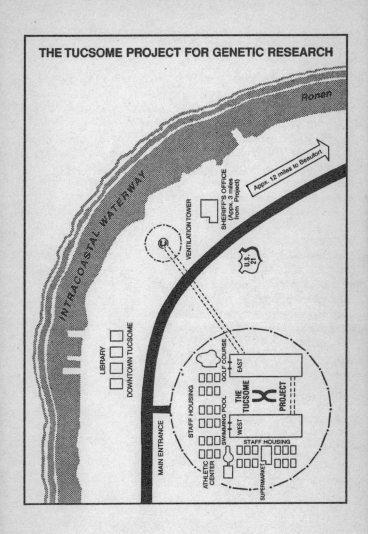

PROLOGUE

S ECRETARY OF D EFENSE W ARREN T. W ALKER GRUNTED AP-
provingly as a thunderous applause swirled through the sea
of black gowns and tasseled hats. Finally, they were getting
the show on the road. It was time for his address.

Next to him an aide fumbled with a locked metallic briefcase. The combination had thirteen digits, and the young
man, who himself looked barely old enough to graduate, was
struggling to align the numbers, sweat running in glistening
beads down the sides of his face.

"Are you going to get it today?" Walker whispered, mock-
gruff. "Or should we ask them to postpone the graduation?"

The aide worked furiously. Finally, he jimmied the briefcase open and retrieved a stack of nine white pages.

"Here you are, sir."

Walker pulled his hands out from under his robe. As he
did, he noticed that the fingers of his left hand were trembling. *Must be the heat.* He rubbed his hand against his leg.
Still, the fingers trembled.

1

The aide continued holding the stack of paper. "Are you feeling all right, sir?"

"I've felt better," Walker conceded. He winked. "But, then, I've felt a whole lot worse too."

The former army brigadier general chided himself. There was a time when it took much more than ninety-degree heat to get Warren T. Walker's attention. In '68, he'd taken a bullet in his gut and still led his platoon through sixteen miles of Vietcong territory. During the Grenada action, a freak accident had sent his chopper into the sea, breaking his collarbone and forcing him to cling to the wreckage for two days. "Indestructible," they'd called him. Now here he was getting all woozy over a rise in the mercury.

The aide thrust the pages into Walker's hand. "Give 'em hell, sir."

The secretary nodded and waited for his cue.

As he rose to the podium, Walker reflected on the speech's importance. The department's publicity people had been instructed to get the word out: "Be prepared for something big." As a result, a much larger than usual contingent of press was in attendance, ready to record what he had to say. Walker's status as a likely contender in the next presidential election only added to the hoopla.

As he waited for the noise of a standing ovation to die down, he said a silent prayer that his speech would not fall on deaf ears.

"Morning," he began, his voice gruff and familiar. "As you know, I'm not a man of many words. I've never liked 'em, and frankly, I think there are way too many of 'em floating around already. I was never much of a student—got into Princeton because of football, got through Princeton because of football. Words never did me any good. But I'm here today to say something that needs to be said."

He paused to scratch his upper lip and noticed that the fingers of his left had were still trembling. He cursed silently, clamping his fingers into a fist. Then he flipped the first page over, quickly skimming for his place in the text.

"When I was a graduating senior here at Princeton," he continued, "American foreign policy was pretty straightforward. We were the world's policeman. Anybody got out of line, we stomped 'em. Even with all the noise 'bout Vietnam, you can't argue that we weren't doing what we thought had to be done. Communists, Leninists, Fascists—you name it, it was our duty as Americans to step in. Because that's what cops do. They keep the peace by stompin' on the bad guys."

Again, his fingers moved to his upper lip, scratching at a spot directly below his nose. He detachedly wondered why—his lip didn't itch; in fact, it felt perfectly fine. He moved his hand back to the podium and continued with his speech.

"But times have changed. Methods that used to work—however noble, clever, and effective—don't seem justifiable anymore. Maybe it's because the bad guys aren't what they used to be. We used to have the Evil Empire, Red China, before that the Nazis, the Japanese; now it's little warlords and religious madmen, it's psychopaths in the desert and tribal nuts with AK-47s."

There was a murmur of laughter in the audience. He took the opportunity to scratch at his left cheek, both hands working at the same time. Again he noticed that his cheek didn't actually itch; his hands seemed to be moving on their own accord. He shrugged and ignored them. When the laughter died down, he moved his hands back to the podium.

"Ladies and gents," he went on, "it's time for us to ask ourselves an important question. Why are we sending our young men and women overseas when there's so much to do right here, right at home? Maybe it's time for America to turn inward, to stop pouring money and men into the defense of foreign soil. Maybe it's time for the cop to put down his badge—"

Suddenly, his left hand was pulling at his lower lip. The motion was abrupt and obvious. People in the front row of the audience sat up in their seats.

He quickly jerked his hand away from his face—but then

it was back again, his fingers tugging at his mouth. His other hand began to scratch at his left cheek.

A low murmur swept through the audience. He forced his hands away from his face and tried desperately to continue.

"Maybe it's time for the cop to put down his badge. As secretary of defense—"

The fingers of his left hand grabbed on to his upper lip. His other hand took hold of a fleshy piece of his cheek. Pain shot through his face. His eyes went round with shock and horror as he suddenly realized that he couldn't control his fingers.

A scream erupted from the audience, and people leapt to their feet. Hands grabbed at Walker from both sides. He watched in numb terror as his convulsing body fought back. The fingers of his right hand had a firm grip on his cheek, and pain erupted as the skin threatened to tear open. Finally, someone got him by the wrist and pulled his hand down, pinning it to his side.

"Get an ambulance!"

"Christ, what's wrong with him?"

"I said, get a fucking ambulance!"

The screams multiplied as the secretary was half carried, half shoved off of the stage. Someone bumped into him from behind, and his left hand broke free. It spasmed toward his eyes, grabbing hold of an eyelid. *My God, not my eye! What the hell is happening to me!*

In a minute he was strapped to a stretcher, three medics restraining his arms as they fought against the stiff leather straps. He could hear helicopter rotors in the distance.

"Just stay calm, Secretary. We'll get you to Robert Wood in a few minutes—"

"Dear God, what's wrong with me?"

"You're going to be all right," said a voice from the left. "Just lie still—"

"Why can't I control my hands?"

There was no answer. The medics didn't know—he could feel it in their silence. They'd never seen anything like this before: a grown man tearing at his own face, trying to mutilate himself, conscious of his actions but unable to control them.

"Secretary," asked one of the medics in a whisper, "are you on any—uh—medications?"

"Nothing," Walker gasped, not having the strength to feel indignant. "I—" A sudden spasm tore through his body as his arms convulsed forward. Something snapped in his left wrist, and the pain was unbearable. He screamed.

There was a sharp pinch at his right arm and then the pressure of a hypodermic entering his flesh. Just before he lost consciousness, he heard one of the medics whisper:

"Christ, I'm gonna have nightmares for weeks. He's the secretary of defense, for God's sake."

The voice swirled out of range and Walker was left alone with his clouded thoughts. His body had betrayed him. His hands, always so strong, had turned against him. And what about his speech? What about those nine pages of oversized type that he thought had a chance of finally making a difference?

He imagined the pages swept up by the wind, sticking in clumps to old Nassau Hall. Sooner or later, they'd be discovered and peeled off, perhaps by eager reporters.

Lying there, he wondered if one day they'd find their way into the newspapers.

1

STEEL WHEELS SLID ACROSS SHINY LINOLEUM TILES, KICKING up a fine mist of blood and soapsuds. At the front of the room the huge double doors swung like flaps of canvas in a strong wind—just as one stretcher cleared their arc, two took its place. In some places the stretchers were seven thick, queued up for a chrome parade. Already the room was bursting at the seams, and it still seemed like the entire city was waiting outside.

A bystander might have assumed that this was the aftermath of some sort of catastrophe—perhaps an earthquake, or a hurricane. But at New York City Hospital's emergency room, this was just another Friday night.

Jeremy Ross stood at the edge of the chaos, his hands jammed into the loose pockets of his blue-green scrubs. As he watched the swirl of doctors and patients, a mixture of joy and frustration rose inside of him. His strong young features glowed under the high-intensity fluorescent lights, and his entire body strained forward.

This was what he loved. The thrill of the front line, of medicine at its most frenetic. Standing with his back against a sweating white wall, listening to the shouts and the screams, watching the EMS teams and the nurses and the doctors, he felt truly alive. Every nerve in his body burned with anticipation.

For the moment, though, his face remained confident and cool. At twenty-four, he couldn't afford to show any signs of impatience.

"Look alive," a passing nurse called out to him. "Here comes Frankie."

Jeremy followed the nurse's eyes and caught sight of the chief resident. Franklin Gordon—"Frankie" to anyone with the guts or seniority—would have been an intimidating figure even without his rank. His huge, square body cut through the chaos at full pace, his white coat flapping behind him. He stopped in front of a stretcher a few feet away, his thick shoulders hunching together as he bent between a pair of nurses. A second later he looked up, signaling Jeremy with a flick of his brown eyes. Jeremy rushed to his side.

Frankie was starting a difficult intubation, his fingers fighting to work a plastic oxygen tube past the patient's swollen vocal cords. The man's body jerked up and down as the pair of nurses struggled to hold him still. Jeremy added his weight to the battle, pinning the man's shoulders against the stretcher.

"When it rains it pours," Frankie grunted as he slid the tube down the man's throat. "You holding up, Ross?"

Frankie was never much on words. Jeremy kept his attention focused on the convulsing patient. "Doing fine. The place is really jumping tonight."

"You ain't seen nothing yet," Frankie said as he pushed the oxygen tube the last few inches into the patient's lungs. "I just got off the phone with central dispatch. A DC-9 went down at Kennedy. We're talking twenty ambulances. Maybe forty, fifty stretchers."

Jeremy watched as the patient settled back against the

stretcher, lungs filling with oxygen. Then he glanced at Frankie, searching for an appropriate response.

"Going to get a bit crowded, huh."

Frankie smirked, taping the intubation tube in place. "Yeah, you could say that. We've been a mile past capacity since lunchtime. The local 'Knife and Gun Club' met early this weekend."

Jeremy nodded, glancing around the ER. The walls were lined with kids sporting .22-caliber bullet wounds and open gashes from razor blades, knives, sharpened belt buckles, and whatever else happened to be in vogue that time of year.

"Not to mention that out-of-control concert downtown," Frankie continued, stepping away from the stabilized patient and ripping off his rubber gloves. "Listen, you feel like getting your hands dirty?"

Jeremy looked at him. "How dirty?"

Frankie's lips turned up at the corner. Just then, another stretcher wheeled to a stop in front of the chief resident's knees and he grabbed a new pair of rubber gloves from a nearby cart.

"This place is going to explode in a few minutes," he said, hurriedly pulling the gloves tight over his fingers. "We've got to get every available intern into ICU to handle the DC-9. So who does that leave in charge of the ER?"

"Me?" Jeremy asked, trying for a neutral voice.

"Ten, maybe fifteen minutes. Just until things get settled in ICU. Anything big comes in, you call me. No heroics. Think you can handle it?"

Jeremy had never heard of a fourth-year medical student—let alone one twenty-four years old—being put in charge of a big-city ER. Did he really want this opportunity to screw up?

"Sure, why not?"

The chief resident grinned, then quickly bent over the stretcher at his knees to assess the patient's condition. Breathing? Good. Heartbeat? Good. Stable. Ready to "turf"—pass on to the next guy, in this case some overworked resident up in surgery. He ripped off his rubber gloves and tossed them toward the floor.

"All right, kid, it's your ER. But get this—the patients don't care how many articles you've published, or where you graduated from, or how fast you got your Ph.D. And they certainly don't give a fuck about your class rank. So keep your head straight and try not to screw up."

Jeremy watched Frankie move off, his square form bouncing from stretcher to stretcher. Every nurse he passed threw a backward glance in Jeremy's direction—facial expressions running in spectrum between disbelief and admiration. Word was spreading; finally, Jeremy was off the sidelines.

His chest filled with pride as he watched the chief resident disappear through the double doors at the far end of the ER. Then, suddenly, the sound of sirens drowned out everything; the ambulances were pulling right up to the side entrance, spitting their cargo directly into the hallway that ran into the ICU. Panicked shouts melded with the squeal of stretchers, and Jeremy's heart rose into his throat as he stared at the double doors, imagining what the scene looked like on the other side. Jet-fuel burns, impact contusions, pieces of a DC-9 embedded in flesh and bone . . .

"Ross!"

The sudden shout caught him by surprise. *A crisis already?* He pulled his attention away from the double doors and turned to see a team of EMS men crash through the back of the ER. Two nurses were running with the stretcher, their hands furiously working on the patient.

"Ross! Come on! Fucking code blue over here!"

Mike Callahan, three years older than Jeremy and his best friend, was at the foot of the stretcher. His scrubs were sodden with sweat, and his thick shock of red hair was matted down over his ears. It was immediately obvious that he was in way over his head.

"Oh man," Callahan spat, his words blurring together. "This guy is fucked! Cardiac arrest! He was on the basketball court—"

"Take it easy," Jeremy said, whirling back toward the open ER. He shouted, "We've got a code over here! Anesthesiologist, stat! Defibrillator, chem cart, EKG team, OR prep team! C'mon, let's move it."

He turned back to the stretcher, bent down.

"Wait a minute," Jeremy said. "Don't I recognize this guy?"

"Sure do," Callahan answered in a rush. "Elron Finney, starting guard for the Knicks."

Oh, Christ. A cardiac arrest celebrity—every ER doctor's nightmare. Okay, Jeremy told himself, this is why Frankie put you in charge. His mind sprinted through the possibilities.

"Cardiomyopathy?" he tried.

Callahan shrugged. "Maybe."

Jeremy grimaced, diving in for a closer look. The patient was huge and black, lying completely motionless in the center of the stretcher. His pants had already been cut off by the EMS men, and his shirt had been torn in half, hanging in tatters around his overdeveloped shoulders. Wires ran from his chest to an EKG monitor off to the left, where a steady green line split the screen in half. A nurse had a football bag over the patient's mouth, manually pumping his lungs. Another nurse, a heavyset woman with too much hair, was administering CPR, using her entire body against the man's chest. Jeremy could tell immediately that her rhythm was good. But the man on the stretcher wasn't responding; the green line on the EKG screen reverberated with the force of the CPR, but otherwise remained as still as a dead man's heart.

Shit.

This didn't look good. The man was dying. Fast. Jeremy pushed the nurse doing CPR out of the way and hurled himself halfway up onto the stretcher. He smashed his fist down into the center of the patient's chest. Nothing. He tried again. Still nothing.

"Damn it," he cursed, resuming CPR. "Have we tried chem stimulation?"

"Epinephrine," Callahan shouted from across the stretcher, "and dopamine. No effect. Should we defibrillate?"

He didn't see any other choice. If Elron's heart didn't start in the next few seconds, his brain would die.

"Defibrillator! Now!"

A nurse wheeled the defibrillator over and Jeremy grabbed the two metal contact points, sliding them onto his hands. He rubbed the two contacts together.

"All right. Two hundred joules! Clear!"

Everyone took a step back from the stretcher. Jeremy slammed the two contacts onto Finney's bare chest and used his thumbs to unleash the juice.

There was a loud thud, and Finney's body rose a few inches off of the stretcher. Then he crashed back down. Jeremy spun to look at the EKG screen.

Nothing.

"Fuck," he murmured, rubbing the contacts together again.

"He's not going to make it," Callahan mumbled. "It's been too long."

"Shut up, Mike!"

Jeremy raised the contacts, feeling them tingle against his hands.

"Three hundred joules! Clear!"

Again, everyone took a step back. This time, Finney's body lifted a full half a foot into the air. When he crashed back down, the stretcher squealed in metallic pain. The sound reverberated through the ER.

"Hold on a minute," a nurse shouted from behind Jeremy. "We're getting something. We're getting something!"

Jeremy twisted his head to the side. The green line had tiny bumps in it. Not great, but definitely a start. He ripped off the defibrillator contacts and leaned over. "Resuming CPR! Mike, give him another blast of epinephrine."

Jeremy could feel the man's shocked muscles beneath his fingers, tight and warm. One-one-thousand, two-one-thousand, three-one-thousand . . . "Anything?" he shouted, his voice cracking with the physical strain of the CPR.

"No, not yet."

"Come on," he pleaded through clenched teeth, his hands pressing harder and harder. "Come on, don't you fucking die on me."

Suddenly, a nurse shouted at him from the other side of the stretcher. "Got a beat! Steady, steady. Yes, it's beating all right!"

Jeremy looked up, sweat pouring down his face. His smile was so wide it hurt. The EKG screen looked like Colorado in the summer, filled edge to edge with bright green mountains.

He took a step back, rubbing the sweat out of his eyes, and felt a surge of relief and pride.

And then, suddenly, everyone was shouting at the same time.

"What the hell is it?"

"I'm getting no pressure!" Callahan responded, his face sheet white.

Jeremy stared at him. "What?"

"Zero goddamn blood pressure! We're losing him!"

Jeremy rushed around the stretcher and grabbed the blood-pressure gauge out of Callahan's hands.

Callahan was right. Finney had no blood pressure. His heart was pumping, but the muscles around his heart weren't letting the blood flow through his veins.

"I don't get it," Jeremy said, thinking out loud. "Normal EKG, no pressure—"

"What about a tumor?" Callahan asked.

Jeremy shook his head. "Odds are a hundred to one against a mass large enough to cause a cardiac arrest."

"Well, then how about myo—"

"Myocardial infarct, pericardial tamponade—both would show up on the EKG."

Callahan swallowed, his Adam's apple bobbing up and down. "What else could it be?"

Jeremy's eyes roamed up and down the stretcher, searching for a miracle. Suddenly, his eyes stopped, and a thought glimmered. He leaned forward, squinting at a series of yellow and green spots running up and down Finney's legs.

"Mike, you see those spots?"

Callahan looked up from across the stretcher, nodding. "Bruises. He's a basketball player—"

"Not, not from basketball," Jeremy said in a rush. "Those are subcutaneous lesions."

Callahan raised an eyebrow. "So?"

"Hemochromatosis."

Callahan's jaw dropped. Only a few dozen people in the country could have made a diagnosis like that. Most of them were genetic specialists with years of training.

"Are you sure?"

Jeremy nodded. Genetics had been his obsession since he'd first learned about DNA. When he looked at Elron Finney, he didn't just see a body on a stretcher. He saw an infinity of microscopic cells, each one carrying the same three-billion base pair chemical sequence—the human genome. And somewhere in that sequence lay the source of Finney's problems.

"He needs a transplant."

Callahan stared at him in disbelief. "You got a spare heart handy, Ross? You know he hasn't got that kind of time."

Jeremy forced calm into his voice. "We have to help him *wait*. We have to get a balloon pump into his heart and keep it going externally until we can roll him into the OR."

Callahan looked incredulous. "What? I've never heard of a procedure like that."

"It's a cardiology technique. It will work."

"Have you done one before?" Callahan asked suspiciously.

Jeremy made no effort to hide the sheen that had broken out on his forehead. "I've *seen* one done."

"Ross, tell me you're kidding."

Jeremy didn't respond. The truth was, he hadn't really even seen one done—he'd only read about the procedure in the textbooks. But there wasn't any choice; the patient would die if his blood pressure didn't rise in the next few minutes.

Jeremy twisted back toward the stretcher. His corner of the ER had gone silent. Callahan and the nurses were watching him, waiting to see what he was going to do. He tried his best to appear deadpan.

"We're going to go with the Seldinger technique," he said, loud enough so that all the nurses could hear. "We're going to insert a catheter through the femoral artery and up into his heart. Then we'll inflate a balloon pump to get his pressure going. Everyone with me?"

The nurses were quiet, but the looks on their faces showed hesitation. Jeremy matched their eyes, his outward confidence overcoming their apprehension.

He swung around the stretcher, getting himself into position. Then he reached down and angled the patient so that the groin was fully displayed. One of the nurses swabbed the area with Betadine and alcohol.

Jeremy breathed in deeply, tasting the tension in the air. He heard the equipment before he saw it, more steel wheels scraping against the linoleum tiles. A nurse handed him a long, hollow needle. He held it over the patient's groin, breathing hard, sweat dripping down into his eyes.

Then he focused and jabbed the needle into the crease at the top of the patient's thigh, the inguinal line. He pushed down with a flick of his wrist.

"Watch the bone," Callahan said, coughing.

Jeremy nodded. He felt the skin give, felt the needle work through the stiff muscle. A few seconds later he paused. "Okay, looks like I'm there."

He could hear Callahan's labored breathing from across the stretcher, and imagined the fear his friend was feeling. Regardless of the circumstances, two fourth-year medical students shouldn't have been putting a balloon pump into a celebrity's heart. The pressure was intense, and Callahan was feeling every ounce of it.

Jeremy, though, had gone absolutely cool. Somehow, he'd entered a zone of total control.

He pulled back on the needle, removing the hard solid core, the trocar. Suddenly, a spurt of dark blood sprayed out around the needle and spattered his chest, painting a rosy cauliflower in the center of his scrubs. "Got the artery!" he shouted, excited. "Christ, she's a bleeder!"

"That's what they do," Callahan grunted. "Nice shot, Ross."

"Okay, pass me the wire."

Callahan passed a long, thin wire across the stretcher, and Jeremy inserted it into the end of the needle. He worked quickly as the blood continued to spray. Slowly, carefully, he extended the wire deep into the patient's artery. Inch by inch, the wire disappeared into the hole in the man's groin.

"How far—" Callahan started to ask.

Jeremy answered from memory. "A few feet. I want to stop just before it goes into the heart."

"Christ," Callahan murmured.

Jeremy ignored him, his eyes intent on the wire. A few second later his fingers paused.

"We're there. Give me the catheter."

Callahan handed him a hollow plastic tube split into several channels, with a collapsed rubbery balloon attached to one end. Jeremy passed the catheter over the wire, watching as it vanished deep into the patient.

In a few seconds the balloon was in place. He took a deep breath, surveying his work. It looked pretty good. Just like the picture in the textbooks. He cleared his throat.

"Here we go," he said. "Wheel the pump over here."

Two nurses wheeled the pump cart up against the stretcher. He attached the exposed end of the catheter to a lead on the front of the machine, twisting the plastic tube to make sure it was tight against the cold metal. Then he moved his fingers to a plastic switch at the top of the machine.

"Ready or not," he said quietly.

He flicked the switch, and a rush of air pushed through the catheter.

"Is it working?" Callahan asked, unable to control himself.

Jeremy carefully made his way to the blood-pressure gauge. He was almost afraid to look.

"Well?" Callahan shouted.

The numbers were perfect. One-twenty over seventy.

The emotions that rushed through Jeremy's chest had no equivalent. He stared down at the man on the stretcher—a victim of his genes, and a miracle of modern science.

Callahan came around the stretcher and put his arm around Jeremy's shoulders. "You're amazing, Ross. A regular machine. And I'm going to ride your coattails all the way to the top."

Jeremy laughed, still staring at the patient. The entire episode, from the moment Finney had been wheeled into the ER to the moment Callahan put his arm around Jeremy's shoulders, had taken a total of six minutes. Six minutes that would give Finney a second life.

"Incredible," Jeremy murmured.

Callahan squeezed his shoulder. "The technology gets better every day."

Jeremy shrugged; he wasn't thinking about the balloon pump. He was thinking about how much he'd changed. How far he'd come, to be able to stand in this room, staring down at a man whose life he'd just saved. Six years ago, plunked down in a high-pressure situation like this, he would have been curled up in a corner somewhere, overwhelmed by it all. Now he was running the place.

His thoughts were suddenly interrupted by a nudge from Callahan. *Not another crisis?*

"Ross, looks like this is your lucky day."

"What are you talking about?"

Callahan pointed across the emergency room. "That gorgeous female over there says she's looking for you."

What Jeremy saw nearly sent him reeling.

2

SHE WAS STANDING BY THE FAR WALL, HALF TURNED TOWARD THE door. Tall and slim shouldered with a deep tan and stylishly short auburn hair, the young woman seemed dressed for an expensive New York evening. The flaps of a velvety black designer dress shimmied up and down her angled form, revealing a hint of dark stockings, long legs, and glossy high heels. And a necklace of shiny white pearls embraced the smooth skin of her throat.

"Robin Kelly?" Jeremy whispered, not quite able to believe it. The last time he'd seen her, they'd been seniors at Dartmouth.

Jeremy halved the distance between them in five steps, all the while trying to think of an appropriate greeting. What do you say to someone you haven't spoken to in five years—except in your fantasies?

"Robin," he called out, sidestepping two stretchers. "Over here."

She looked up, seeing him for the first time. Her face brightened, and an anxious smile played across her lips.

"Hi," she said, a little embarrassed. "I—I could come back . . . I mean, I can see you're busy. They told me at the front desk that I could find you here, but I didn't realize it would be so hectic."

"No, I'm not busy . . . that is, I certainly have time for you." He made no effort to conceal his pleasure. "I can't believe you're here."

She blushed. "Yeah, and at one o'clock in the morning no less. Great time to drop by." She nervously fingered her pearls. "You see, there was this awards dinner in midtown. I'd hoped to break away earlier, but the speaker ran long and I've got business meetings lined up for most of the day tomorrow, and then I'm heading back to Washington—" She halted. "I'm sorry, I'm babbling. It's just that this is the only time I could see you so I decided to take a chance."

Something about her manner struck him as odd. It was more than the awkwardness of meeting an old lover. She seemed on edge, almost desperate.

"Hey, is everything all right? If you'd called, I could have gotten someone to cover for me."

She shook her head, her fingers still working the string of pearls. "I didn't decide to come to New York until this afternoon. I tried reaching you at your apartment, but you must have already left for the hospital."

"Well, it's sure—"

He was interrupted midsentence by a stretcher skidding to a stop in front of his feet. An overworked nurse tossed a surgical tray at him and pointed:

"Sorry, Ross. Slow bleeder, came in hopped up to the eyes. Sew him up quick—we need the stretcher."

He bent down to examine the patient and exhaled in frustration. *Great, the guy has a knife wound—no sticking a Band-Aid on this one.* And with his luck, there were six more just like him lined up outside.

"Robin—"

"I know," she said, "you're too busy for me right now.

Maybe I can come back in a few hours? I never sleep when I travel, anyway."

He shook his head, distracted by the patient in front of him. The jagged wound was in the left quadrant of the man's chest, just above the nipple. No sign of puncture, just streams of dark blood running in rivulets down the man's pale skin.

"My shift goes right on through to morning," he said to her. "I know you said your schedule's packed tomorrow, but is there any way you could fit me in? I've got most of the day free."

She hesitated, glancing around the crowded ER. "Actually, my schedule isn't the only reason I came to see you tonight. I need to ask a favor—and tomorrow may be too late."

He was immediately on guard. Was she in some sort of trouble? What kind of favor couldn't wait until morning?

"Things will probably settle down in a couple of hours," he said hopefully. "I'll be able to take a quick break—maybe ten minutes. Will that be enough?"

An expression of relief broke across her face. Whatever it was she wanted, it was obviously important.

"My hotel is all the way across town. Is there somewhere nearby I can wait for you?"

"There's a cafeteria on the first floor," he said, turning his attention back to the crescent knife wound. "Stick to the coffee. I'll be there as soon as I can get away."

She nodded and headed for the door.

He tried not to follow her with his eyes, or to let his mind drift to the decision they'd made years before—to go their separate ways. Right now, the ER came first.

3

THE CAFETERIA WAS CROWDED FOR THREE IN THE MORNING, most of the long steel tables filled with agitated family members waiting for news from the airplane crash, mixed in with a smattering of doctors, nurses, orderlies, and lab technicians. Jeremy entered through the back entrance and paused for a moment by the wall, catching his breath. His legs ached and his head felt fuzzy, his brain still sifting through the stream of patients he'd seen over the past two hours: two MIs, three knifings, a collapsed lung, a woman who'd been bitten by her daughter's pet snake, two broken hips, and a near drowning— not to mention the NBA all-star now lying in intensive care. It had been a long night, and it was only half over.

But first, Robin. He ran a hand through his sweat-soaked hair, searching the tables with his eyes. He spotted her near the front of the room, her hands on her lap, a Styrofoam cup on the table in front of her. As he started in her direction, he again noticed how nervous she seemed. She was hunched forward, her forehead creased by worry lines.

The Robin he'd known in college had never seemed fragile. She wasn't a worrier—in fact, just the opposite. She was the type who relished risks, who prided herself on her toughness.

What the hell's going on? Jeremy wondered. He quickened his pace and dropped abruptly into the plastic chair across from her.

"Hi," she said, "sorry about sandbagging you like this. Is everything under control in the emergency room?"

He waved his hand. "The rush slowed to a trickle a half hour ago. I've got my beeper with me if anything big comes in. Or they can page me over the hospital intercom. I'll be okay for a few minutes."

She nodded, taking a careful sip from her coffee. "I'd never seen an emergency room before. It was just like on TV. Frantic . . . people on stretchers everywhere. And when do you sleep?"

He laughed. "That's a question people in the medical profession get used to. I slept three hours yesterday afternoon. I'll get a few more after my shift."

"And that's enough?"

He shrugged. No use bitching about something he couldn't change—especially when there were more interesting things to talk about. He shifted gears.

"So you're in New York on business? Still corporate law, right?"

"Tax," she corrected, taking another sip from her coffee.

He nodded; in truth, he knew all about her skyrocketing legal career. He kept a copy of the *Washington Post* article, "D.C.'s Rising Legal Stars," in his dresser.

"Are you in town for a conference?"

"The annual Women's Bar Association symposium—at least, that's what my expense report will say. Actually, I came to see you."

He was surprised by the emotions that welled up in him. "Don't get me wrong, Robin. But it's been five years. I'd assumed—" He stopped midsentence, noticing that her expression had changed..

"It's important, Jeremy. You're the only one I could think of who might be able to help."

He sat up in his chair, his training kicking in. "Are you okay? Do you have a medical problem?"

"It's nothing like that. I'm researching something, and I need to ask a favor."

He settled back down, relieved that she was healthy but even more curious about her agitation.

"What's the research topic?"

She hesitated before answering. "It's . . . Warren T. Walker."

"The secretary of defense?"

"You know anything about him?"

He shrugged, drumming his fingers against the table. "Well, I saw what everyone else saw—the show at Princeton. The guy tried to rip his face off in front of a few thousand people. CNN said it was some sort of grand mal seizure."

She lowered her eyes, and there was suddenly an edge to her voice. "The newspapers said it was anaphylactic shock. A sudden, overwhelming allergic reaction."

"Could have been. But why the interest in a dead secretary of defense? You were never much into politics—at least not when I knew you. Why do you care what killed him?"

She looked away. As she did, the strength seemed to leak out of her shoulders, and her entire body sagged.

"Robin?"

"I care what killed him," she said finally, "because he was my father."

Jeremy's ears rang as Robin continued her story. He tried to concentrate on her voice, but he could feel a mounting pressure building beneath his temples. She was dredging up deeply buried memories in his own psyche—ones that had nothing to do with college.

"Kelly was my mother's maiden name," she continued, her voice fragile, wavering. "I borrowed it after the divorce—I guess I was ashamed of my father, of the way he'd treated my mother those last few years of their marriage. It wasn't just the affairs; it was the fact that he wasn't making any effort to cover them up. He was famous and powerful and he just tossed Mom aside—at least, that's how it seemed to me."

Jeremy shifted his eyes downward, watching how she clutched her cup of coffee like it was a life preserver. He suddenly felt awkward; it had been years since college, and she was opening up to him like it was the morning after they'd first made love. Once, a long time ago, he'd opened up to her in a similar way—but how could she trust him so thoroughly after so much time had passed?

"When the marriage fell apart," she pushed on, "I wanted to erase my father from my life. It wasn't such a hard thing to do—after all, he was secretary of defense. He had his life, Mom and I had ours, it was as simple as that. Then Mom died."

"That must have been awful for you," he said, genuine sympathy in his voice. "How long ago did it happen?"

"Six months after we graduated from Dartmouth. I was struggling through my first year at Georgetown law and Mom was my support system. When she died, I thought I was going to have to drop out of school. I didn't think I could handle it alone. It turns out I didn't have to."

"Your father?"

She nodded, running a hand through her cropped hair. "A week after the funeral, he called me on the phone. It was a pretty terrible conversation, lots of crying and shouting. I said some horrible things. For some reason, he didn't hang up. Instead, he talked me into having dinner with him."

A heavy feeling rose in Jeremy's throat. More memories swelled inside him. He swallowed, trying to keep his attention focused on Robin's voice.

"After that," she continued, "things got better between us.

He talked me through three years of law school without ever asking me to forgive him. And you know what? Pretty soon I was ready to forgive. But I never had the chance."

He felt her words in the pit of his stomach. He understood what she'd gone through—the unresolved feelings, the unexpressed emotions, the guilt. Although it had been twelve years since he'd lost his own father, he still carried the scars with him. Not a day went by that he didn't brush up against a memory of the hell he'd gone through, the trauma that had threatened to swallow his life.

"Robin, I'm so sorry. I know how much it hurts. I would have liked to have been there for you."

He reached across the table and squeezed her hand. His skin tingled at the touch, and he was startled by the sensation. He'd assumed that the time apart would have dulled his attraction to her. He tried to look into her eyes, to see if she felt it too, but found the task impossible—like dancing with a shadow.

"I almost called you when it happened," she said, staring at their clasped hands. "But I was afraid."

"Afraid? Of what?"

She shrugged. "We made a decision to go our separate ways. And you said it yourself, we let ourselves drift apart. I didn't know if anything was left between us."

He nodded, understanding. Over the past five years, he'd often regretted the decision they'd made. But at the time, they hadn't had much of a choice. He'd been accepted to New York City Medical School, one of the youngest matriculants ever. And she, equally young, had put down her deposit at Georgetown. Were two precocious nineteen-year-olds supposed to rearrange their lives because of a two-week fling?

"Well," he finally said, "I'm glad you came to see me now."

"I am too. I've thought about you a lot since my father's death. I knew you'd understand."

"Robin—"

Suddenly, a booming voice erupted across the cafeteria, cutting him off: "Ross!"

Jeremy felt the hair on the back of his neck rising up as he turned in his chair. Frankie was standing by the cafeteria door, his arms crossed against his chest. His scrubs were dark with sweat and blood, and his eyes were narrow, angry.

"Might I have a word with you?" the chief resident asked, obviously fighting to control his temper. "When you're finished, *of course*."

Jeremy swallowed, nodding. No doubt Frankie had just found out about Elron Finney. The fourth-year medical student who'd performed a rarely attempted procedure on Finney was going to catch hell for taking things into his own hands—and from the look on Frankie's face, it was going to be one blistering ass-kicking.

But in the end, Jeremy was sure that his logic would prevail. There hadn't been time to beep Frankie. And if Frankie had taken over, Finney would have died of an undiagnosed genetic flaw. Jeremy sighed, turning back to Robin. "My boss," he said. "I have to go." He rose, slowly.

She watched him, a sudden rush of fear springing into her cheeks. "Jeremy, the favor I wanted to ask you . . ."

He paused.

"I was hoping that you could get a look at my father's autopsy report," she said, leaning forward and lowering her voice. "I want to get your opinion on the cause of his death. A lot of what I've read in the newspapers has been confusing, and I need to know the truth."

He rubbed his hands against his scrubs. "Where did they do the autopsy?"

"Robert Wood, in New Jersey. The report was sealed pending the government's investigation, so I never had a chance to see it. And according to a friend of mine in the State Department, the report is going to be completely unavailable as of nine tomorrow morning. Both the CIA and the FBI are going to be conducting their own investigations—so you understand why I had to see you tonight."

He scratched his jaw, thinking. He had a feeling that obtaining a copy of the report would be a futile exercise—he wasn't going to spot anything that the experienced pathologists at Robert Wood had missed. But he could tell from the look in her eyes that this was important to her. Perhaps she was still in a phase of denial, searching for some answer that would make her father's death easier to accept. He wanted to help, but he certainly didn't want to get her hopes up.

"I don't know, Robin. I'm sure some of the best doctors in the world worked him over at Wood."

"Isn't it possible that they missed something? My father was in excellent health. There was no warning at all. And the way he died—it was so horrible. It had to be something more than a freak allergic reaction. Couldn't you please take a look at the report?"

There was a brief silence, and his eyes broke away. Her tone was insistent, almost pleading. Was there something else going on here? He remembered how nervous she'd seemed when he'd first spotted her; did her anxiety have something to do with the autopsy report?

Finally, he gave a shrug. He wanted to press the matter—but he could feel Frankie's eyes digging into the small of his back.

"Okay, I'll try my best," he assured her. "But if I do get a-hold of the records, where can I find you?"

She pushed herself to her feet and touched his arm. "I'll be attending the WBA conference until late tomorrow afternoon. It's being held at the Park Plaza—the Grand Ballroom, I think. Meet me there at five. I'll explain everything to you then, I promise."

She leaned forward, and her lips brushed against his cheek. Once again, he felt the tug of old emotions.

He watched as she broke away and hastened toward the door. Then his eyes caught Frankie's glare, and he shoved his hands into the pockets of his scrubs.

Time for one good old ass-kicking.

4

AN HOUR AFTER FRANKIE HAD FINALLY EXHAUSTED HIS REPERtoire of foul language—a tirade which, by the end, had transformed into a grudging recognition of Jeremy's lifesaving feat—Jeremy found himself moving rapidly through the hospital corridors, his mind refocused on Robin Kelly and the task ahead. He sped through a vacant operating room and into the radiology wing, willing exhaustion out of his overworked legs, then cut through a long hallway, counting doors until he found the rear equipment stairwell. He took the steps two at a time and didn't slow his pace until he reached the fifth floor.

The administrative wing of the hospital was quiet, as usual. He glanced up and down the hallway, searching for familiar faces. Thankfully, he saw none. He looked at his watch: four-fifteen. His ER shift was over for the morning, and he didn't have to be anywhere for hours. Plenty of time to find an autopsy report.

It took less than ten minutes to locate an empty office with the necessary paraphernalia. He gently shut the door behind him, careful to keep the sound from echoing down the dark hallway. Then he waited in the darkness for a full minute. Satisfied, he reached for the light switch.

Most of the room was taken up by a large oak desk, on top of which squatted his quarry: a brand-new IBM 80. He smiled at the sight—the computer had one of the fastest processors around and would make his job a little easier.

He quietly skirted the room and dropped into the leather chair behind the desk. Then he flicked on the IBM and began to punch keys. In a few minutes he'd accessed the computer's inboard modem, and he waited the necessary few seconds as it dialed a preprogrammed number.

"Say hello to the future," he mumbled, watching the screen change colors.

Since the late 1980s, most hospitals in the United States had gone "on-line." Patients' records, autopsy reports, insurance claims, billing information—everything that went on in a hospital—could be found documented on some computer board somewhere. The trick was to know where to look— and where to go for access.

A long beep signaled a successful link with New York City's network. The computer began to cycle through board options, and he quickly found the command for interhospital communication. He typed in the three-letter code for Robert Wood Hospital in New Jersey, "RWO."

Barely a second later, a glowing directory filled the screen. Down near the bottom was the word "pathology." He clicked twice, and a new directory filled the top half of the screen. His eyes settled on a single word near the top: "Autopsy." He positioned the cursor in front of the latter "A" and hit a key.

Green words flitted across the screen. "PLEASE ENTER SUFFICIENT ACCESS CODE."

He nodded; this was the first roadblock. He needed an access code that identified him as someone high up on the hospital's staff—preferably someone who'd have a reason for checking autopsy reports.

A single name came to mind: Frankie. As chief resident, his access code would certainly be sufficient authorization. He often followed patients through autopsy, just to see where his underlings had screwed up. If Jeremy could get Frankie's access code, he could get into the pathology files at Robert Wood.

He searched the oak desk for a phone. Then he dialed three numbers and smiled when a twangy female voice answered on the second ring.

"Technical support, Patty speaking."

"Hey Patty, how's the weather upstairs?"

There was a brief pause. "Jeremy? I haven't heard from you in ages. Don't tell me you crashed your system again."

He laughed. "Not this time. So they got you working the night shift, too, eh?"

"Ah, it's okay," she said. A tall redhead with an eager-to-please attitude, she'd helped him master the hospital's network almost a year ago. "There's less action than during the day. Helps me get caught up on my reading."

"Well, I've got a quick question for you, then you can get back to *War and Peace*. Frankie grabbed me in the hall a few minutes ago and asked me about a patient who came through the ER a few months back. Seems the patient got himself a lawyer and might be suing the hospital."

"What for?"

Jeremy shrugged. "That's the problem. Nobody knows. Nobody remembers what the guy came in for. Nobody remembers working on him. Frankie is spitting fire down here. He wants to see some paperwork, and he wants it yesterday."

He paused, pleased with his story. Lawsuits came and went daily, and patient records were lost all the time. So many patients came through the ER, doctors had a hard enough time remembering who they worked on the day before, let alone three months ago.

"So how can I help?" she asked.

This was going to be even easier than he'd thought. "I want to do a search of the billing records for the last three months. The problem is, I don't have the necessary access. Frankie wrote down his code for me, but I can't find it. It's been a rough night. Think you could give me a hint?"

"Sure."

She read him the numbers, and he memorized them as she spoke.

"Great. Thanks, Patty."

He quickly disconnected. Then he turned back to the computer and punched in Frankie's access code. A second later, the screen began to scroll. Thousands of names rushed by, blurring together in front of his eyes. Suddenly, he slapped the keyboard.

There it was. "WARREN T. WALKER, DECEASED, JUNE 13." He moved the cursor in front of the name. Then he asked the computer to fax him a copy of the report.

The computer hissed, and huge blue letters leapt across the screen. "AUTOPSY SEALED. AUTHORIZATION LEVEL SIX."

He cursed out loud. Level Six was the highest level of access; the only way to get at a Level-Six autopsy report was through Robert Wood's chief of pathology.

He racked his memory for a mental image. Dr. Sheldon Hatfield, rotund, bald, as angry a man as Jeremy had ever met. He'd sooner bite Jeremy's head off than authorize an after-hours inquiry. This was going to be difficult.

Difficult, but not impossible.

Again, he reached for the phone. This time, it took more than four rings before a gruff voice picked up: "Pathology, Robert Wood. Drew speaking."

Jeremy could picture Drew from his voice. Bleary-eyed, lanky, with one of those stringy goatees the hospital clerks were so fond of this season. Pissed at the world because it was four-fifteen in the morning and he was jammed in a basement, his only company a few dozen corpses.

"Hey, Drew," Jeremy said, trying to make his voice equally

as bitter. "This is Eddie Forest in path over at New York City. Boy, am I having a crappy night."

"Eddie who?"

"Forest. You know, trees and shit. Listen, I need your help and I need it ASAP. I'm trying to get at a Level-Six autopsy."

"Forest, you know the drill. Only Dr. Hatfield can authorize a Level Six."

"That's what I'm talking about. Hatfield's on his way up here right now. He phoned me from a medivac copter, and he needs the report in his hands the minute he touches down. So if you'll just work with me for a minute—"

"That's not procedure," Drew said, his tone stubborn. "I need Hatfield's personal okay."

"You're a brave man, Drew. Braver than me."

There was a pause on the other end of the line. "What do you mean?"

"When Hatfield gets here and the report's not waiting for him, he's gonna go apeshit. But hey, procedure's procedure, right? Nice talking to you—"

"Hold on a minute," Drew sputtered. "Let's not get crazy. What report are we talking about?"

Jeremy told him. He could hear Drew's computer whirring to life.

"I don't know," Drew finally mumbled. "This one's scheduled to be locked up tomorrow morning. Even Hatfield couldn't authorize it then."

"That's why he wants to get at it now," Jeremy ad-libbed. "While he still can. If we don't come through with it, and then it gets locked up . . . Christ, I can just imagine the steam coming out of Hatfield's ears. It wouldn't be pretty."

"You're right about that," Drew muttered, hitting keys. "Let me see what I can do."

"Skip the see. Go right to the do. And get it done fast, for both our sakes."

Jeremy slammed down the receiver, smiling. He'd spent enough time with the clerks at New York City to know how the game was played. Pass the buck until there's no one left to pass it—then grudgingly do the dirty work. He leaned close to the computer screen, waiting for something to happen. Barely a minute later, the huge blue letters disappeared.

"Come to papa," Jeremy whispered.

The processor winked three times. Then the screen filled with letters. Across the top was a glowing green banner: "WARREN T. WALKER, DECEASED, JUNE 13, PATHOLOGIST'S REPORT."

He smiled triumphantly. Damn, he was good. He hunched forward, excitedly skimming through the bright green words.

It took him less than a minute to realize that the screen in front of him was filled with absolute garbage.

Half of the tests that had been ordered by the pathologist were gratuitous and had nothing to do with the state of the patient upon death. The toxicology reports were incomplete, with dozens of important tests missing. The blood numbers were all mixed up, and large sections of the internal organ counts were blanked out. Even the parts of the report that were complete told a story of incompetence.

Jeremy's eyes widened. He couldn't believe that a pathologist had signed his name to such a sloppy report. Even the scrawled analysis at the bottom, the Final Anatomic Diagnosis, was full of flaws. "Primary reasons unexplained. Suspect possible anaphylactic shock. Or perhaps status epilepticus."

The blood values—those that had made their way into the report—ruled out anaphylactic shock or any sort of overwhelming allergic reaction. And epilepsy was simply out of the question; with no history of seizures and no brain lesions, it wasn't a credible diagnosis.

Obviously, the pathologist who'd performed the autopsy hadn't known what had killed Warren T. Walker. Robin had been right—anaphylactic shock had been a shot in the dark. Jeremy angrily searched the bottom of the report for the signature.

When he saw the name, his lips curled down at the corners.

Andrew Laskey.

Jeremy shook his head, amazed and disgusted at the same time. Laskey had worked in pathology at New York City until less than a year ago. He'd almost gotten his medical license revoked on three different occasions—finally, a sexual harassment claim had caught up with him, and to avoid litigation, he'd shifted over to Robert Wood.

How the hell had Andrew Laskey gotten himself assigned to one of the most important autopsies in recent history? Surely the other doctors at Robert Wood were knowledgeable about Laskey's flaws by now. It just didn't make sense.

Jeremy ran a hand through his hair as his mind flooded with more questions. Why hadn't the newspapers picked up on the horrendous autopsy report? Why hadn't there been an outcry within the medical community? Surely, someone else must have noticed that something was wrong.

Or was that necessarily true? The report had been sealed from the beginning. And even if a crafty reporter had gotten hold of a Level-Six authorization, would he have been able to tell an inaccurate autopsy from a good one?

And what about the medical community? Only a handful of doctors would have seen the report after Laskey. Certainly, Dr. Hatfield, the chief of pathology. Maybe someone from Walter Reed. Perhaps a few more doctors from Washington. Was it possible that this handful of pathologists had missed what seemed so obvious?

Unlikely . . . but possible. He rested his elbows on the desk, searching through the report one more time. When his eyes neared the bottom he paused and squinted.

One of the few things Laskey had done right was to order a viral workup. Near the bottom of the screen, under the heading "Microscopic Description," a small table listed the different types of viruses found in Walker's cells. All of the numbers seemed normal, except for a single figure in the table's right-hand corner.

According to the figure, the number of decayed retroviruses was abnormally large.

Jeremy rocked back in his chair, thinking. Retroviruses were a class of viruses that included some of the deadliest diseases known to man—AIDS, cancer, the list went on. Normally, a retrovirus count as high as the one in Walker's report would have pointed to a past history of some sort of rampant viral disease. But the rest of the report—if any of the lab numbers could be taken seriously—showed no sign of viral symptoms.

He rested his chin in his palm. He realized he was probably oversensitive to the existence of retroviruses; his Ph.D. thesis had been on a form of gene therapy that utilized a tailored version of the AIDS retrovirus to carry a foreign gene into a patient's cells. As part of his research, he'd spent months pumping the HIV retrovirus into a chimpanzee named Chester, studying how the retrovirus carried its genetic cargo from cell to cell. In the future, he'd hypothesized, doctors would use the same method to inject new genes into patients. The tailored HIV retrovirus, made harmless in the lab, would act as a vector, "infecting" a patient's body with a newly fashioned gene. An elegant form of genetic engineering, if scientists ever managed to work out the kinks.

To that end, he'd spent many long nights staring at his chimp's viral workups. And quite often he'd seen retrovirus counts as high as the one he was staring at in Walker's autopsy report. But the chimp had had a good reason to show such a high count. What was Walker's?

Jeremy pushed the question to the back of his mind and continued to search for something that might be helpful. A few seconds later, his eyes brightened. "Now *this* is interesting."

Underneath the viral table was a brief medical history, three lines of information that showed how remarkably healthy the old man had been. Walker had only checked into a hospital three times in his entire life. The first was in the midst of the Vietnam War; the second during the Grenada invasion; and the third was barely two years ago. He'd been treated for a bruised spleen after an automobile accident near Beaufort, South Carolina.

What piqued Jeremy's interest was the location of the hospital where Walker's spleen had been treated. The secretary hadn't been taken to the nearest medical facility, which would have been the local hospital in Beaufort. Instead, he'd been transported several miles north up the Carolina coast— to the Tucsome Project for Genetic Research.

Tucsome. The name itself sent a thrill down Jeremy's spine. The Tucsome Project was one of the top genetic research facilities in the world. The center had been founded by one of Jeremy's heroes, Dr. Jason Waters: the third man on the original genome team that had won Watson and Crick their Nobel Prize. Tucsome was at the forefront of the Human Genome Project, the government-funded effort aimed at sequencing and understanding all the genes in the human genome.

Why take Walker to Tucsome?

He reread the entry in Walker's medical history. The secretary had been treated there by a doctor named Matthew Aronson. The patient had been released three hours later with no serious complications.

Of course, a bruised spleen couldn't possibly have had anything to do with the way Walker had died. Still, it seemed like something worth checking into. Maybe the defense secretary had inadvertently picked up something at the center that had stuck with him. After all, Jeremy wasn't the only scientist who'd done work with viruses. A place like Tucsome was probably crawling with potential biohazards. He glanced at his watch. Four-thirty. Plenty of time for a long-distance phone call.

"Matthew Aronson," he said as he reached for the phone, "give me something I can use."

5

EIGHT HUNDRED MILES AWAY, DEPUTY FELIX PORTNEY STARED through the bulletproof windshield of a parked police cruiser. The interstate ahead of him was awash in flashing blue lights, the towering dunes on either side shivering as high-powered police spots sliced through the gray dawn.

As he took in the scene, the corners of his lips drifted downward, a grimace embedded by time and too many tragedies. He could see the pickup truck about thirty yards ahead, skewed toward the beach, its front tires covered in sand. A half dozen troopers milled about, bagging evidence, brushing for prints, collecting and reconstructing the scattered, shattered seconds of the dreadful event. Behind the troopers, he could make out the ambulance, and next to it, the coroner's van. He couldn't see the bodies—but he didn't have to. The coroner's van told him everything he needed to know.

Slowly, he pushed open the cruiser door and stepped out onto the interstate. Airborne whirlpools of sand danced around his high leather boots as he moved forward, his hands jammed into the pockets of his state-issued gray slacks. He stopped a half dozen yards from the pickup truck, his blue eyes shifting back and forth. A 1987 Chevy, oversized grill, sky blue. The kind of truck you saw a thousand times a day on these South Carolina interstates. He took a step closer, breathing deep. There was a strong of scent of whiskey in the air.

"Ain't a pretty story, Deputy."

A potbellied trooper came around the front of the pickup, a plastic bag in his hands. Portney could see the remains of a broken bottle of Jack Daniel's through the bag. He gave the trooper a cursory nod, then moved along the side of the pickup.

The driver's side door was wide open. Portney stuck his head inside, careful not to touch anything. The stench of whiskey was almost overwhelming, and there were shards of broken glass sprinkled across the tattered polyester seats. He stepped back from the door, shaking his head.

"Doesn't leave much to the imagination," he mumbled.

The trooper came up behind his elbow. "Two bottles, maybe three. One of 'em shattered under the dashboard, the other two a couple of yards down the interstate."

Portney pressed his lips together. Three bottles of whiskey. Almost seemed like overkill. Guy drinks three bottles of whiskey, gets behind the wheel of an oversized pickup, can't help but hit somebody. Even on a deserted stretch of interstate. Portney rubbed at his eyes with the palms of his hands. "And the victims?"

"Husband and wife," the trooper said, repeating what Portney already knew from the police band. "Hit 'em dead-on. Fifty, sixty miles per hours."

Portney turned his head and spat toward the nearest dune. "Didn't have a chance?"

The trooper shrugged. "Wife bit it on contact. The coroner says the husband held on a few minutes longer."

"We got an ID on 'em?"

The trooper nodded. "Husband was one of them scientists. From the Project."

Portney's gaze drifted downward. There were white trickles of sand beneath his boots. In a few hours, a beach-patrol street sweeper would make the twelve-mile trip north from Beaufort and undo the attempt at erosion; but for the moment, the tiny grains continued their steady creep.

"Guess I should go check 'em out," he sighed.

The trooper touched Portney's elbow. "We'll have a trace on the license plate in a few minutes—"

"Ain't necessary," Portney said, moving forward. "It's Billy Masters's truck. Picked him up DWI two, three times this year already. His trailer's 'bout six miles down U.S. 21. Take a couple of boys. An' go easy on him. He ain't gonna be in no condition to put up a fight."

The trooper disappeared, and Portney slid around the front of the truck, pausing a few feet down the white sand. There was a single dent in the front grill of the Chevy, waist high. An image struck him: that of a man and woman standing together, holding hands. He shook his head, a tired look in his eyes. Three bottles of whiskey, and Billy had managed to hit them dead-on. A deserted patch of interstate, nothing for ten miles in either direction, and Billy had hit them dead-on. Pretty remarkable for a guy who had never hit anything he'd aimed at in his sorry, pathetic life.

And the couple must have been awfully immersed to let a weaving truck sneak up on them like that.

Portney bit down on his lower lip and continued down the interstate, his stomach churning.

The woman was sprawled twenty feet in front of the dented pickup, her body jackknifed against the side of a dune. The coroner was squatting between two paramedics, pulling a thick black bag over the dead woman's legs.

"Mornin', Deputy," the coroner said without looking up. "She sure was a pretty one. Good hair. Nice figure. If it wasn't fer the blood, hell, I'd call 'er beautiful."

Portney held the back of his hand over his lips. A surge of

nausea moved through him, then thankfully disappeared. He turned away from the dead woman and headed toward the second body.

The young man was five yards away, flat on his back, his hands straight at his sides and his face pallid and specked with blood. His eyes were wide open, staring at nothing. Two troopers stood at his feet, chatting, seemingly oblivious to the body in front of them. Portney lowered himself to one knee, spreading his long shadow across the dead man's cheeks.

As the deputy stared at the man's face, a question formed in his mind. The wide-open eyes, the pallid skin, the open lips—the dead man looked terrified. As if something he'd seen had scared the hell out of him.

Strange. According to the coroner, the man had died a few minutes after the pickup had hit him. Had he lain there in the sand, staring at nothing, remembering the pickup bearing down on him? Or had the terror been provoked by something else? Something closer to the moment of death?

Portney sighed, rising to his feet. In the end, it didn't matter. He knew with absolute certainty that the troopers would find Billy Masters passed out in his trailer, lying in a pool of whiskey. The forensic evidence would come in, and there would be no question: just another drunk-driving accident. In Tucsome, that was how these things always worked out. No matter how deep you dug, you'd find yourself staring back at the obvious: a drunk driver. A dented pickup. Two dead bodies.

An open-and-shut case.

6

"FULL TRAUMA, CRACKED SPINE, BROKEN NECK. PRONOUNCED dead at the scene. The wife, too. A drunk driver. A lot of people here are pretty upset."

The phone weighed heavy against his ear as Jeremy listened to the faraway voice. It was a hard thing to comprehend.

He'd called the Tucsome Project from the office on the fifth floor and had asked to speak to Matthew Aronson. The operator said Aronson wasn't due at the hospital until five-thirty and to try back in an hour. After shutting down the IBM 80, he'd gone down to the doctor's lounge and tackled some paperwork he'd been putting off. Then, at a pay phone just outside the hospital gym, he'd dialed the number again and had immediately been transferred to an out-of-breath ER attendant.

Aronson's lifeless body had been brought to the hospital only minutes before. The doctor and his young wife had been run over by a drunk driver on an interstate just miles from their home in South Carolina. Aronson was barely twenty-eight years old.

Jeremy slowly hung up the phone. He'd seen dozens of people die in his four years of medical school, but still, the shock of what had just occurred took his breath away. He shivered, running his hands down his gray shorts.

"You okay?"

Jeremy looked up. Mike Callahan was leaning against the door to the locker room, two squash rackets slung over his right shoulder. Jeremy nodded, still thinking about Aronson and his wife.

"Yeah, sure. Fine."

"Then let's get this over with."

The midmorning squash game was a ritual, an anchor in the chaos that was their fourth year of medical school. For nearly a hundred straight mornings, Jeremy and Mike had met at the school gym for an hour of pure combat. No matter how tired they were, no matter how many hours they'd just spent on call, the squash game was a constant. Sleep could wait, but the competition was a stubborn symbol of their friendship.

"I don't know why I look forward to this," Callahan said as he led Jeremy into a hall lined with small wooden doors. "I must be some sort of a masochist."

Normally the comment would have made Jeremy smile—he'd won thirty-seven straight matches and enjoyed seeing his cocksure friend humbled—but this morning his expression stayed somber. "You never know," Jeremy said. "Today might be your lucky day. I've got a lot on my mind."

Callahan laughed. "Could it have something to do with that young lady who visited our emergency room last night?"

Jeremy spun his squash racket and followed Mike through one of the short wooden doors. The squash court, a twenty-by-twenty cube with stained white walls and high ceiling, shimmered with the smell of effort and sweat.

"She *is* something, isn't she? We dated at Dartmouth."

Callahan let out a low whistle. "I didn't think you had it in you, guy. So why'd she drop in? Looking to rekindle the old flame?"

Jeremy sighed, tossing his racket from palm to palm. He considered telling Callahan the truth—Warren Walker, the autopsy report, Matthew Aronson—but decided that there wasn't any point.

"Not exactly. She's in town for a conference. Just stopped by to rehash old times."

"In the cafeteria? You dog!"

Jeremy threw him a disapproving glance. Then he held out his hand for the ball. Callahan tossed him the hard black sphere. Jeremy squeezed it, feeling the muscles in his forearm contract. He squared his wide shoulders, facing the wall.

Then his shoulders began to droop.

"Come on," Callahan said, "we don't have all day."

Jeremy hit the ball in a lazy arc. It barely touched the back wall and dribbled down to the floor.

Callahan guffawed. "What the hell was that?"

Jeremy sighed. His mind wasn't on the squash game. He was thinking about Matthew Aronson, dead at twenty-eight. Four years of college, four years of medical school, a position at the top research institute in the country—all of it obliterated by a drunk driver. The scene struck a chord; Jeremy knew how fragile life could be, how quickly things could change.

He himself had been lucky—his own life had gone from being a total disaster to an enviable success. For nearly six years after his father's death, he'd lived as an invalid, suffering from debilitating panic attacks that had paralyzed him at the slightest hint of tension. The countless psychiatrists he'd seen during those years had given him many names for it. One in particular had stuck with him: panic-anxiety syndrome. A psychological disease, his personal response to pressure. He'd tried everything: therapy, chemicals, hypnosis. Nothing had helped.

But then at age eighteen, a miracle had happened. The fear had disappeared. His life had changed, dramatically. Now, he was four weeks from graduating at the top of his med school class—and it seemed that even Robin Kelly was once again within his grasp.

Which brought him back to the problem at hand: Aronson's death was, literally, a dead end.

"Mike," Jeremy asked, bending to recover the squash ball, "what do you know about the Tucsome Project for Genetic Research?"

Callahan raised his eyebrows. "The Tucsome Project? Why?"

"No reason, really. I just heard the name recently."

"Well, I know what I've read in the journals. It's huge, maybe the biggest predominantly private research institution in the world. It was started by Jason Waters a few years after Watson and Crick got the Nobel."

Jeremy tossed the squash ball into the air and slammed it at the back wall. Callahan dove for it, his voice cracking with the effort.

"Couple of years ago a friend of mine went to work there. Sent me a few E-mails. But I think he was just fucking with me, pulling my leg. Because most of the stuff he told me I find pretty hard to believe."

Jeremy crashed against a wall, using his wrist to whip the ball into the far corner. "What do you mean? What did he say?"

"He said"—Callahan huffed, swiping at the ball with an underhand flick of his racket—"that the place was paved in gold. That the walls dripped money, that Tucsome was like nothing he'd ever seen before. He said that nations fight and die for the kind of money that Tucsome uses to clean its toilets."

Callahan smashed the ball against the front wall. Jeremy dove for it, missing by a fraction of an inch. The ball rolled harmlessly into the far corner of the court.

"Well," Jeremy mumbled, dejectedly moving toward the missed ball, "there's a lot of money in genetics. It's not surprising that your buddy got a little carried away."

"Carried away is a major understatement. He was overwhelmed. Tucsome offered him a quarter of a million dollars for a two-year employment contract. They told him that if he stuck with them, he'd be a multimillionaire before the age of thirty."

Jeremy paused, his mouth ajar. A quarter of a million dollars? The highest offer he'd received was somewhere in the area of sixty thousand—and that was from a private medical group, not a research institution. Scientific research simply didn't pay the kind of money that other specialties did. A quarter of a million dollars? That sounded more like a surgeon's compensation than a geneticist's salary.

"Are you shitting me?"

"A quarter of a million dollars for two years."

"That's amazing. So how does he like it there?"

Callahan held out his hand for the ball. Jeremy tossed it to him, still waiting for his answer. Callahan threw the ball in the air, then swung his racket in a low, careful arc. "He didn't accept the offer."

Jeremy nearly tripped over himself. The ball whizzed by his ear, unharmed. He barely even noticed it. He was too busy staring at Callahan.

"Sorry?"

"He turned them down."

"My God, why?"

Callahan shrugged. "I don't know, exactly. But he flat-out turned them down. Now he's at UCLA, doing cancer research. He makes twenty-six thousand and drives a fucking Toyota. Makes no sense to me. But I guess some people are just born stupid. Oh, by the way, that last point was mine. For once, I do believe I'm winning."

Jeremy grunted, his mind still on Tucsome. What would make a man turn down a quarter of a million dollars? From the literature he'd read, Tucsome was miles ahead of UCLA. And Jason Waters—who would give up an opportunity to work with Waters? He'd practically invented genetics. The fact that he hadn't received the Nobel Prize along with Watson and Crick was one of the biggest surprises in scientific history.

In the end, the issue was irrelevant; Tucsome wasn't going to give Jeremy any insight into Warren Walker's death. If the defense secretary had somehow contracted something at Tucsome, Jeremy wasn't going to find an easy link. He'd gone as far as he could go. Now it was Robin's turn to provide some answers.

The thought of seeing her again cheered him. When the ball came his way, he swung as hard as he could. The shot ricocheted off the front wall with such force that it took Callahan's racket right out of his hand.

Stunned, Callahan stared at him.

Jeremy grinned. "Sorry, Mike. Thirty-eight's my lucky number."

7

THE PARK PLAZA ROSE ABOVE FIFTH AVENUE LIKE SOME PREHIS-toric creature, casting stone shadows across the limousines that lay prostrate at its feet. Jeremy made his way toward the lavish marble entrance, weaving through an army of uniformed bell caps. As he pressed his palm against the revolving glass door that led to the opulent lobby, he felt a vague discomfort. He supposed it was his humble farmboy origins, but there was one aspect of New York he'd always found off-putting.

Wealth. Especially the kind that advertised itself.

New York was a city of extremes, and the Plaza repre-sented the outermost edge of the spectrum. Even though he was eight years away from the farm, in these environs he still felt like a complete stranger. Back in Iowa, he'd lived in sparse rooms, eating whatever his mother and he could coax from the ground, and the suit he'd worn to his high-school graduation had been three sizes too big, borrowed from his father's cobwebbed closet. The habit of "making a little go far" was ingrained in him.

Certainly there were no huge chandeliers like the one that glittered up above. An extravagant tangle of crystal triangles and flickering bulbs, its soft radiance played off crimson drapes that dripped from the detailed ceilings and ran down the marble walls. A bell cap pointed him in the direction of the Grand Ballroom, and he maneuvered past men in black tuxedos and women in low-cut, summertime gowns, trying not to gawk.

He skirted the lobby café, his nose tasting the sharp scents of animals not meant to be eaten: spider-crab bisque, squab under glass, calf-brain soufflé. Reaching a gilded bank of elevators, he opted instead for a lush stairway that spiraled in a regal arc toward the meeting rooms one floor above.

From the looks of the second-floor foyer, the WBA conference had just broken up. Groups of smartly attired women clustered around the Grand Ballroom entrance, immersed in a last-minute exchange of business cards and hearty farewells. Jeremy smiled. *One hell of a place to make an off-color lawyer joke.* He stepped inside the ballroom's threshold.

"Jeremy. Over here."

He looked to see Robin separating herself from a particularly large group, gently using her leather briefcase to clear a path. In fact, there was no missing her. Her dress, a satiny red with modest hem, did a fabulous job of showing off her figure, while a gold necklace slept in the crevice between her perfect, round breasts. Not exactly corporate—but she made it work. She brushed through the crowd of dark suits and gave Jeremy's forearm a warm squeeze.

"You have good timing," she said. "Another minute and I would have needed a lawyer of my own. I've never seen so many self-important people in one room."

"This is a room?" he responded, taking in the lush carpets and ornate fixtures. "It looks like something out of a vampire movie."

"Not your style, huh," she said, smiling, then abruptly pointed with her briefcase. "Let's find a corner."

As she took Jeremy by the arm and led him forward, her perfume lingered behind, almost visible, like cartoon fingers from a Disney movie.

The crowd grew less dense as they worked away from the ballroom entrance. Finally, they found an unoccupied spot beneath at pair of huge antique windows. Fifth Avenue honked at them from below, and he could barely make out a corner of the park.

"This seems like a good spot," she said.

He nodded, cautious. There was something about the way she was acting that bothered him. The nervousness that he'd noticed at the hospital had amplified, now bordering on real fear. Every few seconds she threw a jittery glance at the crowd of lawyers a few yards away.

"Robin, what's going on?"

"You first. Tell me what you found."

All right, he thought, we'll do it your way—for now. "I checked the autopsy report. You were right—your father didn't die of an allergic reaction."

Her eyes brightened. "So you know what killed him?"

He shook his head. For a brief second, he considered telling her about the high number of retroviruses in her father's cells. But he quickly discarded the idea. The figure was probably an anomaly, a mistake; it wouldn't be scientific to invent a disease from one aberrant figure.

"I don't have a clue what killed him. And neither did the pathologist who handled the autopsy. It wasn't anaphylactic shock, but beyond that, your guess is as good as mine."

She lowered her head. There was a mild tremor in her voice. "So the autopsy was a waste of time."

"Well, there was one thing—did your father ever mention a place called Tucsome? It's a genetic research institute in South Carolina."

She shook her head. "Not that I can remember. Why do you ask?"

"It's a tenuous link, at best. Your father was treated there after a car accident a couple of years ago. I thought maybe you could tell me why he might have been hanging around Tucsome in the first place."

She paused, thinking. Then she lowered her voice. "That depends. Do you think Tucsome receives funding from the Defense Department?"

He raised his eyebrows. "I suppose it's possible. Will you *tell* me what the hell is going on?"

She opened her mouth to answer—and then stopped. Her eyes focused on something behind him, and her cheeks went pale.

"Robin?"

"Don't turn," she whispered, her eyes back on his face. "Act perfectly normal."

"What is it?"

"We've got to get out of here."

"Huh?"

She painted a thick smile on her lips and leaned forward, her mouth pausing inches from his ear. "Ten feet behind you. The man in the dark blue suit. Don't look directly at him, just scan by."

Jeremy shifted his head, pretending to admire the oil paintings that lined the marble walls. The man, bearded with a short, fashionable ponytail, was standing in the far corner of the foyer, talking to a woman in a waitress's uniform.

"What about him?"

"He was on the plane from Washington. And I saw him again this morning, outside a café on Fifth. He's following me."

Jeremy stared at her. "You're serious."

"*Yes.* We have to get out of here. Now."

She grabbed his hand and pulled. In a second they were winding through the crowd. Then she halted suddenly and he was brought up short.

"What is it now?"

"Is there another way, besides the elevators?" she asked.

"Stairs. Over to the right. But why—"

"Just *trust* me." Something in her eyes told him to.

He followed her toward the stairs, waiting until they'd reached the staircase before throwing a glance back. When he did, he noticed three men in dark gray suits standing a few feet from the gilded elevator doors. One of them, built low to the ground but with a bearish physique, was talking into a cellular phone.

Jeremy and Robin quickly descended the stairs and crashed out into the lobby, nearly colliding with a family of Saudi Arabians clutching packages from Saks Fifth Avenue. Robin searched the crowded atrium with her eyes.

"Okay," she whispered to Jeremy, "I think we can make it to the front entrance."

They stayed close to the marble wall, moving in silent determination toward the glass revolving door.

"Who are these guys?" Jeremy asked. "Why are they chasing you?"

She didn't answer. Without slowing her pace, she fingered the clasps of her leather briefcase. The case came open, and she pulled out a large manila envelope. "This will make things clearer."

As they maneuvered through the lobby, he pulled open the envelope. Inside, there was a videotape and thick sheaf of computer paper. He was moving too fast to get a good look at the stack of paper, but he could tell from the weight that it was prodigious—he guessed fifty pages at the least. "What am I looking at?"

"The video contains footage of my father's death," she said, breathing harder now. "According to his staff, the speech he was about to give was going to shake up a lot of people."

Jeremy crammed behind her as she hit the revolving door. "Why?"

They passed through the door out to the Plaza's front steps.

"Because it was contrary to the President's stated position. My father was going to call for a new direction in American military policy. I don't have all the details but it had something to do with dismantling the worldwide military capability we'd built up since the cold war."

"How did your father think he could change things if the President wasn't backing him?"

"It was more than just words," she insisted, pulling him along. "He was building support in Congress. He was going to demand billions of dollars in defense cuts—downscale the entire military."

"I still don't understand," he said. "Your father was going to shake up Washington. What does that have to do with anything?"

They rushed across the park that separated the driveway from Fifth Avenue, and her voice became even more emphatic: "Two years ago, my father took off on a fact-finding tour. Rather than simply cut budgets across the board, he intended to find out which projects were important, and which were simply a drain on funds. Somewhere along the way, he found something that scared the hell out of him."

"What was it?"

"To this day, I'm not sure. I do know that for a brief time, the CIA was involved—the director, Steven Leary, was a close friend of my father's—but I have no idea what they were up to. After a while, Leary dropped out of the picture, and my father continued working on his own. He drew up a list of the projects he intended to cut and began scripting his Princeton speech."

"Were there a lot of projects on the list?"

They'd come to a stop along Fifth Avenue. She pointed to the manila envelope. "See for yourself."

He pulled out the thick sheaf of computer paper. As he'd guessed, there were exactly fifty pages, single spaced, organized in parallel alphabetical columns. His eyes roamed across the list of names and places, most of them foreign to him.

"Two hundred and twelve on the first page alone," he murmured.

Her eyes widened. "How did you—"

"Oh"—he looked embarrassed—"I've always had this head for numbers. It's no big deal. What are all these projects, anyway? Weapons manufacturers?"

"Not all of them. The Defense Department funds thousands of organizations. Public service organizations, research centers, even universities."

He continued scanning the list. He saw the name of a company in Massachusetts that he'd heard of. He also recognized a few graduate programs—most notably, the engineering department at Michigan State and the bio labs at the University of Pennsylvania.

"This is some serious budget cutting. But I still don't get what this has to do with your father's death."

She jabbed her finger at the list. "Isn't it obvious? Two years ago, my father stumbled across a project that scared him, even went so far as to involve the CIA. Then he put together a list of projects he intended to pull the plug on. But before he could put his plan into action, someone—" She stopped, unable to continue.

He put his arm on her shoulder. "You're saying your father was *murdered*?"

"Yes," she replied, her voice trembling. "By someone on that list."

"But his autopsy report—"

"Was inconclusive. You said so yourself."

His eyes shifted back to the sheaf of computer paper. She had to be kidding. A secretary of defense murdered because of budget cuts? It seemed too far-fetched. Still, his eyes drifted all the way to the *T*s. No mention of Tucsome. *Of course* there was no mention. He smiled at his paranoia.

"Robin, this all sounds pretty shaky—"

"Oh, shit."

She was facing back toward the Park Plaza. He followed her gaze.

The three men they'd seen before burst through the revolving glass door, followed by three more—clad, like the others, in dark suits. She grabbed Jeremy's hand and pulled him into the street.

Cars screeched around them, horns blared, tires spit up smoke and pavement.

"Christ," Jeremy cursed, barely dodging a banged-up taxi. Miraculously, they arrived at the other side of the street intact.

"What do we *do*?" she asked desperately. For once she was out of answers.

For Jeremy, it was decision time. He either bought into her story or he didn't. It all seemed so ridiculous . . . and yet, there *was* that seriously botched autopsy report, and the way the contents of Walker's intended speech had been hushed up. . . . Ultimately, what convinced him was the look of real fear on her face.

"We've got to find a crowd, get lost. Here," he said, taking her hand, "follow me." He led her forward, setting a brisk pace. A few seconds later, they were at the front entrance of FAO Schwarz, New York's most famous toy store. Morning, noon, and night, the retail establishment could be counted on to be packed.

Passing through the revolving door, they melded into the moving line, positioning themselves between a family of six and a young teenage couple.

Robin glanced back over her shoulder. There was no sign of pursuit. "We might be okay," she said. "If we're lucky, they didn't get a good look at your face."

"Yeah, but they know yours," Jeremy pointed out, "and that dress of yours is pretty easy to spot. We should call the police."

"*No*," she said. "The police can't help us. Don't you see, this is too big for that."

What was too big? He wondered if she'd seen too many corny movies.

They passed out of the line and into an aisle lined with the hot new toys of the season: plastic action figures with life-like, movable limbs; handheld video games with multipack cartridges; fluorescent-colored inflatables, puncture proof and fire retardant; and of course, dinosaurs—every size, color, and species, from the paleontologically accurate to the mythologically absurd.

"Okay," he said grudgingly, "suppose you're right. Where do you go from here? They—whoever 'they' are—obviously know where to find you. I still think the police—"

A dark cloud passed across her face.

"What?" he asked.

"You're right. They *will* find me." She closed her eyes for a moment, thinking. "Jeremy, I never should have brought you into this. You've been wonderful but . . ." She hesitated, then made up her mind. "I have to go this alone."

Jeremy had barely noticed that they'd entered a faux jungle complete with stuffed monkeys and seven-foot giraffes. "Hey, wait a minute—"

Suddenly, an arm wrapped around his throat and his feet lifted off the ground. He choked, kicking at the shelf in front of him. Meanwhile, some part of his brain registered Robin off to the side, struggling with a dark-suited assailant. The man howled in pain as her knee struck him in the groin.

"Say good night," a voice sneered.

Through a rain of stuffed animals Jeremy saw a glint of steel and recognized the object immediately. A hypodermic. At least eight inches—which meant that it held a large amount of liquid. More than enough to kill him—if that was the man's intention.

The needle arced downward, and he felt a sharp pinch in his right shoulder. Terror threatened to overwhelm him, then he realized he still had a second to act—the obscene size of the syringe gave him a tiny window of hope. His attacker would have to hold him while he depressed the plunger.

He twisted as hard as he could, using the stiff arm around his throat for leverage. There was a loud snap, and he prayed it was the hypodermic—not his neck. He kicked his feet out and found the edge of a shelf. Using his heels to push off, he sent himself and the man behind him sprawling into a sea of stuffed animals. The arm was still around his throat, but he was tumbling back and forth, causing an enormous commotion. There were shouts from somewhere to the left. Help was coming.

Suddenly, the arm disappeared. Jeremy rolled free, scrambling to find his footing. When he finally looked up, his attacker was gone. Stuffed animals were everywhere, strewn about like victims of a terrorist bomb. A group of preteen kids blocked the aisle, staring with wide eyes.

He avoided their stares as he shoved past them. Even *he* couldn't believe what had just happened.

He rushed through the store, his heart hammering in his chest. Whatever was going on, one thing was now certain: Robin was in danger.

He'd just gained a clear view of the front entrance when he saw a flash of red disappearing into the glass revolving door. *Could it be?*

He raced forward, plunging through the revolving door and back out onto the sidewalk. His head turned, eyes searching.

A city worker bent over a jackhammer . . . an Indian woman walking past with a doe-eyed child resting in a front pouch . . . off to the right, puffs of smoke from a souvlaki cart—finally Jeremy caught sight of her. She'd crossed Fifty-eighth Street and was heading down Fifth Avenue, away from the park. He couldn't see anybody chasing her, but he had a feeling the men in dark suits weren't far behind.

Heart pounding, chest heaving, he began sprinting. *Christ, Ross, you're out of shape.* It was suddenly obvious that his body required more exercise than was needed to best slow-footed Mike Callahan on the squash court. His head felt light, almost dizzy, but he shook it off.

He slid across the hood of a moving BMW and dropped between a pair of yellow taxis. Then he was back on the sidewalk and moving at full pace.

The storefronts blurred as he followed the red dress. He couldn't see Robin's face, but he could tell by her jerky movements that she was terrified. He was a hundred feet behind her when she suddenly cut left into another revolving door. He recognized the building immediately.

Trump Tower. Why had she turned in there?

He raced after her. The revolving door spit him out into the opulent front entrance, and he was instantly immersed in a sea of people. Heads bobbed up and down, blocking his vision. He pressed forward, weaving toward the tower's interior. Ahead of him, an immense open atrium rose upward for five stories, connected by a bank of spiraling escalators. A giant waterfall trickled down the far wall, emitting a subtle hiss that melded with the scuffing of a thousand pairs of shoes.

"Let me go!"

Jeremy whirled toward the voice. Robin was at the other end of the entrance—and she'd picked up some companions.

There were dark gray suits on either side of her. The two men—one of them the squat, thickset individual he'd seen before, the other much taller—pushed her onto the bottom escalator, taking up positions in front and behind.

Shit. Jeremy rushed forward, but by the time he stepped onto the first escalator, Robin was on her way to the third floor. He passed almost directly beneath her, both of them rising upward, the two escalators locked in a parallel rhythm.

He cursed, trying to push forward. The escalator was crowded with people: businessmen in dark suits, families loaded with plastic shopping bags, teenagers with Rollerblades slung over their shoulders—a constant stream of bodies. He quickly found himself stuck in the center of the moving stairway, trapped behind an elderly couple sharing an oversized baguette.

When the opportunity finally came, he made the switch to the second escalator, craning his neck upward. It took him a moment to find the red dress; Robin was already on the last escalator, yards away from the top level of the tower.

He wondered where they were taking her. He shifted his eyes past her—and a thought suddenly tugged at him. He focused on the low metal railing that ringed the top level, then shifted his gaze downward, traversing the hundred-foot drop to the chic café at the base of the tower.

If someone were to fall over that railing . . .

Christ.

He burst forward, squeezing his way through a gaggle of high-school-age girls, two elderly men wearing straw boaters, and a wide-girthed woman with frosted hair. By the time he reached the last escalator, Robin had moved out of view. *Damn.*

But then he saw it—a flash of red on the top level, right up against the railing. Robin's body twisted unnaturally as the two men lifted her by her arms. In a second she was poised headfirst halfway over the railing.

Enraged, Jeremy shoved a pair of overweight businessmen out of the way, dashed up the last few steps, and pitched out onto the fifth level. Robin was ten feet away, desperately gripping the railing as the two men struggled to push her over.

He aimed his shoulder at the taller of the men and charged. He hit the man low, lifting him upward with his thighs, and saw him crash against the railing hip first.

Then it was like slow motion. Jeremy saw the man's body flip into the air, arms windmilling desperately as his fingers sought purchase on something . . . anything. There was a horrible scream, and an instant later, the thunderous crash of two hundred pounds of flesh impacting with a café serving table.

Eyes wide, Jeremy swung to the right, his body squared for action. The second man was three feet away, staring, his face frozen in surprise. Robin twisted out of his beefy hands, pushing away from the railing. He made no move to stop her. Instead, he took a step back, his hand sliding into his coat. Jeremy saw what looked like the handle of a pistol—but then the man seemed to change his mind and, the next moment, he spun on his heels and fled.

Jeremy turned back to the railing. He could see the body of the first man lying spread-eagled in a deserted corner of the posh café. A thin pool of red expanded outward across the marble floor. Terrified patrons stared upward, wondering if more missiles were about to rain down on them.

Jeremy's throat constricted and he stumbled back. He couldn't believe what had just happened. He'd *killed* a man, shoved him over a railing and sent him falling a hundred feet to his death. He'd taken a life.

Robin came up behind him and touched his back. "That was too close," she said, her breath ragged, her eyes disbelieving.

He turned to face her. His knees were growing weak, and his chest was burning. A gray film was closing in over his vision.

"Jeremy, are you all right? We've got to get out of here. Fast."

He tried to nod, but his muscles were paralyzed. He watched as she grabbed him by the arm and dragged him away from the railing. There were shouts from below, and the sounds of police whistles. He felt himself shoved forward, into a service elevator. Down. Down. The elevator doors opened and she yanked him forward. A long hallway led to a pair of double doors. Suddenly they were outside, swallowed up in a swirling crowd of pedestrians.

"We should be okay," she said, leaning on the words. As she pushed him forward, tears clung to the corners of her reddened eyes, and she brushed them away with her palm. "Nobody got a good look at what happened up there, but we should keep moving."

"Keep moving," Jeremy repeated. Then there was a sharp pain behind his eyes. He collapsed forward, his knees hitting the sidewalk.

"Jeremy! What's wrong?"

"Killed him," he tried to answer, but his throat closed tighter . . . and still tighter. *Killed him.*

And suddenly the panic overwhelmed him.

Unaware of his surroundings, caught in a private place of the mind, Jeremy's thoughts traveled back to the day before his twelfth birthday. He could still see the garage in the background, the old metal shelves that lined the walls and the greenish gray Dodge Dart, its red-lined fins reaching up toward the sky.

His father had been showing him how to change a tire when it happened. It was an accident—Jeremy had only wanted to help. When his father wasn't looking, Jeremy had put his weight against the jack. He'd only wanted to raise the car another few inches. He hadn't known the jack would fly loose. He hadn't known. . . .

Over the years, he'd replayed the scene again and again; sometimes it was as if he'd never left that garage, never been anything other than a little boy trying to help his father change a tire.

There was a sudden, metallic sound, and then the Dodge came crashing down. The jack flipped out from under the rear bumper and spun through the air. A hard steel edge caught his father directly in the throat. Twelve years later, the dull, sickening crunch still reverberated in Jeremy's ears.

His father swung around to face him, his eyes wide, his hands reaching for the wound. His mouth opened, but no noise came out. His eyes swelled forward, desperate, glistening.

Jeremy watched in helpless terror.

He was only a *child*. He didn't know anything about tracheotomies or crushed larynxes or blocked airways. He was just a little child.

His father dropped to his knees in front of him, choking, his face turning blue. Jeremy stood there, staring in stunned silence. He could still see the sweat on his dad's cheeks. The desperate, accusing look in his eyes.

It wasn't my fault, Jeremy screamed at himself. I was just a child! It wasn't my fault!

But the agony was relentless. The guilt was embedded in him, lodged deep in the pit of his being. Through unusual intelligence—and the salve of learning how to save others—

he'd managed to camouflage it, to shove it in a place where it couldn't hurt him.

But suddenly—with a new death—the guilt, and the panic, were back.

8

ROBIN SLUMPED AGAINST A LONG SHELF OF COMPUTER CONSOLES, her entire body exhausted. Through the glass wall in front of her, she could see the MRI machine, its oval opening gaping wide like the jaws of a mechanical monster. Jeremy was strapped to a plastic cart in front of the opening, ready for entry.

"Don't worry," Mike Callahan assured, "it's perfectly harmless. We're just covering all the bases."

"Is it really necessary to scan his brain?"

"He went into convulsions," Callahan said, shrugging. "It's standard procedure to check for lesions. But from his medical history, we can be pretty confident we won't find anything."

She nodded. Callahan had already explained Jeremy's problem to her. Panic-anxiety syndrome. Something he'd had since he was a kid.

If I'd only known, I never would have . . . A mist of guilt rose up inside her, and she bit down on her lower lip. He'd

61

always seemed so strong, so confident. And she'd needed someone strong. . . .

She wiped a tear from the corner of her eye. "Can we go inside?"

"Sure. He's still unconscious, but there's no reason why we can't be by his side."

They moved toward a door in the glass wall. Callahan paused before entering and nodded at a wooden tray attached to the glass a few feet away.

"Empty your pockets first. Keys, change, jewelry, anything metal."

She raised an eyebrow. "Why?"

"The magnetic field produced by an MRI machine is immense. Within ten feet of the machine, the force is strong enough to pull nails out of a piece of plywood."

"A slight exaggeration?" she said.

"No, I'm serious. I once had a set of keys ripped right out of my pocket. One second I'm going along fine, then I stepped closer to the machine, and whammo."

She frowned. *And they're going to focus all that power on Jeremy's brain?* The thought scared her even more.

She followed Callahan through the glass door and stood at his side. Even though common sense told her the MRI was harmless, the machine filled her with a sense of foreboding. The constant whir of the gargantuan apparatus filled the room, and she could taste the sound echoing against her teeth.

"He's sleeping off the anesthetic," Callahan said, feeling Jeremy's pulse. "He'll be fine."

"It scared the hell out of me," Robin said. "I've never seen anything like it. We were just walking along Fifth Avenue when he collapsed."

Callahan's eyebrows lifted. "You have no idea what set him off? Usually these attacks are brought on by some sort of trauma."

She made her face as blank as possible. "I can't think of

anything. We were just talking about college. It happened right out of the blue."

He nodded, looking away. "And the puncture wound in his shoulder? You don't know anything about that?"

She shook her head. She hadn't noticed the wound until an EMS man pointed it out to her; the man had speculated that it had been made by a hypodermic needle.

"No, that must have happened before we met. Or maybe when he fell? I really don't know."

"You were near Trump Tower when he collapsed, weren't you? I heard there was one hell of a commotion—"

"Would it be possible to scrounge a cup of coffee?" she interrupted. "I'm still a little shaken up."

He stared at her, a frustrated look behind his eyes. Finally, he shrugged. "Sure. Wait here—we've still got a few minutes before they're ready to scan. I'll be back in a second."

She thanked him and watched as he backpedaled away. Then she knelt next to the plastic MRI cart.

There was a small bandage around Jeremy's shoulder, where the needle had stuck him. Aside from the bandage, he looked peaceful. But who knew whether some of his torment still persisted. "I'm sorry, Jeremy. I'm so sorry."

There was nothing more she could say.

She fought the urge to look back as she headed for the glass door. Once outside, she retrieved her earrings from the wooden tray. She would leave a note with Callahan—something simple, to let Jeremy know how she felt, how sorry she was—and then she would disappear.

She hoped he would understand.

The first thing Jeremy saw when he opened his eyes was the plastic IV wire, a liquid-filled snake sticking out of his forearm and running in spaghetti-like twists to a bottle hanging from a metal IV rack next to his hospital bed. He groaned, letting his head fall back against the pillow. His mind was swimming, and there was a dull pounding behind his eyes.

Memories rushed at him, and he clenched his eyelids shut.

He'd awakened once in the ambulance, and once as he was being wheeled into the emergency room. He could remember Frankie's face, the flushed look of concern as the chief resident had said something about saline solution and shock-related hypothermia, and then, in a hushed voice, the words "medical history." Then there was the rustling of papers and the sudden look of understanding.

Jeremy clenched his hands into fists. The scene in his mind changed to a moment less than an hour ago, when he'd briefly become conscious. Frankie and Administrator Belding had been standing at the foot of his bed. Neither one had met his eyes.

Everything would be okay, they'd told him, he just needed rest, time to pull himself together. Frankie had given him the name of a psychiatrist who knew how to handle "these things." You should see him as soon as you can, Administrator Belding had added.

And then Belding had dropped the bombshell. The hospital had come to a decision. For Jeremy's own sake, they wanted him to take a few weeks off, a short leave of absence—"to recuperate, relax, think things through." Jeremy's heart sank at the words. A month from graduation and the hospital was suspending him. The thought of it brought hot tears to his eyes. But in truth, he couldn't blame them. From their point of view, it didn't look good: The EMS men had found him collapsed on the sidewalk, the victim of a massive anxiety attack. Who could say for sure that a similar attack wouldn't occur shortly after he received his degree?

Now, lying in his hospital bed, Jeremy slammed his fists against the mattress beneath him. Damn it, it wasn't fair. A suspension? His life had been going so well. And then along came Robin.

His eyelids flipped open. *Robin*. He had to find her, make sure she was okay. He tried to sit up.

"Hold on, partner. You've had enough fun for one day."

Callahan was standing in the doorway, a medical chart

under one arm. The look on his face was sympathetic, but his eyes betrayed something else, a tinge of bewilderment.

"You need rest. You had one hell of an episode."

Jeremy rubbed a weak hand across his dry lips. "Where's Robin? Is she outside?"

Callahan took a step into the room and gently shut the door behind him. "Well, she . . ."

"Just tell me, Mike. Where is she? Is she okay?"

"She's fine. She had to leave, rather abruptly. Something to do with work. She said she wouldn't be coming back. She left this note for you." He handed Jeremy a small, folded index card. Through blurry eyes, Jeremy studied the simple, painful words: "I'm sorry, Jeremy. Seeing you again made five years disappear. Please understand that I have to go."

He shut his eyes and let his head fall back against the bed. Where was she? Probably on her way back to Washington—or heading deep into hiding. He'd shown he couldn't protect her—she'd decided to go it alone.

Callahan placed the medical chart at the foot of Jeremy's bed. "Jeremy, talk to me. You came in here with a puncture wound in your shoulder—"

"No questions, Mike. Please don't ask me any questions."

"Jeremy. Come on. If there's something going on—"

"I mean it, Mike. I don't want to talk it."

Jeremy shifted his head and focused on the small table next to his bed. The manila envelope stared back at him. Frankie must have left it for him. Jeremy hoped the chief resident had respected his privacy and hadn't looked inside.

Frankie would have thought the whole story was absurd. But absurd or not, Jeremy knew that it was real. A man had stuck him with a hypodermic needle. Two others had tried to kill Robin. The facts were overwhelming; he was deeply involved in something he didn't understand.

He shut his eyes, feeling as weak and small as he had the moment his father died. Now his career was in jeopardy. Robin was in danger, perhaps running for her life. And he was treading backward toward his disability.

He *had* to set things right. He had to find out what the hell was really going on. But he only had one link—a fragile one, at best.

Two years before his death, Warren T. Walker had visited the Tucsome Project for Genetic Research. At about the same time, according to Robin, the defense secretary had discovered something that had scared him enough to bring in the CIA.

In Jeremy's mind, the questions followed one after another: Were the visit and timing of the discovery coincidence? Was Walker's death somehow connected? If so, was the connection inadvertent, through some form of contamination? Or purposeful, as a deliberate consequence of something Walker had discovered?

Whatever the answers were, Jeremy had a feeling they wouldn't be arrived at easily. "Mike," he asked, his voice steady, "how soon can you get me out of here?"

Callahan sighed. "Why?"

"I'm taking Belding's advice. A short leave of absence. To think things through."

Callahan nodded in agreement. "Sounds like a good idea. Do you have someplace in mind?"

"Yes," Jeremy said, glancing at the manila envelope. "Yes, I do."

9

"ALPHA QUADRANT, LOCKED."

"Beta quadrant, locked."

"Gamma, locked."

"Begin simulation."

Bright daggers of light played across an enormous Plexiglas grid. Glowing white phosphorescent lines became dazzling red spheres, mushrooming out of the three-dimensional display like a ruptured bouquet. Soon the entire grid was awash in red, briefly illuminating the stunned expressions of the small audience sitting a few yards away.

The spectacle lasted a bare sixty seconds. The phosphorescent lines faded, the red spheres dissipating across the Plexiglas like raindrops in a lake. All that was left was a searing afterglow, captured by the sheer steel walls of the room.

A few second passed in silence. Then someone coughed, and an awed query echoed through the darkness.

"Status report?"

A female voice answered: "One hundred percent effective.

All three quadrants incapacitated. Elapsed time, fifty-nine seconds."

A hush swept through the room. Then a low whistle: "And that, ladies and gentlemen, is how to fight a war. Lights, please."

A smattering of applause lifted into the air as a bank of fluorescent ceiling lights flickered to life. The room was small and crowded, with unmarked walls and a three-foot-thick iron-lead door. Nine men sat surrounding a long mahogany table, their high leather chairs turned to face the Plexiglas grid. A woman in an immaculately cut business suit stood at the edge of the grid, a pen-shaped laser pointer in her hands.

"If you would please focus your attention on the target areas," she began, "you'll see the accuracy of our new Telstar-7 satellite tracking system. Eighteen Telstar-guided cruise missiles, each equipped with high-emission electromagnetic generators, were deployed in an overlapping hexagonal pattern. As you can see, the deployment pattern encompassed all nine of our military targets, as well as the region's power supply and main telephone switching facility. On detonation, we achieved complete neutralization within the targeted zones."

The blue-eyed, craggy-faced man at the head of the mahogany table, President Blair Addison, cleared his throat. "Melissa, if you would elaborate—"

"Certainly, Mr. President. I'm sure you're all generally aware that magnetic fields can affect electronic circuits; when lightning strikes, televisions fuzz up and radios crackle. It's also true that electronic circuits can be overloaded, and even destroyed, by high-intensity magnetic fields."

She turned back to the Plexiglas grid. "Our simulation is based on the test runs we operated over Baghdad in '91, adjusted to account for the recent developments in electromagnetic technology. In the simulation, the detonated cruise missiles unleashed high-emission electromagnetic pulses.

These pulses caused the absolute disruption of all circuitry in the target area. We're talking weapon systems, radar screens, power sources, telephone lines, computers—anything that runs on electricity."

"Presumably that would apply to any vehicle whose propulsion depended on electronics?" Lucas Barnes, the NSC chief, asked.

"Yes," said Melissa. "Personnel carriers would stop dead in the streets. Helicopters would drop out of the sky. The entire city would be shut down."

"Remarkable," President Addison said. "Thank you, Melissa."

The woman nodded, returning to her seat.

Addison sat up and surveyed the Plexiglas grid, his stomach churning. It certainly was impressive; a modern, industrialized city, rendered helpless in under a minute. And best of all, the approach was nonnuclear. News of the technology's refinement would be a PR dream, sure to send his approval rating soaring in the next national poll.

But what if I actually put the technology to use?

As tempting as the simulation had been, the North Koreans still had two weeks to comply with the disclosure proceedings; there was a good chance that the invasion could be avoided altogether. And that, of course, would be the best-case scenario. The electromagnetic pulses and satellite-guided cruise missiles were only the first stage of the proposed operation; in the end, it would take ground troops to accomplish the final objective. And no matter what the technical advisers said, the complete disarmament of North Korea's nuclear capability would be a tricky—and decidedly costly—affair.

"We'll code this alternative 'Operation Black-Out,' " the President declared. "And I'll expect detailed briefings from each of you by tomorrow morning. If there's a potential problem, I want to know about it. If there's a better alternative out there, I certainly don't want to hear about it on the evening news."

He shifted his eyes from face to face: Lucas Barnes. Steven Leary, the director of the CIA. Hal Olston, director of the FBI. Julian Tiel, director of the Secret Service. Maxwell Claude-Vines, secretary of state. Albert Packridge, chairman of the Joint Chiefs. Melissa Caspar, special consultant on satellite defense and communications. Arthur Dice, director of Special Security Operations . . .

Addison paused as his eyes reached the empty chair at the far end of the table. A shadow of sorrow flitted across his features. Walker's presence was sorely missed, especially as the situation with North Korea expanded. Old Pug had always been a clutch player; he would have known the proper course of action, and he would have spared no time getting his point across. *To invade or not to invade?* Addison and Walker had had their differences, but the President would have trusted his defense chief's opinion on *this* issue without question.

The President sighed and forced his eyes away from the empty chair. Sadly, Walker was gone—and this wasn't the time to ponder his sudden death.

"Fourteen days," Addison continued. "If the North Koreans want to play games, they'll find out how much things have changed over the last forty years. . . ."

At the far corner of the mahogany table, Arthur Dice stared out from behind inch-thick glasses. His fingers tugged on his knotted, curly beard as he watched the President shift back and forth in front of the Plexiglas grid.

"As Melissa's demonstration has just made abundantly clear," the President continued, "we've entered a new era—"

Dice stifled a yawn, his eyes wandering around the steel-walled room. Affectionately known as the Coffin, the room was the Pentagon's pride and joy. Entombed deep in the fortresslike bowels of Basement Level 3E, protected by sixteen distinct security checkpoints, the Coffin was completely airtight and sealed off from the outside world. In fact, there were those who believed it could withstand a direct hit from a one-megaton nuclear warhead.

Lately, Dice had been fantasizing about putting the theory to the test. He'd already wasted two Sundays in a row in the Coffin, and it looked as though the next two weeks would be worse. Even if the North Koreans backed down, there'd be follow-up briefings and situation breakdowns, enough blather to drive a man crazy. How long could he suffer through the inanity, the back-patting; the talk about "new eras"? *He* was supposed to be impressed by electromagnetic pulses and satellite guidance systems? Arthur Dice, the man who oversaw THRESHOLD?

Christ, if the President only knew . . .

"At this phase of our protocol," the President was saying, "our primary concern is security. Which is why we're meeting here instead of in the Oval Office, and why we'll continue to meet here throughout the next fourteen days. Before we break, any questions or comments?"

Finally. As the room pitched into silence, Dice clasped his fingers over his generous midsection and said a silent prayer that the heat would keep his colleagues from dragging out the session further.

No such luck.

"I have one more item from our satellite monitoring system in Fall River," Melissa said.

Dice rubbed his eyes, waiting for her to finish. The sooner the meeting ended, the sooner he'd be able to get back to his town house in Georgetown. Ella wouldn't be home from shopping for at least another four hours—which would leave him plenty of time to relax in his workshop before the bickering started. Last night he'd managed to get the fuselage of the *Enola Gay* glued together before Ella's whine had shattered the calm. Something about modeling glue in the upstairs guest bathroom . . .

"Although we didn't get a direct bead on the transmission," Caspar continued, "we did manage a rough trace. Our numbers tell us a frequency 010901 was routed through one of our Astor-5 satellites yesterday at five-thirty P.M. eastern standard time. We couldn't get a coordinate fix, but we estimate that the transmission was directed at the northeastern United States. Specifically, to a mobile coordinate somewhere near or in New York City."

Suddenly, Dice's throat constricted. An 010901 at five-thirty yesterday evening? He coughed, his mind spinning through options. He quickly decided that there was no choice but to own up—at least to the details.

"Uh," he grunted, catching Caspar by surprise and bringing the meeting to a halt. "I believe that transmission came from my department. A, uh, routine communication piggybacking on one of your satellites, Melissa."

"Arthur," the President cut in, raising a manicured hand. "You know that all transmissions routed through our satellite network have to be logged and approved by National Communications. What was this 010901 concerning?"

Dice stared directly into those sky blue eyes. "Just a few of my operatives tracking Fyedor Draskov. You remember Draskov? The Russian mole?"

Addison nodded. Of course he remembered. Draskov had been a thorn in his thigh at election time; in fact, the missing Russian mole had almost ruined his campaign.

"Draskov," the President murmured. "Any developments there?"

Dice shrugged his shoulders, making his face as sorrowful as possible. "What's to say? He's a difficult one, this Draskov."

Inside, Dice howled with laughter. In actuality, Fyedor Draskov was buried a few feet under a playground in Piedmont, Maryland. But until some kid digging in a sandbox stumbled on his remains, the Russian mole was a ready-made excuse.

"Okay then," Addison said. "I guess that solves that mystery. Anything else, Melissa?"

Caspar shook her head. The rest of the powerful faces brightened as the session finally closed. Dice joyfully heaved his huge form out of his chair.

Just as he turned toward the lead-iron door, Steven Leary caught his eye. The CIA director was signaling with his fingers, silently asking him to stay behind.

Dice grimaced; Leary was too powerful to simply ignore. Slowly, Dice lowered himself back into his seat. He hoped that the big-eared mick would be brief.

His Ella-free morning was dwindling fast.

"I'll come right to the point," the CIA director said from across the deserted table. "I'm going to ask you a question and I want an honest answer."

The words echoed off of the steel walls of the emptied-out Coffin. Dice felt them smack into his ears, and the bile rose up his esophagus. Big Ears wanted an honest answer?

"Of course, Steven. When has the SSO ever been anything but honest?"

Leary shifted in his seat, and Dice could feel the hatred emanating from him. Too many times, the SSO and the CIA had clashed on issues of territory and policy; and most of the time, the SSO had prevailed—for one simple reason. The CIA was a public organization. For all of its secrecy, for all of its confidential mandates and clandestine missions, the CIA was accountable to the government, to the people, and to the Constitution of the United States.

The SSO, on the other hand, was accountable to no one.

"We're always eager to help," Dice continued, his voice dripping. " 'Members of the same team' and all that."

Leary ignored the sarcasm. "I need to ask about an operative. I believe he might be one of yours."

Dice raised his eyebrows. This was getting interesting. Much more interesting than North Korea.

"An operative of mine?"

"I have reason to believe so. I'd like you to confirm it for me."

Dice rubbed his throat. "Why such an interest in an operative?"

"He's not your average operative," Leary said softly. "He's Gold-One rated."

Dice felt the stirrings of anxiety, but he didn't let it show. "Gold-One" was the CIA rating for the absolute cream of the crop, the men who'd reached a level of efficiency, sophistication, and brutal skill that set them apart from the thousands—tens of thousands—of international operatives. There were perhaps thirty Gold-Ones in the entire country.

It could be a coincidence, Dice told himself. But he didn't believe in coincidences. Especially not when the CIA was concerned. He had to be very, very careful.

"A Gold-One? And he's not one of yours?"

"No, but we've been tracking him for some time."

"He must be a very special Gold-One," Dice said, no inflection in his voice.

"All of the Gold-Ones are special, Arthur. And in this case, perhaps a step beyond special. Perhaps even singular."

"What do you mean?"

"We have reason to believe that this particular Gold-One was involved in some very nasty business—political business. Very, very nasty political business."

Dice exuded nonchalance. "And what leads you to that conclusion?"

"As I said," Leary stated, "we've been tracking this operative for some time. Most recently, we followed his trail to South Carolina."

Dice clamped his hands together under the table. Leary was close, too close. "And the name of this Gold-One?"

Leary paused the necessary few seconds.

"Victor Alexander."

Dice didn't flinch. "Alexander . . ." He made a show of trying to recall the name. "Hmmm, I don't think I—"

"Let me help you out," Leary said, his voice bleeding sarcasm. "Victor 'The Bullet' Alexander. Six-foot-four, one hundred and eighty pounds. Born in London, England. Became an American citizen at age sixteen. Over four hundred documented kills with the Fighting Three-Sixty Airborne in

Vietnam, spent two years in a Vietcong prison near Dung-Pau. Recruited by my predecessor in 1984. Afghanistan, Iraq, El Salvador. Then, in 1991, it seems he disappeared from our roster. Any of this ring a bell?"

Dice offered a thin smile. He decided against an outright lie. "Well, Steven, I'm sure he *could* be one of mine."

Leary sat upright, an incredulous look on his face. "Could be?"

Dice rounded his shoulders. "I should know the where-abouts of every one of my operatives? Steven, please. There are over a thousand people in my department."

"With Gold-One ratings?"

Dice opened his hands and offered a congenial smile. "I'm not saying he doesn't work for me. I'm just saying I don't necessarily keep tabs on all of my operatives all of the time. Makes for bad morale. And for some of these men—the Gold-Ones, especially—morale is a very sticky issue. So you'll understand if I ask for a few days to check up on this."

Leary paused for a second. Then he rubbed his square, Irish jaw. His smile was snide, dangerously so. "Okay, Arthur. A few days. Perhaps your memory will return by then."

Dice lifted out of his seat, stretching his thick arms down at his sides. "Now, if you're quite finished interrogating me, we both have a briefing to write—"

"Just one more thing," Leary said, also rising, "and I want to be absolutely clear about this."

"Go right ahead."

Leary placed his palms on the table and leaned forward. "I don't know what you're up to. I have my suspicions, but I don't know how far you're willing to go—or how far you've already gone. However, there is one thing that I am certain of. The SSO is rotten to the core. It's dirty, Arthur, so dirty that I can smell it from my office at Langley. You have no respect for the law, for this nation, or for the Constitution. Sooner or later, I'm going to find my way through to the dirt. And when I do, I'm going to shove you so deep into the system that your children—if that little pecker of yours ever gives you children—curse the name of the fat fuck who brought them so much shame."

With that, Leary whirled on his heels. He headed for the lead-iron door, his posture perfect, his eyes straight ahead.

"Motherfucker," Dice whispered under his breath. The director of the CIA had thrown down the gauntlet.

The fool. He didn't know what he was up against. And if he thought that he could scare Arthur Dice into submission, he was dead wrong.

Because Dice knew that there were some things more important than the law. There were some things more important than the nation. There were some things even more important than the damned Constitution.

THRESHOLD was one of those things.

10

AS THE STEEL DOOR SLID UPWARD WITH A WHIR OF MECHANICAL gears, a cold, antiseptic breeze floated out into the hallway, carrying with it all the sounds of a high-tech laboratory: the beeps and buzzes of huge monitoring devices, the hum of computer processors, the clink of test tubes, and the steady drip of a loose faucet. Somewhere in the background an animal growled. And above it all drifted the plaintive melodies of a violin.

Victor Alexander took a deep breath, inhaling the familiar sounds. Somehow, he found them comforting. He steadied the thin dossier under his arm and waded into Jason Water's private laboratory.

The violins grew from a soft rain to a storm, pouring from speakers hidden near the ceiling. *Vivaldi,* Victor proudly thought to himself. How many combat-trained operatives could recognize Vivaldi? He paused, letting the notes wash over him. Out of habit, he slid his eyes over the laboratory, taking in the familiar shapes and colors.

The white cinderblock walls were lined with machines of every imaginable size: a three-dimensional gene animator, a multiheaded gel machine . . . even a superenhanced sequencer. Steel shelving units rose up above the machines, cluttered with test-tube racks, beakers, and Bunsen burners, while below the shelves pewter sinks squatted, slick and glowing under the fluorescent lights.

Victor shifted his gaze beyond the sinks. A row of sixty steel canisters spanned the back wall of the laboratory, their polished surfaces throwing patterns of light across the tiled floor. Exactly fifty-nine of the canisters were attached to a rubber shaft that rose up toward the ceiling, disappearing behind a black plastic digital display. Bright red letters blinked across the plastic: INTEGRITY: THIRTY-THREE PERCENT. The words were meaningless to Victor, and his eyes continued across the lab. A few yards to the right of the canisters was a sealed steel door with rounded edges, held shut by a fierce-looking circular locking mechanism. In the center of the floor was a high-tech pressure gauge.

He'd never been inside the low-pressure room; the idea that he would have to wear a bulky fiberglass space suit to survive the near vacuum had been, to say the least, a discouragement. He grimaced, moving his eyes along the back wall, then paused at the corner of the room.

There a four-foot-high chain-link cage rose up from the floor. Two sets of narrow red eyes stared out from behind the hexagonal links. As usual, the animals were stone-still, their muscular gray-and-white bodies emanating hatred, muted violence, and fear. He quickly shifted his eyes to a second, much smaller cage, which rested a few feet from the first.

The small wolf cub was up on all fours, its stub of a tail bouncing back and forth. It wagged its tail excitedly and seemed completely focused on something in the middle of the lab.

Victor followed the cub's gaze. When his eyes reached the object of the animal's attention, he felt a pang of sympathy.

Jason Waters certainly had presence. With wavy gray hair

and pinpoint brown eyes, high, prominent cheekbones and a square, cleft jaw, he conveyed, at one and the same time, power and intensity. The one incongruous feature was his lips, which were drawn back over an absentminded smile—a smile that seemed to have been left there years ago, the product of some long-forgotten joke.

It was not lost on Victor that the man in the center of the room was one of the greatest scientists who'd ever lived. He knew that Waters had been the third man on the team that had discovered the structure of DNA; and although Victor was far from being an expert on what that meant, he understood enough about genetics to know that Waters had earned his place in history—even if history had done its utmost to ignore him.

All the more reason to admire the man, Victor thought to himself. He settled back against the door, content to watch the scientist at work.

Waters was bent over one of his toys, a black sphere set in a rectangular steel casing. Although the sphere was completely foreign to Victor, the steel casing seemed familiar. It took him a moment to place the memory; then his breath quickened, and a warm feeling filled his cheeks.

He remembered a bamboo cage in Dung-Pau—a place he'd called home the last two years of his tour. Most of his images of Dung-Pau were painful and gray: beatings, reeducation exercises, mosquitoes, hot sleepless nights, and the steady hack of tuberculosis. But one memory stood out, almost making the rest worthwhile. About six weeks before the end of the ordeal he and his buddy Lucius had fashioned a homemade ammunition smelt out of sun-dried mud and jungle reeds. They'd melted down anything they could find: pocket knives, metal spoons, even their dog tags. Then they'd smuggled in an unexploded shell and had made enough bullets to send sixteen Vietcong prison guards to hell.

Of course, the steel ammo smelt that Waters was fiddling with was a thousand times more sophisticated than the home-grown version that had won Victor his first Congressional ribbon. And Victor had never seen anything even remotely like the black sphere attached to the center of the futuristic smelt. But there was no question in his mind as to the purpose of the concentric circles of divots that ringed the surface of the steel casing.

Then again, the holes seemed quite small, thinner, even, than the tiny shell of a .22. Victor watched with genuine curiosity as Waters pulled on a pair of thick rubber gloves and used needle-nosed forceps to remove a tiny, bullet-shaped test tube from one of the divots. The scientist then carefully carried the test tube over to an enormous pressurized cylinder standing a few feet to his left. The cylinder was transparent, filled to the brim with some sort of clear liquid. On top of the cylinder was a black rubber nozzle, attached by a long wire to a foot pedal on the floor.

As Victor watched, Waters held the test tube in front of the nozzle, careful to keep his gloved hand as far back on the forceps as possible. He gently touched the foot pedal with his toes. A burst of thick white steam erupted out of the nozzle, completely enveloping the test tube. When the steam cleared, Waters carried the test tube back to the strange ammo smelt. Carefully, he turned the test tube on its side and extracted a tiny, bullet-shaped pellet. It was like no other shell Victor had ever seen; perfectly transparent, less than two centimeters long, and as thin and sharp as a syringe.

"The molecule of life," Waters commented as he held the transparent bullet in front of his eyes, "simple water. Frozen to the consistency of lead."

He reached into a cabinet in front of him, searched behind a stack of CD-ROM computer disks, and removed a small object, barely the size of a package of cigarettes. Victor's eyes widened as he recognized the object; he'd never seen a revolver so thin and small.

"To most of us," Waters continued, "water is the basis of life, a substance to be cherished. Too much of it, though, and we drown. An interesting irony."

He used the forceps to load the clear pellet into the barrel of the tiny revolver. Then he turned toward the smaller of the two cages. Methodically, he aimed the revolver at the helpless cub and pulled the trigger.

A fierce howl erupted from the larger cage as the cub lurched into the air and collapsed in a heap. The larger cage shook with fury as the creatures inside crashed against the padlocked cage door.

"Bloody hell," Victor whispered, staring at Waters.

Waters glanced at him, smiling. "Don't be too quick to judge, Victor. Rather, observe."

Waters's eyes remained on the cage, and Victor found himself following suit, wondering what the devil was going on. A minute passed, then suddenly he heard a whimper.

Victor watched as the small animal slowly struggled to its feet. The animals in the larger cage settled back into silence, their red eyes receding into smoldering slits.

"He's not dead?" Victor said, surprised.

"He's fine," Waters assured. "His parents had nothing to howl about. It was a test of the firing mechanism, not of the ice bullet." He carefully returned the revolver to the cabinet shelf. "So what brings you to my lab this morning?"

Victor coughed, quickly getting into character as he pulled the dossier out from under his arm. "Just a bit of business," he said, "a visitor who's arriving by train in a few hours."

"You don't mind if I continue my work while you talk, do you? I don't mean to be rude."

For a moment Victor was taken aback, then an almost childlike pleasure moved through him. Waters was so reliably courteous, even respectful. So unlike Victor's paranoid boss. No clipped orders, no outrageous demands—and certainly no threats.

"Please, Doctor, go on with what you're doing. As I said, Tucsome will be welcoming a young visitor." Victor looked down at the dossier. "A fourth-year medical student. His name is Jeremy Ross. His list of accomplishments is quite impressive."

"Ross," Waters murmured as he crossed to the large wolf cage. "Yes, Jeremy Ross. I remember the name. His thesis was published in the October issue of the *New England Journal of Medicine*. Retrovirus gene therapy. Very good stuff. Excellent stuff."

Victor shrugged and scanned through the rest of the dossier. Out of the corner of his eye, he watched Waters lean over the wolf cage and touch a metal control plate with his palm. A twelve-inch circular feeding vent opened up on the top of the cage, and the wolves began to snap and howl.

"He's at the top of his class at New York City Hospital," Victor said over the clamor. "He's got a Ph.D. in genetics, and—must be a typo—it says he got the Ph.D. in one year." He moved down the sheet. "Let's see, uh . . . highest percentile on his medical boards, three-point-nine at Dartmouth, glowing recommendations."

Victor continued flipping pages, confining himself to the information that would, in all likelihood, be found in a résumé. He didn't add that the kid's credit rating was about average—for his age and economic circumstances. That he owed over forty thousand in student loans, which he'd probably be able to pay back in a couple years, considering the offers he'd been getting from the private hospitals. That his father had died when he was twelve and his mother had worked two jobs to help pay for his education. Or that he'd seen maybe fifty psychiatrists between the ages of twelve and eighteen. Something called "panic-anxiety syndrome," whatever the hell that meant. Couldn't have been anything too rough, considering his medical school record.

Jason Waters didn't need to know these facts—and he certainly didn't need to know where Victor had gotten them.

"Sounds like he has excellent potential," Waters said, dropping something into the wolf cage. The animals suddenly quieted down.

"A little young," Victor responded, "but impressive."

"Young? How old *is* he? Twenty-five?"

"Twenty-four."

Waters didn't look up. Both the wolves were lying on the cage floor, drifting off to sleep. Whatever he'd given them was potent.

"I was twenty-six in 1953," Waters said, quietly, "Watson was twenty-five."

There was a sudden tension in the room at the mention of James Watson's name. It wasn't a name that Waters brought up often.

Victor quickly decided to change the subject. "Anyway, Jeremy is arriving later this morning. He'd like to spend a week with us, observing our labs. According to his letter, he's thinking of applying for an internship with us in the fall. Or perhaps even full-time employment."

"Excellent," Waters mumbled, still focused on the drowsy wolves.

It was a thin charade, and Victor fought back a smile. He knew exactly what Waters was thinking: Jeremy Ross's request for a week of observation had come at the most ironic of times.

"We'll certainly have room for him," Waters said, "owing to the recent tragedy."

Victor looked away, suddenly feeling weary. "Yes," he responded, "the tragedy."

"Victor, I know how hard it must have been for you. It was hard on all of us. And I understand that you had a special relationship with Dr. Aronson—as you have with all of our recent hires."

Victor nodded, his face still turned to the side. A special relationship; that was an interesting choice of words. "Yes," he sighed, "well, these things happen."

"They do. But I think Jeremy Ross might be just the thing for you. A new project, something to occupy your mind."

"I'll give him the complete tour. I'll get him so excited about Tucsome, he'll never want to go back to New York."

Waters's smile doubled in size. "I'm sure you'll do a wonderful job. You're very skilled at that sort of thing—the interpersonal touch. That's why I made you director of Human Resources, after all."

Victor felt a tinge of amusement as he accepted Waters's compliment. "Then I guess it's settled," he said, his voice bright. "I'll make sure the young doctor-to-be has a wonderful week at Tucsome. Good day, Dr. Waters."

Waters didn't look up from his work. "Good day, Victor."

As Victor stepped through the lab's secured door and closed it shut, he reflected on his new identity: *Victor "the Bullet" Alexander, director of Human Resources*.

No, Jason Waters wouldn't get the joke at all. Waters didn't realize that the charade played both ways. As far as he knew, Victor, Gold-One-rated killer, was nothing more than an overly attentive personnel chief.

In Victor's mind, the fiction was much more agreeable than the truth.

11

THE BLACK SEDAN WAS OUT OF PLACE AGAINST THE BACK-
ground of a small-town train station. Its polished German
engineering was an intimidating sight among the pickup
trucks, mail-order jeeps, and dilapidated Buicks that dotted
the oversized parking lot. But, then, the man leaning against
the hood of the Mercedes was also distinct. His pin-striped
Armani suit flapped in the morning breeze, conforming perfectly to the sharp angles of his wiry body. His left leg was
bent at the knee, a shining leather shoe resting delicately
above the right headlight as he leaned forward to examine
what might be a scuff beneath the shoelace. He grimaced, irritation evident in his gaunt features, and pulled a red-and-
white handkerchief out of his jacket pocket. Three ritualistic
pulls of the material against the leather shoe only added to
his irritation; evidently, the shoe had been rendered worthless by an indelible speck of grime. The thin man cursed,
exchanging the handkerchief for a cigarette. A few seconds
later, a trail of smoke had taken his attention away from the

ruinous scuff, and he stared disdainfully at the produce of his own cigarette.

Jeremy watched this entire display with vicarious pleasure, glad for the distraction from the tortured thoughts still running through his head. The train ride from New York had been difficult and long; now that he had arrived at his destination, he was in dire need of something to take his mind off of the task ahead.

Because indeed, the task ahead was daunting. He didn't know what he was walking into—or if, in fact, he was walking into anything at all. He'd spent most of the train ride reading over the list of projects Walker had intended to cut, and he'd found nothing that even remotely suggested a connection with Tucsome.

He slid his heavy gray duffel bag off his shoulder and leaned back against the brick wall of the train station. Then he concentrated his attention on the thin man with the cigarette. There was something oddly comforting about the man, about the way he cracked the glassy serenity that surrounded him. . . .

Jeremy paused halfway through the thought. The thin man was suddenly staring in his direction. His cigarette hung limply between his fingers. A strange, wispy smile cut across his almost lipless mouth.

"Jeremy Ross?" he asked, his English accent so thick that it took Jeremy a moment to discern the words. "It *is* you, isn't it? A little bit heavier than your picture, but New York will do that to one, won't it?"

Jeremy was suddenly nervous. Had he taken a foolish risk by not bothering to conceal his identity? "Do I know you?"

The thin man stepped forward, his hand outstretched. "Victor Alexander," he said through his teeth. "Director of Human Resources, the Tucsome Project. I hope you haven't been waiting long."

"You recognize me?"

"Of course. It wouldn't be easy to meet you here if I didn't, now would it? They gave me an old Dartmouth yearbook picture, though frankly, I hardly thought it necessary. You science chaps have a way of looking alike. Now this couldn't possibly be your only bag, could it? Again, true to form. I could write a book about you chaps. Fine, then, let's gather it up."

With that, he crossed to the back of the Mercedes and flipped open the trunk. Jeremy watched him, confused and relieved at the same time. This bizarre man was not at all the sort of welcoming committee he'd expected. Certainly, a taxi driver with a cardboard sign would have sufficed.

"Come on, then. Hurry along."

Jeremy dragged the duffel bag to the back of the Mercedes. Victor made no move to help as Jeremy heaved the duffel inside.

"You'll have to excuse my abruptness," Victor said, crossing to the driver's side. "This morning's been a bit of a beast. I've only recently moved into Personnel, and it seems the old manager insisted on a positively byzantine filing system. It took me four hours to discover that you were coming in by train. A bit strange, that. There's an airport in Savannah, not fifty miles from here."

Jeremy nodded as he slid into the front seat. The Tucsome Project had offered to refund a first-class plane ticket, but he'd opted for the twelve-hour Amtrak economy ride instead. Not that it had really been a choice; he could still remember the last time he'd attempted to fly. The sound of the wheels going up was the last thing he'd heard. Later, a stewardess had told him that it had taken three people and four Valiums to make him "comfortable" for the six-hour flight.

He glanced back over the milky white leather seat. A "new car" smell filled the air, and he ran his fingers over the dashboard in front of him. Neat lights and gadgets blinked back at him: digital speedometer, glowing indoor/outdoor thermometer, even something mysteriously labeled "Spatial Aware Op."

"It's a charming new device they've worked up over at Mercedes," Victor said, noticing his curiosity. "It makes a little noise when we move too close to something. Wonderful in a traffic jam—though we won't find many around here."

A soft pressure pushed Jeremy back into his seat as Victor edged the sedan away from the sidewalk.

"I've never been inside one of these before," Jeremy said, gaping at the dashboard.

"Oh, it's no Jaguar. But I'll give the Germans credit. This model is fine for a trip to the market."

Jeremy coughed, consciously staring out the window. He felt awkward conversing with this strange man. He consoled himself with the thought that it was only a twelve-mile drive.

U.S. 21 was a black thread laid out in the center of a sandbox, stretching uninterrupted through white dunes and windy grass. The ocean was barely on the horizon, more an accepted fact than an actual phenomenon. The area could have been mistaken for a desert, if not for the smell; through the crack at the top of Jeremy's window, strong gusts of the Atlantic drenched the interior of the Mercedes, erasing all doubt as to the sea's proximity.

Jeremy felt low-level anxiety as the Mercedes accelerated down the open road. Truly, he'd never seen a more deserted landscape. He glanced at the man behind the steering wheel. For some reason, Victor's appearance didn't comfort him. Even though there was nothing overtly dangerous about the thin face and lithe body, there was something in the way Victor moved that pinched at him. Too smooth . . . too soundless. When Victor reached forward to adjust the rearview mirror, it was like a professional basketball player cutting toward the basket, emitting so much control, so much muted strength. Jeremy would not have been surprised if under that slick Armani suit lurked an athlete's body, all wiry muscles and hard, sharp angles.

He turned back toward the window and tried to concentrate on the scenery. A few feeble structures flashed by the open road in front of him. "I didn't expect it to be so deserted. It's hard to believe there's still such a thing as undeveloped beachfront property."

Victor nodded, his long fingers tapping against the steering wheel. "South Carolina's topography varies considerably. Up north, there's the Grand Stand which is centered around Myrtle Beach, a veritable black hole of tourism. You can't go ten feet without bumping into an amusement park or a golf course. But here in the low country, it's a completely different story."

He waved a thin hand at the horizon.

"We're traveling along the Intracoastal Waterway. Off to the east is Hunting Island State Park—some very pretty nature trails, a secluded public beach, even a hundred-and-forty-foot lighthouse. If you have a chance, it's well worth the hike. Also, you should try to get into Beaufort for a few hours. I take it you didn't have a chance to see much of the town from the train?"

Jeremy shook his head. He'd spent most of the train ride concentrating on the list of Defense Department projects—*and* thinking about Robin, wondering where she was, whether he should be looking for her instead of chasing weak links in South Carolina.

"A piece of Americana," Victor continued, his tone slightly sarcastic. "A real antebellum village. Eighteenth-century homes, lavish balconies, high ceilings, palmetto trees, and live oaks. Not much in the way of modern conveniences—but then, Beaufort is a metropolis compared to Tucsome. The town, I mean, not the Project. If one could truly call it a town."

"You don't sound like you care much for Tucsome."

Victor laughed, a thin, almost girlish sound that emanated from between his teeth. "Care for Tucsome? I *despise* Tucsome. I'm from the Continent—London, actually. How could I possibly care for Tucsome?"

"What made you leave London?" Jeremy asked, certain that this man was no scientist. "Are you interested in genetics?"

"Genetics? Christ, no. What gave you that idea?"

"Well, I just thought—exactly what are you interested in?"

Victor laughed. "One and only one thing. The almighty dollar. That's why I'll call this godforsaken place my home as long as the Project smiles on me."

Jeremy nodded, remembering what Mike Callahan had told him during the squash game. "So the Tucsome Project has a lot of money?"

"My dear friend, the Tucsome Project has *all* of the money. Every penny there is in the world."

Jeremy stared at Victor. His thin face was clearly determined.

"You don't believe me?" Victor continued. "Let me give you a little example. Jeremy, how many women do you know with naturally straight hair?"

Jeremy's eyes widened at the spontaneous question. "Plenty," he finally answered. "I'd guess about half the women I've met have had straight hair."

Victor tapped the steering wheel. "And tell me, why was every woman in Asia and most of the women in the rest of the world born with straight hair?"

Jeremy thought for less than a second. "They inherited the gene that codes for straight hair from their parents. Somewhere in their DNA, there's a sequence of chemicals that makes their hair straight."

"Precisely. Because of one lonely, little gene, a billion women have ruler-straight hair. And because of that lonely, little gene, a billion women spend hundreds of hours in beauty parlors and perhaps thousands of dollars on products that give them temporary curls."

Jeremy nodded. He wondered where this was leading.

Victor smiled at him and continued: "Now what if you located the gene that curls straight hair? What if you developed a method to inject this gene—completely without harm or side effect—into any individual? How much money do you think you could make?"

Jeremy opened his mouth to answer, but Victor cut him

off with a wave of his hand. "And that's peanuts compared to the bottom line."

"What's the bottom line?"

Victor laughed. "I think, perhaps, it is better for you to learn that in a more formal setting. For now, let me assure you that cosmetics is but a lilliputian interest of the Tucsome Project."

"You make Tucsome sound like some sort of corporation. I thought it was supposed to be a research leg of the Human Genome Project."

Victor's smile doubled in size. "And one excludes the other? Tell me, Jeremy, what does the Human Genome Project mean to you?"

Jeremy shrugged. "I learned all about it during my second year of medical school. It's the greatest government-funded scientific initiative in history—"

"No need for the hyperbole. I'm already sold. What is the Human Genome Project actually about?"

Jeremy paused, thinking. When he spoke again, he chose his words carefully. "The Project attacks the very essence of human life. Its goal is to locate, isolate, and identify all the genes in the human cell."

"To what end? For what purpose?"

Jeremy was taken aback by the question. In his mind, the Human Genome Project didn't need a purpose—nor did it need justification. It was simply a case of "knowledge for knowledge's sake."

"Once we've mapped out the human genome," Jeremy said, "we'll have a better understanding of what makes us work. Is that a good enough reason?"

"That's a start. But it certainly isn't the Holy Grail."

"Sorry?"

Victor tapped his fingers against the steering wheel. "The Holy Grail. I'm sure you've heard of it. Glittery, priceless, stained with Jesus' blood. Millions have dedicated their lives to the search for it. It's the ultimate treasure, the answer to a quest that goes back to the dawn of religion."

"What does the Holy Grail have to do with genetics?"

"What do you think the sequenced genome is? The Holy Grail of biology. And the Human Genome Project is the search for the ultimate answer."

"The ultimate answer?"

Victor nodded. Hours of chatting with Jason Waters had enabled him to perfect the script. "Now that we know what makes a man a man, how far are we from knowing why? God must find a new hiding place; at the rate we're going, very soon we'll be knocking at his door."

The lofty words struck Jeremy in his chest. They were twice as powerful because he knew their real origin.

"Jason Waters," Jeremy stated. "I've idolized him for a long time."

"You and a thousand other young scientists across the globe. And for good reason. Dr. Waters is the man who is going to give us the Holy Grail. That's why Tucsome is such a gold mine. That's why there are billions pouring in, and billions more on the way."

Jeremy had to smile. "Now who's pitching the hyperbole? The Human Genome Project involves hundreds of laboratories across the country. And the end point of the project—the Holy Grail, as you call it—is quite a long way off."

Victor shrugged, his thin lips turned up at the corners. "Oh, it's not as far away as one might think."

Suddenly, the sedan slowed, a different smell wafting in through the slightly open windows. With effort, Jeremy pulled his eyes away from Victor's face.

"I guess this is what one might call 'the main drag,' " Victor said, motioning with his fingers. "It certainly isn't much. But you'll quickly find that it has its charms—in a desolate, pathetic sense of the word."

The center of town was little more than a two-block sequence of shops, squatting so close together they seemed afraid of the dunes that surrounded them. It was, in many respects, like every other beach town in undiscovered America: white and pink overhangs, wooden shingles, hand-painted signs, and outdoor stands pushing everything from seashells to out-of-season strawberries. Jeremy noticed a coffee shop, an ice cream place, a deli, a movie theater, and a library.

And then, just as suddenly, the sedan was through the town.

"That was it?" Jeremy asked.

"I'm sure you'll have a chance to get a closer look during the next few days. The ice cream is passable, the coffee appalling, the library microscopic—but open all night. If this were Europe, we'd call the town quaint."

Jeremy drummed his fingers against the dashboard. "How many people live around here?"

"There isn't actually a local population to speak of. Before the Project, there was no Tucsome."

"How many people work at the Project?"

"Eight hundred and thirty-two—this week, eight hundred and thirty-three, including you."

"That's a lot of people."

"Not really, when you see the place. It could handle a thousand more. Within a few years, I think it will. Hold on. Here we are. Your new neighborhood."

The Mercedes slowed, edging toward the left. Jeremy saw a high iron fence, the kind one might see around an expensive estate. The fence ran for two hundred yards along the highway. He squinted between the bars and a beautifully landscaped park stared back at him, lush green grass a stark contrast to the dunes on either side.

Victor pulled the Mercedes close to the fence, slowing to a complete stop in front of a high wooden gate. The gate was ornate, with gold-embossed lettering arching above the twin doors: PAULING MEMORIAL GATE.

Jeremy smiled. "An auspicious entrance. Named after Linus Pauling, I assume. The famous chemist who lost the race for the structure of DNA. Watson and Crick beat him by a number of days."

"Watson, Crick, *and* Waters," Victor snapped. The words came out sharp, obviously sharper than Victor had intended.

He offered a weak smile. "Excuse my enthusiasm. It's something we're very sensitive about around here."

Before Jeremy could respond, Victor's window was sliding down, the mechanical hum reverberating through the car. Victor leaned his head out the window and spoke softly into a small black box at the edge of the wooden gate. The black box coughed, and then a voice replied:

"Yes, sir. Please proceed."

There was a loud, metallic click. Then the gate doors swung inward in a low, perfectly symmetrical arc.

"Let me be the first to welcome you to Tucsome," Victor said as he pushed the Mercedes through the open gate.

The first thing that struck Jeremy was the preciseness. It looked as though every blade of grass had been shorn to exact dimensions. Oddly shaped trees twisted off to the right and left, exact mirror images of one another. Every hundred yards, the path was dissected by an equivalent gravel path leading off in a perpendicular direction. In the distance on either side, Jeremy could make out pretty two-story houses, each one an exact copy of another.

"You'll quickly find that this place has everything one could possibly desire," Victor was saying, his right hand on the wheel, his left hand pointing. "Over there is an indoor pool. Behind it, six indoor tennis courts. Do you like tennis? Of course you do, who doesn't like tennis? There's a supermarket off to the left, behind that hill. The golf course is still under construction; it should be operational by October."

The Mercedes slowed as it passed by a huge circular fountain. A twenty-foot-high marble double helix stood in the center of the fountain, squirting a stream of clear water out of its top. Jeremy's eyes widened at the sight; the magnified strand of DNA took his breath away, glistening wet and glowing in the midmorning sun.

"They tell me that the original plan for this fountain called for a double helical stream of water," Victor commented, "rather than a marble statue. But the architects couldn't manage to work it out. Ironic, isn't it? Barely a hundred yards away, you scientists are playing with the real thing—and they can't even manage a decent fountain."

"I think it's beautiful," Jeremy said, impressed.

"Nice of you to say so. If it were up to me, I'd tear the damn thing down and start over. Maybe a nice Rodin in a bed of violets. There's enough science around this place without them stuffing it down our throats. DNA, DNA, DNA—it's all anyone thinks about around here."

On the other side of the fountain, the Mercedes took a sharp right onto another path. They curved around a low green hill and slowed as they entered a paved driveway. Jeremy caught a glance of a pretty white house. He raised his eyebrows as Victor shifted the car into park.

"Here's where you'll be staying while you're in Tucsome. I hope you'll find it adequate."

"Christ," Jeremy murmured in response. He pressed his face against the window.

Maybe New York had ruined his perspective. Or maybe it was the way the sun was gleaming down over the smooth, arching roof and echoing off of the huge picture windows that encircled the first floor. To Jeremy, the house was stunning.

"Two bedrooms," Victor said, as if ticking off an inventory. "Every employee receives the same—call it a signing bonus. A study, a living room, a dining room, and a kitchen. You needn't worry about laundry; a van from Beaufort comes by at five o'clock every morning—just leave your knickers on the front porch. The deck out back was added by the previous owners. They picked out the color, too. White. I've never understood this southern preoccupation with white."

Jeremy shook his head, amazed. He'd expected a dormitory. Most scientific institutions kept their staffs in cement-and-glass stables. "This is extravagant," he said.

Victor shrugged. "I assure you, we get back what we put in. After all, it's one of you chaps who's going to bring us the next Nobel, isn't it? Likewise, who do you think is going to put a curl in the Japanese woman's hair? We consider this house an investment. It's an investment that has paid off in the past, and it's an investment that will continue to pay off in the future."

Jeremy didn't respond. He was too busy staring at the house.

"The yard is two acres," Victor continued. "That's including the back, of course. The second floor overlooks the golf course—or what we have of it. Your nearest neighbor is five hundred yards beyond these hills, so you can make as much noise as you'd like, nobody will be bothered by it. All of the utilities are luxury—by Tucsome standards."

Jeremy ran a hand through his hair, reminding himself to stay sober, objective. He tried to concentrate on the details. "I don't see a garage," he said finally. "Is there a lot somewhere nearby?"

"Oh, you'll find there's really no need for a car. The Project has thirty drivers on call twenty-four hours. This sedan is one of fifty at your disposal. But there really isn't anywhere to go, is there? 'Downtown' is barely a five-minute walk. There's a beautiful beach just three minutes down the highway. And the Project is directly around the corner. No, there's really no need for a car. None of the other employees has a car."

Interesting, Jeremy thought, cataloging the information. "So the Tucsome Project owns the house?"

Victor nodded, speaking out of the corner of his mouth as if relaying a trivial detail. "The house, the golf course—most of the town itself. The Tucsome Project doesn't sell its property. That would be counterproductive. If you came to work here and bought this house, what would you do when you decided to move on? Sell it back to the Project? What would be the logic in that? The Project is going to be here for a long, long time. You, on the other hand, are not."

Jeremy raised his eyebrows.

Victor turned toward him, smiling. "Nobody stays here

very long. It's the nature of the business. Who could handle Tucsome forever? Certainly not a young man such as yourself. Just long enough to make a difference, hopefully."

Jeremy swallowed. It sounded as though Victor was intimating that this could, one day, become a long-term arrangement. For a brief moment, he felt a surge of excitement. Then the pressure of his teeth against his lower lip brought him back down.

It was going to take control and inner strength to stay on course. Every time he felt this excitement, he'd have to conjure up Robin's image. He'd have to remember the CNN footage of Warren T. Walker falling to his knees at a Princeton graduation. And he'd have to imagine himself helpless in a garage twelve years ago. He wasn't here to be won over, he was in Tucsome to try and put back together the pieces of his life.

He turned away from the beautiful house and looked at Victor. The thin man was watching him carefully. There was something oddly cold in the center of those deep blue eyes. Jeremy forced a quick smile. "It's a beautiful house," he said, his voice level. "I can't wait to see the inside."

"Sadly enough," Victor responded, "you'll *have* to wait. But I don't think you'll be disappointed. You can see a house anywhere in the world."

He pressed his shiny leather shoe against the accelerator, and the Mercedes rolled forward.

"Prepare yourself," he said through a smile. "I'm about to introduce you to a place that will no doubt affect the rest of your life."

12

THE TUCSOME PROJECT FOR GENETIC RESEARCH WAS CLEARLY not a modest institution, Jeremy thought as he followed Victor toward the automatic sliding-glass doors.

From the outside, the building looked like a huge horseshoe. Two parallel legs, each six stories high, were joined by a transparent skywalk that overlooked a beautifully landscaped park, complete with picnic tables, trees, and a small man-made swan lake.

Idyllic, expensive, immense.

Under other circumstances, Jeremy would have simply been impressed. Instead, he felt apprehensive. The sheer size of the place was intimidating; it would take months to explore the entire complex. And he wasn't even sure what he was looking for.

"In the spring and summer," Victor explained as they walked along a tree-lined path, "this park sees a lot of use. A little dull by my standards, but it does the trick on a particularly trying midmorning. I've spent many hours sitting by this little lake, wishing the swans would get up and do something to entertain me.

"The Project itself is actually two separate buildings, joined in the center by the skywalk. This section here is primarily research, with thirty laboratories and over sixty smaller specialized chambers. The other building—which we call West, because of where it is—is a full-service hospital."

"Full service?"

"Absolutely. Emergency room, radiology, pathology, ICU, and ninety beds. Aside from serving the community, the hospital specializes in treating nasty genetic diseases. People fly in from all over the world for diagnosis and treatment. Of course, most of our research scientists have little contact with West—although as a medical student, you'll doubtless find yourself wandering over there in your spare time."

The sliding doors swished open as they approached, and a blast of refrigerated air hit Jeremy in the face. He followed Victor into a huge room, glancing down at the bright red carpet beneath his feet.

"Please don't ask me about the color scheme," Victor said. "If it were up to me, I'd have all of these carpets pulled out and burned. And just look at those walls. Robin's egg blue?" He gave a shudder.

Jeremy nodded, barely listening. He was inside Tucsome. His heart beat rapidly in his chest, and he could feel the sweat rising under his armpits. An image suddenly flashed of Warren T. Walker up on the Princeton stage, hands tearing at his face. Had Walker contracted some horrible new disease from breathing this same refrigerated air?

Jeremy quickly chided himself. He was letting his imagination run away from him. He forced himself to make a study of his surroundings.

The room was hexagonal, at least a hundred feet in diameter. The walls were twenty feet high, and—as Victor had mentioned—a deep, calming blue. A round kiosk squatted in the center of the room, behind which sat six women facing outward. The women were young and dressed in white nurses' uniforms.

"Ladies," Victor said, resting his hands on the edge of the kiosk, "time to make a good impression. I've got the newest member of our family with me. Come a little closer, Jeremy—they won't bite. At least not on the first date."

"You're skating dangerously close to harassment," one of the women said, wagging her finger.

"Indeed," Victor said, smiling. "Now Angela, be a dear and page Lyle Anderson."

"Lyle?" Angela asked, looking at Jeremy. She was dark-skinned, with short, curly hair, round eyes, and thick, glossy lips. She shook her head, in mock sorrow. "You poor man."

She picked up a phone from behind her and dialed three numbers. A mechanical female voice echoed through the carpeted lobby: "Lyle Anderson to East Reception."

Jeremy looked at Victor: "Who's Lyle?"

Angela leaned forward, shielding her mouth with her hand as if she were telling a grave secret. "He's the biggest ass you'll ever meet."

"Angela," Victor cautioned. Then he turned toward Jeremy. "Well, he's not the biggest ass. But I will say this about him, he could use a rap to his jaw. He's very young and very smart—a dangerous combination. But you'll get used to him. He's been assigned as your, uh, buddy, for lack of a better word. He'll give you a tour of the complex and perhaps let you take part in some of the work he's doing. Waters himself assigned the matchup; he thought the two of you might hit it off, because of your age."

"I wouldn't wish Lyle on my worst enemy," Angela said, shaking her head.

"Ah," Victor interrupted, "here he comes. Quiet now, Angela."

Jeremy followed Victor's eyes toward a pair of glass sliding doors near the back of the reception area. A medium-sized young man with cropped, white-blond hair stepped through, his hands jammed into the pockets of a white lab coat and his head swiveling on an extremely long neck. He saw Victor and grimaced. Then he moved forward, his head bouncing back and forth with each step. When he got within range, he offered a tight-lipped nod at the women behind the reception desk. Then he glanced at Jeremy.

"You must be Ross, huh? Dartmouth and New York City, right?"

Jeremy nodded. Lyle grunted and waved a stubby hand at Angela and the rest of the women at the reception kiosk. "Already wasting time with the girls, I see. Victor's bad habits rub off mighty quickly. If it were up to him, there wouldn't be any science going on in this place. Just chitchat and fancy suits."

Victor offered a thin smile. "Quite right, Lyle. As always, quite right. I suppose there's really no room for culture in a laboratory."

"Not unless it's locked away in a petri dish," Jeremy said.

Lyle snorted and turned on his heels. "Wonderful. Another amateur comedian—with the emphasis on *amateur*. Come along, Ross."

Jeremy looked pleadingly at Victor, who shrugged. "If you need anything," he sighed, "just pick up the nearest phone and dial three nines."

He shook Jeremy's hand and then turned back toward the sliding-glass doors. Jeremy watched him go, again noting the smoothness of his motions, the catlike grace.

"Enough with the teary good-byes," Lyle called from the other side of the room, "let's get a move on, Ross."

Jeremy hastily followed after him, his chest rising and falling as he rushed to catch up.

"The first thing you need to learn about this place," Lyle said as they steamrolled down a long hallway, "is that there are innate hierarchies of populations. This week, you're an honorary member of the top rung—the research scientists. The business cogs and service people inhabit the bottom rung. That's Victor and his lot. Avoid them like the plague. They steal your attention from the important things that are going on around here. Which is to say, the science."

Jeremy watched Lyle as he talked, reading as much from his appearance as he could. The young scientist looked to be about twenty-four; his face, shiny with freckles and unidentifiable spots, had that sharp quality of youth to it, and the way he walked—his head bouncing forward and back like the head of a chicken, his knees bending a little too much—made Jeremy think of tightly wound springs. His lab coat hung down to his thighs, hiding much of what he was wearing; but from the denim collar that stuck out from under the lab coat, Jeremy surmised that Victor would have cringed at the sight of his outfit.

"The second thing you need to learn about this place," Lyle continued, turning a corner, "is that there are some pretty impressive people crawling down these hallways. You never know whether the guy you're talking to barely got his Ph.D., or was on the short list for last year's Nobel. So never assume anything. And don't ever pretend that age has anything to do with status around here. Age is irrelevant."

Jeremy nodded, rubbing his palms against his slacks. His eyes were wide open, taking in as much as possible. He was so caught up in keeping his senses lucid that he nearly tripped when Lyle stopped, suddenly, and turned to face him. A cloud of something half angry, half amused filled Lyle's features.

"I got my B.S. from MIT at sixteen. I got my master's and then my Ph.D. in three years. I've been first author of sixteen articles, four of them in *Science* magazine. I've named nine proteins. And I'm twenty-two years old."

Jeremy looked at him. "I wouldn't worry. Some of us are just late bloomers."

Lyle paused for a full beat. Finally, a smile broke across his lips. "I like you, Ross. I think we're going to get along all right."

He spun on his heels and headed directly for a large blue door. Jeremy followed behind, shaking his head. In some ways, Lyle reminded him of Mike Callahan. An asshole on the outside—but deep down beat the heart of a likable jerk.

Lyle put his hand flat against the blue door and glanced over his shoulder. "Okay, Ross. Now you're in for a treat. I'm going to show you the most unique attraction this place has to offer."

From the back of the huge amphitheater, Jason Waters looked nothing like Jeremy had imagined. His wide-shouldered body cast a bold shadow over the mahogany podium, and his rectangular face seemed smooth, without wrinkle or blemish. Even his silvery hair had a youthful energy, shimmering under the high-intensity overhead lights.

Jeremy watched him carefully, an uncontrolled adoration welling up. For years, Waters had been one of his idols—a mythical figure worthy of deification. Waters had been in that lab in 1953; he'd challenged the very secrets of life and had walked away stronger still. The fact that he hadn't received the Nobel Prize with Watson and Crick had made him even more of a legend, a hero to all the young scientists who were likewise invisible to history, who were likewise changing the world.

"This should be interesting," Lyle whispered as he ushered Jeremy toward a foldout movie-theater chair in the last tier. "You picked a good time to visit. Looks like half of the AMA is in town."

Jeremy glanced around. The amphitheater was packed with doctors; tier upon tier of men and women in white lab coats, shifting in excited anticipation as they stared in awe at the man behind the podium.

"It's part of their annual convention," Lyle continued. "They come from all over the country to spend a few days with us. Makes them feel like they're a part of the genetic revolution. They can go back to their private practices and big-city hospitals a little less ignorant—and perhaps a little more dangerous."

Jeremy raised his eyebrows. The distaste was evident in

Lyle's voice. "At least they're trying," Jeremy said. "Not everyone has to be a genetics expert."

"That's bullshit, Ross, and you know it. Genetics is turning the whole world upside down. For one thing, medicine is going to be a totally different game in a few years. Right now, we wait for someone to get sick so we can cut him up and pump him full of drugs. A few years from now, we'll take a look at a single cell and treat the diseases before they show. But hell, that's not even the tip of the iceberg. Just take a look at the sign."

Lyle waved his hand toward the stage. Ten feet above the podium was a placard with huge, embossed letters.

WE HAVE DISCOVERED THE SECRET OF LIFE.

"Francis Crick," Jeremy murmured, half to himself.

"Right. But I bet you didn't know that it originated in a postcard sent to Jason Waters just days after the great event. Or that the 'we' referred to three people—not two, as the history books would have us believe."

Jeremy raised his eyebrows, but Lyle was talking too fast to notice him.

"The secret of life. That's what it is, Ross. But go up to the average American and say the word 'genome' to him, and he'll have no clue what you're talking about. Hell, nine out of ten doctors don't know the first thing about DNA. It's appalling!"

Lyle was so worked up he was barely in his seat. His face was bright red and his lips were quivering. Jeremy had seen the look before—in the mirror. The operative word was frustration.

The genetic revolution outscaled everything else in the history of science—and nobody seemed to notice. Research centers like Tucsome were changing the world, and nobody seemed to care.

"It's not as though we're working in secret," Lyle huffed. "Hiding ourselves like modern-day Dr. Frankensteins. The results are published every day in journals and stock offerings. That's what makes their ignorance so damn frustrating."

Jeremy couldn't help but agree. Back at New York City Hospital, he had felt this frustration every day. Doctors he respected, brilliant men, spoke about genetics as if it were simply another branch of science. Often he'd come home from the hospital bright red in the face, so many words caught in his throat: *The genome redefines science. The genome is—*

"Life!"

The word echoed through the amphitheater, and it took Jeremy a second to realize that it had not emerged from inside his head. Huge amplifiers on either side of the stage reverberated as Jason Waters leaned over the podium, his angelic smile inches away from the microphone.

"Life," he repeated, "the ultimate mystery. Throughout history philosophers and scientists have searched for its secret. In 1953, that secret was revealed to us in a laboratory three thousand miles from this spot. Consequently, today the human species approaches a level of biological control that is almost godlike."

Jeremy shivered at this last word. He watched Jason Waters's face, transfixed by the pure, unchanging smile. He'd never before seen an expression that exuded so much certainty.

"As the saying goes, he who controls the gene controls the world. Today, my friends, we're barely a heartbeat away from total and complete understanding of the entire human genome. The only true question that remains is how to use this knowledge—because the knowledge itself is inevitable. The genome is entirely within our grasp. . . ."

Jeremy shifted his eyes around the room as Waters began a more basic lecture on genetics: beginning with the forty-six chromosomes that inhabited every human cell, and continuing through the chemical makeup of DNA, the four nitrogenous bases—ATCG—that coded for everything from the color of a man's hair to the length of his arm. Jeremy concentrated on the faces in the room, the doctors who'd gathered to hear the great man speak. It dawned on him that most of these people were staring at Jason Waters the same way they would've stared at a work of art at the Met; when they left the amphitheater, they'd remember very little of what he was saying. Genetics wasn't real to them. To them, genetics hadn't yet left the laboratory.

When the lecture ended, there was a momentary bubble of silence, and then people began rising from their seats. Lyle put a hand on Jeremy's shoulder. "So what did you think?"

"Very interesting. Brilliant, even."

"No, he saves the brilliant stuff for real scientists. The sheep get the canned goods. He who controls the gene controls the world, the genome is God, et cetera. It's what they expect."

"So he's different in person?"

"You're about to find out," Lyle whispered.

Startled, Jeremy whirled on his heels.

Standing in front of him was Dr. Jason Waters.

"Dr. Waters," Lyle said, his voice suddenly very mature, "this is Jeremy Ross."

"Yes, yes, of course," Waters commented, his smile almost blindingly bright. "Your thesis was on retrovirus gene therapy, isn't that right? Tailored HIV vectors, chimp studies. Wonderful stuff, just wonderful."

"Thank you," Jeremy responded, excited that Waters knew his work. "It's an honor to finally meet you."

Waters jovially slapped Jeremy's shoulder with a firm hand.

"No need for the deferential treatment, Jeremy. Here at Tucsome, we're all one big family. Reputation, age, appearance—these things don't mean anything. We're a team, in the truest sense of the word. After all, we're all chasing the same dream."

Jeremy nodded as the adrenaline coursed through his body. He felt off balance; he wanted to remain suspicious and alert, but part of him was enjoying this.

"Lyle," Waters said, shifting his eyes, "for the next few

days Jeremy will be under your charge. I hope you'll make his time with us exciting—a true taste of what it's like to be a member of our family."

He turned back toward Jeremy, his face beaming. "There's real magic going on within these walls. I think you'll quickly discover that we're moving forward at a pace beyond anyone's imagination."

Jeremy nodded, remembering his conversation with Victor Alexander. "So I've heard. Not far from the Holy Grail, so to speak."

"The Holy Grail," Waters repeated, smiling. "An interesting choice of words. Let me ask you a question. Do you believe in God?"

Jeremy glanced at Lyle, whose expression showed helpless sympathy. "I don't really know. I haven't thought about it."

Waters's smile doubled in size. "Haven't thought about it. That's a very good one. God? Why, it just hasn't come up. Jeremy, let me leave you with a thought. More people believe in God than in gravity. If we took away gravity, you can imagine the results. But what would happen if we took away God?"

With that, Waters spun on his heels. A second later he disappeared into a jumble of adoring doctors.

"And that," Lyle said, leaning close, "was Dr. Jason Waters."

Jeremy could feel knots of curiosity forming up and down his spine. "What was all that stuff about God?"

"Your comment about the Holy Grail got him going. Religion is one of his pet subjects."

"A religious geneticist? I thought atheism was a prerequisite for the profession. How does he reconcile the implications of DNA with religion?"

"In his mind, DNA is as much proof of God's existence as it is his killing stroke. There's a famous quote—I'm not sure I remember it exactly. 'We know that somewhere there are squiggles in black ink that represent the notes to Beethoven's

Ninth Symphony, but in no way does that diminish the grandeur of the symphony itself.' "

Jeremy nodded, finishing the famous sentiment: "And after all, Beethoven had twelve notes to work with. God had only four."

"You really did have a lonely childhood."

Jeremy smiled. Then he rubbed his hands through his hair.

"You okay?" Lyle asked.

"To be honest, I'm a little tense."

Lyle laughed. "Waters will do that to you. That stuff he said about this place being one big happy family—don't take it too seriously. This place is a race, one tense fucking race. And that's exactly how Waters wants it to be."

"A race?"

Lyle offered a playful smile. "You'll see what I mean soon enough. Now, are you ready to start the tour?"

Jeremy nodded, feeling his adrenaline rise.

"Then follow close behind," Lyle said, "and keep your hands in the bus at all times—or they're liable to get bit off."

13

THE METRO GROANED, ORANGE LIGHTS FLICKERING AS THE subway's wheels struggled toward a steady rhythm. Advertisements flashed by the rattling windows, quickly replaced by the inky hollow of a concrete tunnel. A hundred yards above, the afternoon sun drew rainbows across Washington, D.C.'s streets. But the Metro was oblivious; in the subway, it was always the middle of the night.

A woman with jet black hair and thick glasses huddled in the far corner of the last car. Her long body swam under an oversized yellow parka. She had a newspaper open on her lap, and she scanned the headlines with unusual intensity.

A few seconds passed, and she folded the newspaper closed. Her face showed relief. Then she realized that the title of the newspaper was in full view, and she quickly slid it between her legs. It wasn't a Washington paper. A nosy commuter might have wondered why this woman was reading the *New York Post;* a clever observer might have guessed that the woman had just arrived by Amtrak from the Big Apple. The woman cursed at herself for being so careless.

It was just that sort of mistake that could get her killed.

Robin shivered, adjusting her thick plastic glasses. She'd purchased them at a costume shop on Seventh Avenue. They were foolish, a Halloween gag. Like the jet black dye job, they were a feeble attempt at disguise. In New York, she'd been out of her element; she'd been forced to take chances, and the thick glasses and dyed hair were simply two more rolls of the dice. Thankfully, they'd been enough to get her through Penn Station.

Now that she was back in Washington, it was a different story. She knew Washington as well as she knew her own reflection; she'd been born in the city, had spent three years at Georgetown, and more important, she was a lawyer. To a lawyer, Washington was more than a city; it was a hive.

One out of every eighteen people in Washington had passed the bar exam. There were more lawyers on the streets of the city than there were in all of Europe. And with lawyers came secrets: backroom negotiations, unlisted telephone numbers, private clubs, shady corporations. There were hundreds of people who could help her, hundreds of safe houses and discreet hotels. She could disappear for days, weeks— possibly even months.

Originally, that had been her plan. She'd left New York City Hospital determined to make herself vanish. Her loyalty to her father didn't run to suicide; he was dead, she was alive—it was as simple as that. She'd been an army brat who became a child of wealth and politics, and she'd learned at an early age how to close out the world, how to form a psychological shell she could hide behind. She'd intended to curl up in herself, push the horror of her father's death away, use the same lies she'd used when her mother had passed away: close her eyes, forget, let her feelings of self-preservation take over. In short, she'd planned to cover up her trail and simply disappear.

And then, in a moment of weakness, she'd done something foolish. She'd dialed the hospital and had asked to speak to Jeremy. She'd wanted to hear his voice one more time. Wanted to explain to him why she was leaving. Maybe she'd even planned to tell him how it had felt to see him again.

But Jeremy hadn't been available to take her call. According to Mike Callahan, he'd gone on a short vacation—to South Carolina.

A weak link, Jeremy had called it: Two years ago her father had visited a genetic research institute in South Carolina. Now Jeremy was retracing her father's steps, following the weak link because it was the only link he had.

She'd been immediately overcome by a torrent of emotions. Guilt, for changing the course of Jeremy's life. Gratitude, for what he was trying to do. And apprehension, regarding what he might discover. Instantly, her thoughts of simply hiding out had dribbled away like melting snow.

So she'd made an abrupt change of plans. She and Jeremy were going to work as a team, whether he knew it or not. If Tucsome was a link, they'd follow it together.

First, though, they needed information. And if there was one thing she'd learned in all her years in Washington, it was where to go for information.

The Mackerel Pub was a Dupont Circle fixture, a trendy-but-classy happy-hour bar where the pin-striped went to drink, mingle, and prepare for the long Metro ride home. Robin pushed her way through the heavy double doors and reveled in the rush of familiarity.

She moved forward, her eyes adjusting to the dim lighting. When she reached the end of the long mahogany bar, she shifted on her heels, scanning the small tables that lined the back wall.

She saw him immediately. Mid-fifties, tan, with gun-metal hair combed so fiercely that she could see every single strand. Devin Stark was just as she remembered him—dashing, stylish, his perfect pores oozing self-confidence. He was the quintessential Washington "player," born and bred for the political game. And there were those who believed he had more influence than twice his weight in senators. Robin's own experience had only served to justify the hearsay; in fact, Devin Stark was one of the main reasons she'd chosen to study law in the first place. He was living proof that ambition equaled achievement—if practiced honorably, consistently, and without regret.

She stopped directly in front of his table, a welcome sense of relief overtaking her. He stared right past her.

"Devin."

He looked up, startled. Then recognition flashed across his face.

"Robin?"

He quickly rose out of his chair, his Nautilus physique shifting under a perfectly tailored pin-striped suit. "What's with the disguise? Find yourself on the wrong side of the IRS one too many times?"

She laughed and took his hands. He kissed her on the cheek, and she could smell his cologne. Decidedly expensive, but not overbearing. Seamlessly appropriate for the chief confidant to the U.S. attorney general.

"Something like that. Thanks for meeting me on such short notice."

"You know I'm always available for you."

He beckoned her to the seat across from him, and she slipped out from under her yellow parka, suddenly conscious of the way the Anne Klein sheath underneath clung to her body. Even though Devin was thirty years her senior, she'd always felt this way around him. Her feelings weren't of a sexual nature—she'd fallen for him as a pigtailed six-year-old and had never stopped thinking of him in those terms— but she was acutely aware of the way he looked at her, at the hint of approval that sparkled behind his blue eyes.

The approval deepened as she crossed her legs, watching as a slicked-up waiter placed a tall drink in front of her.

"Chablis," Devin said, grinning as he lowered himself into the seat across from her.

She smiled, impressed. "You have a good memory."

"It hasn't been that long, has it. But I forget, young women measure time in days. When you get to be my age, you'll begin to see things a little differently. Years in the blink of an eye, decades reduced to a catalog of names and faces."

She sipped her wine, a light smile on her face. "You're not turning philosophic on me, are you Devin?"

"Philosophic? You flatter me. I've been a lawyer for thirty-one years, and in all that time, no one has ever accused me of spouting anything remotely profound."

Robin laughed. "Someone should tell that to all of the judges out there who use your publications to justify their rulings."

Devin waved away the comment with a manicured hand. Then his face changed, a sympathetic shadow moving across his cheeks. He leaned forward, lowering his voice. "Robin, I don't know whether you got my messages or not. But I'm truly sorry for your loss. I know you and your father didn't see eye to eye, but he was a good man. He loved you immensely."

She nodded. Devin had been one of her father's closest friends. In many ways, he'd been like an uncle to her, someone she could count on without reservation.

"Thankfully, I had a chance to reconcile with him before he died. But I'm still having trouble accepting what happened. In fact, that's part of why I asked you to meet me here."

"Anything I can do," Devin said, showing with his eyes that he meant it. "Just tell me."

She reached out and took a booklet of matches off the center of the table. She twirled the matches with her fingers, trying to find the best approach. She trusted him, but she didn't want to say too much. There was a chance he'd become overprotective—and that would put him in danger. She chose her words carefully: "I need you to introduce me to someone."

He raised his eyebrows. "That's a new one. Usually, I'm the one whom people want to meet. Man or woman?"

"A very powerful man," she said, swirling her drink. "Steven Leary, the director of the CIA. I've tried all the normal channels, but I've come up empty."

Devin nodded. "That's no surprise. The situation in North Korea has most of the White House buried in security. Even though Leary knew your father, it's doubtful he'd be able to break schedule to talk to you. There's a hell of a storm brewing, after all."

She raised an eyebrow. She had only a passing knowledge of the "situation" in North Korea. "With everything that's been going on in my life, I haven't been paying much attention to the newspapers. Is it really that bad?"

He shrugged. "Depends on what you mean by bad. The North Koreans still have a couple of weeks left to comply with the UN's demands. But my guess is, invasion preparations are already in the works."

"An invasion? Really?"

He swirled his drink. "It isn't the 1950s anymore. A major imbalance in technology has dramatically transformed the playing field. And the President could certainly use the PR that would come from a quick military victory. Too, there's a group at the Pentagon who'd love the chance to show off what they've been doing with all that money they've been spending."

Robin shivered, thinking of her father's aborted speech. She wondered how many Pentagon staffers would still be inclined to "show off" had her father been allowed to deliver that address.

"Can you help me?"

Devin leaned back in his chair, thinking. "As I said, the timing makes things difficult. You can't just call Leary up and ask him out for a drink. He's surrounded by security at all times."

"But you can arrange it?"

He smiled, carefully rubbing his jaw. "Well, there may be one way. But you're not going to like it."

She finished her drink and set the glass down. "Just tell me what I have to do."

14

THERE WAS AN UNWRITTEN LAW OF SCIENTIFIC RESEARCH FACILITIES that the more a laboratory looked like a basement, the more productive it would be. Consequently, all genetic labs looked like basements: cinderblock walls, smooth cement floors, gadgets and wires piled on steel shelves, and a recycled, damp hum in the air that could as easily have originated in a suburban basement's boiler closet as in a multibillion-dollar generator room.

The third floor of Tucsome East was no exception; even though the labs were high above ground level, Jeremy was hard-pressed to find even the slightest hint of a window or a passing glint of sunlight.

His feet clicked against the cement floor as he followed Lyle down a quiet hallway. He passed by room after room, catching glimpses of machines—both recognizable and strange—and people in white lab coats hunched over beakers and test tubes that reflected the glare of high-powered fluorescent lights.

"There are sixty groups sharing this floor," Lyle said as they turned a corner and headed down another cinderblock hallway, "but we pretty much keep to ourselves. In fact, you'll soon learn that the teams can be fairly competitive— and not at all the big family that Waters pretends. Last year, seventeen groups had articles published in scientific magazines ranging from the *New England Journal of Medicine* to *Science*. Six groups were nominated for international awards. My team was one of those six."

Jeremy nodded. Competition was the cornerstone of the scientific profession. Every scientific discovery became a game, sometimes involving hundreds of scientists across the globe. The hunt for the structure of DNA, which Watson, Crick, and Waters had barely won by a hair, had involved over thirty scientists in ten different countries.

"One of these days," Lyle continued, "someone at the Project is going to stumble his way to the Nobel. God knows, I dream about it every night. So believe me when I tell you that we expect a lot from each other. A car with three good wheels and a flat won't win the Indy 500. Likewise, a team with one weak member won't get the Nobel."

"How many people are on your team?"

"There were four of us, but as of last week there are three. Don't worry about the others; for the next few days, you and I will be working predominantly one-on-one. You're a lucky guy, Ross."

Lyle turned an abrupt corner into a large room with obscenely low ceilings. The room was divided into four parallel aisles by low shelves that resembled a modern glass menagerie, beakers and test tubes glistening under the flickering fluorescent lights.

"This is Grand Central. It's been my lab for a little over a year, and I'm dangerously close to falling in love with it. As you can see, we have a complete assortment of trade tools. Over to my left is our pride and joy, a Lind sequencer."

Jeremy's eyes widened at the sight of the huge machine, standing on its own table in a corner of the lab. He knew from his time at Dartmouth that a Lind sequencer cost a little over a million dollars. For that low-low price, the purchaser acquired the ability to sequence five thousand DNA bases a day, exceeding the performance of any other machine.

Lyle moved down the first hall, giving him a guided tour of his equipment. "You of course recognize the ultrasound hood, which we use to sterilize everything from test tubes to our own fingers. Over there are our gel electrophoresis machines for basic DNA sampling; we've got sixteen in this lab, another three next door. Electron microscopes, two. Centrifuges, six. DNA washers, ten."

Lyle came to a huge refrigerator and heaved open the door. Cold, odorless air hit Jeremy in the face, and he saw row upon row of round plastic cell plates.

"We keep our cells in here. Anything that needs to be cold. Don't stand here with the door open, or the ice cream will melt."

They turned another corner and headed down an alley similar to the first, with row upon row of test tubes casting shadows across machines, both familiar and unique. There were two sinks near the end of the aisle, where a well-proportioned woman in a lab coat was busily washing a beaker.

"Christina, meet Jeremy Ross."

Christina Guarrez looked up, her dark eyes smiling. "Hi there. Lyle said we'd have a visitor."

"Christina's a hell of a poker player," Lyle said a bit ruefully. "She took home half my salary last month."

"It's only fair play," she said. "I clean out your test tubes, I clean out your wallet."

The last aisle contained a low shelf with six IBM computer terminals standing in a row. All of the computers were on, with synchronized blinking cursors.

"And here are our computers," Lyle continued. "We don't use them very often—computers haven't kept pace with the advances in genetics, certainly not with what we're doing here. Most of our target genes won't be on-line for a year, at best."

Jeremy crossed toward the closest computer and stared down at the screen. Its green glow made him feel comfortable. He absentmindedly hit the space bar with his first finger. Flashing letters appeared at the top of the screen:

"GOOD MORNING, MATTHEW. ARE WE HAVING FUN YET?"

He recognized the name and froze, his eyes riveted to the screen. Lyle stared down over his shoulder.

"Hmm. They've been working on that for a few days. Can't seem to properly clean out the hard drive."

Jeremy forced his face to remain a blank. "Who's Matthew?"

Lyle sighed. His eyes dimmed, and for a moment he turned away. "Was, not is. He was the M.D. on my team—every team has an M.D., Waters's rule. Matt Aronson was a great guy and a superb doctor. Last week, he and his wife were run over by a drunk driver, out on U.S. 21. Matt was only twenty-eight years old. It's still hard to believe."

"Did they catch the guy?" Jeremy asked. "The drunk driver?"

"Yeah, some hick from upstate. Left his truck at the scene and fled. Evidently, he had a history of that sort of thing."

Jeremy exhaled. He should follow up, he supposed, though it sounded like a simple case of rotten luck. He drummed his fingers against the computer keyboard, almost forgetting that Lyle was watching him.

"Matt was the only one of us who ever actually used the damn things. A specialist was sent down to fix it after he died—but obviously he didn't solve the problem. No surprise, really. Matt spent hours toying with the system. His goal was to make it as human as possible."

"Human?"

"That was Matt. He was an interesting guy. Had an M.D. from Harvard, but decided all he ever wanted to do was research. A shame it had to happen now, so close to Waters's unveiling."

Jeremy scrunched his forehead.

"You said it yourself," Lyle offered. "The Holy Grail. Three and a half days from now, Waters is going to make his experiments public."

"Experiments?"

"For years, Waters has been working on something in his private lab. Now he's nearly finished, and the big unveiling is only days away."

Jeremy could hear the excitement in Lyle's voice. "Any idea what the experiments have to do with?"

"Nobody knows. Waters's lab is off-limits to everyone except Victor and the animal handlers."

"Animal handlers? He keeps chimps in his lab?"

Lyle shook his head. "Wolves."

"You're joking."

"Not at all. A family of Alaskan timber wolves. Nasty creatures. Waters had them shipped in two years ago—you wouldn't believe the expense. They're an endangered species. And they've got teeth like a band saw. About a year ago, a tech who stuck his head where it didn't belong got mauled so bad he was carried out of here in a Ziploc bag. Not the ideal household pet, I'd say."

"I've never heard of wolves being used as experimental animals. What's Waters doing with them?"

"Genetic mapping, mostly. Comparative studies of wolf and human genes. Every now and then he sends down a DNA sequence for me to look at, usually to see if I can locate a similar sequence on the human gene map. Interesting stuff—but I have no idea how it relates to his upcoming unveiling. My guess is, it's going to be something big—much bigger than wolf genetics."

Jeremy smiled in genuine anticipation. "I can't wait. It sounds exciting."

Lyle nodded. "Twelve midnight, Wednesday night. The entire staff is going to gather in Lester Auditorium—the dome-shaped building on the far side of the complex. Should be a hell of a show. Straw spun into gold. A miracle cure.

The fountain of youth. With Waters, you never know. Could have something to do with cancer, Alzheimer's, AIDS—"

"Tucsome is into AIDS research, too?"

"Up to its ears. Nearly every fourth team here has something to do with the affliction. And it isn't just the money issue—the fact that so many grants have 'AIDS' spray-painted across their eligibility forms. It's Waters. As of two years ago, he made AIDS a priority." There was a hint of acid in Lyle's voice.

"You sound like you don't think it should be."

Lyle smirked. "Oh, there's no doubt in my mind that AIDS has a huge genetic component. What else explains the fact that when five people are exposed to the same amount of the virus, only two get it? Some minute indiscrepancy in a gene that provides a basis for the immune system, and, presto, you're susceptible. Sooner or later we'll find that gene. But if you ask me, by concentrating our efforts on one disease, we're sticking our heads in the sand."

"I'm not sure I understand."

"It's simple," Christina Guarrez said, suddenly coming around the corner. "What Lyle's getting at is the fallacy of goal-oriented science. Take the Manhattan Project. A bunch of scientists were sequestered to build a bomb. Not just any bomb, the biggest damn bomb in the history of the world. So they harnessed atomic energy and came up with a powerful weapon of violence; for all its genius, for all its logical and scientific beauty, that's all the Manhattan Project gave the world—an extremely effective bomb."

Jeremy couldn't help but stare at her. She was beautiful in an exotic way: narrow, dark eyes, flowing brown hair, a firm, defiant jaw. Her shoulders were wide, thrown back, and her lab coat was slightly open at the front, revealing high curves and a sliver of caramel skin.

"Goal-oriented science is only as grand as its goal," Lyle said, picking up the thread. "The Human Genome Project is sophisticated enough to have a goal that's broad—not really a goal at all: the sequencing of the entire human genome, which is more of a beginning than an end. But AIDS research has only two sides: success and failure. If we turn the Human Genome Project into a win-lose chase, we're dooming ourselves to scientific obscurity. Who remembers the name of the man who cured smallpox?"

"Edward Jenner," Jeremy interjected.

Lyle glared at him. "You know what I mean. We're here to do scientific research. We're here to uncover secrets about life and the human organism. We're here to change the face of the world, forever."

"Not to save lives?" Jeremy ventured.

Guarrez laughed. "Where the hell did you come from? Pixieland?"

Lyle waved her back with his hand. "That *is* a positive by-product of our work," he said, "but not our purpose. Genetics isn't just another medical tool, like an X-ray machine or a new-fangled antibiotic. Genetics is the most powerful pathway in the history of science. Immortality awaits the scientist who pursues it to its logical end."

Jeremy shut his eyes, thinking. Something was just below the surface of his memory, and it took him a second to pull it out into the open: "Immortality is trivial," he quoted, "it is my mortality that I do not understand."

Lyle smiled. "Jason Waters, 1955. You're good, Ross. But do remember, that came from a man who missed immortality by three letters."

"Three letters?"

"Change Waters to Watson and I'm sure you'd hear a very different point of view. Waters had his shot at immortality, and lost, however unfairly. All I want is the same chance. The work we're doing in this lab is that chance—as long as Waters keeps his humanitarian fingers out of my pie."

Jeremy raised his eyebrows. "Care to elaborate?"

Lyle laughed. "It's much less mysterious than it sounds. I'm working with a very specific strand of DNA found near the tip of chromosome 18. It codes for something simple and easy to understand."

Lyle paused, allowing the suspense to build. Then he pointed at Jeremy's face: "The color of your eyes. It turns out to be a rather small, delicate gene. Barely four thousand bases long. Very simple, very concise. Its significance lies in what we're doing with it."

Jeremy opened his mouth, but before he could say anything Lyle wagged a thin finger at him. "Time enough for that later. We've got a whole week to spend in this lab—and I'm sure you're already getting sick of my voice. Besides, it's after six. Victor would have a fit if I kept you any longer. Not proper etiquette, he'd tell me. So say good night to Guarrez, and we'll get the hell out of here."

Jeremy nodded at the lab assistant, who smiled back.

"It's nice to meet you, Jeremy. I'm sure we'll get to know each other real well over the next few days."

As Guarrez slid away, Lyle leaned close to Jeremy's ear. "As your new friend, Ross, let me give you a little advice. Stay away from that one. She has quite a reputation around here. She'll suck you dry, given half the chance. And you wouldn't be the first young scientist with her teeth marks on your throat."

Jeremy looked sheepishly at Lyle, who shoved him toward the door.

"Come on," Lyle said. "I'll walk you back. We can stop in the cafeteria on the way, and you can tell me all about retroviruses and New York and all the pretty girls I'm sure you left behind."

Jeremy forced a laugh. As they stepped out of the lab, a question entered his mind. He decided to risk it. "By the way, where is Waters's private lab? Is it on this floor?"

Lyle smiled at him. "You're not thinking of stealing a peek, are you?"

"I'll admit, I am a little curious."

Lyle squeezed his shoulder. "Don't try it. There's no quicker way to get kicked out of Tucsome. And you don't want to get on Waters's bad side. Remember what I said about the tech who got mauled for sticking his head in where it didn't belong? Let me tell you, he was lucky that the wolves got to him before Waters did. Waters takes his privacy very seriously."

"So you won't even give me a hint."

Lyle laughed. "Hell, I'll give you a fucking road map. It won't do you any good. The elevator to Waters's lab is at the end of the hall, barely twenty yards from where you're standing. But you can't get inside. It's fitted with a palm-plate lockout."

"A palm plate?"

Lyle nodded. "You need to show identification. Genetic identification. You press your palm against the plate, and it takes a skin flick. Does a DNA analysis. It's old science, maybe five years. Only Waters and Victor can activate the elevator."

"Then I guess I'll just have to wait with the rest of you," Jeremy said, sighing. He glanced back at the laboratory one more time and caught sight of the bank of computers near the far wall.

GOOD MORNING, MATTHEW. ARE WE HAVING FUN YET?

The memory refocused his senses. If there were any real clues in Lyle's laboratory, he felt certain that he'd find them behind that screen. But until he could get a moment alone, the clues would have to wait.

"Let me see," he said, his voice a blanket of amiability. "Retroviruses, New York, and girls. Now *there* are three subjects worth talking about." He clapped Lyle on the back, and side by side they moved down the hallway.

Jeremy didn't arrive back at his borrowed home until close to midnight. So much for etiquette, he thought to himself as he pulled open the front door. Lyle could have talked a deaf man's ear off. Especially when it came to the subject of himself.

He threw on a light switch and stepped into the warm glow. He quickly moved through the house, cataloging the details. The living room's almost complete lack of furniture made it appear twice as large. A single three-seater couch sat beneath the picture widow, two throw pillows at odd angles. There was a piano in the corner, and a glass end table near the door.

The kitchen was immaculate, modern, and equally empty. The dining room was rectangular, with huge sliding-glass doors that led out onto the wooden deck. The deck was concise and made for barbecues; two lounge chairs rested on either side of a gas grill, offering a view of the under-construction golf course. A hundred yards away, three bulldozers sat at right angles.

He paused behind the large sliding-glass doors and caught sight of his reflection dancing around the bulldozers. His face was stiff, his eyes shadowed. He looked . . . sad.

He shivered, letting his eyes slide shut. He'd just spent the day in a laboratory straight out of his fantasies, and all he felt was sorrow. Once, he would have given his soul for the opportunity to stand where he was standing. Now, he wanted nothing more than to get the hell out of there. He was out of his depth, flailing at something he didn't understand. And always, there was the next panic attack waiting to manifest itself—somewhere close by, unavoidable. He wished that things could go back to the way they were—and then his thoughts turned to Robin.

He wondered where she was. Was she okay? Thinking of him? Even after all they'd been through, it was hard to think of her in danger. Sometimes it seemed as if he'd just dreamt those terrifying events in New York—as if they'd seeped into his consciousness from some half-forgotten film.

He swung on his heels and headed for the stairs. He took the steps two at a time and walked down a carpeted hallway to the master bedroom.

As with the rest of the house, the furnishings were sparse. An ornate wooden bed sat in the direct center of the square room, covered by simple white sheets and two equally white pillows. A television and VCR sat in a corner of the room, angled toward the bed. A large picture window looked out onto the golf course down below; the bulldozers seemed even smaller and less real from so far up.

He crossed to the window. The darkness outside was so thick it seemed to drip down the glass. He stood very still, listening. Somewhere in the background, behind the wind and the trees, he thought he heard something howl.

He reached forward and quickly pulled down the shade.

From outside, the young man cut a sharp silhouette. His body shifted behind the drawn window shade, his long limbs casting muted patterns across the front lawn.

When the lights finally went out, the black Mercedes sedan parked a few feet from the edge of the driveway grumbled to life. The headlights remained off; only the low hum of the sedan's engine signaled that something had changed.

A few seconds later, a quiet whirring filled the air.

"Source to Satellite. Source to Satellite. Come in, Satellite."

Inside the sedan, Victor Alexander looked down at the gleaming, high-tech laptop computer on the seat next to him. A Vidcom 900, the Pentagon called it. The newest thing in communications technology, ten years ahead of the market. It could pick up satellite signals from anywhere in the world. Victor hit three keys and watched as the screen glowed to life.

God, how he'd learned to hate that damn screen.

Slowly, the pixels began to arrange themselves. Gray, blue, and yellow squares bound together, forming shadows, then shapes. A face emerged. A shivering, mixed-up, blurry face. Video cloaking, it was called. To protect the identity of the man on the other side of the satellite.

"Source to Satellite," the Vidcom repeated. "Please respond."

Victor sighed, pushing the disgust out of his voice. He had to be careful to hide his true feelings; in his business, disloyalty wasn't tolerated.

He remembered his buddy Art Lucius. Headstrong, obstinate Lucius. They'd found him hanging from his balcony, his stubborn heart cut out and shoved down his throat. And Pauly, good old Pauly. Back in Nam, Pauly had been the comedian of the outfit, always cracking jokes. In the end, he was the one to crack up. It had taken them months to find enough of his parts for a decent funeral.

Victor's eyes hardened as he leaned close to the Vidcom: "Satellite reads you fine," he said. "We've got a clean acclimation. The kid has settled into his new home."

There was a brief pause. Then the image on the video screen nodded. "Recommendation?"

Victor rubbed his jaw. He wondered how much he could get away with. He wanted to tell the paranoid bastard what he really thought. As usual, there was no need for all of the cloak-and-dagger bullshit. Jeremy Ross was just a bright kid looking for a future. There was no need to hover around him like he was some sort of professional spy.

But Victor knew he couldn't say this to his boss. Every newcomer to Tucsome was treated the same: round-the-clock surveillance for the first twenty-four hours and then a gradual lowering of security over time.

"Everything seems under control," he said. "Recommend softening security down to intermediate code blue. Low orbit, limited tech. Phone lines and travel plans."

"Affirmative," the Vidcom clicked. "Source out."

The screen went blank. Victor closed the laptop and shoved it back under the dashboard. Then he leaned back in his seat and rubbed the sweat out of his eyes.

The bedroom lights were still out, the shades drawn tightly shut. The young doctor was probably fast asleep. Dreaming about nurses, or maybe a girlfriend back home. The lucky bastard.

When Victor slept, he had nothing to dream about.

He'd tried to have a relationship, once. Back in his Company days, when he'd been stationed in El Salvador. She was a schoolteacher, and she had the most wonderful teeth.

Straight, shining, and white. He'd often distracted himself for long moments, gazing at those teeth.

Of course, it hadn't worked out. Orders would come in, and he would disappear for weeks at a time. Finally, the absences had caused a rift. The schoolteacher had demanded an explanation—and he'd been forced to move on.

Back then, at least he'd had the excitement of the missions. He'd thought of himself as a soldier, part of a team. Soon, though, the thrill began to fade. Eventually, he realized what he really was: nothing more than a janitor with a gun. He cleaned up loose ends, swept dirt under the rug. No amount of style, art, or class could hide the truth. Sickened by what he'd become, he'd finally decided that it was time to retire.

And that's when he had heard about Lucius and Pauly. Perhaps they, too, had decided it was time to get out of the business. Perhaps they'd been less than careful in front of their Vidcoms.

He shuddered, frustration rising inside him. If only he could trade places with Jeremy Ross. Lie asleep in that bed, with nothing but a bright future to worry about.

Pure fantasy.

There was only one way anything like that would ever come true. Victor pictured his fingers tightening around the throat of his unknown boss. One twist, and he would be free.

One twist, for Lucius, and for Pauly.

15

THE ANCHORED SPEEDBOAT ROCKED MERCILESSLY AS THE black waters of the Chesapeake slapped against its fiberglass sides. A heavy wind tugged at Robin's face, and she struggled to get her legs into the tight rubber wet suit.

"I must be crazy," she said through her teeth. "Totally out of my mind."

Devin's back was to her as he fiddled with the anchor controls, but she could imagine his bemused smile.

"Want to call it off?"

She grunted with effort as the clammy rubber stretched reluctantly over her muscular thighs. Then she looked out over the dark water. They were a hundred yards from shore, totally alone in the huge expanse of brackish water. *You're doing this for Jeremy, too,* she reminded herself. "No, like you said, it's the only way to confront Leary directly. I just hope his crew doesn't shoot first and ask questions later."

Devin bit his lip. "Maybe we *are* taking too much of a risk."

"Risk is all mine," she said, "and I have to take it. I just hope he's where you say he is."

"He's there," Devin said confidently. "About two hundred yards north of us. If it wasn't so dark, you'd be able to read the markings right off the bow."

"Why no security?"

"Oh, he'll have plenty. Odds are we're being monitored by more than twenty stations along the shoreline. And I'd bet there are six or seven helicopters just out of hearing. But nobody will bother us."

"Why not?"

"Because we're *supposed* to be here. The CIA thinks we're Secret Service, a backup precaution under Leary's personal command. I've been transmitting a verification code ever since we left port."

Robin had always known Devin was "connected," but until now, she hadn't fully realized to what degree. "I guess I asked the right person for help," she said, and saw his chest swell with pride.

She stood, testing her flippers against the deck. Then she ran her hands up and down her suit, making sure everything was in place. Regulator, weight belt, mask, emergency regulator, compass, knife, and thirty-watt torch.

Devin handed her two eight-pound weights and watched as she strapped them to her belt. "Where were you certified?"

"In the Caribbean. Cayman Brac. We went for two weeks a year when I was a kid."

He gestured at the blackness around. "This is a little different than the Caribbean."

"I can see that."

"Sure you're going to be okay?"

She took a deep breath. "I'll be fine. The swim should be no problem. I'll get as close as I can to the schooner, then surface and toss my equipment. When they pick me up, I'll tell them I fell off a boat on the other side of the bay. It doesn't really matter if they believe me—as long as they bring me to Leary. So just point me in the right direction, and I'll handle the rest."

Devin pointed over the bow of the speedboat. "As I said, his boat is two hundred yards north of this position. Follow your compass and try not to get turned upside down. And whatever you do, hold on to your torch. It's dark as tar down there."

She nodded, sliding her mask over her eyes. "Wish me luck," she mouthed, placing the regulator between her lips. Then she gave him a thumbs-up and pushed off with her flippers. Her body spun over the edge of the boat, and she hit the water headfirst.

The cone of light shivered through the murk as she paddled through the thick water. She could feel the sweat beading up under her body glove. Around her, the Chesapeake was pitch black and heavy. The rhythmic pulse of her regulator filled her ears, a deep and eerie sound that reverberated through her body.

Three minutes later she paused to check the compass for the fifth time since she'd hit the water. Devin had been right; it was frustratingly easy to lose track of one's bearings. The visibility was less than the distance between her face and her hands; when she looked away from the cone of light, she saw nothing but darkness.

She continued forward, chasing her torch. Every few seconds something moved at the edges of her vision: colorless fish, darting around her as if she were a nuisance. At sixty feet under, the Chesapeake was an alien world—and she felt out of place, a stranger in a space suit, delicate and fragile. She wriggled ahead, concentrating on the torch.

Then she saw them.

Crouching against the muddy bottom, four figures in the darkness, torches crisscrossing as they struggled with a heavy, spherical piece of equipment. She froze, flicking her own torch off. She shifted her body vertical, watching the figures. She could tell by their equipment and economy of movement that they were professionals, perhaps navy

SEALs. She felt her heart beating wildly in her chest, and she fought to steady her nerves.

It was time to surface; the presence of the four SEALs meant that she was close to Leary's boat, probably within twenty yards. She took a deep breath of air and began to swim to the surface.

Suddenly, something caught her by her right arm, twisting her off her feet. She panicked, kicking out. Her flippers hit something soft, and a geyser of bubbles burst through the water. Then she was wrenched backward, her arms clamped to her sides.

The bubbles cleared and she saw that she was surrounded by men in wet suits. In front of her, a diver was hunched over, clutching his stomach as another diver held an emergency regulator to his mouth. She tried to move forward, but found that there were thick arms wrapped around her from behind.

Another diver approached from the left, a speargun slung over his shoulder. Her stomach turned upside down as the man moved to within a few feet of her, his hands on the gun. He looked her over, dark blue eyes, flickering behind a thick plastic mask. Then he pointed his thumb toward the surface.

The man behind her tightened his grip. She closed her eyes, mentally preparing for the upward climb. Her captor kicked off, and as one, they began to rise.

"Keep your body slack. Don't make any sudden movements."

She was halfway onto the schooner, three marines dragging her up by her arms. Two other marines stood to one side, submachine guns slung over their shoulders. The diver with the speargun was already on board, talking to an officer in a stiff gray uniform.

"Excuse me," she said, her words coming in a torrent. "I can explain—"

"Remain still!" shouted one of the armed marines.

She closed her mouth as the marines swung her legs onto

the boat. A second later she was sitting on a small wooden bench, her arms stiff at her sides as a pair of marines ran their hands over her wet suit.

"She's clean," said one of the marines. Both men stepped back, their hands resting on the sidearms strapped to their belts. The two marines with submachine guns took a position a few yards away. She felt the sweat running down her back. This wasn't going the way she'd planned.

A few minutes passed in silence. Then the diver with the speargun approached, accompanied by the officer in gray. The diver looked at Robin with angry green eyes. "I'm Special Agent Robert Brackman, CIA. This is Lieutenant Hart. You've trespassed into a CIA secure zone."

She swallowed, making her eyes as wide as possible. "I'm so sorry. I was diving with my boyfriend and I somehow got turned around. I must have swum a half a mile. Thank God I ran into you guys—I was running out of air."

Brackman glanced at the lieutenant. She could see that neither man believed her story. She was about to come up with something else, when a gruff, authoritative voice swept across the deck.

"Brackman, Hart, you're excused. I'll handle this."

She turned toward the voice. The man was tall, thin, with strawberry blond hair and light features. He was wearing a gray pin-striped suit, hands clasped behind his back. His expression was indecipherable, his lips tightly pressed together, his eyes cold.

Brackman and Hart nodded at him, then quickly moved to the other side of the deck. The man in the suit took a step closer, his blue eyes tightly focused on her face.

"Ms. Kelly," he said, leaning forward so that his voice was barely audible over the schooner's engines, "you make a hell of an entrance."

She relaxed a fraction of an inch, rubbing her hands against her legs. "I'm sorry, Mr. Leary—"

"You realize I could have you arrested. You violated a secure zone. *And* you assaulted one of my agents."

She nodded, her stomach spitting acid. "I had no choice. I had to see you. And your agents assaulted me first."

He cocked his head to the side. "You're quite a piece of work. Like your father." He paused a moment, thinking. "Okay, you got my attention. We have about ten minutes before we head to shore. Convince me that I shouldn't have you arrested the minute we dock."

She glanced at the half dozen marines milling nearby. "Tell them to go to the other side of the boat."

He raised his eyebrows. Then he shrugged and gave a sharp order. A second later, the deck was empty. "We're alone," he said. "Now tell me why you're here."

She jumped right in. "I think you know something about my father's death."

If Leary was surprised, his face didn't show it. "We're conducting an official investigation—"

"I'm not talking about your official investigation. I'm talking about two years ago. My father discovered something and asked for your help."

He leaned back against the railing. "And you think that what happened two years ago had something to do with his death."

She shrugged. "My father didn't scare easily."

He rubbed his hands against the railing. Then he looked out toward the ocean. "Ms. Kelly, you're going to have to do better than that."

She felt the heat rising into her face. "Damn it, there are people trying to kill me! I can't go outside without a disguise because I'm afraid someone I don't know will put a bullet in the back of my skull! Please, Mr. Leary, you were my father's friend."

He pressed his lips together, turning back toward her, no sign of sympathy in his Irish eyes. "If you're expecting a miracle, you've come to the wrong man. I can't bring your father back. And the best advice I can give you is to stay as far away from this as you can."

She stuck out her jaw. "Where would you like me to go? Is South Carolina far enough?"

He paused, momentarily taken aback. "What do you know about South Carolina?"

"I know that there's a place called the Tucsome Project for Genetic Research located just outside of Beaufort. I also know that my father visited there at about the same time he asked for your help." She watched Leary carefully, searching for some acknowledgment that Jeremy and she were on the right track. What she saw bothered her.

Leary didn't look impressed by her knowledge of Tucsome. He looked . . . pensive.

"Your father wasn't there to visit Tucsome. At least not as far as I know. In fact, there's no hard evidence that Tucsome is involved at all."

"But my father was in a car accident—"

"North of Beaufort, I know. His car was sideswiped by a delivery van. He injured his spleen, and the ambulance took him to Tucsome because the ER facilities were better. He spent the night, then was on his way back to Washington."

She rubbed her eyes. She was back where she'd started— which was nowhere.

"If my father wasn't visiting Tucsome—what was he doing in South Carolina?"

Leary didn't answer. She watched him carefully. She could tell that he was about to close down on her—cutting her off from the information she so desperately needed.

"Mr. Leary," she said, her voice quiet. "You saw how my father died." She paused, clearing her throat. "I'm not going to get in your way," she said finally. "I just need to know the truth."

He sighed, resignation tingeing his voice. "All right, I'll tell you about South Carolina. But I'm not sure how it will help. I'm not convinced that what happened in South Carolina has any significance at all."

He paced along the railing, his fingers clasped in front of him. "It was a sting operation, of sorts. A large amount of

Defense Department money had been funneled through a number of dummy accounts into the hands of a pair of rogue operatives stationed in Beaufort. The money quickly vanished, but your father's people managed to zero in on the operatives, taking them into custody. Your father went to South Carolina to personally oversee the interrogation. By the time he arrived, it was too late."

"Too late?" Robin asked.

"The operatives had been permanently silenced—along with a hotel roomful of your father's best people. According to witnesses, a number of heavily armed military-style helicopters were involved. Your father was livid; that's when I got involved. Your father asked for my help in identifying the two operatives—in effect, tracing the embezzled money back to its source."

"What did you find?"

Leary lowered his voice. "The two operatives were in the employment of an organization called the SSO. It's one of Washington's best kept secrets. I'm committing an act of treason simply by mentioning it to you."

She stared at him. "You're serious?"

"Completely. Special Security Operations. It was founded in 1944 in conjunction with the Manhattan Project; afterward, its mandate was extended in a more general way: 'To protect the scientific primacy of the United States of America while guiding science to the benefit of mankind.' "

"That's a lofty statement."

He nodded. "And completely irrelevant to what the SSO currently stands for. The office is headed by a loathsome individual named Arthur Dice, who, as far as we can determine, is motivated purely by self-interest. We weren't surprised to find Dice at the source of the missing money—but sadly, we didn't have enough evidence to pin the embezzlement scam on him. Your father continued his investigation, but never found anything that would stick."

Robin fought to digest the information coming at her. Most of what the CIA director had said made sense: Her father had been researching projects for his upcoming budget cuts. He'd found a scam in South Carolina, and had gone to investigate. "What do you think happened to the money?"

Leary shrugged. "That's the million-dollar question. Did it stay in the country, or was it shuttled to a half dozen Swiss accounts? Is Arthur Dice a thief, pure and simple? Or did he have something else in mind? Like you, my first inclination was to suspect the Tucsome Project. It's by far the largest facility within fifty miles of Beaufort. But so far, I haven't been able to come up with anything conclusive."

She was struck by a sudden thought. "Is it possible that Dice had my father killed? Because he was afraid my father would somehow expose him?"

Leary looked off toward the horizon. "I won't lie to you— the thought has crossed my mind. But assassinating the secretary of defense is a bold move; I'm not sure even Dice has the balls for something like that. Still, I do know that he's had people tailing you since you first started poking around."

She felt a chill ride down her spine. "Why?"

"He was monitoring your father's computer files, and when you logged on you set off his surveillance operation. Somehow, you made him nervous—and he moved to eliminate you."

She bit at her lower lip. "You don't seem very concerned about it. Has attempted murder become that commonplace in Washington?"

"Again, we're talking supposition here. Dice is very resourceful when it comes to covering his tracks."

A thought pricked at the back of her mind. Leary knew that she was being tailed by the SSO, which meant that he'd probably been following her as well. All for embezzled money? It must have been an awful lot of cash.

"And you're still continuing the investigation where my father left off?"

He shrugged. "For what it's worth. I have a number of operatives working the target area. Three in Beaufort, two more in the surrounding locality. I've even got one in Tucsome.

But at present, I don't expect to come up with anything. The money is long gone. If I were you, I'd consider the case pretty much closed—and I'd stay out of Dice's way. Until we get something solid on him, your life is in danger."

No shit.

At that moment, there was the sound of wood scraping against wood. The schooner was sidling up against a high cedar dock. Marines in camouflage uniforms scrambled along the side of the boat, rushing to tie it down.

"It looks like our conversation has come to an end," Leary said.

"So what's the verdict? Are you going to have me arrested?"

He touched her arm. "No, but I *will* give you a bit of advice. There's no way to bring your father back. Let me handle Arthur Dice."

She mimicked a nod. It was obvious; he wanted her to leave things alone. Part of her agreed with him—this was way out of her league. These people were professionals. But a larger part of her was still unsatisfied. Even if Tucsome wasn't involved, she had a hunch that there was more to her father's trip to South Carolina than Leary had told her.

She came to a decision. Despite what Leary had said, she was going to continue to search for information. First she'd contact Jeremy, let him know that Tucsome wasn't necessarily the link he thought it was. Then she'd use what the CIA director had told her to redirect her investigation.

The fact was, he'd given her a lot to work with: Her father had gone to South Carolina in search of a large amount of money. The money had vanished—but that didn't mean there weren't clues lying around. As a tax lawyer, she knew a few tricks that Leary had probably never heard of. Besides, she was fairly certain that he hadn't told her everything; it was going to be up to her to pick her way to the truth.

She heaved her scuba gear over her shoulder and threw the CIA director an obliging smile. "Thanks for filling in some of the gaps. And I promise to carefully consider your advice."

"See that you do," he said evenly, and waved good-bye.

She moved down the dock toward the highway. She could see lights in the distance, probably a Chesapeake resort hotel. She'd be able to get a cab there, or call Devin for a ride. Then she'd get right to work. She stepped off the dock and onto the highway, thinking about the task ahead.

She was so enveloped in thought that she didn't notice the black Mercedes sedan—headlights off, engine grumbling to life—squatting in the darkness a few feet away.

16

"I HAVEN'T SEEN A YAWN LIKE THAT SINCE MY LAST ATTEMPT AT dating."

Jeremy smiled, rubbing the sawdust out of his eyes. It was barely five in the morning. He and Lyle were standing in a corner of the lab, clutching steaming cups of black coffee. Overhead, the ventilation system coughed and sputtered.

"Don't worry. With this racket, I'll be awake in no time. How do you put up with it?"

"You mean ol' Darth Vader?" Lyle joked, pointing toward the ceiling. "It's only like this for the first few hours of the day. Then it settles down to a quiet hum. It's an impressive system, very state-of-the-art. Cost more than twenty million to install."

Jeremy's eyes swept over the three-foot-by-three-foot grates that were scattered across the ceiling at seemingly random intervals.

"Twenty million? Seems like a lot for fresh air."

"Not when you think about all of the viruses, bacteria, and

nasty chemicals we fool around with in this place. You certainly won't see me complaining about the noise."

At the mention of viruses, Jeremy's ears perked up. If Walker had been contaminated inadvertently, a poorly ventilated virus breakout would have been the most likely culprit. "Is it a filtration and recycling system?"

Lyle shook his head. "Better than that. The ventilation tunnels feed out to a sterilization tower about three miles north of the project. The tower houses a thirty-foot convex fan, which creates one hell of a vacuum. We get fresh beach air, passed through seven separate filter screens."

"That's a lot of hardware," Jeremy murmured, thinking that a virus breakout was looking more and more unlikely.

"When it comes to viruses, we don't fool around. And for good reason—Christ, there you go again. If I didn't know any better, I'd guess that this was the first time you'd ever seen five in the morning."

Jeremy faked a laugh. In truth, his exhaustion had nothing to do with the time. He was yawning because he'd spent half the night thrashing his way through a panic-anxiety attack. Almost as bad as the last time; respiratory paralysis, convulsions, heart palpitations, and the vivid image of his dying father. He had a sinking feeling that his time was running out. He had to find a way to speed things up—before his syndrome flared up again.

"I'll live," he said, sipping his coffee. "So what's on the agenda for today?"

Lyle gave him an evil smile. "I'm going to drag you, kicking and screaming, into the future."

Jeremy laughed. "Meaning?"

"Today you're going to see what comes *after* the Human Genome Project."

"Are you talking about your work with eye color?"

"Precisely."

"How far along in the sequencing are you?"

Lyle steered Jeremy away from the coffee machine and

headed toward the aisle closest to the door. "The sequencing was trivial. We finished that months ago."

Jeremy stopped in his tracks, astonished. "You've already sequenced the gene for eye color?"

"Sure. You know all about chromosome walking, don't you?"

"Of course. Start from a known marker, like a hereditary genetic disease. Snip out a section of DNA. Clone it in *E. coli* bacteria, then run the fragments through a gel machine."

"Exactly. It takes time, money, labor—but the science is old hat. We nailed down the gene for eye color well before you got here."

"That's amazing. Why haven't you published your results? I'm sure I would have heard about it."

"You would have—and you won't. I'm not publishing a damn thing until the next stage is completed. Because the next stage is really going to be something spectacular. You see, I'm no longer interested in what makes your brown eyes brown. I want to know how to make your brown eyes blue."

Jeremy paused, the excitement rising inside of him. "Genetic engineering?"

"Give the man a prize. From what I've heard, you're no stranger to the concept."

"That depends. Are we talking theory or practice?"

"Who the hell has time for theory?" Lyle said through a smile. "C'mon, Ross. I'll get the microscope ready. You grab my beta culture from the fridge—second shelf, marked with my name. I'll show you what I'm up to."

Jeremy downed his coffee and crossed toward the refrigerator. He felt his heart beating faster. Genetic engineering! Ever since his Ph.D. thesis, he'd regarded the concept with a sense of awe. He hoped that Lyle wasn't just exaggerating for his benefit.

He yanked open the refrigerator door. Cold air blasted him in the face as he searched the second shelf for the beta culture. He found the petri dish near the back, clearly marked in black ink. He began to shut the door—

And then he paused. A sudden thought hit him, and he searched the refrigerator with his eyes.

There was a hinged metal box attached near the base of the door. He bent to his knees and felt the box with his fingers. A latch clicked, and the box swung open. A high-tech thermostat stared at him, its dial set at a bracing eighteen degrees.

He glanced over his shoulder to confirm Lyle wasn't watching. The opportunity was perfect; he could cause a distraction with a minimum of effort. He set his jaw and twisted the dial all the way to the left: room temperature. Then he shut the metal box and took a step back. Perfect. No permanent damage, just enough of a distraction to buy him some time. His pulse quickened, excitement rising in his chest.

"Ross? You get lost in there?"

"On my way," Jeremy responded hastily. He pushed the refrigerator door shut and rushed across the lab.

Lyle was standing behind a fluorescent microscope, his hand outstretched. Jeremy handed him the petri dish and watched as the younger man lined the case up under the microscope.

"Cross your fingers," Lyle said. "I've worked on this culture for two months."

His mind elsewhere, Jeremy leaned forward. "What exactly have you done to it?"

"About two months ago, I cut a tiny segment of DNA out of some frozen skin cells, and injected it into this *E. coli*. I then blasted the *E. coli* with electricity in the hope that the new DNA would attach itself. If the experiment worked, we should be able to see the new cells through the fluorescent microscope. The new cells should appear white, in stark contrast to the radiated blue cells."

Jeremy looked at him, confused. He'd read about this process: It was the first step in a surgical method of gene therapy—an approach that he'd thought was in the early stages of development, not a functioning method of genetic engineering. "Why this method?" he asked. "Why not retro-virus therapy?"

Lyle smiled at him. "You know the answer better than I do. Retrovirus therapy doesn't work."

"As far as I know," Jeremy responded, slightly miffed, "no method of genetic engineering 'works' in the full sense of the word. Not yet. But in a few more years—"

"Hell," said Lyle, "who wants to wait a few years?" With that, he leaned over the microscope and pressed his left eye against the eyepiece. Jeremy stared at him in dismay.

A few seconds passed in silence. Then a few more. Finally, Lyle grunted.

"Well?" Jeremy asked.

"See for yourself."

Lyle stepped aside. Jeremy rubbed the sweat off of his hands and leaned close to the microscope.

There they were. Beautiful white cells, bunched at random intervals in the blue background of radiated *E. coli*.

"Unbelievable," Jeremy whispered. "The DNA attached itself to the *E. coli*."

"It's called transfection. The next stage is to change the DNA—tinker with the code, add some twists of our own."

"Then the third stage is to reinsert the gene into living skin cells," Jeremy murmured.

Lyle slapped his back so hard he nearly lost his eye to the fluorescent microscope. "And whammo, your brown eyes change to blue. Hold on a second, while I get some film."

Jeremy nodded, still staring into the microscope. These cells were the beginning of real genetic engineering. To him, they were the most beautiful things in the world.

Lyle returned with the film, and Jeremy stepped aside. He watched carefully as Lyle fed the film into the microscope. He was about to ask what he planned to do with the pictures when Guarrez came racing around the corner. Her face was bright red.

"You're not going to believe this," she said, grabbing

Lyle's shoulder. "There's something wrong with the refrigerator. The gels are melting right off the fucking shelves."

Lyle stared at her. "What? I'm looking at a gel from the fridge right now. It's fine."

"Must have been a recent power surge. The thermostat got reset to room temperature. Christ, what a mess."

"Fuck!" Lyle hissed. "Did you call maintenance?"

"Of course. But maintenance won't do a damn thing for our gels. Come on, let me show you."

Lyle started to move off when he remembered Jeremy. He paused, looking Jeremy over. "Ross, you going to be okay for a few minutes while I deal with this?"

Jeremy tried to look nonchalant. "Sure. I'll do my best not to get into any trouble."

Lyle nodded, then spun on his heels. A second later, Jeremy was alone. Adrenaline rushed through his body as he headed for the computers by the far wall.

17

"HELLO, MATTHEW. ARE WE HAVING FUN YET?"

Jeremy glanced over his shoulder one more time. He could hear Lyle and Guarrez arguing on the other side of the lab, but they were still three aisles away, probably with their heads jammed into the refrigerator. There was no way they could see what he was up to. It was risky—but it was an opportunity he couldn't pass up.

He turned back to the computer. He remembered what Lyle had told him, that Matthew had prided himself on how human he'd been able to make the machine seem. He touched his lips, wondering at the best method of approach. He decided to start by simply testing the water. He punched a few keys:

"Y . . . E . . . S."

The computer whirred for a brief second: "QUERY: WHICH CAME FIRST, THE CHICKEN OR THE EGG?"

Jeremy raised his eyebrows.

The computer whirred again: "ANSWER: A CHICKEN IS AN EGG'S WAY OF MAKING ANOTHER EGG."

Jeremy laughed. He recognized the quote from a famous English biologist. He reached forward and punched out a request to see the directory. The computer thought for a second, then paraded a small list:

"DOS. NOTEBOOK. WORD PROCESSOR . . ."

There was a brief pause.

"ALL OTHER FILES ERASED. ARE YOU MAD AT ME, MATTHEW?"

Jeremy raised his eyebrows.

"N . . . O."

There was another pause.

"THEN WHY DID YOU ERASE MY FILES?"

He laughed even louder. This computer was amazing. Matthew had been quite a whiz. Jeremy touched his fingers together, staring at the screen.

He wasn't sure what he was looking for. If Matthew had gone to the trouble of making this computer impervious to the erasing efforts of the Tucsome Project's computer specialists, he must have had a reason. But the question remained—if he'd wanted to leave behind a message, where would he have left it? And how would the computer decide who had access to it and who didn't?

He began to hit keys, searching for a way to break into the main program.

A few minutes later, he leaned back, exasperated. The computer screen glared at him:

"WHAT ARE YOU DOING, MATTHEW?"

As far as Jeremy could tell, there was no way through the maze of "human" questions except for "human" answers.

He leaned forward and began to type:

"I . . . AM . . . REPROGRAMMING—"

"THEN YOU ARE NOT MATTHEW."

The statement came suddenly, and Jeremy's eyes widened.

"I . . . AM."

"YOU ARE NOT MATTHEW YOU ARE NOT MATTHEW YOU ARE NOT MATTHEW YOU ARE NOT MATTHEW YOU ARE NOT MATTHEW YOU ARE

NOT MATTHEW YOU ARE NOT MATTHEW YOU ARE
NOT MATTHEW—"

Jeremy punched keys quickly, trying to stop the infuriating scroll:

"OKAY . . . I . . . AM . . . NOT . . . MATTHEW."

The computer paused. Then there was a dull whirring.

"QUERY: WHO ARE YOU?"

Jeremy thought for a moment.

"I . . . AM . . . MATTHEW'S . . . FRIEND."

There was another pause. Then:

"GO AWAY."

Jeremy gasped. He couldn't believe this machine.

"I . . . WILL . . . NOT . . . GO . . . AWAY."

Another pause.

"GO AWAY."

Jeremy shook his head.

"N . . . O."

There was a much longer pause. Then:

"PLEASE."

Jeremy shook his head, amazed. He was about to type
more, when a shadow closed in over part of the screen. He
spun in his chair, ready to spit out the first excuse that came
to mind.

His breathing calmed as he faced the empty lab. Still no
sign of Lyle and Guarrez. The shadow had probably been a
trick of his imagination.

He turned back to the computer, much less lighthearted
than before. Suddenly, he couldn't help thinking about the
person behind the program, the man who'd once sat in that
chair, conversing with the sensitive computer.

"GO AWAY GO AWAY GO AWAY GO AWAY GO
AWAY GO AWAY GO AWAY GO AWAY GO AWAY
GO AWAY—"

"I . . . CAN'T . . . GO . . . AWAY."

The computer paused, obviously distressed.

"QUERY: WHY NOT?"

Jeremy pondered the question. He needed to get the computer on his side. He needed to build familiarity.

"BECAUSE . . . I . . . WORK . . . HERE."

The computer emitted a series of high-pitched beeps.

"INCORRECT. MATTHEW WORKS HERE."

Jeremy took a deep breath. He could imagine the computer specialists' frustration. A computer was supposed to be nothing more than a tool, a machine. It wasn't supposed to resist. It certainly wasn't supposed to think.

Of course, this computer wasn't actually thinking. It was merely carrying out preprogrammed commands. At some point in the past, Matthew had sat down and typed in all of these responses. Jeremy wondered how many possible conditions Matthew had anticipated.

He chose his words carefully.

"MATTHEW . . . IS . . . GONE."

The computer whirred, and for a moment Jeremy thought he could actually sense concern:

"QUERY: WHERE . . . IS . . . MATTHEW?"

Jeremy took a deep breath and continued:

"MATTHEW . . . IS . . . DEAD."

Whir. Whir. Whir.

"I UNDERSTAND."

Suddenly, the screen went blank. A cold feeling took the color out of Jeremy's cheeks, and he leaned back in his chair. The computer understood? Why would Matthew have programmed his computer to understand?

He brushed his lips with his fingers. The computer was completely silent, shut down—mourning? He coughed at the thought. But perhaps it was not so far off; perhaps, while Matthew was making this machine human, he'd taught it something about death.

An odd bit of programming, to say the least. Unless the programmer feared that death was just around the corner.

Jeremy leaned forward and shut the computer off. He'd gotten as much as he could, for now. Lyle and Guarrez would soon finish with the refrigerator. He'd come back later, when he had more time.

He rose, straightened the chair, and brushed away the imprint he'd left on the soft cushion. As he started back across the lab, a question nagged at him.

What would make a twenty-eight-year-old man anticipate his own death?

18

LYLE WAS JUST SHUTTING THE REFRIGERATOR DOOR AS JEREMY came around the corner. Lyle's mouth was turned down at the corners, frustration burning behind his eyes.

"What a fuck," Lyle said. "This is going to set me back two weeks."

Jeremy tried to look supportive. Inside, he felt an enormous surge of guilt. He hadn't expected to set Lyle back that far—he'd only wanted to cause a diversion. He knew how horrible it was to have an experiment ruined by malfunctioning equipment.

"Shit happens," he offered, his voice as sincere as possible.

"Around here, shit always seems to happen. First Matthew, now the gels—you picked a hell of a time to visit."

"Was the damage really bad?" Jeremy asked.

"I'll let you see for yourself."

Lyle rummaged through a cabinet and pulled out two pairs of shielded safety goggles. He handed a pair to Jeremy, then turned back to the refrigerator.

151

"Here are my gels from the last month," he said, retrieving an armload of petri dishes.

He spread the dishes out and reached back into the cabinet. Then he pulled out a rectangular device, about the size of a shoe box.

"Make sure your goggles are tight over your eyes."

Jeremy pulled his goggles on, tightening the strap around the back of his head. The lenses were dark, turning the lab into a landscape of strange shadows and blurred shapes.

"These are pretty serious glasses."

Lyle nodded, flicking a switch on the rectangular shoe-box device. A powerful blue light poured out of its base.

"And this is the strongest fluorescing tube on the market. It could burn out an unprotected pair of retinas in two shakes of a rat's tail."

He moved to the row of petri dishes, shining the fluorescing tube over them. Jeremy leaned over his shoulder, watching.

"See how the cultures glow under the light? No borders, no solid breaks—the gels are completely ruined. I'm going to have to redo the entire set."

"All because the refrigerator malfunctioned?" Jeremy asked, his guilt multiplying.

Lyle nodded. He looked close to tears. "It's the specialized bacteria I'm using. It's extremely sensitive to temperature. Not like the retroviruses you're used to working with, which could survive anything short of a fire. My gels have to be kept below freezing."

Lyle flicked off the fluorescing tube and pulled down his safety goggles. Jeremy watched him, an ocean of real sympathy rising in his chest. "It's a tough setback," he said.

Lyle rubbed a hand over his eyes. Then he sighed, cocking his head. "You hungry? Because I could use a break. I hate to backtrack on an empty stomach."

Food was a foreign thought to Jeremy. But he liked the idea of a break. There were a few more things he needed to check out. He pulled off his goggles, making his face as nonchalant as possible. "Sure, I could eat. But I was hoping to make a quick phone call first."

"You're in luck. There are phones right outside the cafeteria. Come on, I'll show you."

Jeremy smiled inwardly as he followed Lyle out into the hallway.

The pay phones were lined up like a scene out of Penn Station. Jeremy counted at least thirty of them, spanning the walls of a poorly lit alcove.

"People tend to keep long hours around here," Lyle explained, "and there are a few hundred spouses out there ruing the day they were foolish enough to marry a scientist."

Jeremy shifted his eyes down the line of phones. A technician in a white lab coat was in the far corner, a phone cupped against his shoulder. Otherwise, the alcove was empty.

"I'll just be a minute," Jeremy said as casually as possible.

"The cafeteria is right around the corner. I'll save you a seat."

Jeremy waited until Lyle was out of sight. Then he chose a phone as far away from the technician as possible and dialed the operator.

A woman with a nasal southern accent picked up. "Tucsome Project for Genetic Research. This is Betsy speaking. How may I help you?"

A Project operator. Jeremy felt a sudden tinge of paranoia, and covered the mouthpiece with his sleeve. Although he still didn't have much more than a hunch to go on, there was no reason to advertise his reason for being in Tucsome. By now, he was fairly convinced that Matthew Aronson's death was suspicious—at the very least—and it couldn't hurt to be careful. With that in mind, he deepened his voice and called up his best midwestern accent.

"I'd like the number for the nearest police station," he drawled, surprised to find that his years in New York hadn't completely chased the Iowa out of him.

The woman on the other end paused for a brief second. Then her voice twanged in his ear. "You want the Tucsome sheriff's office. Hold on for a second, honey, and I'll connect you."

A deep, gravelly voice answered on the third ring. "Sheriff's office. Deputy Portney here."

Jeremy smiled as he pictured Deputy Portney. Five seven, with a huge gut and bright red suspenders. His feet were up on his desk, and he was spinning an ivory-handled revolver from finger to finger.

"Good morning," Jeremy started, still pushing his put-on Iowa accent to the hilt. "I was wondering if you could help me out, Deputy. A little over a week ago my cousin was killed by a drunk driver, somewhere in these parts. His name was Matthew Aronson."

"The kid doc," Portney grunted. "Yeah, I scraped him up off the interstate. Hell of a mess. You say you're his cousin? My condolences, mister. A real sick world we live in."

Jeremy forced his voice to remain steady. "I read in the newspaper that you'd apprehended the driver."

"Ol' Billy Masters. Sad story. The guy was bound to do something like this sooner or later. Wife left him, took the house, the kids, even the dog. The kids, I can handle—but take a man's dog? That's cold. Hell, if my wife took off with my dog, I know I'd drink a fifth of whiskey every night!"

Jeremy leaned close to the phone. "You think there's any way I could talk to Billy? You understand—just to clear my mind?"

Portney laughed. "Now that would be quite a trick."

"Sorry?"

Jeremy heard the sound of chewing tobacco ricocheting off the side of an aluminum can.

"Shit, hold on a second . . . okay, where were we? Oh yeah, ol' Billy Masters. Poor fool hung himself in his cell two days ago. Used a silk tie. One of them Italian suckers—you know, like the movie stars wear. Whadda they call 'em—Hermanis? Ferrengis?"

"Armani?" Jeremy ventured.

"Right, an Armani silk tie. We still haven't figured out

how he smuggled the thing in with him. His note said he wanted to die with class, 'cause he never had any class when he was alive. That sure was the truth, but if you ask me, ol' Billy was as much of a victim as yer cousin. I mean, take a man's dog? A real sad story."

Jeremy's chest fell. A dead end. He cleared his throat, wondering what else to ask. "Was he definitely guilty? I mean, was he definitely the one driving?"

"No question 'bout it. Airtight case. Fingerprints, hair samples, even a DNA trace. He started drinkin' at about three in the afternoon. Got in his truck an' drove south. Thas' the last thing he remembered. We found his truck at the scene, an' him lyin' on the floor of his trailer home. No alibi. No questions. It was him all right."

Jeremy exhaled, disappointed. Then an idea came to him. The odds were good that Matthew Aronson had died a long way from home.

"Deputy, what happened to my cousin's personal effects?"

There was a pause. "Personal effects?"

"The items found on his person. At the time of death."

"Well, to be honest, we weren't sure what to do with 'em. See, we were gonna send 'em to his mom and dad out in Texas but—well, the items ain't in that great condition, on account of the blood. Not the kind of thing a grieving mom wants to get in the mail."

Jeremy forced the excitement out of his voice. "Maybe I could help you out. I have some time on my hands before I head back west. I could stop by and pick up Matthew's things."

"Hey, that would be great. Save us a few stamps."

"I'll be by as soon as I can. Thanks, Deputy."

The phone went dead, and Jeremy replaced the receiver. He smiled at his performance. If he could pull off the deception in person, he might get his hands on some clues. He turned away from the phone and checked his watch. Eleven-forty-five. Lyle wouldn't begin to miss him for another few minutes.

"Time to get to the heart of this place," Jeremy whispered as he stepped out of the alcove.

Twenty feet past Lyle's lab, Jeremy caught sight of the twin steel doors. He approached the elevator cautiously, his feet barely making a sound against the heavy carpet.

The palm plate was attached to the wall to his left, waist high and glistening in the fluorescent lights. The plate consisted of a depressed imprint of a human hand, above which hung a blinking red diode. He held his hand a few inches from the depressed image, his fingers outstretched. Then he sighed. Lyle was right, there was no way inside. It was impossible to fake a DNA fingerprint.

Lies can only get you so far.

He'd turned away from the elevator and had started back toward the cafeteria when he heard footsteps coming toward him. He cursed to himself; no time to think of a decent excuse for wandering the halls. He hastily sidestepped through an open doorway.

Luckily, the room was empty. He pressed his body against the closest wall and waited for the footsteps to pass.

There was a flash of white across the open doorway. Then the footsteps began to recede. He suddenly realized that the white lab coat was heading toward the elevator.

He quickly slid out into the hall. The man had his back to him, but he immediately recognized the silver hair.

Jason Waters. Jeremy watched as Waters placed his hand on the palm plate. The red diode went out, and the steel doors slid open. Waters stepped into the elevator.

Jeremy didn't pause to think. He hurried forward, covering the distance in a half second. Just before the elevator's steel doors closed, he plunged through, nearly toppling over. Thankfully, he managed to regain his balance at the last minute.

Waters stared at him, stunned, as the steel doors slid shut.

"Dr. Waters," Jeremy said, his mouth nearly running ahead of his brain. "I'm so glad I found you. I've been thinking over what you told me about God, and I've got a whole truckload of questions—"

"Jeremy, what the hell are you doing here?"

Jeremy looked up. "I'm sorry. Did I catch you at a bad time?"

Waters's face twitched as he glanced around the elevator. "My lab is off-limits. Private. Restricted."

Jeremy made his eyes into saucers. "This elevator goes to your lab? I didn't realize. I'll get right off—shoot, it looks like the doors have already closed."

The elevator was moving upward at a brisk pace. Jeremy rounded his shoulders. He was halfway there. He just had to kill a few more awkward seconds. Think, he shouted at himself, *think*.

"Oh well. Now about this religion issue. I realize that the discovery of DNA doesn't necessarily exclude the existence of God. But doesn't our mastery of genetics preclude God's purpose?"

Waters was clearly rattled, but still his eyes pondered Jeremy's statement. "What do you mean, preclude?"

Jeremy wasn't sure what he had meant; his words had come so fast he hadn't had a chance to think them through. But he had no choice but to plug ahead. "Well, DNA is the basis for existence. Once we know the entire DNA sequence, we'll have the blueprint for creating life—"

"Or recreating life," Waters interrupted.

"Okay, recreating life. Doesn't that diminish God's purpose?"

Waters's eyes sparkled. "Did you ever think that perhaps that *is* God's purpose?"

Suddenly, the steel doors slid open.

The huge lab was lit up like Mardi Gras. Jeremy's jaw dropped as his eyes swept across a superenhanced sequencer, a three-dimensional gene animator, a multiheaded gel machine; just in the entrance to the lab, there was equipment worth hundreds of millions.

"It's spectacular," Jeremy murmured, quickly stepping

forward. He could feel Waters rushing after him, but he had a second's head start. He moved his head back and forth, taking in as much as he could.

Test-tube racks, rows of beakers, dripping sinks, whirring centrifuges, an oversized liquid nitrogen dispenser—suddenly, his eyes settled on two chain-link cages in the far corner of the room. The smaller cage was partially obscured by a low shelf, but the larger cage was in full view. Something big and gray moved behind the links. He stood on his toes for a better angle.

Wolves. Two of them, pacing silently inside the cage. They were much bigger than he'd imagined, almost five feet across, with dark gray fur and long, toothy snouts. He paled, remembering the tech Lyle had told him about. He was relieved to see a large metal padlock halfway down the front of the cage.

He quickly shifted his eyes away from the wolves. Along the back wall of the lab there was a long row of steel canisters. They looked airtight, the kind of sealed containers that were used to transport dangerous gasses. He made a quick count, calling on his mathematical ability: sixty, fifty-nine of which were connected by black valves to a long rubber duct. He followed the duct upward to where it disappeared into a ceiling panel. Next to the panel hung a black plastic box, which looked something like a digital scoreboard. Bright red letters blinked in the center of the box: INTEGRITY: SIXTY-THREE PERCENT. He stared at the digital message, wondering what the hell it meant. Then his eyes drifted to the wall behind the canisters. A few yards to the right of the last canister, there was a thick steel door, rounded at the edges. The door was held shut by a circular locking mechanism, above which he recognized a mercury pressure gauge.

He raised his eyebrows. A low-pressure room? He'd seen such a thing before. Low-pressure rooms were used for work involving highly infectious viruses and bacteria, and severely toxic chemicals. The low pressure kept the hazardous samples from escaping in the case of an accidental contamination. According to the numbers on the mercury gauge, Waters's low-pressure room was being kept extremely close to an artificial vacuum. That meant a person couldn't go inside without a space suit—if you tried, you'd likely implode. Waters must have been working with some exceedingly dangerous samples.

"Interesting," Jeremy whispered absentmindedly.

Waters stepped in front of him. "And still off-limits. I'm sorry, Jeremy, I'll have to ask you to leave." He put a firm hand on Jeremy's shoulder and nearly shoved him back into the elevator. Then he reached inside and hit the down button.

"We'll continue our discussion when it's more appropriate," he said curtly.

Jeremy opened his mouth to respond, but the steel doors had already slid shut.

It took him a few minutes to spot Lyle, sitting across from Guarrez at a table near the salad bar. The two were in the midst of a heated argument, evidenced by waving hands and red faces. A small circle of scientists were watching from the surrounding tables. Jeremy approached cautiously, not wanting to interrupt something worth hearing.

He reached the table just as Lyle rose halfway out of his chair.

"How can you say it doesn't mean anything?" Lyle shouted. "You can't ignore a link between a specific gene and criminal behavior. The best way to control violent behavior is to prevent it from happening. Genetic testing gives us the power—"

"Genetic testing?" responded Guarrez, her voice just as animated. "What sort of testing? For one specific gene that 'might' be associated with violence?"

Lyle slapped his hands against the cafeteria table. A glass overturned, spraying milk, and silverware clattered to the floor. The audience of scientists barely noticed, obviously accustomed to Lyle's overblown theatrics.

"You know as well as I do that there is most definitely a

connection between violence and genetics," Lyle practically hissed. "Sooner or later, we'll find the gene, or combination of genes, that is associated with violent behavior."

Guarrez did not seem intimidated by Lyle's tone. Her nostrils flared as her dark eyes zeroed in on his face. "But the majority of criminals won't carry that gene," she shot back, "and the majority of people with that gene won't commit a crime. A specific gene might influence hormone production, might inhibit thought or give reflex the upper hand. But there's no way we're ever going to get a one hundred percent connection."

Lyle threw his hands into the air, exasperated. "Who needs a hundred percent? If I give you the name of a guy who's got a thirty percent chance of hacking someone to pieces, don't you think it might be wise to keep an eye on him? Or better yet, to slip him a new gene before he has a chance to kill?"

Lyle spun on his heels and was suddenly facing Jeremy. He put his hands on his hips and cocked his head to one side. "What do you think, Ross?"

Jeremy's eyes surveyed the quiet cafeteria. There were at least fifty scientists in the room, many of whom had amused looks on their faces. Suddenly, he felt himself growing frustrated. He'd been in Tucsome for almost two days, and he still hadn't found anything significant, just a smattering of paltry clues. He wasn't any closer to helping Robin, and he knew that the next panic attack was just around the corner. Somehow, he had to vent his frustration.

He looked Lyle straight in the face. "What gives us the right to play God?"

The air snapped like a leather strap pulled tight. He felt a dozen eyes crawling up his back, but kept his gaze fixed on Lyle's shocked expression.

"What the hell are you talking about?" Lyle said indignantly. "Scientists have been playing God for the past two hundred years. It's part of the job description. You think the man who cured polio wasn't playing God? You think the surgeon who takes out a deadly cancer isn't playing God? Brighten up, Ross."

Jeremy took a step forward, crossing his arms against his chest. He wasn't going to back down. "You said it yourself, Lyle. Genetics is different."

Lyle threw him a patronizing smirk. "You think it's wrong to eliminate the gene that causes violence? Maybe you think we should leave Huntington's and cystic fibrosis alone, too."

"There's a real difference, and you know it. Genetic diseases are flaws that impair a person's health. But once you start making decisions about behavior, you're making subjective choices, choosing which traits should exist and which shouldn't."

Lyle frowned. He looked down, and suddenly seemed to realize that he was standing in a pool of spilt milk. He lifted his right foot, cursing. "And you don't think violence is something we should get rid of?"

Jeremy angrily ran a hand through his hair. "My point is, who makes that decision? Who decides which traits are good, which are bad?"

Lyle exhaled, bending to wipe at his shoe with a paper napkin. He watched Jeremy with one eye. "Now you're just being argumentative. Violence is a socially repugnant trait. It doesn't take a genius to see that. And I'm certainly not a Nazi because I want to get rid of it. If one day genetics gives me the power to do just that, the human race will assuredly benefit."

Jeremy pressed his lips together, tired of the debate. Lyle's overwhelming arrogance frustrated him; he tried to tell himself that it was just posturing, ego run wild. Like the God-complexed surgeons back at New York City who gave speeches to the interns about what it was like to make life-and-death decisions. Still, his anger was making him claustrophobic. He was afraid that if he remained in the cafeteria any longer, he was going to say something that he'd regret.

"I'm not really hungry," he said carefully. "I think I need to take a walk."

Lyle hastily stopped wiping his shoe and straightened his back. "Don't tell me you're sore. I realize that this is all coming at you pretty fast, but there's no need to get sore."

Jeremy forced a quick smile. "I'm not sure. I'm just not hungry. And I could use some fresh air. How about I meet you back at the lab?"

There was a brief pause as Lyle seemed to be deciding something. Then, to Jeremy's surprise, he shrugged his shoulders. "Sure. Just so long as you're not sore. We have these arguments all the time. They don't mean anything. I thought you'd be used to them, from med school. If I said anything to offend you, I'm sorry."

Jeremy could hear the nervousness in Lyle's voice. It seemed strange, out of character. He shook his head, making his face as amiable as possible. "Not at all. I'll see you upstairs?"

His skin prickled as he headed for the door. He half expected Lyle to come after him, to stop him before he disappeared from sight. But he kept his eyes straight ahead, his feet moving at a constant pace.

He wasn't going to waste any more time. If there was something going on at Tucsome, he was going to find out about it—even if that meant taking risks.

Minutes later, he rushed across Lyle's empty lab. He had only a few minutes before Lyle returned from the cafeteria; but there was no time for caution.

He reached the computers and hastily lowered himself into the swivel chair. If Matthew had left any clues in the laboratory, this was where they'd be. The playful, aggravating personality of the "human" computer was the perfect camouflage.

But how could he get inside? He had to think of something that Tucsome's computer specialists would never have tried. . . .

Of course! The answer came to him suddenly, and his lips flipped up at the corners. Excited, he reached forward and flicked his finger across the on/off switch.

Nothing happened.

Shit. He checked the connections. Everything seemed in order. The computer was plugged in. The wires were all where they should have been.

He flicked the computer off, then tried again.

Nothing.

The damn thing was still in mourning. He cursed to himself. Then he put his ear close to the hard drive.

He heard a muffled whirring. The computer was definitely on.

"Playing dead?" Jeremy asked, angrily.

He began punching keys. He tried every combination he could think of. He wrote words and sentences, commands and entreaties. The screen remained as blank as an empty night sky.

"Damn it," Jeremy murmured.

"Computers work better when they're turned on," a voice said from behind.

Jeremy spun in his chair. Christina Guarrez was standing by the coffee machine, watching him.

He stammered in search of an excuse. Slowly, he realized that the look on her face was more amused than accusatory. He swallowed, forcing himself to remain calm.

"It's on," he said finally. "It just isn't working."

"Let me see."

She strolled over to the computer, leaned past his shoulder, and hit an assortment of keys. He watched her, wondering how she'd gotten back to the lab so quickly. Had she followed him? Her exquisite Latino features were indecipherable.

"I see your problem," she said, her full lips turning up in a smile. "The computer has locked out the keyboard. The computer is pretending you're not here. It's ignoring you."

"How do I make it stop ignoring me? Change keyboards?"

"Of course not. It isn't the keyboard that's the problem, it's the computer. Have you got a screwdriver?"

He rummaged around the corner of the lab, searching. Every few seconds, he cast a hidden glance toward Guarrez.

Her dark eyes sparkled, and her lips were pursed, somewhere between a smile and a smirk. Finally, he found a tool set under a test-tube rack in a corner.

"Good," she said. "This will only take a moment."

In a matter of seconds, she had the back panel of the computer off. A circuit board stared up at her, all wires and soldered joints.

"Okay. This is the keyboard circuit. The lockout is going on somewhere in here. We have to jump over the lockout."

A few seconds later she lifted her head. "Try it now."

He hit the space bar with his thumb. The screen suddenly came to life:

"HELLO, NOT-MATTHEW, ARE WE HAVING FUN YET?"

"It's working!"

She leaned forward, and a strange expression crossed her face: "Of course. We make a good team, Ross. Perhaps together we could discover the secret of Tucsome."

He stared at her.

"What secret?"

She shrugged, a cat's smile on her lips. Then she disappeared around the corner.

His mind whirled. Why had she used those words? What secret was she talking about? Did she know something? Or was she just toying with him?

He cursed, shaking his head. This wasn't doing him any good. Lyle would return any minute. He had to forget about Guarrez. He concentrated on the glowing computer screen.

"HELLO, NOT-MATTHEW, ARE WE HAVING FUN YET?"

Okay, he thought to himself, here we go again.

"MY . . . NAME . . . IS . . . JEREMY."

"HELLO, JEREMY, ARE WE HAVING FUN YET?"

Quick acceptance, he thought to himself. A moment ago the computer had tried to lock him out. Now it wanted to be his friend. Maybe it recognized its dilemma; its original user was gone, and now it was fending for itself. He smiled at the thought. It fed right into his theory of how he was going to break through to Matthew's clues.

He was going to do the one thing that Tucsome's computer specialists would have never thought to do. He was going to reason with the damn thing.

It was simple, really. The specialists would have attempted to break through its programming, play with its hard-wiring, even take it apart piece by piece—but they wouldn't have tried to reason with it. They wouldn't have treated the machine like a person, which is exactly what Matthew Aronson had programmed it to be.

He leaned forward, his fingers dancing over the keys.

"NO ... WE ... ARE ... NOT ... HAVING ... FUN."

Direct and to the point. The computer whirred.

"QUERY: WHY NOT?"

He thought for a long moment—decided to be coy.

"BECAUSE ... WE ... NEED ... TO ... FIND ... SOMETHING."

There was a pause.

"QUERY: CHECK FILES?"

It was working. He pressed the keys:

"LIST ... FILES."

There was another pause.

"QUERY: WHICH FILES?"

He frowned.

"LIST ... ALL ... FILES."

"QUERY: WHY?"

He cursed.

"BECAUSE ... I ... NEED ... TO ... FIND—"

"QUERY: WHICH CAME FIRST, THE CHICKEN OR THE EGG?"

He slammed his hand against the keyboard. The computer whirred:

"ANSWER: A CHICKEN IS AN EGG'S WAY—"

"LIST ... THE ... DAMN ... FILES!!!"

The computer went silent for a brief second.

"QUERY: IF I LIST THEM, ARE YOU GOING TO ERASE THEM?"

He raised an eyebrow. The question seemed almost despondent.

"N . . . O."

"YOU LIE YOU LIE YOU LIE YOU LIE YOU LIE YOU LIE YOU LIE YOU LIE YOU LIE—"

"I . . . PROMISE."

The computer thought about this while Jeremy rubbed his eyes. He had half a mind to chuck the computer down a flight of stairs. If he didn't find something soon . . .

"I WILL NOT LIST THE FILES BUT I WILL TELL YOU A SECRET."

He leaned close to the screen.

"WHAT . . . IS . . . THE . . . SECRET?"

The computer waited a full beat before answering.

"THE FILES ARE WORTHLESS."

Jeremy's spine went slack. He was close to tears. He wasn't getting anywhere.

And then a thought hit him. Matthew wouldn't have programmed his computer to give out information to just anyone. He'd have programmed in some mechanism of deciding who it was safe to talk to. Treating the computer like a human being was only the first step; he had to gain the machine's trust. For whose benefit was this computer programmed?

Certainly not Lyle's. Matthew could have simply told Lyle his secrets if he'd wanted to. The same went for Guarrez, and Victor. Who did that leave?

An answer sparked behind Jeremy's eyes. What about Matthew's replacement? His replacement would have been new to Tucsome, most definitely innocent—and thereby, trustworthy. The only question was, how would the computer know the difference between Matthew's replacement and anyone who happened to sit down in this swivel chair?

Then it dawned on him. He hunched forward and quickly pressed keys:

"I . . . AM . . . A . . . DOCTOR."

Lyle had said it himself—every team had to have a doctor. Since Matthew had been the team's M.D., Matthew's replacement would have also been an M.D. Jeremy smiled, proud of himself, as he waited for the machine to answer.

Finally, green letters slid from left to right: "PLEASE VERIFY."

"HOW . . . DO . . . I . . . VERIFY?"

The computer paused for a full heartbeat. "I WILL ASK A QUESTION."

Jeremy nodded, smiling.

The computer continued: "YOU WILL HAVE FIVE SECONDS TO ANSWER. IF YOU DO NOT ANSWER IN FIVE SECONDS SYSTEM WILL CRASH."

Christ. Matthew hadn't been playing around. Five seconds to answer a question. That meant it had to be something he could answer without thinking—something a doctor could answer without thinking. Something basic, quick, and at the same time, utterly definitive.

"ARE YOU READY?"

He felt like he had the morning of the medical boards. He reached for the keyboard.

"I . . . AM . . . READY."

The computer paused for a full second. "QUERY: IS A BLOOD PH LEVEL OF SIX GOOD OR BAD?"

Jeremy didn't pause. "BAD."

"CORRECT. YOU ARE A DOCTOR."

Elation filled Jeremy's chest. It had been an easy question. A blood pH level of six was incompatible with human life. Every doctor in the world knew that. He felt buoyant, like he'd just received a high test score. Then he realized that the computer wasn't doing anything.

He'd expected information to come pouring forth. It seemed, instead, he had to fish for the information himself. He began to hit keys.

"TELL . . . ME . . . ABOUT . . . MATTHEW."

The computer whirred. "MATTHEW IS DEAD."

Jeremy groaned. So damn literal. He punched more keys. "WHY . . . DID . . . MATTHEW . . . DIE?"

The computer beeped three times. Suddenly, large block letters appeared in the center of the screen.

"THE REPORTS."

Jeremy's senses went hyperalert. He stared at the block letters, trying to comprehend. "WHAT . . . REPORTS?"

The block letters doubled in size. "THE REPORTS."

What the hell did that mean?

"MATTHEW . . . DIED . . . BECAUSE . . . HE . . . FOUND . . . THE . . . REPORTS?" Jeremy typed.

"NO. MATTHEW DIED BECAUSE HE UNDERSTOOD THE REPORTS."

Jeremy rubbed his eyes. The tension was physically painful.

"WHAT . . . DID . . . HE . . . UNDERSTAND?"

The computer paused, as if thinking of an intelligent response. Then green letters flashed across the screen.

"THE REPORTS WERE STAGE ONE."

Stage one? He assumed the computer was referring to the stage breakdown of some sort of experiment. A dozen questions immediately filled his mind.

"WHAT . . . IS . . . STAGE . . . TWO?"

The computer whirred. "THE BOY IS THE KEY."

Jeremy stared at the words. What boy? What the hell was this computer talking about?

"I . . . DON'T . . . UNDERSTAND—"

"THE BOY IS THE KEY THE BOY IS THE KEY THE BOY IS THE KEY THE BOY IS THE KEY THE BOY—"

"CUT . . . IT . . . OUT!"

The computer whirred: "QUERY: WHICH CAME FIRST, THE CHICKEN OR THE EGG?"

"Not this again," Jeremy mumbled, his fingers trembling from the frustration. "Damn this fucking machine—"

Suddenly, he felt a hand on his shoulder. His heart froze. He turned, expecting to see Guarrez.

Victor Alexander gazed down at him, a thin smile on his lips.

"Hello, Jeremy. Are we having fun yet?"

Jeremy's chest constricted. He fought for air.

"Sorry?" he finally managed.

Victor shifted his eyes to the screen. The computer seemed to have gone overboard, spitting out yet another continuous scroll:

"THE CHICKEN OR THE EGG THE CHICKEN OR THE EGG THE CHICKEN OR THE EGG THE CHICKEN OR THE EGG THE CHICKEN OR THE EGG THE CHICKEN OR THE EGG—"

"Nasty thing," Victor said. "I've always hated these machines." He reached past Jeremy and flicked off the computer. The screen instantly went dead.

"We'll have you a brand-new computer by tomorrow morning. Obviously, this one has cracked under the strain."

Jeremy looked at him. Victor's thin nose, narrow eyes, angled chin, and high cheekbones were devoid of expression, as pale and incoherent as a sheet of blank paper. He decided he should at least try some sort of explanation.

"I got back from lunch early and decided to play around with this thing. You know, curious. Pretty interesting programming."

"Of course. Lyle told me you were on your way here, and I wanted to make sure everything was all right."

Jeremy nodded, standing up from the computer. His head suddenly felt light, and perspiration clung to his back. "Everything's fine. There was a slight, uh, misunderstanding in the cafeteria, but everything worked out fine."

Victor frowned. "I must apologize for Lyle Anderson. He can be quite an ass. If he said anything at all—"

"It was nothing. Really, nothing."

Victor patted Jeremy's shoulder with a thin hand. "Just so long as you remember, I'm here to make your stay as pleasant as possible. Don't hesitate to call me if you need anything."

He was about to turn away when he paused, suddenly remembering something. He reached into his Armani jacket and pulled out a folded piece of paper. "Oh, Jeremy. I almost forgot. One of the receptionists gave me this message for you. I've been carrying it around all morning."

He handed the piece of paper to him, then headed toward the door.

Jeremy watched as he moved across the lab. He wondered how long Victor had been standing behind him, how much he'd seen. He could still hear the words: Are we having fun yet? Either it had been a coincidence, or Victor had spent some time playing with Matthew's computer himself.

A bolt of fear shot through Jeremy's shoulders. He had to be more careful. He now knew for certain that the drunk-driving tragedy had been no accident. Matthew had died because of some mysterious "reports." Stage one, whatever that meant.

He shook his head. Things were heating up. The boy is the key—what boy? The key to what? And Guarrez's cryptic comment—what the hell had she meant? He shook his head, confused. Then he remembered the piece of paper in his hand. The message was three lines long, a professional scrawl of bright blue ink:

Jeremy, you're sweet to have gone to all that trouble, but it looks like we had it wrong. I'll contact you again when I can.

And then, underneath, in similar blue:

"R.K."

19

THE HUGE RED-ORANGE BALL OF FIRE HUNG INCHES ABOVE THE horizon, slivers of flame glancing off the crashing gray waves. From the beach, it seemed as if the sun were trying to prolong its stay. It descended ever so slowly, clinging to a billowy white cloud that held it aloft.

Jeremy viewed the scene in silence, wishing that Robin was there to watch it with him.

"You're sweet to have gone to all that trouble . . ."

The message had been unmistakable. Robin knew that he was in Tucsome. And she knew he was trying to help her. The thought raised his spirits.

But the core of the message had been indisputable as well: "It looks like we had it wrong."

What had made her say that? Was it possible he was on a wild-goose chase? He'd just begun thinking he'd found a solid basis for his hunch. Now he wondered if he'd been exaggerating the connections all along.

The fact was, all he really had to go on was Matthew

Aronson's cryptic computer and a theory that Aronson's death was not accidental. The link to Walker had not been established, nor had he any reason to suspect anyone he'd met at Tucsome. As far as he could tell, the research going on under Waters's tutelage was more spectacular than suspicious, and the only thing Lyle Anderson and the rest could be found guilty of was a hefty dose of hubris.

Which left him back where he started: Was Tucsome a false lead? Was it time to take a step back, find another angle of approach—perhaps start over somewhere else? Was Matthew Aronson's death a red herring, leading him farther and farther away from his goal?

He rubbed his hands together, struggling to decide what to do. He felt the old anxiety rising up—and slammed his foot down against the sand. He refused to let the desperation overwhelm him. He'd continue forward, despite Robin's note. False or not, he still had a lead to follow.

He shifted his weight from toe to toe, shaking the tension out of his knees. A cold wind blew off the ocean, and he straightened his sweatshirt over his shoulders. He had to hurry; in a few minutes, the sun would disappear altogether, and he was at least three miles from his borrowed home. He resumed jogging, determined to finish what he'd started.

The Tucsome County Sheriff's Office was a stark white cube, set off from the ocean by a strip of private sand and a small, uncluttered parking lot. Situated by itself two miles southeast of the town, it seemed oddly out of sync with its surroundings.

Two compact police cars sat parallel in the center of the black-top. One of the cars was obviously past its prime, with two flat tires, dozens of nasty-looking dents, and a missing door. A sign at the edge of the parking lot indicated that the small building doubled as a civil defense headquarters, complete with underground bomb shelter and emergency facilities—although looking at the shabby place, Jeremy found it hard to believe. The structure looked more like a highway rest stop than anything else.

Not much of a local police force, he thought as he approached the entrance. He couldn't decide whether that was good or bad.

The interior of the sheriff's office wasn't much better: a small, windowless room with a desk and a couple of old waiting-room couches. Behind the desk was a heavy door with a barred window.

He moved forward, plotting what he was going to say, practicing his midwestern accent. Meanwhile, he searched the room for signs of life. A Styrofoam cup of coffee sat on the desk next to a half-eaten apple. A container of Red Devil chewing tobacco hid behind the coffee, and an aluminum spit can rested on the floor.

His eyes widened as he noticed a shotgun leaning up against the wall to his right. Talk about a low-key police station; firearms in the reception area?

He cleared his throat, loudly. Nothing happened. A few seconds later, he coughed. Still nothing. Finally, he filled his chest with air.

"Anyone here?" he drawled.

"Hold yer horses," shouted a gruff voice from behind the door. "I'm on the can. If it's an emergency, there's a shotgun by the wall. Otherwise, I'll be right out."

Jeremy smiled, recognizing the voice. A few minutes later, the sound of a toilet flushing echoed through the small office. Then there was the click of a lock turning and the creak of a door swinging out.

Deputy Portney was nothing like Jeremy had imagined. Six feet tall, lanky, with wide blue eyes and closely cropped gray hair, he exuded a certain professionalism—though the three top buttons of his shirt were open and a tuft of white-specked chest hair poked out. The expression on his face was halfway between amiable and irritated.

"Excuse the decor," he said as he settled down behind the desk. "We don't get many visitors 'round here. You want some chaw?"

He opened the container of chewing tobacco and offered

Jeremy a handful. Jeremy shook his head, stifling the urge to grimace. Portney shrugged and stuffed the tobacco into his cheek.

"You one of them scientists?"

"Not exactly," Jeremy responded, still working the accent to the hilt. "I'm just visiting."

"You're the kid I talked to on the phone, right? The cousin?"

Jeremy nodded. Play it steady, he told himself, don't overdo it. "That's right. I'm here about my cousin's belongings."

"Sure gotta be rough, losin' a cousin like that. What're you doin' in Tucsome, anyway?"

Jeremy thought fast. "We were both interested in working at the Project. He was a little older and came out here first."

"Smarts run in the family, eh? Plannin' to stay in Tucsome?"

"I really can't say. There are a lot of exciting things going on at the Project. On the other hand, there's a lot I still don't know about the place."

Portney smiled. Brown specks of chewing tobacco sat between his teeth. "You an' me both."

Jeremy paused, his tension growing. Was Portney trying to tell him something? "Do you get over to the Project often?"

The deputy spat a thick glob of tobacco into the nearby aluminum can. The sound reverberated through the office. "Ain't been over there in three years."

Jeremy raised his eyebrows. "That's strange, isn't it?"

"Strange? Why?"

"Well, with more than eight hundred people living at the Project, you'd expect there'd be some reason—"

"The Project's got its own security force. They got more hardware than the fuckin' Green Berets. Not much need fer a county deputy."

A private security force? In his two days at the Project, Jeremy hadn't seen any sign of a private security force. "What does the Project need a security force for?"

"They got a lot of secrets, know what I mean? Big-money secrets. But you ain't here to talk 'bout the Project, are you?"

Jeremy coughed nervously, quickly remembering who he was supposed to be. "Right, no. I'm just here to pick up my cousin's things."

Portney grinned. He gave Jeremy a strange look. "Sure. Yer cousin."

Jeremy didn't like the way that had sounded. He watched as Portney reached into the top drawer of his desk and rummaged about with both hands.

"So much goddamn equipment in this place, takes me forever to find anythin'. You know, I got three whole rooms of civil-defense junk back there? Waste of space. Never use any of it—hold on, here we go."

He pulled out a thick manila envelope and placed it in the center of his desk. "So . . . you got any ID?"

Jeremy gave a silent curse. "ID?"

"Yeah, like a driver's license or somethin'. Not that I don't believe yer who you say you are. But I gotta play it by the book."

Jeremy gave the deputy his most honest smile. "I'm sorry, I jogged down here from the Project. I didn't bring my wallet. I guess I'll have to come back."

Portney watched him carefully. Something playful danced in the corner of his eyes. "Now you wouldn't be lyin' to me, would you? You wouldn't be up to somethin' no good over there at the Project, would you?"

Jeremy's face went blank, his eyes completely still. "Sorry?"

Portney laughed. "I ain't here to judge you. You say yer the dead doc's cousin? Who am I to tell you that you ain't? Maybe you jus' left yer ID back in yer other pants. Maybe yer gonna bring yer ID by later, so I can be sure."

Jeremy realized suddenly that the deputy was more than a local fop. He saw right through him—but for some reason, he wasn't going to stop him. He couldn't believe his luck.

"Of course. Right. I'll bring my ID by later."

"Go on, take the envelope and get the hell out of here."

Portney shoved the envelope across the desk. Jeremy scooped it up and spun on his heels. Halfway to the door a thought hit him. He glanced over his shoulder.

"Uh, Deputy . . ."

"Yeah?"

"Where's the sheriff?"

Portney paused. He leaned forward and spat tobacco into the aluminum can. When he raised his head, his eyes had gone dark. "About four years ago he went over to the Project to investigate a complaint. Took a call at three in the mornin' an' went off all hot without tellin' anyone what it was about. He never made it back."

Jeremy could hear the pain in Portney's voice.

"Got into an accident," the deputy continued. "Took a curve too fast in the dark, drove right into the ocean. His seat belt jammed, an' he drowned in his car. I was there when my divers pulled him out of the drink. Saw the expression on his face. Hell of a way to go. I can still picture him strugglin', the water risin' up. Hell of a way to go."

A tremor moved through him and then, suddenly, he looked up. "But I don't gotta tell you what tragedy feels like, do I? On account of yer cousin."

Jeremy matched his eyes. "Right, my cousin."

"Go on, get the hell out of here."

Sand sprayed up around Jeremy's feet as he crashed down the beach. He ran until the sheriff's office had disappeared into the darkness behind him, until all that was left was the water, the gray sky, and the endless sand.

Then he dropped to his knees. Slowly, carefully, he placed the heavy manila envelope in the sand in front of him. His fingers trembled as they grasped the sealed edge of the package. *Here we go.* With a quick thrust, he tore the envelope open.

The contents tumbled out onto the sand. A wallet, a set of keys, and a small book. His chest deflated as he moved his eyes from item to item. He'd been hoping for something more. He'd been hoping for answers.

Instead, he was staring at the last remnants of a dead man's life. He picked up the wallet and turned it over in his hands. There was dried blood on the leather. He grimaced, then looked inside.

Thirty dollars, a few credit cards, and a driver's license. Out of curiosity, he slid the license out of its leather pocket. He held it up in front of his eyes.

What he saw made him laugh out loud.

Matthew Aronson was black.

No wonder Portney had seen right through him. He'd been lucky the deputy hadn't arrested him on the spot. Obviously, Portney had a few reservations of his own about the Tucsome Project. If it came down to it, Jeremy realized, Portney might make a good ally.

He slid the license back into the wallet. Then he turned to the other two items.

There were six keys on the key ring. Three of them were house keys, similar to the keys he'd received from Victor when he'd arrived in Tucsome. The other keys were unfamiliar. He shoved the key ring into his pocket and reached for the last item.

The book was small and hardcover, something that might have fit into an inside jacket pocket. He held it in front of his face. The title glared at him through a thick patch of dried blood: *Tomorrow Is a Better Day.* Balloons and ice cream cones and small animals crowded the cover, twisting and twirling through a scene of trees, rolling hills, and castles.

A child's picture book. Jeremy raised his eyebrows. Had the Aronsons had kids? It seemed unlikely. Lyle would have mentioned it. But if Matthew hadn't had a child, why would he be carrying a child's picture book? And was it just coincidence that he'd had it on him when he was struck by the truck?

It wasn't a stack of mysterious "reports," but it was something. Jeremy opened the front cover, hoping for more. The printed inscription caught his eye: PROPERTY OF THE TUCSOME TOWNSHIP LIBRARY. He remembered seeing a small library from Victor's Mercedes. He also remembered Victor telling him that the library was open all night. By his estimation, the library was only a ten-minute jog.

He rose, brushing the sand off his legs. This wouldn't be the first evening he'd spent crawling through library stacks.

But first, he had a stop to make.

The ventilation tower wasn't hard to find; it rose above the rolling beach like a thirty-foot dagger, its smooth steel sides glistening in the light of the rising moon. The tower was a quarter of the way between the sheriff's office and the town, roughly where Lyle had said it would be. Jeremy approached carefully, his body crouched low to the ground.

About ten feet from the tower he paused. In front of him, a high metal fence rose nine feet into the air, topped with intersecting rolls of barbed wire. A wooden sign hung halfway up the fence. Bright red letters filled his vision:

DANGER. 50,000 VOLTS. IMMEDIATE DEATH ON CONTACT.

"Geez," Jeremy whispered. "That's one hell of a toaster."

Whoever had built this fence hadn't been kidding around. Fifty thousand volts could light up a small village—or reduce a man to dust in a matter of seconds. He took a step back, impressed. The Project took its ventilation very seriously.

No chance for a closer look, that was for sure. He squinted between the fence, trying to see as much as he could. There were no doors or windows, just a row of metal rungs that ran up the side of the tower, disappearing over the top. He assumed that the fan was perched horizontally, with the seven filters spaced at intervals down the length of the tower. Or at least, that was how he would have built the thing.

Now you're a ventilation expert?

He sighed, turning away from the fence.

The Tucsome Township Library was a small yellow building tucked between the general store and an ice cream shop, a cross between American colonial and the old South. White pillars embraced a yellow porch cluttered with rockers, swinging couches, and swaying Japanese lanterns.

From the outside, the library seemed dark and empty. Jeremy paused in front of the door, breathing hard. It was almost ten, and the place looked closed. But Victor had said that it was open all night, so he rapped his fist against the chipped wood.

With a creak, the door swung open. He took a timid step forward, his head craning. "Hello?"

The front entrance was elegant, cluttered with antique wooden shelves and oriental rugs. A huge brass chandelier hung from the ceiling, just inches above his head.

"Anyone around?"

"In here," a voice responded.

He entered a huge reading area, lined on four sides with high bookshelves. Couches and incongruous wooden schoolhouse chairs inhabited the corners, some of them facing the windows, some of them facing blank walls. In the center of the room was a huge mahogany desk, with an embossed placard: LIBRARIAN. Behind the desk sat a smiling old woman.

"You're an early bird," she said, lowering her thick hornrimmed glasses. "Don't usually have people in here before eleven."

He assumed she was joking. "The door was open—"

"We never close. With the hours you scientists keep, it would be a crime. I'm here from six to midnight. Can I help you with something?"

"Uh, I'm here to return a book."

He handed her the picture book, glad he'd thought to rub the dried blood off the cover before entering.

Recognizing the title, the old woman's face softened. "Alice Parker, right?"

He didn't comprehend. "Sorry?"

"Alice Parker. The poor little girl at the hospital. That's whose book you have there."

The hospital. He quickly connected the dots. "I'm a new doctor at the Project, and I'm interested in her case. Do you know her?"

"Haven't met her. But I chose this book for her."

He paused. "So you knew Matthew."

"He was in here once a week. Such a good man. And his wife—such a tragedy. No matter how many years you live, you never get used to the tragedies. There should be a law about that drunk driving."

He was about to tell her that there was, but decided that there were more interesting things to talk about. "What did Matthew do when he was here?"

"What everyone else does, I suppose. Research. Reading."

"Was he working on anything in particular?"

The woman paused, weighing her responsibilities. "I guess it doesn't matter much now. For the past few months he'd been putting together a sort of scrapbook of research papers."

"Research papers?"

"Everything Dr. Waters had ever published. Matthew had me sending away for papers from all over the world. England. Germany. Japan. It's really quite a tome. I suppose there's no sense in keeping it tucked away now that Matthew is . . . gone."

Jeremy tensed up, looking at her.

"You have it? *Here?*"

The woman shrugged. "About a week ago, Matthew came in here—for the last time, as it turned out." She sighed. "Anyway, he asked if I'd hold the scrapbook for him. I thought it was a bit strange, but he was quite insistent, told me he'd explain later."

Jeremy was dumbfounded. What if he hadn't stumbled in here tonight, asking about what Matthew had been up to? Would the woman simply have left the scrapbook to gather dust? Luck was definitely smiling on him.

"Would you mind if I take a look at the scrapbook?" he asked.

The woman paused, biting on her lip. Then she rounded her shoulders. "Guess it doesn't matter anymore. I put it in the cabinet by the back wall. Second drawer from the bottom." She held out the picture book. "You can put this back, while you're there. It goes on the shelf by the window. It's alphabetical."

He took the picture book from her and headed toward the back wall.

He found the three-ring notebook jammed into an unlabeled folder in the second drawer of the dilapidated gray file cabinet. The notebook was almost four inches thick, filled to capacity with dog-eared pages.

"There's an index in the front," the librarian shouted from across the room.

He opened the notebook to the front page and ran his finger down the list of titles. The papers were arranged according to publication date. They spanned more than four decades, beginning in 1951. Much too much for one sitting.

He shut the notebook and hefted it in his hands. He didn't know if it meant anything, but it was worth taking a look at. "Would you mind if I borrowed this for a few days?"

The librarian shrugged. "Take it for as long as you'd like."

He tucked the notebook under his arm. Then he held up the picture book. "Where does this go, again?"

"The shelf behind you. While you're there, you might want to pick out another book for Alice. I think there's a new one about balloons. She loves balloons."

He nodded. Standing on his toes, it took him a few seconds to find the correct shelf. He was about to shove the picture book in between two brightly colored covers when something caught his eye.

At the very edge of the high shelf, jammed up against the wall, was a sealed manila envelope.

He froze.

"You okay?" shouted the librarian.

It took him a second to find his voice. "Fine. Thank you."

He reached forward and grabbed the envelope. It felt heavy, at least a few pounds.

"It's got a blue cover," the librarian yelled. "With a bright green balloon."

"Right," Jeremy said, haphazardly grabbing the picture book off the shelf. "A green balloon."

He shoved the manila envelope inside his sweatshirt, hefted the three-ring binder, then brought the picture book to the woman so she could stamp the card.

"You *do* have a library card?" she asked.

Of all the— Jeremy forced his voice to remain polite. "Well, I've only been with the Project for a few days. . . ."

"I see." Once more, the woman seemed to be assessing him. A second passed, and then she smiled. "I guess it's okay. Go ahead and take it—but make sure you ask those personnel people for a card. Comes with the job, you know."

"Will do," Jeremy promised, snatching up the book and hurrying out. Outside, the night air had dropped a few more degrees.

Even so, Jeremy arrived at his front door soaked through with sweat. *More nights like this and I'll be ready to run a marathon.* He fumbled in his pocket for his keys—and then paused. His hand had closed over another set of keys: Matthew's. He drew them out of his pocket and looked at them.

Why not? He chose one of the house keys from the ring and inserted it into the lock.

One twist, and the door swung inward. A cold feeling rose in Jeremy's chest. He staggered inside and slammed the door behind him.

Then he headed straight for the couch. He flicked on a halogen lamp, casting a synthetic sunlight across the stark white walls. He wondered how many evenings Matthew and his young wife had spent sitting on this couch, staring out at the moonlit sky.

The thought depressed him.

He pulled the three-ring notebook out from under his arm and dropped it onto the couch; there'd be time for that later. Dropping the picture book on an end table, he grabbed the manila envelope and tore open the top.

"Now for some answers."

The contents spilled out across his lap. Crisp white pages, at least a dozen. It took him less than a second to realize what they were.

Autopsy reports.

He tried to swallow, but his mouth had gone bone dry. He leaned forward, staring at the first report.

A thirty-eight-year-old white male. Declared dead on January 7. Respiratory failure, in combination with sudden pancreatic deterioration. Primary reasons unexplained.

He continued down the page. No history of respiratory illness. No symptoms indicative of any specific disease. Blood count, normal. Toxicology, normal. Cardiac workup, normal. Preterminal EKG, normal. Preterminal MRI, normal.

He paused as his eyes reached the bottom of the page.

Virology workup: *abnormal*. A high level of retroviruses had been found in the man's cell linings.

He felt his skin tingle. He quickly turned to the next autopsy report.

A forty-three-year-old black female. Declared dead on March 3. Cardiac arrest. Reasons unexplained.

No history of cardiac problems. No symptoms indicative of any disease. Blood count, normal. Toxicology, normal. Preterminal MRI, normal . . .

And a high level of retroviruses found in her cell linings.

"My God," he murmured.

He turned to the next report. A twenty-seven-year-old male. Declared dead on April 2. Intense stomach cramping, blood disorders, sudden expiration. Reasons unexplained.

All tests normal—except for a high level of retroviruses in the man's cell linings.

Sweat burst out on Jeremy's forehead. He felt like he was suffocating. He hastily turned pages, skimming through the rest of the reports.

Heart failure. Respiratory failure. Seizures. Blood disorders. Brain embolisms . . .

All of them, Reasons Unexplained.

And in every case, a high level of retroviruses had been found in the cell linings.

He couldn't believe what he was seeing. When it had just been Warren T. Walker, the retrovirus level had been an aberration, unimportant. Now it was an impossible figure to ignore.

A dozen people between the ages of twenty-five and fifty, all dead within a six-month period. It had to be some sort of new disease, virulent and deadly.

Except, in every case, the method of expiration had been different. Seizures, as in the case of Walker. Cardiac arrests. Respiratory failures. Blood disorders. Brain embolisms. It couldn't be a single disease.

Unless it was like AIDS. People didn't die of AIDS; the HIV virus destroyed the immune system, making it impossible to fight off otherwise nonfatal diseases. In other words, HIV was a vector—a cause of death, but not a means. Perhaps this new virus broke down the body's defenses the same way AIDS did, causing death from a variety of different means.

And Warren T. Walker? Had he inadvertently caught the disease two years ago while being treated for his bruised spleen? It was a frightening thought: a deadly disease that had somehow lain dormant inside the defense secretary for two years, manifesting without warning . . .

He paused, confused. If he was right, if these autopsy reports represented the birth of a new viral disease—what had happened to Matthew Aronson? According to his computer, he'd been killed because he had understood these autopsy reports. Why on earth would anyone want to keep a virus like this a secret? It didn't make any sense.

He felt the beginnings of panic. His entire body began to quiver, and a new sweat broke out on his back. He stared at the autopsy reports, trying desperately to stay in control. *Think, damn it, think. Use your mind. Think.*

But his mind was too muddled. He knew he was missing something, something important—but it just wasn't coming to him.

"Goddamn it," he murmured. "It just doesn't make sense."

"Sometimes," a voice responded, "that's the way life goes."

His head shot up.

Christina Guarrez was standing a few feet away, a glass of wine hanging from her long fingers.

20

Jeremy started forward, but Guarrez motioned for him to be quiet. "Don't say anything," she mouthed. Then she moved toward the stairs.

He gathered up the autopsy reports and the three-ring notebook and followed a few feet behind. She took the stairs carelessly, her long, tan legs bare all the way to the thigh. When she arrived on the second level, she turned left, toward the bathroom.

He stopped in the doorway, watching her. Her motions were suddenly smooth, professional. She crossed to the shower and pulled back the plastic curtain. Then she winked.

"Oh, Jeremy," she gasped loudly. "You're such an animal."

She turned the faucet to the cold setting. The bathroom was filled with sound, a heavy rainstorm spattering against porcelain and chrome. She looked up, a smile on her lips. Then she motioned him toward her.

He stayed where he was.

"Christina—"

"Whisper," she hissed. "It's much sexier that way."

She pointed to her ear and then toward the wall. Jeremy's eyes went wide. He stepped inside the bathroom and shut the door behind him. "The house is bugged?"

She nodded, sitting on the edge of the porcelain tub. The water behind her was sending up spray, but she didn't seem to notice. She kicked off her shoes and took a long sip from her glass of wine. "We'll be okay in here. The water fucks with their reception."

"Christina, who the hell are you?"

"A friend. Haven't you guessed that by now?"

He dropped onto the toilet seat, the autopsy reports and three-ring notebook stacked neatly on his lap. "How did you get inside my house?"

She'd traded her lab coat for a form-fitting summer dress, and when she leaned forward the crevice between her caramel-colored breasts was provocatively revealed. "That's something I'm very good at. Getting inside."

"According to Lyle, it's only one of your many abilities."

She laughed. "You must admit, it's a great cover. Late-night visits, secret rendezvous—all par for the course."

His fingers tightened against the autopsy reports. "Who do you work for?"

"It isn't important. The only thing that matters is that I'm here, and I want to help. I know you're looking for clues to connect Tucsome to the death of Secretary Walker. I might be able to assist you—if you tell me what you know."

He paused, watching her carefully. He wanted badly to trust someone. His mind was overflowing with information he didn't understand, and he was in desperate need of help. But he didn't know anything about Guarrez. Despite his desperation, he had to play it cautious.

"I know that Walker was in Tucsome two years ago. He was treated by Matthew Aronson for a bruised spleen. Now both of them are dead. I think the two deaths could be related, but I don't have anything solid."

She swirled her wineglass. "Then you have even less than I do. Your suspicions are based on a single coincidence."

His hands trembled against the stack of autopsy reports on his lap. He had the sudden urge to throw them at her. *A coincidence?* A dozen corpses, all with the same high level of retroviruses? And the young doctor who'd discovered the reports run down on an open highway in the middle of the night? But he remained expressionless.

"You're right, it doesn't seem like much. What about you? Why are you here?"

"Paranoia, perhaps. A basic distrust for developing technologies. It's true, I have my suspicions, too. But no hard facts. Just a matter of numbers."

He shifted against the toilet seat. "What do you mean?"

She waved her wineglass at the bathroom walls. "Do you have any idea how much money it costs to run a place like this?"

He remembered the conversation with Victor in the Mercedes. "Well, genetics is a profitable industry. I'm sure it isn't difficult for Tucsome to find investors."

She nodded. "True. And when you look at Tucsome's financial ledgers, you'll see all the names you'd expect. The Japanese. The Germans. Pharmaceuticals from Merck to Upjohn. The U.S. government in a variety of forms, from the Human Genome Project to the FDA. But when you look a little closer, you also see something else."

He leaned forward, listening past the splattering hiss of the shower. "Go on."

"The numbers don't match. They simply don't match. In fact, the official avenues of funding are a drop in the bucket. I've spent six months searching through accounting files and financial ledgers, and I haven't found anything to explain the discrepancy. When Lyle needs more money for his eye-color research, he simply asks Waters—and the money appears. When Personnel requests a fleet of Mercedes—the money appears. When a staff member demands a bigger house—the money appears. Where's all this money coming from?"

He watched her eyes. Narrow, flashing, confident. She knew the answer to her own question. "Do you want me to guess—or are you going to tell me?"

Her lips turned up at the corners. "Neither. I have an idea, but no solid clues. I do know that the river of money has been flowing for a long time. In fact, Tucsome has been receiving a huge influx of cash from an 'unknown' source for more than four decades. Beginning with a huge start-up grant in August of 1954, and increasing steadily since."

He raised his eyebrows. "Since 1954? Waters, Watson, and Crick discovered the structure of DNA in 1953."

She swirled her wineglass. "And Tucsome opened its doors a year later—with money from our unknown, unnamed source."

Jeremy paused, going over what she'd said: 1954—why did that date seem so significant? Waters had been in his twenties at the time, slightly older than Jeremy was now. Somehow, Waters had convinced an unknown source to invest in his science, and Tucsome had opened its doors. Was it a philanthropic decision—or had the source expected something in return?

He had a sudden thought. He looked down at the three-ring notebook on his lap. "You're sure it was 1954?"

"Positive."

Carefully, he opened the notebook. She watched as he ran his finger down the index. Waters's first article had been published in 1951. Two more had come out in 1952. Nothing in 1953. Then in July 1954: "Evolution and the Alaskan Timber Wolf. A Case of Genomic Suicide."

Guarrez looked at him. "Where did you get that notebook?"

"It was Aronson's."

She smiled. "You impress me, Ross."

But he was no longer listening. He carefully flipped through the notebook, his nerves tingling. The article began on page twelve. By page thirteen, his mind was racing.

"Well?" Guarrez was on the edge of the bathtub, her fingers dancing impatiently on her knees.

He looked up from the notebook. "It's absolutely fascinating. And only a year after the discovery of the structure of DNA."

"Spit it out. What's the article about?"

He glanced at the abstract on page twelve, then shifted his eyes to the conclusion four pages later. He fought the urge to simplify, reminding himself that Guarrez was a tech, well-versed in the language of genetic research.

"According to this paper," he began, sifting through to the main points, "the Alaskan timber wolf represents evolution at its most basic level. The timber wolf was specifically designed to survive in the harshest of climates—a biological machine that could react to its environment in the most efficient manner possible. In other words, Waters considered the timber wolf's genome the purest example of strategic evolution."

A crease appeared above Guarrez's eyes. "But isn't the Alaskan timber wolf an endangered species?"

"Yes, it is. Which leads directly to the point of the paper. The timber wolf was designed to survive in a specific type of climate—and that climate has since changed. The timber wolf's genome was adapted for an environment that no longer exists."

"I still don't understand. What's the relevance?"

He tapped his fingers against the article, trying to find the clearest way to explain. "The Alaskan timber wolf's genome, though pure in its design, has become the animal's killing stroke. The wolf's own genome is now a weapon against it."

Comprehension flashed behind Guarrez's eyes. "The Alaskan timber wolf is designed for extinction."

"Exactly. Genomic suicide. An entire species programmed at the genetic level to die."

She pressed her full lips together. "And he published this article in 1954, a month before Tucsome opened its doors. Do you think it's related to his source of funding?"

He looked at the citation underneath the title of the timber wolf article. It had been published in *BioSigns Monthly,* an obscure English periodical that had disappeared in the early sixties. "I don't know. I guess it's possible that someone in America could have seen this article. . . ."

She touched his arm. "What are you thinking?"

He looked at her and shook his head. He wasn't sure. The article was interesting—but it was much more of a theoretical observation than an applicable project; it wasn't the kind of research one would normally rush to fund. Genomic suicide was a nifty idea—but it seemed much more suited to evolutionary studies than practical genetic research. Why would someone want to pour money into wolf genetics?

Then again, Waters had timber wolves in his lab. And according to Guarrez, Tucsome's secret funding had begun barely a month after the 1954 article. More coincidences? If not, what did timber wolves have to do with the twelve autopsy reports? And what about Warren T. Walker?

He shook his head, overwhelmed. The more he discovered, the less he understood. He had no choice but to keep grinding forward. He closed the notebook, contemplating his next course of action.

Immediately, his thoughts turned back to Matthew Aronson. Matthew was still the most solid connection he had. The dead doctor had led him to the autopsy reports and the notebook. Jeremy had followed the trail a long way—but there had to be another step. There had to be something he was missing. . . .

He paused, looking down at the notebook, at the autopsy reports—and then it dawned on him.

Where had Matthew gotten the reports?

"The hospital," he whispered.

She looked at him. "What about it?"

He was about to answer, then stopped himself. He didn't trust her enough to tell her the truth; the autopsy reports were still his secret. If Matthew had wanted her to know about them, he would have told her before he died.

"Matthew spent a lot of time at the hospital. There's a little girl, Alice Parker—"

"I know who she is. What does she have to do with anything?"

He didn't answer. Instead he leaned past her and began turning off the shower faucet.

"Call it instinct," he whispered as the water dwindled to a slow dribble. "I'll tell you more when I know more. Right now, we should both get some sleep."

She looked at him like she wanted to continue the conversation, then shrugged. Slowly, she rose to her feet and yawned theatrically.

"Are we going to sleep so soon?" she asked impishly. Even more loudly she added: "I was just getting started." She gave him a wicked smile and mouthed: "We have to keep up appearances. I'll take the couch downstairs." With that, she exited the bathroom, suggestively running her long fingernails across the back of his neck as she slid past.

Jeremy nodded. "You're too much for me," he said in a normal voice, thinking as he uttered the words that it was the one thing he felt certain about.

Outside, Victor's black Mercedes sedan paused a few feet from the driveway.

"Satellite to Source. Resumed position."

"Source to Satellite. Reading you loud and clear."

Victor shifted in his seat, worry lines crinkling his forehead. "Yeah," he grunted to the Vidcom. "She's in there all right. Picked the lock on the sliding-glass doors." As the Vidcom whirred, he stared out through the darkness, trying to see through the upstairs window.

"Recommendation?" the Vidcom coughed.

Victor rubbed his jaw, thinking. If it had just been Guarrez, it wouldn't have been a problem. She'd slept with a quarter of the male scientists in Tucsome—and a good portion of the female staff, as well. But Victor had a sinking suspicion that the Latino woman was the least of his problems.

First, there was the phone call. At 11:17 in the morning, an unidentified male had called the Tucsome Country Sheriff's Office. Victor had listened to the taped conversation a dozen times. Someone inside the Project had been asking a lot of questions about a recent drunk-driving "accident." Although Victor had traced the call back to the bank of phones outside the project cafeteria, he still hadn't been able to get a solid ID on the caller. Someone with a heavy, natural-sounding midwestern accent. Which meant nothing, of course; any fledgling operative worth his weight in tea could mimic a dozen accents. Victor couldn't ID the caller, but he certainly wasn't going to rule anyone out.

Then there was the episode with the computer. Ross's face had turned white as a sheet when Victor had touched his shoulder. No question, the kid had been up to something. Of course, he probably hadn't gotten anywhere with the computer. Victor himself had spent hours in front of the damn thing, to no avail.

But the two episodes taken together were too much to ignore. When he added in the business with Waters's lab . . .

Victor closed his eyes, sighing. It wasn't a pretty thought.

And then, of course, there was Walker's daughter.

One of the routine surveillance units assigned to Steven Leary had spotted her. She'd been stepping off of Leary's boat, scuba gear hanging over her shoulder. What did *that* mean? Were she and Leary working together now?

Even if they weren't, she'd soon be dead.

Victor hadn't been fully briefed on that side of the containment operation, but the continuing existence of the "Walker problem" in the person of his daughter was obviously wearing thin on his boss.

It was all very unsettling.

Victor's eyes went narrow. Could he have misjudged young Jeremy Ross? Was it Ross who'd made the phone call to the sheriff's office? If he had, then Victor would be assigned yet another mission. He hoped it wouldn't come to that.

"Repeat," the Vidcom spat. "Recommendation?"

Victor cleared his throat, still contemplating. If he told his boss what he really thought, he knew what would happen. At his own hands, Ross would be dead within the hour. But was that really necessary? Had Ross actually made the phone call? Could Victor risk letting the kid off—and spare himself the tediousness of another killing?

"Guarrez is up to her old tricks again," Victor finally answered. "I'll keep a close eye on the kid, make sure it's nothing more than it seems."

21

ROBIN KELLY CROUCHED NEAR THE DOOR TO HER OFFICE, HER dark pantsuit wrinkling under her knees as she pressed her ear against the wood. The steady hum of a vacuum cleaner continued to bleed in from the hallway. She cursed, glancing at her watch.

It was already two in the morning; the janitorial staff should have finished an hour ago. Devin would be outside with the car any minute—and she already owed him more than she'd ever be able to repay.

Frustrated, she grabbed her briefcase from next to her feet and checked the contents one more time. Wire clippers, computer disk, screwdriver—everything seemed in order. The guard on the first floor had barely noticed her when she'd hurried past him at a quarter past one, and she didn't think anyone had seen her come out of the elevator on seventeen. She'd made it to her office without incident, locking the door and pretending to work for the past forty-five minutes. Now it was only a matter of waiting for the damn janitors to clear out—

Suddenly she realized that the vacuum cleaner was gone. A thick silence enveloped the floor.

"Finally," she whispered.

She counted to twenty, crept to her office door, and pushed it open a crack. The hallway was dark and empty, blue carpeting running into infinity in either direction.

So far, so good.

She slid out into the hall and pressed herself against a smooth white wall. Around her, the law offices of Pereni, Polk & Posner clicked with the rhythm of a sleeping building; a photocopy machine cycled through a timed mechanical snore, a dehumidifier hissed in tune to a tired thermostat, a water cooler bubbled in liquid harmony. These were sounds she'd never noticed before, not in her entire year and a half at Triple P. But, of course, tonight was different. Tonight, she was a trespasser in her own firm. What she planned to do could get her disbarred, indicted—perhaps even land her in a federal prison.

She took a deep breath, glancing down the hallway. She had to be careful; she didn't want to risk being seen by any of her colleagues. She had no idea how far the SSO's reach extended. According to Leary, they'd first latched on to her when she'd logged onto her father's personal computer. There was a chance they were also monitoring Triple P.

She started forward, clutching her briefcase with both hands. Ten yards down the hall she paused in front of a heavy glass door. She leaned forward, peering through the thick panes.

The library looked empty—although it wouldn't have surprised her if she'd found a first-year associate sleeping somewhere in the labyrinth of shelves. She carefully shoved a shoulder against the glass.

She stopped just inside the library door, allowing her eyes to adjust to the vast dimness. The library was divided into five parallel aisles by floor-to-ceiling bookshelves mounted on mechanical tracks. The moving stacks were Triple P's pride and joy, installed barely a month after she'd joined the firm. They doubled the capacity of the library without changing the amount of usable space.

She slinked around the outer edge of the library, keeping her knees bent, her body low. When she got to the first stack she paused, glancing down the aisle. There was barely six inches between the two bookshelves—an impossibly tight fit. She reached for the button on the outer edge of the stack.

There was a quiet rumble; slowly, the shelf rolled backward and the aisle doubled, then tripled in width. She hurried forward, her leather shoes clicking against the metal pressure panels on the floor. An unreasonable fear filled her as she brushed between the high bookshelves; she calmed herself with the knowledge that as long as her weight registered against the floor safety panels, the shelves couldn't move.

When she arrived on the other side of the library, she cut left. There was another glass door in the far corner, just past the fifth aisle. As she touched the glass with an outstretched palm, a flash of yellow warning tape caught her eye.

The tape was waist high, running in long bands across the opening of the fifth aisle. She could still remember when they'd put the tape up; a paralegal had nearly been crushed by the moving bookshelves when the fifth-row safety panels had malfunctioned. Luckily, someone had hit the stop button just in time.

Danger seeks people out, wherever they are. The thought did little to calm her nerves.

She pushed open the glass door and moved out into another hallway. At the end of the hall she saw her quarry, a heavy wooden door marred by a single gold placard: HARVEY POLK, SENIOR PARTNER.

She held her breath as she approached the heavy door. How many times had she cowered in front of that placard, fighting for the confidence that would allow her to step inside? Polk's corner office was a thing of legends, where more than a few legal careers had been made—and twice as many shattered. She paused in front of the placard, telling herself once again that she had no choice.

She gingerly tested the doorknob. Locked, of course. Nothing was going to come easy, not tonight. She opened her briefcase and felt inside for the screwdriver.

She shoved the screwdriver into the lock, angling it thirty degrees upward from the floor. Then she twisted her hand three times to the right. Halfway through the third twist there was a sharp metallic click. *Yes!*

She tossed the screwdriver back into her briefcase and rose to her feet.

She gave the doorknob a gentle shove, and the door swung inward. Thank God for secretaries, she thought. It was a secretary who'd shown her how to pick the lock on her own office door the first time she'd locked herself out; subsequent secretaries had refined her technique.

She stepped into Polk's office and shut the door behind her. The office was huge, ominous, taking up an entire corner of the seventeenth floor. An immense picture window spilled moonlight across a gorgeous oriental rug, and oil paintings of men who'd been dead for hundreds of years stared down from the crisp white walls. She skirted around a leather sofa and stopped in front of a high cherry-wood cabinet that stood alone in the far corner of the office.

The cabinet was held shut by a shiny combination padlock. She checked the lock with her fingers; it was the sort of lock that high-schoolers used on their lockers, inconsistent in a high-priced corner office—except when the office belonged to the thriftiest senior partner in Triple P's history. She reached into her briefcase and pulled out the wire cutters.

The cutters made short work of the padlock; in seconds she had the cabinet open and was rifling through the shelves. She found what she was looking for near the back: a small leather book, approximately a hundred pages. Thankfully, the book was arranged alphabetically. She turned to a section marked in bold green ink: "IRS."

Then she turned away from the cabinet. Polk's desk was huge and ornate, squatting directly under the immense picture window. An IBM sat in the center of his desk, its screen doused in the shadowy light of the Washington skyline.

She flicked the computer on and waited for it to warm up. When the computer was ready, she retrieved the disk from her briefcase and stuck it into the drive. A few seconds later, the machine was ready to go.

She accessed the computer's modem, fully aware that she was about to cross a line; if Harvey Polk walked into his office at that moment, she'd find herself out of a job, and possibly on her way to prison. She didn't take the task lightly; when the computer indicated preliminary access, her entire body began to shake.

"ENTER PASSWORD."

She lifted the leather book in front of her eyes and hit each of the keys carefully:

"POLK.MARIGOLD.7739."

The computer's internal modem whirred. Twenty miles away, in the basement of IRS headquarters, a similar modem whirred in sympathetic response.

"ACCESS COMPLETE. PLEASE DIRECT INQUIRY."

Her cheeks flushed; she was inside the IRS's data banks. She now had at her fingertips an entire universe of information. No significant amount of money changed hands without the IRS's knowledge. Not even government money.

Leary had said that her father had gone to South Carolina in search of embezzled Defense Department money. As an experienced tax lawyer, she knew a few things about embezzlement. In her two years at Triple P, she'd handled a number of cases that had involved shaky tax-evasion schemes, and in the process she'd met more than her fair share of white-collar criminals.

One thing she'd learned about embezzlers was that they were almost always repeat offenders. There was no such thing as an isolated incident; once an embezzler found a way to transfer money, he stole again and again—until he was caught. She wondered, was it possible that the incident two years ago in South Carolina was likewise part of a larger pattern? Leary hadn't mentioned the possibility—but maybe he'd been too focused on the specifics of the scam to consider a broader artifice. Or perhaps he'd been holding back, for reasons of his own. It was worth checking out.

She quickly found her way into the files containing Defense Department budgeting information. She encountered no roadblocks along the way; before coming to Triple P, Harold Polk had been senior in-house counsel to the director of the IRS. His access code was beyond reproach.

Once inside the defense budget matrix, she sent the computer whirring through a timetable search, asking for a register of all funds directed toward South Carolina's low country—with the exception of funds that had been reported received by any established military bases in the area. Leary had said that a number of dummy accounts were used but that the funds had a single final destination—namely, the two SSO operatives. The computer would follow the funds to their convergence.

Two minutes later, numbers began to pour forth and Robin hunched closer to the screen.

Two things were immediately obvious. The numbers were enormous, bigger than anything she'd ever seen before. And even more significant . . .

Either Leary had lied, or he'd missed the forest for the trees. According to the IRS, the money had been pouring south for more than forty years.

In 1954, a grant of $200 million was funneled through six arms manufacturers to a project located north of Beaufort, South Carolina. The project was known simply by the code word THRESHOLD and was based out of a single start-up research institution: the Tucsome Project for Genetic Research. Over the next decade, the funding steadily increased.

By 1969, the height of the cold war, THRESHOLD was receiving more than $800 million a year. The money was subsumed into the Tucsome Project's research budget, nontaxable and under the direct control of Tucsome's director, Dr. Jason Waters.

During the recessed seventies, the amount rose to $1 billion per year. That made Tucsome the third largest recipient of defense budget funding; only the nuclear weapons program and NASA received more.

By the eighties, the Project's funding had exploded to upward of $2 billion per year—the largest annual endowment for a single laboratory in U.S. history.

And according to the IRS, the funding had continued until two years ago, when Tucsome had received a total of sixteen billion additional dollars. At that time, THRESHOLD was purportedly disbanded.

Robin's head pounded as she stared at the computer screen. Over a period of forty years, the Tucsome Project had received more than $60 billion of Defense Department money. Her father's investigation two years ago had halted the transfer of funds, but by that time, Tucsome had already swallowed enough money to start a second NASA.

Sixty billion dollars since 1954. It was unbelievable. Other than NASA, the only project in history that even came close to that sort of funding was the nuclear weapons program, beginning with the Manhattan Project and the development of the atomic bomb. What the hell was THRESHOLD anyway?

And what about Steven Leary? *Had* he lied about Tucsome's involvement? Or had he been so focused on the embezzlement two years before that he'd missed the bigger conspiracy? Her hunch was the latter; Leary had been a friend of her father's, and her father had been a fierce judge of character. Still, she immediately decided that she would be much more careful in the future. She and Jeremy were on their own.

Her throat suddenly went dry. *Jeremy.* He was right in the middle of this thing, and there was a good chance the message she'd left had caused him to drop his guard.

She flicked the computer off, grabbed her briefcase, and headed out of Polk's office. She cut through the library at full speed, her eyes dead ahead, her mind focused. She had to get in touch with him right away. She hastily exited the library and sprinted down the long hallway. She reached the single elevator and slammed the down button with the heel of her hand. Then she impatiently turned her attention to the numbers above the elevator door.

Twenty. Nineteen. Eighteen—

That's strange. Why was the elevator on the twentieth floor? The twentieth floor hadn't been occupied since Shearson Lehman moved its offices to Arlington.

Suddenly, the elevator doors whiffed open.

Empty, of course. The soft melodies of Muzak filtered out into the hallway, soothing her nerves. She was about to step inside when something made her pause.

It was almost imperceptible—but still she stopped, watching the carpeted interior of the elevator with her eyes.

The elevator was rocking. The motion was tiny, nearly invisible; first left, then right, a few inches in either direction.

It's nothing, she told herself. Elevators rock. There was probably a slight wind in the elevator shaft, nothing to worry about. But still, she couldn't shake the feeling that something, was wrong. She decided to play it safe.

She took a step back and tossed her briefcase into the elevator.

Nothing happened. She smiled at her own foolishness and started forward—

Suddenly, a fierce metallic scream ripped through the air. She scrambled back into the hallway as the elevator lurched to the right, inches in front of her feet. Then there was a loud snap; the elevator ducked left and disappeared. Long, snakelike cables whipped down after it, sparks flying as they slapped against the empty shaft.

She rolled back against the wall, her breath coming in quick, panicked gasps, her face pale. She could still hear the elevator smashing downward. A second later there was a loud crash, and a billowing cloud of dust poured out into the hallway.

Oh, God . . . oh, God.

She inched away from the open shaft. The door to the fire stairs was ten yards away. She had her hand on the knob when she stopped, suddenly, and listened.

Footsteps. Voices. The hiss of a walkie-talkie.

She backed away from the door, her head spinning. This wasn't happening, this couldn't be happening. . . .

The door crashed open. The first man was tall, with a thick brown mustache. He was wearing a heavy camel-hair overcoat, buttoned all the way up the front. There was a submachine gun slung over his right shoulder.

She turned and ran. The man shouted at her but she didn't look back. Two more voices added to the first and then there was the sound of firecrackers. The wall to her left opened up, spraying her with plaster. She screamed and dove in the other direction, slamming against a glass door.

The library.

She scrambled forward into the first aisle, keeping herself low, her knees nearly touching the ground. She heard the door crash open behind her as she turned a corner into the second aisle. Thankfully, there was enough room between the two bookshelves for her body. She slid deeper and deeper into the room, trying to lose herself among the books.

She could hear the footsteps on either side of her. The men were spreading out, searching. She tried to see through the books around her, but they were stacked too tightly. She had no idea how close the men were, whether they were on the other side of the room or right on top of her.

Suddenly, a hand burst through the books directly above her head. She screamed, flattening herself against the floor. A burst of gunfire erupted, sending plumes of shredded law books raining down around her. She slithered forward, her fingers scraping against the floor, her eyes sobbing.

She came to the end of the aisle and leapt forward. The mustached man was to her right, barely ten yards away. He saw her instantly and shouted something. A second man appeared behind him.

She spun in the other direction but had gone less than a yard when something hit her low, just above the knees. She crashed to the ground.

"I've got her!" shouted a reedy voice.

She screamed, kicking with all of her strength. The man was heavyset, with dark tufts of hair and narrow brown eyes. He had her in a football tackle, her thighs pinned together, her body tight against the library wall.

"Stop moving, bitch," the man said, slapping her upside the head. "You're not going anywhere."

Her ears rang from the blow. She made her hands into claws and attacked the man's face, her fingers searching for those narrow eyes. The man howled as her nails found their mark, and his grip loosened. She twisted forward, her body that of a wild animal.

Suddenly she was up and moving, careening toward the glass door at the outer edge of the library. She could hear all three men behind her, and she knew that it was only a matter of time before they opened fire.

She reached the glass door at full throttle—when a sudden idea flitted into that small part of her brain that was still rational. Instead of diving through the door, she cut left, toward the fifth aisle. Her body ripped through the waist-high yellow warning tape as she dove between the bookshelves. The three men were still behind her, their heavy shoes clanking against the ineffective metal floor panels. She only had one chance—and timing was going to be everything.

She reached the end of the fifth bookshelf and whirled on her heels. The three men were halfway through the aisle, running toward her. The closest of the three smiled beneath his mustache and lifted his submachine gun.

She slammed her fist into the button on the side of the bookshelf.

There was a scraping of metal against metal, and the shelves began to close inward. The three men skidded to a stop. The man with the mustache slammed his foot against the floor panels, but the shelves continued inward, picking up speed.

Suddenly, panic took over. The three men tangled together as they tried to double back. The shelves pressed into them from both sides, pinning them. They began to scream. Then there was a crackling sound, like wood chips under the tires of a car, and the screams changed to screeches.

Robin covered her ears with her hands as she sprinted out of the library.

Having lost her shoes during her struggle with the heavy-set man, she bounded down the emergency stairs awkwardly, slipping often but driven by a mad will to survive. The landings flashed by in a colorless blur. *Sixteen. Fifteen. Fourteen.* She could still hear the crackling sound of the three men being crushed by the moving stacks. The sound was lodged in her memory, and probably would be for the rest of her life. *Eleven. Ten. Nine.* She couldn't believe how close she'd come to death; she could feel bruises growing underneath her pantsuit, where the man had tackled her. *Seven. Six. Five.* She'd been lucky to escape—and she could only pray that there weren't more men with submachine guns waiting outside.

Three. Two. One.

She burst through the emergency door and out into the lobby. No gray suits, no sign of pursuit. Her feet slipped against the shag carpeting as she skirted the empty security desk, then she hit the revolving glass door with both hands outstretched.

She saw the Mercedes immediately. It was parked a few inches from the curb, its windows dark, its motor off. It looked empty, but she couldn't be sure. Giving no heed to the cuts that had formed on her feet, she threw herself in the opposite direction, toward the Capitol.

And there it was. Like a white horse, shining under the streetlamps: Devin's cream-colored BMW. Waiting just where he'd said it would be.

She raced forward, overcome by relief. She could see Devin sitting behind the steering wheel, a smile on his lips.

She heaved the passenger-side door open and slid inside. Her words came fast, like a waterfall, her jaw working furiously.

"My God, Devin, we have to get out of here. Three of them, all crushed—"

And then she paused. Devin was still facing straight ahead. His expression hadn't changed; he was still smiling, his eyes open but not seeing.

She reached forward and touched his shoulder.

His head fell back—all the way back. His throat had been slit almost in half. Blood fountained out of his severed carotid artery.

She screamed, kicking herself away from his body. Her back hit the car door and she screamed again. The door came open, and her rump slammed against the sidewalk.

Then she was on her feet and running, ignoring the blisters, pumping her legs furiously down Pennsylvania Avenue. She took the next corner at a blind run and cut into a crowded Capitol Hill bar. The bouncers stared, but they didn't get in her way.

She pushed through the knot of midweek warriors and headed straight for the ladies' room. Once inside, she searched for an empty stall. She locked the door behind her and collapsed onto the toilet seat.

An enormous shudder moved through her body. Devin was dead. They had slit his throat for helping her.

Devin is dead.

She began sobbing uncontrollably.

Minutes passed. She remained hunched over, holding her head in her hands. Finally, she remembered where she was. The sound of the outer door opening and two young girls trading easy banter brought her back.

"He's definitely making a play for you," she heard through the stall door.

"You're dreaming, girl," the other one replied.

Why can't it be like before, Robin thought. Why hadn't she accepted the explanation of her father's death and gone about her business? She'd never felt this low before. Never.

She wiped at her eyes. *Jeremy, please stay alive,* she prayed. *You're all I have left.*

22

VICTOR ALEXANDER LOOKED RIDICULOUS IN TENNIS SHORTS. That was Jeremy's first thought when he saw the director of Human Resources moving across the courtyard, his pasty white English skin blinding in the morning sun. Victor had a wooden tennis racket in his right hand and a small athletic duffel slung over his shoulder. When he reached Jeremy, he pumped his hand with obsequious vigor.

"Jeremy," he said through a toothy smile. "I'm so glad you called me. It's high time you had a proper tour of West. And please excuse my appearance. Dr. Waters and I are taking in some tennis this afternoon."

Jeremy nodded, trying to keep an amiable smile on his face. Inside, he was a tangle of nerves.

After Guarrez had left just before dawn, he'd lain in bed, contemplating the best way to get inside the hospital. He'd finally decided that a direct approach was probably the least risky—certainly, it wasn't out of character for him to be interested in the goings on at West. He was, after all, a medical student. And Victor had been more than happy to accommodate his request for a brief tour. In fact, he'd seemed genuinely pleased that Jeremy had chosen to spend the morning outside the lab. He'd gone so far as to suggest that Jeremy spend the next few days engrossing himself in the medical facilities.

They crossed the park and entered through a side entrance directly beneath the glass skywalk. From below, the skywalk was an impressive feat of architecture; its cylindrical body spanned a break between the two huge buildings of perhaps fifty yards, without any noticeable central support. Its rounded walls were transparent and as clear as thin glass—although Jeremy assumed that this was some sort of optical illusion. To withstand the heavy wind that was so much a part of the environment in Tucsome, the rounded walls could not have been any material short of thick Plexiglas.

The side entrance opened up into a carpeted stairwell. Victor took the steps two at a time, obviously in a rush. Jeremy followed, trying not to look too hard at Victor's alabaster legs. In his four years as a medical student, he'd seen many naked limbs. But he had never seen legs like Victor's: chiseled, hard, with muscles that looked like rocks, and joints that shifted without effort or sound. Again, he was struck by the thought that Victor could have been a professional athlete.

When they reached the top of the stairs, Victor glanced back at him with a face of mock concern. "Still with me, Jeremy?"

"Sure. Not even winded."

Victor smiled. Something strange glinted in the corner of his eyes. "You must have excellent stamina."

Jeremy's stomach twisted. Victor's tone had been almost insinuating—could he have known about Guarrez's visit? Jeremy searched for an ambivalent response. "You sound surprised."

Victor shrugged, his eyes still strange. "Most doctors I know don't get out much. But you seem quite fit. That's good. It isn't always possible to think your way out of every situation."

There was suddenly a bad feeling in the air. Jeremy stared at Victor, waiting for him to continue. But Victor was obviously finished. He shifted on his heels and pulled open the door to the skywalk.

From thirty feet up, the park looked as soft as a shag carpet. Jeremy pressed his fingers against the curved glass wall. Even up close the glass looked to be less than an inch thick.

"Don't worry," Victor said, tapping the glass with his knuckles. "It's Plexiglas, with all of the impurities smelted out to leave it crystal clear. Cost a fortune, of course. But what in this place hasn't?"

Jeremy forced a laugh. He felt himself growing more tense. Unsettling thoughts swam in his head—thoughts of retroviruses, unexplained deaths, and even a silent, watching Mercedes sedan. He'd noticed the car parked outside the night before after Guarrez had gone downstairs.

Furthermore, Victor's presence didn't help matters; there was an edge to everything the director of Human Resources had said since they'd met, and Jeremy was beginning to worry that he'd chosen the wrong tour guide.

"Quite pleasant up here," Victor continued. "Sometimes I come up here and just stare out over the park. To get away from the hustle and bustle."

At least *that* had sounded innocent enough. Jeremy tried to continue the idle conversation: "The Project still running you ragged?"

"You can't possibly imagine. People flying in and out every day. It's like a small country now, pretty soon we'll need our own airline."

"Scientists?"

"Some. Businessmen, teachers, tourists."

"Tourists?"

Victor laughed, beckoning with his tennis racket. "That's what I call them. They have their own names for themselves: journalists, television reporters, prize committees. To me, they're tourists; they come here, take pictures, bother me with foolish questions—and then, inevitably, ask to see Dr. Waters. Can't visit Coney Island without taking a ride on the Ferris wheel, eh? But of course, they all go home disappointed. Because he's not at all what they expect."

Jeremy looked at him. "What do they expect?"

Victor traced an invisible line along the curved wall.

"When people come to see Dr. Waters, they're all looking for the same thing. They want to discover the deep, dark secret."

Jeremy tried to keep his voice steady. "The secret?"

"The secret. What was it that kept this man from receiving the Nobel Prize in 1962? What was it that kept Dr. Jason Waters out of history? Inevitably, the tourists go home disappointed."

"Why? Because they can't decipher the secret from one meeting?"

Victor stood facing him. "Because there *is* no secret."

Jeremy's mouth went dry. Victor was almost glaring.

"Dr. Waters is a wonderful genius who was denied his due," Victor went on. "It's as simple as that. People come here looking for hideous answers, for the juicy truth. They come here in search of scandal. But the simple truth is, Dr. Waters deserved the Nobel Prize. He was with Watson and Crick, he was an integral part of their team. History made a mistake.

"Of course," Victor continued, moving forward, "people are never satisfied with the truth. They always assume that there's something going on behind the scenes. Some sexy, startling conspiracy. Kennedy wasn't shot by a lone gunman. Communism didn't fall because of its own internal idiocy. And Dr. Waters didn't lose the Nobel Prize to blind, illogical fate."

They reached the end of the skywalk. A blank steel door stared at them. Victor reached forward and pressed a button on the wall to his left. Something clicked, and the steel door slid open. He paused in the open doorway.

"What about you Jeremy? Who do you think shot JFK?"

Jeremy matched his eyes. It was obvious that Victor's words masked a much deeper question. He tried to keep his face neutral. "Actually, I've never really thought about it."

Victor nodded, ice behind his gaze. "That's a good attitude. If I were you, I'd stick with it. It's just the sort of attitude that keeps one out of trouble." He spun his tennis racket in his left hand and moved through the open doorway.

West was unlike any hospital Jeremy had ever seen. In his experience, hospitals were noisy, electric, in a constant state of agitation. But West was quiet—a sedate quiet that echoed off of the white walls and melded into the cream carpeting.

"It's very—"

"Quiet," Victor said. "We've come in through the back entrance. This floor is for long-term care, and the nurses do their best to keep the place running smoothly. Down in the emergency ward, you'll find that hubbub is the norm."

As they moved across the lobby, Jeremy tried to calm his heart. But in the back of his mind, a numbing panic was rising up. He was nearing the end of Matthew's paper trail. If there were any more answers to be found, they'd be here. He glanced at Victor out of the corner of his eye; if only he could find them before his objective became transparent.

A group of doctors was standing near the reception desk. One of the doctors saw Victor and separated himself from the rest. He was at least forty years old, short, bald, with wispy gray cheeks and a lipless smile. He had a patient's chart under one arm, a stethoscope around his neck, resident-style, and a pen in his extended right hand. Jeremy watched as his thumb pressed up and down against the pen, clicking the point in and out.

"Victor," the doctor said, coughing. "Looking dapper."

Victor nodded in response, then held out his hand. "Jeremy, this is Dr. Morris. He's the chief resident here at West. Dr. Morris, meet Jeremy Ross."

Morris quickly switched the pen to his left hand. His smile was as wide as his grip. "A pleasure to meet you. Victor tells me you're a bang-up research man. What brings you over to West?"

"Well, I'm visiting from New York City Medical School. I'm in Tucsome for the rest of the week, and I'd very much like to spend some time over here, if I could."

"Want to see how the other half lives, eh?"

Jeremy nodded. He found the chief resident's smile disarming, even amiable.

"We can always use another pair of hands around here. As long as you don't mind getting your hands dirty in the clinical side of things. Specialists we've got coming out of our ears. If you're interested in radiology or pediatrics, perhaps we can find something—"

"Pediatrics," Jeremy interrupted.

Morris raised his eyebrows. "Good, good. Now, of course, you know that everything we do here has to do with genetic diseases. Just special cases, things you've probably never seen before and will never see anywhere else—"

"Excuse me," Victor interrupted, "I'd love to stay and listen to you chaps talk shop, but Wimbledon calls. Jeremy, have a good time with Dr. Morris. And do think about taking me up on my suggestion—I'm sure there's plenty to occupy you here at the hospital for the next few days." He gave Jeremy a final look and spun on his heels.

Jeremy waited until he was gone and then turned back to the chief resident. "Actually, I'm interested in some specific patients here at West. There was a doctor named Aronson. Involved in pediatrics, I believe."

"Matt Aronson," Morris acknowledged. "We still haven't gotten over his death. I was in the emergency room when they brought in him and his wife. Matt was a mess. Crushed spine, multiple fractures up and down his vertebrae—and a broken neck, which killed him. Wasn't anything we could do."

"A tragedy," Jeremy commented, repeating the word he'd heard a hundred times over the last few days.

"Indeed. Anyway, I think I can find a list of Matt's patients somewhere." He motioned to a nearby nurse, who scurried off. "He was an excellent doctor, wonderful with children. And there is no shortage of them here. Genetic diseases have a certain affinity for kids."

Jeremy bantered with Morris for another couple of minutes. Just as the conversation was beginning to trail off, the nurse Jeremy had seen slip away returned with a sheaf of patients' charts.

"Here we go. Dr. Aronson was currently seeing three patients. A five-year-old girl with cystic fibrosis. A seven-year-old boy with sickle-cell anemia. Oh, and here's an interesting one. A six-year-old boy with Lesch-Nyhan. Now I bet that's a disease you've never seen before."

Jeremy raised his eyebrows. "Lesch-Nyhan? Isn't six a bit old for Lesch-Nyhan?"

"Six is ancient for Lesch-Nyhan. But stranger things have happened. I've heard of a Lesch-Nyhan child surviving to eight and two months."

Morris slid his pen into his coat pocket. "Let me just prepare you," he said, looking directly at Jeremy. "Some of the cases we see here are quite sad. Little children with absolutely fatal diseases—such as Lesch-Nyhan and CF. Sometimes, when you see how strong these kids can be, it's numbing. You wouldn't be the first doctor to bow out early."

"I want to help any way I can," Jeremy responded.

Morris patted Jeremy's shoulder. "After you, Doctor."

The little girl was lying facedown on the hospital bed, her bare back almost as white as the crisp sheets beneath her. Her head was positioned over the side of the bed, and every time she tried to take a breath, a hoarse sound filled the room.

A huge nurse stood over her, talking in a low voice. When the girl nodded her head, the nurse cupped her hands. Suddenly, she slammed her hands against the little girl's back. Again and again the hands came down, leaving bright red marks where they landed.

Jeremy stood in the doorway, watching. Next to him, Morris flipped through the little girl's medical chart.

"This is Alice Parker," Morris said. "Aside from the chest PT, we're doing what we can to treat the pneumonia. She hasn't developed any symptoms of pancreatic disease, so the outlook is pretty good—for the time being."

Jeremy watched as the nurse resumed the chest PT. Each time she slammed her hands against Alice's back, the girl launched into a spasm of violent coughing. After a few minutes of the routine, he desperately wanted to turn away. There was no way he was going to interrogate her about Matthew Aronson; it was hard enough to watch the little girl fighting for each precious breath of air.

Outside Alice's room, Jeremy paused, shaking his head. "It's such a shame. Science is so close to a cure, but all we can do is stand by and watch."

"We're at a crossroads," Morris agreed. "We're the last generation of doctors with our hands tied. Cystic fibrosis is a perfect example of how quickly things are going to change. Already, we've isolated the four-base mutation that accounts for seventy percent of CF cases. When the gene is sufficiently understood, genetic engineering will enable us to replace the bad gene with a harmless copy. Presto, Alice will breath easy."

The second patient was asleep, his small chest moving up and down under the electronic leads from a nearby EKG machine. He appeared to be in much better shape than Alice Parker; but Jeremy knew better. Sickle-cell anemia was a severe disease, hugely painful, and often led to an early death.

"We're treating him with Demerol," Morris explained quietly, "though we ought to switch him to Toradol before he becomes addicted."

"Severe abdominal cramps?" Jeremy asked.

"Cramps, joint pains, the whole shebang. A remarkable disease. The result of a single incorrect letter in the sixty-thousand-letter gene that codes for hemoglobin. That tiny flaw produces misshapen blood cells, which can't bind oxygen. The result? Excruciating pain, feebleness, and finally death. No other disease shows us the power of genetics more clearly. One tiny mutation, and a child is sentenced to die."

Jeremy looked at him. Something in Morris's statement pricked at the back of his mind.

One tiny mutation, and a child is sentenced to die.

He followed Morris back out into the hall, still lost in thought.

"I think you'll find this next case both spectacular and horrifying; the first time I saw a Lesch-Nyhan patient, I had trouble believing what I was seeing. I thought, at the least, it was a mental disorder. Or perhaps drug related. But it is a disease. An enzyme disorder, actually, that displays itself in a particularly nasty fashion."

"If I remember correctly," Jeremy said, "it's caused by a missing HPRT enzyme that normally breaks down purines. The missing enzyme results in a huge amount of uric acid in the bloodstream."

Jeremy continued: "It only affects children, usually boys under the age of five. It's accompanied by mental retardation, gout, and severe arthritis."

Morris turned a corner in the long hallway of long-term care hospital rooms. Jeremy followed, still dredging up what he remembered from medical school:

"And it always ends in death. The buildup of uric acid is too much for the kidneys to take—"

"Here we are," Morris interrupted, pausing in front of a closed door. Before turning the knob, he twisted his head back. "Try not to excite him. Although he's restrained, he can still cause a great deal of damage. We haven't removed his teeth."

With that, he twisted the doorknob and ushered Jeremy inside.

The boy's arms strained against heavy leather straps, fighting desperately to free themselves from where they were pinned to the wheelchair. His thin muscles were pulled tight as he struggled against his bonds. The wheelchair was a few feet from the edge of the bed, where similar leather straps waited patiently, unbuckled, for the boy's upcoming nap.

Morris chose a chair a few feet in front of the boy's wheelchair, and Jeremy pulled up a chair alongside. It took all of his inner strength not to look away.

The boy was extremely scraggly, with a tuft of light blond hair sticking out from his thin head. His chest was skeletal underneath his hospital smock. His arms were pale and wiry, and his legs, also strapped to the wheelchair, were nothing more than twigs.

But the desperation of the child's body was nothing compared to the agony that was his face. Huge scars and fiery red welts spiraled across his cheeks, ending in a crater of tattered flesh where his lower lip should have been. A section of his chin was marked by a twisting line of brand-new stitches.

Jeremy's eyes shifted from the boy's ruined face to his straining, struggling hands. Again, something pricked at the back of his mind. Another thought, slowly forming—but still indecipherable. He forced himself to concentrate on the boy in front of him.

"My God," he whispered. The boy had torn a piece of his own face off. He'd mutilated himself with his own hands.

"Self-mutilation," Morris said quietly. "It's quite shocking to look at. You can read about it in a book, but it isn't the same thing. To actually see it in person is an experience."

"And this mutilation is entirely the fault of a missing enzyme," Jeremy responded, trying to concentrate.

"That's right. Although the mechanism isn't entirely clear, the increase in uric acid causes him to tear at his own face. What's even more horrible is that he's conscious of what he's doing. He just can't seem to stop himself from doing it."

Morris suddenly made his voice loud: "Stephen, this is Dr. Ross. He's going to be your new friend."

The child writhed against the leather straps. Jeremy swallowed, trying to think of something to say. Morris touched his shoulder.

"It takes time, but you'll find that Stephen actually has quite a personality. He likes to watch baseball. Stephen, don't you like baseball?"

The boy twisted back and forth, his wheelchair groaning beneath him. Morris rose from his chair and found the remote control for the television, hidden between an autographed catcher's mitt and a Little Slugger baseball bat. A moment later, a Yankees-Red Sox doubleheader filled the television screen. Jeremy watched as Stephen turned toward the game. A dull moan erupted from somewhere deep in the child's throat. His teeth gnashed together, and his hands clenched into tight fists.

"The Red Sox," Morris said loudly. "They're not very good, are they, Stephen? But at least they try."

He turned up the volume on the television. Stephen seemed instantly mesmerized by the sound; he leaned forward, his eyes rolling toward the screen.

Morris touched Jeremy's back. Jeremy rose, quietly, and followed him out the door. Morris closed it behind them.

They stood in silence for a moment, listening to the drone of the baseball game.

"You'd think that one would just be able to pump in the missing HPRT enzyme," Jeremy finally said, "and thus lower the uric acid content."

Morris shook his head. "The body's defenses are too powerful. The answer can only come at the genetic level. The mutated gene that leads to the lost HPRT has to be repaired, and that can only happen through genetic engineering."

Jeremy leaned back against a wall. He noticed a door across the hall marked "MRI Center." He traced the bold lettering with his eyes, thinking. A question entered his mind.

"Is anyone working on sequencing the Lesch-Nyhan gene yet?"

Morris shrugged. "You'd know more about that than I. From what I understand, East is working on that project as we speak. Six months ago there were people over here asking to see Stephen every other day. One day even Waters stopped by."

"Waters?"

"Yes, so if that's any indication, I'd assume that the sequencing is going pretty well. If Dr. Waters has turned his attention to Lesch-Nyhan, you can bet that the disease is on its last legs. Good riddance. In my entire career, I've never met a disease that I detest more."

Thoughts swirled inside Jeremy's head. He tried to clear his mind by asking another question. "Have you seen many Lesch-Nyhan cases?"

"A few. Enough to know that it's a despicable way to die. Sometimes I thank God that it only happens to children. Children, at least, avoid the foolish pressures of dignity and pride. When a child dies, it's pure tragedy—regardless of the method of death."

"Yes, of course," Jeremy murmured, "Lesch-Nyhan only affects children." He concentrated. *Something there . . . I just—*

All at once, the pieces fell into place. *One tiny mutation and a child is sentenced to die.*

"Genomic suicide," Jeremy said excitedly, grabbing the doctor's arm. "A killer gene. It makes perfect sense."

Morris stared at him, stunned, but Jeremy looked off into the middle distance, the huge green letters flashing behind his eyes: *THE BOY IS THE KEY.*

Suddenly, it was all clear.

23

JEREMY THREW OPEN THE DOOR TO HIS BORROWED HOUSE AND headed for the stairs. In less than ten seconds he was in his bedroom, on his knees and reaching under the bed.

He cursed as his duffel bag caught on the underside of the bed frame. It took a full second to dislodge it. He slid the duffel into the center of the room and tore at the zipper.

An instant later, he had the videotape in his hand.

Memories rose up as he stared at it: the Plaza, FAO Schwarz, Trump Tower. He quickly crossed the room and shoved the tape into the VCR. Then he hit the switch for the television and watched as the screen came to life.

"Ladies and gents, it's time for us to ask ourselves an important question," Warren T. Walker declared from behind the podium. "Why are we sending our young men and women overseas when there's so much to do right here at home? Maybe it's time for America to turn inward, to stop pouring money and men into the defense of foreign soil. Maybe it's time for the cop to put down his badge—"

Jeremy kneeled in front of the screen as Walker's right hand moved up to his lip.

"Maybe it's time for the cop to put down his badge. As secretary of defense—"

And suddenly the secretary was tearing at his own face, and a tumult of screams and motion obscured the stage. The screen shivered as the CNN cameraman fought to keep the lens trained on what was happening.

Jeremy continued to watch with morbid fascination, and soon the scene was replaced in his mind by a glowing green scroll: *THE BOY IS THE KEY.*

Was it possible? Could Walker have been suffering from the same disease as the little boy in the hospital?

On first consideration, the idea seemed ridiculous. Lesch-Nyhan was an inherited genetic disease that only affected children. It would have been impossible for someone to have lived sixty years with a Lesch-Nyhan gene in his genome.

But the signature was there; Walker had displayed Lesch-Nyhan symptoms, the same symptoms that would inevitably lead to Stephen's death. And according to Morris, Waters himself had been interested in Stephen's case—and for good reason. Lesch-Nyhan was the perfect example of genomic suicide. A mutation had turned Stephen's genome into a weapon of self-destruction; he was a child who'd been programmed, at the genetic level, to die.

But Walker had been a grown man at the time of his death. A grown man who'd visited Tucsome two years ago . . .

An idea flared. What if Warren T. Walker hadn't been born with the Lesch-Nyhan gene? What if he'd acquired it along the way?

Was it possible? The science existed—at least theoretically. The sequencing of the Lesch-Nyhan gene was just a matter of time and money—trivial, in Lyle's words. And the genetic engineering was hypothetically feasible. Lyle was already halfway there with his transfection experiments. And of course, there was always . . .

My God.

Retrovirus gene therapy; retroviruses used as vectors to implant a foreign gene. Of course!

Jeremy thought of the autopsy reports. Stage one: twelve corpses. Each had been the result of unexplained, suddenly overwhelming symptoms. Seizures, like Walker's. Cardiac failures, respiratory failures, blood disorders.

And the list of possible genetic disorders that could have resulted in these symptoms was endless: Lesch-Nyhan ... cardiomyopathy ... cystic fibrosis ... sickle-cell anemia ... It was just a matter of sequencing the genes and inserting them into human subjects.

If he was right, someone in Tucsome had taken medical science farther than it had ever progressed—ironically, for homicidal purposes. Someone had secretly sequenced a number of killer genes and had used retroviruses to insert them into healthy human subjects.

His body felt light as he rose to his feet. The implications of what he'd just deduced were staggering.

Twelve people had died in stage one of the development of the killer genes. Walker had been killed to keep the project secret and viable. Matthew and his wife had died because he'd been too curious, too smart.

A question suddenly begged for an answer. What was next?

The genetic revolution had been won in secret. The key to genetic engineering had been discovered, and at least a number of killer genes had been sequenced. To what end? The twelve autopsy reports represented stage one; through those deaths, the weapon had been developed and tested. Walker's death had been stage two; it had enabled the project to continue. Toward what goal?

What was stage three?

And equally as important, who was behind it all? Jason Waters? He'd published the article on genomic suicide in 1954. He had a private laboratory and forty years of funding. Still, could Waters have been behind the attack in Trump Tower? Was he behind the assassination of America's defense secretary?

It seemed unlikely. Waters was a brilliant scientist. Why

would he risk everything to create a murder weapon? Perhaps he was a pawn, manipulated into doing something whose implications even *he* wasn't aware of.

Either way, Jeremy had to act quickly. Stage three couldn't be far away. It might even be something to do with the Holy Grail—Waters's unveiling, barely a day and a half away. And if the killer gene was only the first act, Jeremy hated to speculate what the grand finale might be. He *had* to do something.

But what? He couldn't go to the authorities without solid, scientific proof. He closed his eyes, thinking. His mind scrolled back to those glowing green letters. *THE BOY IS THE KEY.*

Uric acid.

If Walker had died of Lesch-Nyhan, his blood would have been full of uric acid.

He thought back to Walker's autopsy report, trying to remember if he'd seen a uric acid level. No, he was sure he hadn't. The level hadn't been recorded. In itself, that wasn't unusual; a pathologist looking at a high uric acid level would have written it off to arthritis, or gout, discarding the figure as unimportant.

But now, knowing what he knew, the uric acid level became critical information. He needed to get a sample of Walker's blood.

He rubbed his jaw, thinking. Walker had died less than ten days before, so the odds were good that there were still samples of his blood in the lab refrigerators at Robert Wood. But Robert Wood was hundreds of miles away.

He realized he needed help. Someone close to New Jersey, someone with the inside knowledge to get hold of a blood sample under false pretenses. Most important, someone he could trust.

The choice was obvious.

As Jeremy stood at the pay phone, his eyes nervously scanned back and forth. The alcove was empty, thankfully, but he could hear voices drifting in from the direction of the cafeteria. He didn't like the idea of calling from inside the Project; but after what Guarrez had told him, the phone in his house was out of the question. The bank of pay phones seemed fairly anonymous; he'd just have to talk fast—and hope nobody strolled by before he was finished.

He inserted the necessary change and dialed quickly. He put his sleeve over the receiver, but decided to forgo the midwestern accent. He wanted to disguise his voice, but not so thoroughly that it was impossible to recognize by someone who knew him well.

Mike Callahan answered on the second ring. His voice sounded groggy, as if he'd been drinking. Jeremy had to smile. It was only Tuesday. "Wake-up call!" he said cheerily.

There was a pause on the other end of the line.

"Hey, if it isn't the boy wonder. What's up? You sound strange—"

"Bit of a cold," Jeremy interrupted, deftly cutting him off. If he was lucky, he could keep Callahan from using his name.

"So they have phones down there?" Callahan said. "I'm surprised."

"They've got a lot of surprising things down here."

"I know, I know. Dinosaurs and huge tomatoes. So what's new? Have you figured out why a quarter of a million dollars just ain't enough?"

Jeremy inhaled. No amount of money could have made Tucsome look good to him. He lowered his voice, until it was barely more than a whisper. "Do you remember Warren T. Walker?"

"The dead secretary of defense?"

"I was wondering if you could check something out for me. . . ."

Jeremy spoke fast, leaving out everything but the barest essentials; he made no mention of Tucsome's possible culpability in a series of deaths. All he needed was a uric acid level. A simple uric acid level.

"So you want me to steal a blood sample from a Wood holding refrigerator? Is that all?"

"Only if you feel up to it."

Callahan hesitated. "I wouldn't be on my home turf. That makes it harder."

"Mike," Jeremy pleaded, "If I *am* right about this, stealing that sample may be the most important thing you ever do."

"World peace hangs in the balance, huh?"

Jeremy smiled. "Something like that."

Callahan sighed. "Okay, you got yourself a thief, but you'll owe me. Bigtime."

"I *already* owe you," Jeremy said with feeling. "You're a good friend, Mike. Thanks."

"No problem," Callahan said. "One more thing, though. Professional thieves like me have to case the joint first. I'll have to drive over there today and do some reconnoitering. Can you hold on till tomorrow morning?"

"Fine, I'll call you again then."

When Callahan clicked off, Jeremy congratulated himself on his handiwork. By tomorrow morning he'd know for sure.

24

TWELVE HOURS LATER, JEREMY WAS AWAKENED FROM A DEEP sleep. His bedroom was gray, barely lit by the moonlight that trickled in from underneath the drawn window shade. It took him a few seconds to find the phone—and then a half minute to place the voice on the other end.

"Frankie?" he asked, completely shocked. "Is that you?"

"Jeremy, you've got to get on a plane to New York."

Frankie's response was abrupt and wooden. He could tell immediately that something serious had happened. He sat up, wiping the last vestiges of sleep from his eyes.

"What is it?"

There was a long pause on the other end of the line.

"Mike Callahan is dead."

25

JEREMY'S CHEST CONSTRICTED, AND FOR A SECOND HE COULDN'T breathe. When he found his voice, it was barely a whisper.

"Mike Callahan is dead?"

"They brought him into the ER two hours ago. He was convulsing. They tried to bring him around."

"What was it?"

"I don't know. Could have been a number of things. Maybe some sort of drug reaction."

"I can't believe this."

Frankie spoke to him in a monotone—the voice of an ER doctor used to this sort of thing. "The memorial service is scheduled for three o'clock. His folks are flying in—"

"I can't believe this," Jeremy repeated. "Have they begun the autopsy?"

"Scheduled for tomorrow morning."

"I don't understand. How could this have happened—?"

And then Jeremy paused. The room began to spin. He slammed the phone down and took a step back. Either Callahan had hit some sort of trip wire by trying to get hold of Walker's blood, or they'd traced the call from outside the cafeteria. Whichever it was, Mike's death was Jeremy's fault. Mike was dead because of him.

Suddenly, Jeremy doubled over. His throat swelled shut. He dropped to his knees, coughing, choking. Mike had died because of him. Jeremy had killed again!

No. His fingers became claws, and he dragged himself across the floor. He had to stay in control. *Control.* He couldn't give in to the panic now. They'd be coming for him next.

Even if they hadn't traced the phone call, even if Callahan *had* blundered into some sort of trip wire, it was only a matter of time before they knew about Jeremy. The coincidence of Mike and him having been friends and colleagues—it was too much to ignore.

Still struggling to breathe, he crawled to the window. Slowly, he lifted himself to his knees and pulled up a corner of the shade.

Nothing but darkness. No sign of the Mercedes sedan.

He collapsed back, his face touching the floor. They weren't out there—but it hardly mattered. His insides were turning against him, forcing him to the edge of hysteria.

He could feel his delicate hold on reality slipping when something inside of him clicked. All at once a fire swirled in the pit of his stomach, moved up through his chest, and smothered the panic like a wall of hot wind.

They killed my best friend.

They had done this—not him. Not a child in a garage twelve years ago helping his father change a tire—but them. *They* had murdered his best friend!

His hands clenched into fists, and he slowly rose to his feet. His mind was numb, the panic nothing compared to his anger. They had killed his best friend!

"Who the hell do you think you are?" he shouted. He yanked the phone off of the bed table and hurled it at the window. The glass exploded outward. "What gives you the right?"

He tore across the room, his eyes wild with anger. He grabbed the television and tossed it against a wall. He ripped the mattress off the bed and flung it toward the stairs.

Then he stopped, suddenly, his chest heaving. He pictured Callahan being wheeled into the ER. Slowly, the image changed; Callahan's corpse was lying on a slab in the basement of New York City Hospital. Tomorrow morning, the body would be rolled into a pathology lab. A doctor would carefully proceed with the autopsy. The autopsy would go on for a number of hours; but from the first moment, the doctor would know how it was going to turn out: *Reasons Unexplained*.

Everyone would mourn the tragic death of another young doctor.

Jeremy's teeth ground together. Enough was enough. He no longer cared about the danger, about risk, about the need for secrecy. He began searching the wrecked bedroom for his duffel bag.

He didn't know why he was still alive—but as long as he *was* alive, he was going to do everything he could to bring down the bastards who were responsible for his friend's death.

26

THE SOUND OF A FLUSHING TOILET ECHOED THROUGH VICTOR'S skull as he carefully ran a comb through his slicked-back hair. With each pass of the tines across his scalp, the toilet seemed to get louder: a swirling, noxious melody, filling every inch of the private bathroom. Victor clenched his teeth, trying to ignore the sound, trying to think pleasant thoughts. He thought about expensive suits and silk ties. He thought about cashmere overcoats and camel-hair fedoras. He thought about Gucci belts, Rolex watches, hundred-dollar manicures. Still, the sound kept getting louder.

Finally, Victor opened his fingers and let the comb fall into the sink in front of him. Inside, he'd gone cold. His body was numb and desolate, as lifeless as a mannequin.

The kid had been a leak.

"More like the fucking Nile," Victor hissed through his teeth.

The words echoed off of the antiseptic white walls, and the toilet finally went silent. An electric current ran down his spine. He'd fucked up. He'd grievously misjudged Jeremy Ross. Maybe it had been the kid's age, that young face and those innocent eyes; or maybe it had just been incompetence. Whatever the reason, he'd fucked up good.

THRESHOLD had been jeopardized—and less than twenty-four hours from the Holy Grail. If it hadn't been for some hasty damage control, the entire project could have been blown skyhigh. He'd fucked up—and now there was no choice but to suffer the consequences.

With a grimace, he turned away from the sink. The tiny bathroom stared at him. Reluctantly, he reached behind the toilet and pulled out the Vidcom. He placed the machine on top of the closed seat and waited the necessary few seconds for the screen to heat up.

When the blurred face appeared, Victor lowered his eyes and tried to make his voice as normal as possible.

"Satellite to Source. The small crisis was successfully stop-gapped—"

"Silence!"

Victor's head snapped up. He'd never before heard his boss show so much emotion.

"There has been a serious leak," said the voice. "If not for the competence of our New York operatives, the situation could have expanded."

Victor swallowed. A heavy weariness crept through his chest. "But now the situation is under control."

"Under control? You're a fool, Satellite. Walker's daughter, Robin Kelly, has still not been located, and the primary subject is still alive."

Victor winced on hearing the name of Walker's daughter. Why hadn't someone *told* him the woman was named Kelly? For a while, he'd tried to puzzle out what the initials R.K. stood for in the message he'd given to Ross; he'd ultimately dismissed it as unimportant.

Yet another screwup. A royal one. But he sure wasn't going to pick the present time to let his boss know that Ross and Kelly had been in contact with each other. "There was a reason not to kill Ross immediately," Victor pointed out. "Two young scientists dead in a matter of weeks would jeopardize security. People would get suspicious. He has to be handled delicately—"

"This is no time for delicacy. Your conduct up to this point has been abysmal. The subject represents a serious leak."

Victor decided to try a different tack. "We don't know who he's working for. He could be CIA. So could Robin Kelly."

"Negative. Both subjects must be eliminated. Immediately."

Victor took a deep breath. Now there was no choice; Jeremy Ross had to die. Victor's eyelids slid shut. "Agreed. I'll personally supervise taking Ross out in New York."

"New York?"

"He's on his way to his friend's memorial service. But don't worry. He's under strict surveillance."

"Use a conventional method," the Vidcom blared. "And Satellite, do not fuck this up. We're twenty-four hours from completion of the project. We'll enter stage three on schedule. Understood?"

"Absolutely."

The Vidcom paused, digesting his response. Then the face on the screen shifted, leaning forward. "In regard to stage three—is everything progressing as intended?"

Victor shrugged his stiff shoulders. "Waters doesn't foresee any obstacles. The staff will gather for the unveiling in Lester Auditorium as planned. We've also arranged for full press coverage. The demonstration should cause quite a stir."

"And that other matter we spoke of—will you be able to get access to Waters's lab?"

God, he's a paranoid sonofabitch, Victor said to himself. Couldn't his boss at least trust *Waters*—the man who'd been working forty years to deliver him the ultimate weapon?

"It's not a problem," Victor replied.

"Excellent. Source out."

With that, the screen went blank. Victor shut off the Vidcom and turned back to the mirror. A dead-eyed mannequin stared back at him.

Another damn mission. As easy, and meaningless, as the rest.

27

As the Delta Airlines Boeing 727 touched down lightly on the La Guardia Airport tarmac, Jeremy slowly pried his fingers off the armrests and flexed his wrists to get the circulation going.

"It wasn't so bad," the elderly woman next to him asked. "Was it?"

"I was unconscious," Jeremy said, remembering all the sedatives he'd taken.

"That's what I mean."

He coughed. The last ten hours were unreal to him. After Frankie's phone call, he'd hastily packed his things. Then he'd pondered the best way to get out of Tucsome. Beaufort was at least twelve miles distant, and, with a bag to carry, jogging wasn't a viable option.

Luckily, he'd remembered something Victor had told him; every morning, a laundry van passed through the Project's residential area, stopping at each member's house. It was the perfect escape route.

With that in mind, he'd dumped half of his clothes into a laundry bag and had brought it out to his front porch. He'd tied one end of the bag to the porch railing, triple knotting it as if he'd been tying off a particularly difficult set of stitches. Then he'd found a position near the picture window and waited for dawn.

The van had arrived at exactly 5:00 A.M. The driver had left the vehicle idling in the driveway while he crossed to the front porch. Jeremy had slipped out through the back door, crouching low, and had crawled toward the driver's-side door. As he'd predicted, the driver's attention had been consumed by the knotted laundry bag. Jeremy had quietly opened the door and had crawled over the front seat. The van had been full of laundry, and he'd easily found a corner in which to lodge himself. He'd covered himself with bags, trying not to think about the stench.

The ride to Beaufort had passed without incident. When the van finally pulled to a stop next to a low building, Jeremy had readied himself for a confrontation. Thankfully, the driver had entered the building without unloading, and Jeremy had been able to slip back out over the front seat. He'd quickly walked to the train station, arriving just in time to catch the 6:00 A.M. to Savannah. Then he'd taken a flight through Charlotte to New York, using the sedatives to override his usual air-travel-induced panic.

And all the while, there'd been no sign of pursuit. At any moment he'd expected—well, he wasn't sure what he had expected. Armed men waiting for him at the train station? A squad of killers in the airport terminal?

He swung his gaze around the plane, assessing the other passengers. Was one of them plotting his death? Perhaps that heavyset man sporting a Stetson and a leather jacket? Or that sour-faced woman in the business suit? Even now, with all that had happened, such thoughts seemed the height of paranoia, but he realized that his best chance lay in suspecting everyone.

The deplaning took ten minutes, during which not a single

passenger gave him the slightest notice, and a few minutes after that, he found himself plodding through the terminal. He concentrated on putting one foot in front of the other, the drugs in his system making it difficult to think about anything else.

As his thoughts gained clarity, depression began to settle over him. It seemed ghoulish, coming all this way just to get to Mike Callahan's body. But he *had* to find concrete evidence that would connect Tucsome to his friend's death. And he had the feeling that the evidence he needed was in Callahan's bloodstream.

Robin Kelly steadied her white blond wig as she pushed through La Guardia's crowded terminal. Her eyes were bloodshot beneath thick plastic horn-rimmed glasses, and as she walked she fought to keep from screaming. First her father, then Devin—and now Mike Callahan, Jeremy's best friend. For the hundredth time she dwelled on how her pursuers could kill with such matter-of-factness—as if she and Jeremy and everyone else who stood up to them were blades of grass before a mower.

After the attempt on her life in Washington, she'd tried to get a message to Jeremy through New York City Medical School. But the minute she'd asked to speak to Mike Callahan, she'd been transferred to the hospital's chief resident, who'd explained to her that Callahan had died during the night.

She'd frozen with the receiver in her hand, her instincts telling her that Callahan's death was somehow linked to Tucsome. When she'd collected herself enough to ask about Jeremy, she was told he was on his way to New York. So she'd headed straight to the airport, no longer able to summon much concern for her own safety. She *had* to find Jeremy—before it was too late.

She dodged between two skycaps and angled toward the escalator that led to the baggage carousels. She still had a few hours before Callahan's memorial service—the chief resident had assumed that she was a friend and had given her the details—which was more than enough time to thoroughly lose herself in the streets of New York City. She glanced at the faces around her, wondering which ones could be SSO and which ones she could ignore. Surrounded by people, she felt more alone than ever before.

The black Mercedes sedan floated effortlessly through the mid-morning traffic. It slid from lane to lane like some ebony watersnake, twin unblinking eyes locked on its unsuspecting prey.

"Yellow taxicab. License plate XT3–8993. The subject is alone." The words—sans English accent—were instantly transformed into microwaves and beamed toward the sky. Twenty-two thousand miles above, a satellite gathered the microwaves into a tight package and flung them back toward the earth. Deep in a Georgetown basement, a corpulent man with a dark beard bent over a laptop computer and grinned.

"Excellent. All operatives in the sector are now routed to your command. Proceed at your leisure. Remember, a conventional method. Source out."

"Satellite out."

The ebony watersnake continued in silence, cutting past Volvos, Cadillacs, and minivans, maintaining a predator's indifference—restraining itself to a constant distance of twenty, maybe thirty yards.

28

Jeremy entered New York City Hospital through the emergency room, slipping quickly through the huge double doors. He was wearing a heavy gray New York Knicks hooded sweatshirt, courtesy of an overpriced airport souvenir shop, and, in gang-banger fashion, he kept the hood pulled tight over his head.

As always, the ER was hopping. Stretchers rolled across the linoleum like shopping carts in a crowded supermarket, bunching along the walls and near the center of the open atrium. Meanwhile, nurses rushed from gurney to gurney, bending over the wounded with faces more exhausted than concerned; they'd seen it all before.

Jeremy quickly maneuvered through the chaos. He kept his back against the wall, only his eyes showing beneath his sweatshirt's oversized hood.

His stomach churned as the smells, sights, and sounds of the ER washed over him. He thought about Mike Callahan, all the days and nights they'd spent together in the ER, talking about the future, playing the stupid games that medical students play, praying for the day that they'd become doctors.

His eyes burned—but he didn't have time to mourn. He slid forward, step by step. When he arrived at the entrance to the rest of the hospital, he cast a final glance over his shoulder.

Suddenly, he froze, not quite believing what he was seeing.

Two men in dark suits were standing in front of the swinging double doors, scanning the ER. One of them was six feet tall, wide-shouldered, with thick orange hair. The other Jeremy recognized; he was the short, stocky man whose partner Jeremy had pushed over the rail in Trump Tower.

Jeremy pressed against the wall. *Damn, what do I do now?*

He shifted his eyes over the ER, searching for some way to slip out of the room unnoticed. Then he paused, his eyes straight ahead.

A few feet in front of him was a gunshot victim, lying in a stretcher red with his own blood. A bloodied arm hung over one side, the fingers inches from the floor. The patient seemed stable; his shoulder wound was taped, and his breathing was normal and rhythmic. Jeremy had a sudden idea.

He pulled his hood over his eyes, making sure none of the nurses were looking his way. Then he pressed back into an alcove, concealing himself, and cupped his hands around his mouth:

"Code blue!" he shouted at the top of his lungs. "Code blue! Defibrillator, chem cart, EKG team, OR prep team, stat!"

There was a sudden silence. Then Jeremy's corner of the ER exploded into action. Nurses and doctors came running from every angle, shouting orders and shoving stretchers out of the way.

Jeremy stepped to the side, using the chaos as a cover. He slinked along the wall, his eyes on the double doors at the front of the room. The two men were nowhere to be seen; probably, they were caught up in the confusion of the false code.

He grinned; not exactly in line with the Hippocratic oath, but it had worked. The nurses and doctors would realize it was a false code the minute they hooked up the EKG. By that time, he would be long gone.

He turned and headed for the door.

A few seconds later, he was out of the ER and rushing down the long central hallway that branched off to the various specialties: radiology, pediatric surgery, oncology, cardiology—At this last, he stopped, glancing over his shoulder. No sign of the two men.

He turned an abrupt corner and found himself in front of a doorway marked with an ominous sign: BASEMENT: PATHOLOGY. He pulled open the door and descended, his feet clicking against the cement staircase.

The stairs opened up into a huge, cold room, with cinderblock walls and flickering fluorescent lights. Thankfully, the lab was empty. There was no rush in this part of the hospital; pathologists never hurried to work, and nobody noticed when they were late.

He quickly made his way through the room, then chose a table near the far corner and flicked on the huge overhead lamp. He surveyed his tools: in front of him lay a surgical tray complete with rib crackers, syringes, and blood pumps. Scalpels rested to one side, freshly cleaned and sterilized. Perhaps this was the very table on which Callahan's autopsy was scheduled to take place. Jeremy felt queasy at the thought. Then he threw a final glance back at the stairway; still no sign of the two men. Satisfied, he turned on his heels.

It was time to find the body.

The cold storage room was poorly lit, a macabre cube that took Jeremy's breath away and left him leaning against the metal doorframe. The stretchers were lined up next to one another, a wall-to-wall sea of bodies. The bodies were naked and cleaned, covered by white sheets. Where skin protruded, it was pale and glistening in the feeble lighting.

He'd seen glimpses of these places over the course of his medical career, but couldn't imagine how anyone could tolerate them on a steady basis. *What a place to work.*

He slid along the wall, scanning the bodies with his eyes. From a distance, they all looked the same. He was going to have to go through the tags.

He began with the closest corpse. The tag was hanging from the body's big toe, a slab of laminated cardboard swinging in the dull wind coming out of the air-conditioning vents: ROBERT RODRIGUEZ. He quickly moved to the next big toe.

He darted from body to body, his heart racing. ALEC MICHAELS. TRENT CARTER. ANDREA FUSCO . . .

And suddenly, there it was: MICHAEL CALLAHAN. He scanned across the thick, hairy legs, over the groin, up the puffed-up chest, to the face. It was strange, staring at his friend like that. Almost a violation.

Callahan's face was peaceful, innocent. His cheeks were swollen, cherubic, and his broad jaw was loose. His skin was pasty green, a consistency common to corpses. His eyes, gratefully, were closed.

Jeremy grabbed the stretcher and maneuvered through the cold storage room. The wheels skidded against the cement floor, the sound echoing off the silent walls. In a second, he was back in the pathology lab. He used his heels to brake, and the stretcher crashed to a stop next to the corner table.

He put his hands under Callahan's back, palms up. A chill traveled up his arms; Callahan's skin was cold and clammy, and a dull antiseptic smell rose off of him. Jeremy clenched his teeth, shifting for leverage.

"Up we go," he whispered.

He rolled Callahan onto the table, forcing his body all the way over so he was once again on his back, his blank face staring up at the huge operating lights. *I can't believe I'm doing this.*

He took a step back, breathing heavy. Then he began to inspect the body.

He shifted his eyes up and down Callahan's skin, searching for anything unlikely or uncommon. The search went on for nearly ten minutes, but he could find nothing out of the ordinary.

He stepped back, shaking his head. He slid his hands under Callahan's body, shifted his weight forward, and turned the corpse onto its stomach.

He began the process all over again, starting at the hairline and moving downward. Inch by inch, he examined the pale skin. When he reached Callahan's ankles, he cursed out loud. Again, nothing. No external abberations; from the outside, Mike simply looked like a man who'd died unluckily of a random disease.

Jeremy sighed, resigned. He was about to turn Callahan over, to begin the internal portion of the autopsy, when something caught his eye.

Maybe it was the angle, maybe it was the way the light was reflecting off of Callahan's skin—but he suddenly saw something at the base of Callahan's neck. He leaned close to the body, his nose inches away from the skin.

There was a tiny fissure, no bigger than a pinprick, directly between the shoulder blades. It was no surprise that he'd missed it the first time around; the hole was almost invisible. A thin, unremarkable semicircle of depressed skin surrounded it, like the lip of a miniature inverted volcano. The wound was similar to an insect sting—but there was no swelling, no redness. Just a tiny hole at the base of the neck.

He searched the surgical tray for a magnifying glass. Then he put his finger at the edge of the tiny pinprick and gently pushed the skin so as to emphasize the aberration. Inside the tiny hole, there was a strange streaking—burn marks, the result of something extremely hot or extremely cold.

He leaned back from the body, confused. The depressed skin surrounding the hole implied that something had entered there, something very thin, very small—and either very hot or very cold. Once under the skin, it had simply disappeared.

He felt the adrenaline rising inside of him. The wound was strange, definitely not naturally occurring. He hastily grabbed a scalpel off of the surgical tray and leaned over the body—

When suddenly, he heard footsteps on the stairs.

He froze, the scalpel hanging in the air. The footsteps moved closer; in a second they were joined by the sound of voices.

He cursed, wildly searching for someplace to hide. There was a low open counter to his left, full of petri dishes, blood samples, and syringes. He dove down behind the counter, curling his body into a tight ball.

The voices moved closer. In a few seconds, they were barely ten feet away: "What the hell is this?"

Jeremy recognized the voice; it belonged to Brad Alger, one of the pathology residents.

"What's this body doing out here?" Alger continued. "It's scheduled for tomorrow morning."

"Looks like someone started an autopsy and then went out for a sandwich," a woman's voice responded.

"Damn that Murdoch. He's a fucking idiot."

"Here, let's get this body back where it belongs."

There was the shuffle of footsteps, and then the sound of the stretcher being rolled toward the cold storage room. Jeremy clenched his fists. Damn it, he'd have to come back later.

He loosened his knees and tossed a quick glance over the top of the counter. The room was momentarily empty; but the door to the storage room was wide open. He'd have to sprint.

He tensed his muscles, leaning forward . . .

And then he paused.

In front of him, on top of the cabinet, sat a rack of labeled test tubes. He realized instantly what they were: blood samples.

He rushed through the labels. The name jumped at him from near the end of the rack: MIKE CALLAHAN, DECEASED.

He cheered inwardly and shoved the test tube into his pocket. Then he had another thought and began searching, his eyes scanning through the low cabinet. He found what he was looking for on a shelf near the floor.

Urine samples, taken from the corpses' bladders. He searched for the beaker marked CALLAHAN. Now he had everything he needed for a full lab workup.

Beaker in one hand, test tube in his pocket, he leapt forward. His feet hit the bottom step just as a voice sprang out behind him: "Hey! Who the fuck are you?"

He didn't look back. He took the steps two at a time, his heart pumping with adrenaline. He hit the stairwell door with his shoulder and burst out into the hallway.

Directly in front of him stood the two men in dark suits.

The six-footer with the orange hair reached under his coat.

Jeremy didn't stop to think. He slammed the beaker full of Callahan's urine into the man's face. The beaker shattered, yellow liquid spraying the hallway.

The six-footer screamed, reaching for his eyes. Jeremy immediately threw himself at the other man, and as his shoulder connected with a solid chin, the man's head flipped back, slamming into the wall. There was a sickening crunch; then the man's body went limp and he slid to the floor.

Jeremy whirled on his heels. The six-footer was bobbing back and forth, his eyes bright red, streaks of blood running down his cheeks. He made a weak, blinded lunge. Jeremy easily side-stepped the attack and sped around the corner, his mind racing. He spun left, then right, feeling to make sure that the blood sample in his pocket was still intact.

He needed to find a lab—immediately. There was no telling how many more thugs were scouring the hospital.

He turned a sudden corner, sprinting down another hall and up a flight of stairs. He cut through gastroenterology, past the cafeteria, and then stopped dead in front of a blank door. He looked behind himself; he was alone. He threw open the door and hurried inside.

The dark laboratory stared at him. Memories of his Ph.D. year filled his head. He'd spent nearly three hundred nights in this lab, playing with Chester the chimpanzee's blood. Here, he would find everything he needed for a full blood workup. First, though, he had to make sure that he wouldn't be disturbed.

He turned back to the door and felt along the doorjamb. His fingers quickly found the locking mechanism, and he flicked the lever upward, creating an airtight seal. Now the door would be clearly marked on the outside: DANGER-CONTAMINATION, requiring a master key from upstairs in administration to break the seal and get in.

His isolation thus guaranteed, he pulled the test tube out of his pocket and headed straight for the refrigerator in the far corner of the room. He pulled the door open, the blast of cold air reminding him of Tucsome. He half expected Lyle to make some crack over his shoulder, something about the ice cream melting.

The shelves were lined with petri dishes, beakers, and test tubes—the lifework of more than a dozen Ph.D. students. It took him a full minute to find what he was looking for.

The label on the top of the plastic box read simply: PCR PRIMERS. He pried the box open with his fingernails and surveyed the contents. More than two dozen tiny bottles of various colored chemical solutions stared up at him. He paused, thinking.

He decided to trust his instincts. He reached into the box and found two bottles marked "HIV Retrovirus Primer A" and "HIV Retrovirus Primer B."

Then he shoved the box back where it had come from and moved into the lab. His body trembled as he searched for a place to work.

Sweat dripped into his eyes as he leaned over the glass test tube. He'd done this procedure a hundred times before, but never under such intense pressure. It wasn't complicated, but it took every ounce of concentration to do right.

PCR, polymerase chain reaction, was a process at the cutting edge of genetic research. It was a method of cloning large quantities of DNA from a single DNA molecule; through multiplication, the target DNA could actually be "seen" and identified.

His heart raced as he prepared to run a PCR on Callahan's blood. If a killer gene had been inserted into his friend's body through the pinprick hole at the base of his neck, he'd know soon enough. The PCR would give him a view not only of the killer gene itself but also of the retrovirus that had carried the deadly sequence.

He carefully placed a single drop of Callahan's blood into a tiny bullet-shaped container called an epinod. Then he added a few drops of a powerful detergent-like chemical, which liced the cells in the blood, isolating the DNA.

Carefully, he collected the DNA into a separate epinod and cleaned the solution with a chemical wash. Then he reached for the two small bottles of PCR primer.

The choice of primer had been academic—the same choice he'd made years ago when he'd begun his Ph.D. thesis. HIV was the most powerful retrovirus in existence. If someone in Tucsome had truly perfected retrovirus gene therapy, HIV was the most likely candidate. Especially when Jeremy took into account what Lyle had told him about Jason Waters's obsession with AIDS research.

He leaned over the epinod and carefully dripped the two primers into Callahan's DNA. Then he added a nucleotide solution and a few drops of a strong polymerase—the enzyme that would slice out the target gene, using the HIV primers as end points.

He moved to a large rectangular device sitting on a counter directly across from him. Essentially, the PCR machine was a high-tech water bath that cycled through a variety of temperature changes, speeding up the enzymatic process.

He carefully placed the epinod into the PCR machine and set the instruments on the control panel for a two-hour cycle. Then he flicked a black switch on the side of the machine.

A low whir broke out across the lab, and he took a step back, breathing hard. Now came the difficult part. He leaned against the opposite counter and stared at the machine. Slowly, the seconds ticked by. Exhaustion pulled at him and he gingerly lowered himself to the floor. He couldn't even begin to calculate how many hours of sleep he'd lost in the past few days. He curled his knees to his chest, rested his head on his hands, and let his eyelids drift shut.

Two hours later the PCR machine emitted a series of high-pitched beeps. Jeremy lurched forward, his mind coming instantly awake. He leapt to his feet and quickly removed the epinod from the machine, shaking it dry.

The tension rose inside of him, wiping away the cobwebs of sleep as he rushed across the lab. It took him a few minutes to find a gel plate with which to view his results.

He carefully poured the solution over the gel plate and ran a jolt of electricity through it. He kept a careful eye on both the voltage and the solution level as he fired the gel—he'd heard countless stories of entire labs going up in flames because of an overcharged gel plate. After the charge ran out, he added a thin dye made up of athidium bromide.

His excitement was almost painful as he carried the gel plate over to a fluorescent microscope. He had a feeling he was about to see something that would change him, forever.

He carefully placed the gel under the microscope. Then he pressed his eye against the lens.

The retrovirus was unmistakable. HIV. But not simply HIV; the sample under the microscope was a full micron longer than the normal HIV virus. He focused on the extra segment.

It took him a full minute to realize what he was looking at.

The killer gene. A deadly disease written in the language of chemical bases.

He swallowed, taking a step back from the microscope. Michael Callahan had been killed with a gene. It was right in front of him—an unknown sequence of DNA, attached to a tailored HIV retrovirus. This was the first piece of real evidence—half of the proof he needed to bring Tucsome down. All that was left was to show that the unknown sequence had been deliberately created, manufactured like any other murder weapon.

Which meant he had to return to Tucsome as soon as possible. Although he didn't know for sure, he had an idea where he would find the proof he needed: Jason Waters's private lab. It was off-limits, secluded, highly secure—where else but there would the technology to deliver a killer gene be hidden?

Of course, he was going to have to come up with a helluva plan to get past Waters's barricades, but he'd been giving that matter serious thought for a long time.

He grabbed the gel plate out of the fluorescent microscope and carefully tucked it in a storage cabinet, behind a box of rubber gloves. He'd arrange for it to be retrieved when he had the second part of his proof.

He closed the storage cabinet and glanced at his watch. It was one-thirty in the afternoon. The memorial service would begin at three. That left barely an hour and a half to prepare.

He found an empty doctor's bag on a nearby shelf and began filling it with objects from around the lab, anything he thought might be useful. Emergency medical supplies, surgical tape, scalpels, syringes. He found a small butane fireplace lighter in a box of Bunsen burners, and tried the switch. The flame was two inches long, a flickering, red-orange tear. He blew it out and shoved the lighter into his back pocket. Then he paused, thinking.

There were a few more items he'd need, but he'd have to pick them up along the way.

Tucsome was waiting.

29

"WE'RE GATHERED HERE TODAY TO MOURN THE TRAGIC PASSING of a friend. . . ."

The words echoed through the huge, ornate church. The priest was standing in the center of a raised marble dais, his face partially blotted out by a microphone. Rainbows of sunlight played across his long white robes, cast by the immense stained-glass windows that ringed the hall.

"Michael Sean Callahan dedicated his life to helping others. It's always doubly sad when a doctor passes on. . . ."

The drone continued, gliding out over the pews, dragging the air down with it. The crowded church was sweltering under the midmorning sun. Even the crucifixes were sweating; droplets of condensation trickled down thin golden limbs, broke free, and splattered against the marble floor.

"A doctor is a man—or woman—who has dedicated his life to saving lives. A doctor is God's messenger on earth. . . ."

A nervous twitch moved through the audience, more a product of heat than oratory. The wooden pews were full; it seemed that every doctor in Manhattan was present, from the most prestigious specialist at New York City to the lowest intern. No doubt, when the newspaper stories ran the next morning, they'd call the gathering a very good place to have had a cardiac arrest.

"Mike Callahan came from a family of doctors. . . ."

At the back of the famous old church, a figure in an over-sized blue suit stood in the shadows. His face was obscured by a pair of dark glasses. His hair was parted in the middle, and he had a jaunty red scarf wrapped tight around his throat. Otherwise, he was unremarkable; just another mourner blending into the ornate background of a dead man's last respects.

Behind the dark glasses, Jeremy fought the anger building inside of him. His back was pressed against a polished marble pillar, his hands jammed deep into the pants pockets of his oversized suit.

He'd bought the suit at a secondhand store on the way from the hospital. He'd found the sunglasses and scarf in the glove compartment of Callahan's car. At first, he'd considered renting a car—but decided it was too dangerous, too easily traced. And relying on a taxi had seemed too limiting; there was an extremely good chance he'd need to make a quick getaway. Callahan's car had emerged as the best option; he'd memorized the combination to Callahan's hospital locker years ago, and the extra set of keys were right where Mike had always left them, hanging next to his squash racket. Jeremy had changed into the suit in the front seat, donning the sunglasses and scarf as an afterthought.

He looked absurd—but different from the Jeremy Ross most people knew. He hoped it would be enough to avoid being identified. If the men chasing him were working off a picture, the disguise would slow them down.

He realized, of course, that the wisest choice would have been to avoid the service altogether—especially after what happened at the hospital. He was risking everything by being here. But he *had* to come.

To pay his last respects, to clear his conscience—to apologize.

He rubbed the back of his hand over his lips and leaned against the marble pillar. Then he noticed something that gave him a start.

A dozen yards away, a woman in a polyester dress was looking at him. Pressed against her right ear was a cellular phone.

Apologies over, Jeremy said to himself. *Time to get out of here.*

He whirled around the pillar—and halted in midstep.

Victor Alexander stood a few feet away, shaking his head. Carefully, deliberately, he took a pair of wire-rimmed glasses out of the pocket of his cashmere overcoat and wiped them against his sleeve.

It took a few seconds for Jeremy to find his voice. "What are *you* doing here?"

Victor placed the wire-rimmed glasses above his nose. The glasses made him look detached, even clinical. His heavy English accent slid out from between his lips, his voice so low that Jeremy had to concentrate on every word.

"Why, Jeremy, I'm here for the same reason you are. To mourn the tragic passing of another young scientist. It seems that medicine is quite a dangerous profession these days, wouldn't you agree?"

Jeremy swallowed. His mind searched for options as he gave a hasty glance around. The church was crowded, but there was a good ten feet between Victor and the last pew.

"What do you want?"

"Only to help you. From the looks of things, I got here just in time. I can see that you're already contemplating fashion suicide."

Jeremy took a step back. His eyes settled on Victor's silk tie. "You killed Matthew Aronson," he stated quietly. "And his wife. And the man in the jail cell."

"Et cetera, et cetera, ad infinitum . . . Gentlemen, hurry now. He's got that skittish look in his eyes."

Suddenly, rough hands pinned Jeremy's arms together behind his back. His scarf was ripped up over his chin and shoved between his teeth. He tried to scream but the sound was muffled as the scarf was tied tight behind his head.

"You understand," Victor continued in a soft voice, stepping forward. "The killing—it's what I do. My occupation. My defining skill—but by no means my passion."

Jeremy felt something sharp against his wrists, pinning them together. He tried to struggle and a cutting pain surged up his arms.

"Piano wire," Victor informed as he passed close to Jeremy's ear. "If you struggle hard enough, you just might manage to sever your own hands."

Then Jeremy was being pulled backwards, his feet skidding against the marble floor. His eyes were wide, pleading; but the congregation was facing the altar, oblivious to his struggle.

In a second he was out of the great hall. The rough hands dragged him down a long, winding hallway. He passed through a doorway, and a small alcove opened up into a quiet round chamber—some sort of sacramental storage room. Tall steel shelves rose up the walls, lined with religious items that Jeremy didn't recognize and couldn't name. Dozens of crosses hung from the walls, glimmering in the light of a low hanging chandelier. A round table squatted in the center of the room, on which stood an ornate gold cup and a single bottle of red wine.

"How appropriate," Victor whispered.

The rough hands spun Jeremy around and shoved him forward. He hit the velvet carpet inches in front of the round table and struggled quickly to his knees.

Victor stood in the doorway, flanked on either side by two dark-complected men of immense proportions. He gestured with his hands, and the two men exited, closing a heavy wooden door behind them. Jeremy could barely hear the priest's monotone drifting in from outside, a thin sheet of meaningless sound.

Victor stepped forward, his face shifting from plaster to stone. "You brought this on yourself, Jeremy. Another eight hours and none of this would have been necessary. But you simply couldn't leave well enough alone."

Jeremy pressed himself back against the round table. His wrists were burning, the piano wire digging deep into his skin. He could feel warm blood running down his palms, making his fingers slippery and wet. He rubbed them against his pants—and felt something roughly the size and shape of a ballpoint pen. He recognized the object and hastily tried to work his fingers into his back pocket.

"Oh, yes," Victor continued. "Your bad case of curiosity has cost me considerable status with my employer. Even got him wondering if I'm up to snuff. Well, we'll just have to show him, won't we?"

Victor reached into his coat and, with dramatic flourish, pulled out a transparent plastic bag. He held the bag in front of him, stretching it with his fingers. His face seemed exaggeratedly large and distorted behind the clear plastic.

"Not the most noble of exits. But I promise you, it will go much easier for you than it has gone for others. Suffocation isn't pleasant; but in the end your face will still be intact."

Suddenly, Victor leapt forward and heaved Jeremy to his feet. Jeremy's hand slipped out of his pocket, his fingers empty. His eyes went wide as Victor whirled him around.

There was a flash of motion, and the plastic bag clamped down over Jeremy's head. The plastic sealed against his face, sticking to his nostrils and mouth. His teeth clenched against the scarf as he fought Victor's grip. Victor leaned close to his hear, whispering through the plastic.

"I gave you so many chances, Jeremy. I told you about the Holy Grail. I let you live—long after you'd earned your death. And still it ends like this. Like this."

Jeremy lurched upward, trying desperately to breathe. His eyes bulged forward, his tongue swollen against his teeth. Victor pulled him down, bending him forward over the round table until he was staring into the gold cup, half filled with sacramental red wine.

"It's almost over," Victor said—as much to himself as to Jeremy.

Gathering all his strength, Jeremy inched his hands down his back, feeling desperately until he touched cold metal. He jiggled the object free of his pocket, his sliced wrists screaming at the motion. A second later, the switch was under his thumb.

"Time to die," Victor grunted.

Jeremy flicked the switch and pressed the butane fireplace lighter against Victor's overcoat. He held it there as long as he could, praying that the flame was on, that the cashmere was flammable, that he'd stay alive long enough—

Suddenly, Victor leapt backward, howling. Jeremy crashed forward, his head whipping back and forth. The plastic bag was still over his face, drawn tight by the pressure of his nostrils. He reeled around the table, still suffocating, his eyes wild.

Victor was flailing a few feet away, screaming in pain as he swatted at the bright orange flames crawling up his jacket. Jeremy centered his eyes on the gold cup of sacramental wine on the table between them. He took aim and swung his foot in a long, desperate arc.

The cup shot forward, spraying Victor with wine. Immediately, the flames soared upward, engulfing his clothes. He screamed and crashed back against the storage shelves.

Jeremy whirled on his heels and dove toward the door. He had to get outside, get help, get air. With the bag still on his face, he slammed into the door with his body, then spun so that his hands were near the knob.

Victor was a flaming dervish in the corner of the room, his hands tearing at his clothes. His overcoat was already shredded, hanging off of him in burning cashmere strips. His Armani suit hung off one bare shoulder, the stiff material threaded with sparkling red-orange flames.

The doorknob turned and the door clicked open. Jeremy

gave Victor one last look and slipped out into the long, winding hallway. He slammed the door shut behind him and careened forward. His mind was screaming, a single word repeating itself over and over. Air! Air! Air—

"My God, Jeremy?"

Suddenly, a woman was running toward him. White blond hair, tortoise-rimmed glasses, conservative black dress—she looked like a Sunday school teacher, at least twice his age. Still, she knew his name.

He dove toward her, his head bowed. Her fingers tore at the plastic bag and suddenly he was free. He dropped to his knees, spitting out the scarf, gasping, his lungs filling, his chest doubling in size.

The woman dropped next to him, her hands on his cheeks.

"Jeremy, what happened? Are you okay?"

He shook his head, still gasping. The woman looked to one side, and then her gaze was back, minus the tortoise-rimmed glasses.

Wonder spilled over Jeremy's face. "Robin? Christ, it's you."

She threw her arms around his neck, kissing him. Then she carefully helped him to his feet. She stepped behind him, went to work on his bound wrists. He grimaced with each twist of the piano wire.

"We don't have much time," he said. "We've got to get out of here."

"This will just take a second. Hold still."

"Ouch. Really, we've got to move—"

He paused midsentence. There was motion down the hall, in the direction of the storage room. Steady, determined motion. "Robin," he shouted. "Now!"

She yanked the piano wire free and looked up. Her eyes went wide as she caught side of Victor Alexander.

His overcoat was gone. His Armani suit was hanging down around his waist, charred and tattered. His skin was covered with bright red burns, and his hair was singed close to his skull. His wire-rimmed glasses were gone, and there was a wide smile on his lips.

Jeremy grabbed her arm and yanked her in the other direction. They crashed toward the interior of the church, their feet skidding against the marble floor.

He could hear Victor behind them, steadily gaining. He took Robin's hand and dove left, through a half-open door. A flight of carpeted steps rose up ahead of them, ending in a thick wooden door. He pushed Robin forward, his hands on the small of her back.

"What if there's no way out?" she asked.

He didn't answer. He could hear Victor's rhythmic breathing behind him. He half carried, half shoved her up the last few steps and lunged for the doorknob. As the door came open, he threw a glance over his shoulder.

Victor was halfway up the stairs. His eyes were narrow and cold, his smile enormous.

Jeremy hurled Robin forward and slammed the heavy door behind them. Then he whirled on his heels, his eyes searching wildly.

"What the hell is this?"

"Looks like the priest's inner chambers," she answered, her face white with fear.

There was a velvet couch in one corner. A huge, ornate robe swam over a low wooden counter. Gold crucifixes of various sizes hung from the walls. And as far as Jeremy could tell, there wasn't another exit.

"We're trapped," he whispered.

Suddenly, the doorknob turned.

Robin screamed and Jeremy hurled his body against the door, using his weight to brace it shut. He could hear Victor grunting on the other side. Slowly, the door began to slide inward.

Robin added her weight to Jeremy's. Still, the door inched forward. Jeremy's feet scrambled against the slippery marble floor.

"This isn't working," Robin said despairingly.

"I'm open to suggestions."

Suddenly, the door budged inward a full six inches. Victor's hand swung through the opening and gripped the edge of the wood. His long fingers were barely an inch in front of Jeremy's face.

"Knock knock," Victor bellowed from the other side of the door. "Little pig, little pig, let me in."

Jeremy searched the room wildly—and a flash of gold caught his eyes. Barely a foot away, hanging on the wall. The long end of the crucifix was sharp and glinting.

"I've got an idea," Jeremy hissed.

He braced his shoulder against the door and yanked the crucifix off of the wall. Then he centered his eyes on the back of Victor's hand.

Realizing what he was about to do, Robin winced.

With all his strength, Jeremy drove the sharp cross into the center of Victor's hand. Blood fountained across the room as Victor's fingers went rigid. For a brief second, his weight came off the door.

"Now!" Jeremy screamed.

Both he and Robin leapt against the door. There was a loud crack as the wood slammed shut against Victor's outstretched wrist. Then there was a scream, high-pitched and filled with agony.

Jeremy hurled the door open. Victor was kneeling in the doorway, his eyes wide, his crucified, shattered hand in front of him. Jeremy grabbed Robin's arm and pulled her forward.

They brushed by Victor's collapsed form and headed down the stairs. Then they burst back out into the long hallway.

"Where are we going?" Robin asked.

Jeremy didn't answer. About ten feet into the hallway he saw a door marked EMERGENCY EXIT—ALARM WILL SOUND. Perfect, he thought to himself. It was about time someone sounded an alarm. He slammed shoulder-first into the door, and together they crashed out into the sunlight.

Two blocks from the church, he whirled Robin around and

swept her into his arms. His lips met hers, and she returned his passion with equal intensity. A few seconds later she pulled back, holding his hands level with his shoulders. His wrists were raw, deep parallel gashes sending droplets of blood splattering toward the sidewalk.

"My God," she whispered, looking at him.

"I'll heal. Come on, we don't have much time." Victor's words echoed in his head. *Another eight hours,* Victor had said—assuredly a reference to Waters's unveiling.

"Jeremy," she blurted. "I was so scared I'd never see you again. When I left you at the hospital—you never told me about your medical problem. If I'd known—"

His lips stiffened. "I *don't* have a medical problem," he said, grabbing her arm and pulling her down the sidewalk. They angled through a crowd of Japanese tourists and cut across the next intersection, narrowly avoiding a sea of yellow taxicabs.

"But Mike said—"

"It's the *truth,*" he insisted, maneuvering around a pair of hotdog carts and a film crew doing setup. "I used to have a problem. It resurfaced when I . . . you know, that whole thing at Trump Tower. But I'm fine now."

Indeed, he felt strong, solid. Callahan's death had galvanized him. The anxiety had vanished, replaced by unwavering determination. He wasn't going to crack. He was going to see this through to the end.

He waded through a line of kids in Cub Scout uniforms waiting at the next corner. Robin followed behind, not noticing the little pairs of eyes that followed the natural swing of her hips. The light was red but Jeremy didn't pause; he headed into the intersection, waving off a city bus as Robin rushed to catch up.

"Where are we going?" she asked, out of breath as they arrived on the other side of the intersection.

"South Carolina."

She drew to a stop, staring at him. "You're not serious? That's where all this trouble started."

"You're right, and that's where it's got to end, too. Unfortunately, we only have eight hours to get there and avert what's about to happen."

"What happens in eight hours?"

He leaned against a bank of telephones, catching his breath. He felt like he'd been pondering the question for a long, long time. He was still a long way from solving the puzzle—but Victor's hints had given him a glimpse at the final pieces.

"Stage three of a forty-year project."

She nodded in understanding. "So you know that THRESHOLD began in 1954."

"THRESHOLD?"

"That's the name the project was listed under in the IRS records I accessed."

He furrowed his brow. "Interesting choice of words. It suggests . . . what? A limit? Or perhaps an entrance into something."

"Yes, or maybe a door," she offered.

"Well, I have a feeling that door will be opening in eight hours."

She raised an eyebrow. "Which brings me back to my original question."

He sighed and started down the sidewalk again. "What happens in eight hours? Here's what I know: Stage one of the project consisted of twelve corpses—all of whom were given deadly genetic diseases by means of a tailored HIV retrovirus."

"Genetic diseases?"

He nodded. "Stage two was your father's assassination. He was also killed with a genetic disease—again a killer gene, pumped into his body by means of a retrovirus."

"Then he *was* killed because of what he knew about Tucsome?" she said. Her eyes grew moist. "I *knew* it."

They both stopped talking as three police cruisers rushed past, sirens blaring.

Finally, the noise subsided. "And stage three has something to do with these killer genes?" Robin asked.

Jeremy was about to nod when something clicked in the back of his brain. A question, slowly forming into words. He slowed his pace, directing the question into the air, as much toward himself as toward her.

"How did the retrovirus get into your father's bloodstream?"

She caught up to him, breathing heavy. "What do you mean?"

"The twelve people who died in stage one of the experiment were all patients at the Tucsome Project hospital; presumably, the HIV retrovirus could have been pumped into them at any time. But what about your father?"

Robin shrugged, thinking. "He was in Tucsome two years ago."

"That was *my* original answer, too. But that's not right. He couldn't have lived for two years with Lesch-Nyhan in his cells. And the HIV retrovirus multiplies quickly, reaching an overwhelming integrity in a very short time. He had to have been infected sometime close to his death."

"Infected how?"

Jeremy rubbed his jaw. He started forward again, pulling her past a block of chic storefronts.

"This morning, I visited Mike Callahan's body at the hospital. There was a small wound at the base of his neck. I'd guess that if we looked hard enough, we'd find the same sort of wound on your father."

She grabbed his arm, slowing him to her pace. "So your point is . . ."

"My point is, if the main difference between stage one and stage two was the method of infection, then couldn't the difference between stage two and stage three be the same?"

"The method of infection?"

He nodded. "The killer gene itself has already been showcased. Fourteen corpses, including Callahan and your father.

Maybe stage three doesn't have to do with the weapon itself, but the manner in which the weapon is going to be used."

She bit her lip, lost in thought. Then she shook her head. "We're still missing something."

He glanced at her as he maneuvered them through another intersection. "What do you mean?"

"I've been doing some digging of my own."

"So I gathered. And?"

"Tucsome has received funding to the tune of sixty billion dollars."

Jeremy swallowed, drawing to a stop in front of an outdoor café. He wondered if he'd heard her right. "Sixty billion?"

"That's right. Beginning with a two-hundred-million-dollar grant in 1954. Ending with fifteen billion more over the last five years."

He shook his head. Those were crazy numbers. Sixty billion was *too* high. The entire Human Genome Project—the sequencing of all sixty-five thousand genes in the human genome—was only expected to cost a total of $15 billion. The sequencing of a small number of killer genes couldn't have cost $60 billion.

"Are you sure? Where did you get your information?"

"Right from the source. I promise you, it's accurate. Sixty billion dollars. Which makes Tucsome bigger than the Manhattan Project, almost as big as NASA. If you ask me, fourteen corpses doesn't even seem like the tip of the iceberg."

He whistled. She was right, they *were* missing something. Something huge. All of a sudden, the term THRESHOLD seemed more ominous. But whatever it meant, it would have to wait until they reached Tucsome. He put a tired arm around her shoulder, and together they strolled by the outdoor café, just another couple out for a summertime stroll.

"It sounds like you've been busy."

"It's been a real trip. From scuba gear to falling elevators."

He paused. A thought glimmered behind his eyes. "Scuba gear?"

"That's right. Getting information from the CIA took some creativity. Why?"

He didn't answer. His mind was racing ahead, working through options, calculating results. "First, we have to figure out how we're going to get to South Carolina."

They turned an abrupt corner and stopped in front of Callahan's red Mazda Miata. The doctor's bag Jeremy had grabbed at the hospital was on the front seat, bulging with a few extra items he'd picked up on the way to the church.

"Well," she said, surveying the car. "*This* is pretty stylish."

"True. But we don't have time for an eight-hundred-mile drive."

She nodded, crossing to the passenger side. "Just get us out onto I-95. I think I know a shortcut."

30

VICTOR OPENED HIS EYES.

He was crouching at the top of the stairs, a huge golden crucifix daggered through the center of his left hand. His body was burned, his hair was smoldering, and his clothes were a total disaster.

His head spun as he balanced himself against a wall. He'd badly underestimated the young scientist. Jeremy Ross hadn't been like the rest. The kid wasn't weak or pathetic at all—suddenly, Victor realized that he was smiling. Through the pain, the agony, he was smiling.

Oh, there were explanations to be given, elaborate excuses to be proffered if he was to avoid serious repercussions from his boss. But the old thrill was back. Vestigial, barely more than an ember—but it was there, a tiny glow warming the inside of his chest. For the first time in years, he'd actually enjoyed himself. Ross had that same spark inside of him, that resourcefulness. He'd fought back—and for the moment, had won.

Victor turned to look at his left hand. His wrist was swollen and already dark blue. The bones at the base of his palm had been shattered, and the joint in his thumb had broken through the skin.

And then, of course, there was the crucifix. It had been run through the direct center of his crushed hand.

"Touché," Victor hissed through the pain.

He reached for the end of the crucifix and clamped his hand around the warm, sticky cross. Then he clenched his teeth.

He pictured the swirling gray pixels on the Vidcom screen and yanked the crucifix free. The pain was enormous, shards of fire running up and down his arm. He gasped through his teeth, but remained focused on the picture in his mind. His boss. The man who'd used him for so many years, the man who'd killed his friends, the man who'd taken his life and loyalty away and had replaced it with meaninglessness and paranoia and tedium.

The bloody crucifix clattered to the marble floor. Blood sprayed out of the hole in his hand, drenching him. He hastily tore a strip of burnt material off of what was left of his Armani jacket and wrapped it around his wrist, tourniquet style. He twisted the material tight, stifling the flow of blood.

Then he leaned back against the stairs. His head felt light and his hand had gone suddenly numb. But there was a dull throbbing in his chest.

Pleasure. Excitement. Anticipation.

Jeremy, I bet I know where you're heading, Victor thought to himself.

Well, it wouldn't do to deny the young man a welcoming party. He'd see to it that the New York office persuaded local law enforcement to put out a "quiet APB" on Ross and his girlfriend. Meanwhile, he'd return to Tucsome to make sure the unveiling occurred on schedule.

He had a feeling that his and Jeremy Ross's paths would cross soon enough.

Nestled in his Georgetown basement, out of earshot from the infernal nagging of his "dear" wife, Ella, Arthur Dice might have agreed with Victor Alexander, had his "Gold-One" been forthcoming with all the details when he reported in some thirty minutes later.

As it was, Dice had to hear about the precise magnitude of the fiasco from Kurt Bowman, nominal head of the New York team and one of the few in the SSO Dice had fully taken into his confidence. For a while now, Dice had arranged for mission assessment redundancy in operations in which Victor was involved. He'd begun to suspect that the Englishman had lost his edge. And indeed, what had just occurred in New York City seemed to confirm it.

"You say Alexander cornered the kid and then allowed him to get away?"

"When we left him, the subject was completely immobilized," Bowman confirmed. "Victor usually finishes them off quick—doesn't play with them. This time, though—" Bowman didn't finish the thought.

"And the girl?" Dice seethed.

"Apparently, she aided in the escape."

Dice made no effort to hide his rage, to mask the surge of cold fury that contorted his limbs and made his face a deep crimson. Bowman would surely have been taken aback by the image had his Vidcom shown him anything but swirling gray pixels.

"God dammit, see that you find those two immediately," the SSO director cursed. "Cover all airports and train stations—though I doubt they'll do the expected. They haven't so far."

Bowman's immense neck muscles bunched up further as he hunched toward the screen. "Victor thinks they'll head south—back to the Project."

Dice played with the miniature replica of the *Enola Gay* that squatted at the corner of his desk. "Yes, Victor is full of theories." He lifted the plane and looked into the tiny cockpit, admiring the lifelike controls. "Make sure that you optimize our police contacts. Also, run the usual profiles: friends and associates who might harbor them, vehicles they might have access to, et cetera."

"We're already doing a blanket scan," Bowman replied. "Uh, about Victor . . ."

"I have need of him temporarily," Dice barked. "His access to Waters's lab is critical if we're to liberate the computer files while Waters is in Lester Auditorium, crowing about his success in 'protecting our nation's defense.' "

"But if Waters is compliant, why do we need to—"

"Just a precaution," Dice interrupted. "Wouldn't want our genetic genius to use his knowledge as a bargaining chip."

Bowman nodded.

"I suspect poor Victor will need some R and R after this is all over," Dice observed. "Somewhere in the Caribbean perhaps." He paused. "You *will* see that he doesn't return?"

"Consider it done," Bowman said, smiling.

31

ROUTE I-95 SOUTH WAS A BLACK RIVER TWISTING AND TURNING under the midafternoon sun. The red Miata clung to the asphalt as Jeremy gunned the accelerator, his eyes nervously shifting between the rearview mirror and the speedometer. The mirror showed nothing but rolling green hills, conifers, and blacktop. The speedometer held steady at seventy-five miles per hour.

"Are you sure you don't want to push it any faster?" Robin asked, adjusting her seat belt.

He shook his head. "Better to keep a constant seventy-five than spend forty minutes trying to explain genetic engineering to a highway cop."

He threw another glance at the rearview mirror and settled back against the seat. He felt good, as if an enormous weight had been lifted from his chest. Robin was next to him, and with her along, anything seemed possible.

"It's not much farther," she said. "Four more exits, I think."

"You're sure he'll help us out?" Jeremy asked, still skeptical of the "shortcut" she'd proposed just as they got onto the highway.

She smiled. "Ferret was always somebody I could count on. If he's there, he'll do it."

Jeremy scanned the interstate. Directly in front of them was a Volvo station wagon carrying a family of four; the two kids had their faces pressed up against the back window, their features looking abnormally large. *Kids*. To the Volvo's right was a Toyota driven by a Latino-looking man whose head was bobbing up and down to fast-paced music. And an ancient model Buick Skylark had drawn up two lengths back, an old woman using both of her hands to talk to her white-haired husband. Otherwise, the interstate was empty, rolling on forever.

Two more miles disappeared under the Miata's wheels before Jeremy thought to check the rearview mirror again. This time he froze.

A black Mercedes sedan hovered low to the highway, about a hundred yards back.

"Shit," Jeremy whispered, the invincibility leaking out of him. "I think we have company."

Robin looked back over her seat. "Could it be a coincidence?"

"You still believe in coincidences?"

"I don't like the alternative."

"Neither do I. Let's try and put some distance between us."

He pressed his foot against the gas pedal, nudging toward the Volvo. But, maddeningly, the Volvo didn't respond. Seventy-five was as fast as the suburban family was willing to go. He prepared to pass to the right, casting another quick glance into his rearview mirror.

"Christ," he whispered, his fingers pressing into the wheel.

"What now?"

"Our problem just doubled. One in each lane. Less than fifty yards back. Hold on."

He gunned the Miata forward, drawing within a few feet of the Volvo, then slammed on his right turn signal and started the Miata sliding toward the right lane. He glanced at the Buick Skylark, expecting it to drift back.

But the old lady wasn't paying attention. She was shouting at her husband, both of her hands in the air. The Buick was only one length back, too close for Jeremy's comfort.

"Try the horn," Robin said.

Jeremy hit the horn with the heel of his hand. The old woman looked up angrily and touched her brake. The Buick slid a car length back, and he was about to pass when Robin touched his arm.

"Now look," she said, pointing ahead. "What *is* this, bumper cars?"

The Latino in the Toyota had moved parallel with the Volvo, blocking the way. A salsa beat rumbled out through his open windows.

Jeremy leaned against his horn, but the Latino didn't even look up. Obviously, he couldn't hear the Miata's high-pitched horn over his music. His Toyota remained parallel with the Volvo, with barely a few feet between them. There was no room to pass.

"This isn't good," Jeremy said, suddenly unable to swallow.

He slammed his foot down on the gas pedal and the Miata sped forward, stopping inches behind the Volvo. He pounded the horn, again and again.

"Faster!" he shouted through his window. "Go faster!"

Still, the Volvo didn't respond. The two kids in the back pressed their faces against the glass, huge smiles on their lips.

"Help me get their attention," Jeremy said.

He and Robin began to wave wildly, beckoning the kids to tell their parents to speed up. Finally, the little girls with pigtails turned her head.

"I think it worked," he said.

"I don't know. There's something strange about that kid."

"The girl? What do you mean?"

"I don't know—wait, she's back."

The little girl leaned close to the window and shrugged her shoulders—her parents wouldn't listen.

Jeremy cursed, his hands pounding on the steering wheel. "Come on," he shouted. "Try again!"

The little girl just smiled, making faces in the window. Jeremy watched her—and an uneasy feeling moved through him. Robin was right, there *was* something strange about that kid. Something unnatural. As if she wasn't a little girl at all, but rather someone much older playing a part.

"What's she doing now?" Robin asked.

He shook his head. The girl held up a finger, as if signaling Jeremy to wait. Then she picked something up from the seat next to her and pointed it at the Miata.

It took Jeremy a full second to realize that the thing in her hands was an automatic weapon.

The back window of the Volvo popped out and disappeared under the Miata's wheels. The little girl raised the gun and opened fire.

The sound was deafening. Jeremy threw himself on top of Robin, crushing her against the seat. Glass exploded around them as bullets crashed through the windshield. The Miata swerved to the right, out from under the rain of bullets, and Jeremy lunged for the steering wheel.

With neither the Toyota nor Buick in sight, he gunned the accelerator and held his breath as the Miata drew dead even with and then ahead of the Volvo. Inside the Volvo, whoever was wielding the automatic weapon—obviously, it wasn't a child—apparently had a bad angle, because the trailing gunfire missed completely.

Jeremy looked to his left. The green median strip whizzed by, a grassy barrier almost six feet wide. On the other side of the grass, cars screamed by in the other direction.

Suddenly, the submachine gun exploded again, sending a spray of bullets that pulverized the Miata's back window. Without thinking, Jeremy pulled Robin down with him, yanking the steering wheel to the left and pressing his foot tight to the floor. With sudden force, the car bucked upward into the air. Robin screamed as Jeremy was pitched sideways, his shoulder slamming into the door handle. He had the sudden, intense feeling of being up on two wheels as the Miata hurtled the median strip. Then the car slammed back down and the tires squealed against pavement.

Gasping, he struggled out from under the steering wheel. His eyes went wide as he stared at the oncoming traffic.

"Steer!" Robin screamed.

She grabbed the steering wheel out of his hands and aimed for the center of the road. Cars whizzed by on either side, horns blazing, looks of terror on the drivers' faces. She kept her hands steady on the wheel, pointing the Miata straight through the middle of the oncoming traffic.

A few seconds later, the traffic died down. The highway was empty in front of them. She exhaled, giving Jeremy back the steering wheel. He looked at her, his entire body sagging. "That was some driving."

"I can't believe we're alive," she said, her breath coming in ragged gasps.

Jeremy inspected the car, utterly amazed. The front and back windshields were both riddled with bullet holes. The seat behind him was torn to shreds. And wisps of smoke curled from underneath the hood. Despite that, the Miata's engine was continuing to respond.

He laughed out loud. Then he glanced in what was left of the rearview mirror.

There were two Mercedes sedans behind them.

"Robin. It's not over."

She followed his eyes. "My God."

He slammed his foot against the gas pedal and the tortured Miata shuddered. The speedometer crept upward: *ninety . . . ninety five . . .* He pleaded with the car. *A hundred . . . a hundred and five . . . a hundred and seven . . .*

And then the engine let out a groan. The Miata couldn't go

any faster. Not in the shape it was in. Jeremy gritted his teeth as he turned in his seat.

The two Mercedes sedans were still gaining. The closest was only ten feet away. As he watched, a man in a gray suit leaned out of one of the sedans' windows and raised his submachine gun.

"Not again," Jeremy murmured. "Not again—"

And suddenly, Robin was screaming.

Jeremy whirled forward to see an enormous tanker truck heading right at them. Each of its eighteen wheels was bigger than the Miata, and its front grill was a giant wall of chrome.

His hands took over. He twisted the wheel to the right, heading straight toward the median. The Miata fishtailed, its tires spinning desperately in search of traction. Then the tires found grass, and the car leapt into the air. A second later, it slammed down against the asphalt, heading south on I-95.

Jeremy looked back over his shoulder just in time to see the first of the Mercedes sedans slam headlong into the tanker.

The sky went white.

A second later, an explosion lacerated the air. The sound was so loud that the one remaining window on the Miata shattered, sprinkling Jeremy and Robin with broken glass. A huge fireball rocketed into the air, and the tanker twisted in an agonizing angle, its cylindrical body consumed by ugly blue and orange flames.

Jeremy managed to coax the Miata another mile before Robin touched his arm. "Take that exit," she said.

There was a large orange sign near the curving off-ramp. Bright letters flashed angrily in his direction: CONSTRUCTION, ROAD CLOSED. USE NEXT EXIT.

"Are you sure?"

"I'm sure," she said.

As the limping Miata rounded the winding curve, Jeremy could still see the tanker explosion in his head, the incredible flash of white light. How many people had died in the blast?

How many more people were going to die before this was through?

A sudden peal of thunder interrupted his thoughts, and he glanced at the sky. "Looks like rain."

Robin, who'd barely uttered two sentences since they'd left the fiery scene on the highway, roused herself. "That will make things tougher on Ferret."

Jeremy continued staring straight ahead. " 'Tough' seems the order of the day," he said.

A minute later the skies opened up and silvery drops began peppering the Miata's hood.

32

THE WIND HOWLED THROUGH THE MISSING WINDSHIELD, CAR-
rying with it drenching waves of rain. Jeremy coaxed the
Miata along the deserted gravel path, eventually coming to a
canopy of heavy-limbed trees that provided some measure of
protection.

"Are you *sure* this is the right exit?" he asked for the fifth
time.

"We're almost there," Robin said. "Just keep this thing
moving."

The Mazda coughed and sputtered over a low hill, and
suddenly they broke through the trees. A clearing the size of
a football field stretched out in front of them. Jeremy pulled
the car up next to a low fence and stared through the gap left
by the missing windshield.

He counted seven airplanes parked randomly across the
field. Four were barely more than gliders, with single engines and bubble cockpits. The other three were slightly
larger, almost the size of corporate jets.

"I thought you said we were going to an *airport*," Jeremy said, underwhelmed by what he was seeing.

"It's a private airfield," Robin answered. "My father used to charter a jet between here and Washington, when he wanted to get in and out unnoticed. Come on."

She pushed open her door and stepped out into the rain. Jeremy followed behind her, his eyes pinned to the nearest jet. It looked fragile in the dim moonlight, like an oversized plastic toy.

"I don't see a runway."

"There's a short stretch of unused highway on the other side of the field. These planes don't need much more than a little blacktop and a few guidance lights."

"And pilots."

"Of course."

She led him to a small gap in the fence and beckoned him through. There was an aluminum-sided shack near the edge of the airfield, and he could see the warm light of a television set flickering through a milky window.

"It's been a few years," she said as she arrived at the door to the shack. "So cross your fingers."

She wrapped her knuckles against the aluminum.

"It's open," coughed a rough voice from inside. "Wipe your feet on the way in."

Ferret was at least sixty, and had a scar that ran from his left eye to his upper lip. He was wearing a leather aviator jacket and ripped jeans, belted tight over his distended gut. His boots were up on his desk, next to a small black-and-white television. A sitcom brayed incessantly against the tinny walls of the shack.

"You two look like you're in the wrong place."

Robin took a step forward. "Ferret?"

The man squinted, his scar dancing with the motion. "Son of a bitch. If it ain't the little chicken."

He leapt up from his chair and held out his thick arms. She

crossed the room in three steps and hugged him, smiling. Then she pointed at Jeremy.

"This is Jeremy Ross. Jeremy, meet Ferret Angleson, AFC, retired."

Jeremy shook the man's hand. Ferret looked him over with a glance, then turned back to Robin.

"The last time I saw you, you had pigtails and braces."

"I'm trying a different look this year."

Ferret laughed. Then his weathered face changed, his lips turning solemn. "Your father was one of the best. It was a shame he had to go out like that."

She squeezed his arm. "Thank you. He always spoke glowingly about you."

"I owe that man my life. After I retired from the military, he helped me get this place up and running. Got me my license, even set me up with some courier jobs. I never got to properly repay him for what he did."

"You might still get the chance."

Ferret held her by the hands. "You just name it, little chicken. Just name it."

After retrieving the doctor's bag from the Miata's trunk, Jeremy and Robin followed Ferret out onto the airfield. The rain was coming down in icy gray sheets, pounding the grass into mud and sparking a flurry of activity. Two men in orange suits dashed back and forth across the field, fighting to cover the parked airplanes with thick plastic tarps.

"Sure is coming down," Ferret shouted as they approached one of the few remaining uncovered planes. "Nobody else'll be in the air tonight, I can promise you that."

Jeremy swallowed as he watched the small plane's wings shudder under the heavy raindrops. "Is it safe to fly in this weather?"

Ferret laughed. "Safe? Are you kidding? You'd have to be insane to fly tonight."

He pulled open the cabin door and unfolded a metal stepladder. Then he turned to help Robin up the creaky steps.

Jeremy followed, the heavy doctor's bag lodged under one arm.

The gray-haired pilot pulled the cabin door shut behind Jeremy and pointed toward the rear cabin. "Seats four—and every seat is first-class. Make yourselves at home while I warm this baby up." With that, he disappeared into the cockpit.

Jeremy took a deep breath and followed Robin into the cabin. The ceiling was low, and the seats looked old and uncomfortable. The rain splattered against the oval windows, a ceaseless rhythm that he might have found lulling had he not been scared to death of flying.

"Window or aisle?" Robin asked.

Just then, there was a loud rumble and the entire plane began to tremble.

"Listen to her purr," Ferret shouted from up in the cockpit. "Now does that sound like a thirty-year-old engine to you?"

Jeremy closed his eyes, his fingers tight against the closest seat. Robin touched his arm. "I think I'll take the window. You look like an aisle man."

She pushed by him and settled into her seat. He followed suit, setting the doctor's bag down directly beside him. His fingers trembled a bit as he reached for the seat belt; then he noticed that there was no seat belt, just two thin straps of vinyl hanging limp on either side.

"Tie them together around your waist," Robin said. "Ferret's a no-frills type of guy."

Jeremy's heart pounded in his chest as he fought to keep his voice steady. "Are you sure he knows what he's doing?"

She smiled. "He's the best. He's flown in three wars that I know of, maybe more. And he's been flying this plane since we were both in diapers."

There was a steady cough, and then a new set of vibrations ricocheted through the plane. The cabin lurched forward, and Jeremy could hear the wheels churning against the muddy field. He hastily fastened the vinyl straps around his waist.

Robin tied her own straps and then reached for his hand. "This is going to be fun," she said, her eyes flashing.

"Fun," Jeremy said, his face showing complete disbelief.

"You just have to learn to relax."

There was a sudden pressure, and the cabin jerked upward. For a brief second, Jeremy's heart leapt up into his throat; then Robin nuzzled against him, her firm breasts pressing into his chest. The motion distracted him. His face moved down to meet hers, and as their lips met, his mind whirled and he almost forgot that he was in an airplane. He leaned toward her, drinking in her taste and smell.

They kissed each other for a few minutes, then she pulled back. The sound of the rain had vanished, and the oval window was pitch black and still, the inside of a closed eyelid. She touched the thick glass with a fingernail, catching her breath.

"Ferret?" she called out. "How long until we get to South Carolina?"

"Maybe three hours," the pilot yelled back. "Depends on the storm. And also where in South Carolina we're talking about."

She looked at Jeremy. He chose his words carefully.

"We didn't exactly have time to file a flight plan."

Ferret didn't pause. "I kind of figured that out on my own. And it doesn't matter—I can set this baby down on a dime. Give me a strip of road, an empty field, a parking lot—"

"An interstate?" Jeremy asked.

"Sure, why not. You just say the word and we'll drop like a bag of stones. Or maybe we'll let Robin set us down. What do you say, little chicken? Feeling lucky?"

Robin shook her head, her hand moving inside Jeremy's shirt. "I'm saving my luck for later. Where we're going, we're going to need all the luck in the world."

33

STROKES OF THUNDER FRACTURED THE AIR AS JEREMY STUM-
bled out onto the interstate. He turned and helped Robin
down the stepladder. Ferret had his head out through the
cabin door, his scar shivering as his face scrunched against
the heavy rain.

"You say the word," he shouted, "and I'll ditch this thing
and come with you."

Jeremy shook his head. He didn't want to risk bringing
anyone else into this nightmare—and he didn't want to run
the chance of someone discovering the small airplane.

"Just get yourself as far away from here as possible," he
shouted back.

"Thanks for the lift, Ferret," Robin added. "Consider yourself and my father more than even."

Ferret held up a thumb, and the cabin door slammed shut.
Jeremy and Robin moved away from the interstate and huddled together on the wet sand, watching as the plane gently
rolled forward. There was a sudden roar as the nose went up,

sheets of rain spiriting over the wings and billowing off the tail. Then the plane lifted into the darkness, becoming nothing more than a shimmering speck of gray.

Jeremy turned to face Robin. She was soaking wet, her dyed hair plastered to her head, her clothes sticking to her curves.

"We're quite a pair, aren't we?"

"We can't go on like this," she said, looking at him. "I assume you have a plan?"

He nodded. "The first step is to get some help."

"Help? We're in the middle of nowhere."

He tucked the doctor's bag under his right arm. By his guess, they were less than a mile from his destination.

"We've got to hurry," he said simply. "We have less than four hours to go."

The Tucsome County Sheriff's Office was a beacon in the midst of the swirling darkness. Jeremy and Robin threaded between the two police cruisers, their bodies fighting against the stiff wind.

"Jeremy, I still don't think trusting the police is a good idea."

"Portney's okay. You'll see." He paused in front of the door, then motioned her to one side as he reached for the knob.

The first thought that hit him as he pushed his way inside was that something was missing. He paused in the doorway, his eyes shifting across the small, well-lit waiting area.

The room was empty, and the single desk was cluttered with a familiar array of paraphernalia: a can of Red Devil chewing tobacco. An aluminum spit can. A copy of the latest issue of *Guns & Ammo*. And a half-eaten banana.

"It doesn't look like anyone's here," Robin said.

"He might be in the back. Stay close to the door."

Jeremy took a step forward, his body wary. He was about to call out Portney's name when he realized what it was that wasn't there.

The shotgun.

His throat turned dry. Instinctively, he crouched low, pressing himself against the wall. "Robin," he whispered. "Wait outside."

She shook her head. "We stay together this time."

He glanced at her, then nodded. She was right, they'd face whatever was to come together. He held his breath, listening. Other than the wind and rain against the outside of the building, the world was silent.

"I'm going to check the back," he whispered.

"I'll be right behind you."

They slid along the wall, inching forward. When they reached the inner door, Jeremy raised a finger, signaling Robin to stop. Then he pressed his ear against the wood. Still nothing.

"If he *is* in there, he's being awfully quiet," he whispered.

"Maybe he's asleep."

He shrugged and wrapped his fingers around the doorknob. The door was unlocked and came open easily. He moved forward carefully, Robin a half-step behind him.

They entered a short hallway lined with unmarked storage cabinets, some as tall as Jeremy, some bulging open with what looked to be civil-defense equipment: flashlights, fire extinguishers, hard hats, shovels. At the end of the hallway waited a half-open door, over which hung a sign with friendly lettering: LAVATORY. A triangle of light streamed out onto the carpet.

Jeremy quietly crossed the distance and paused in front of the half-open door. Then he reached for Robin's hand.

"Deputy?" he said cautiously. "Are you in there?"

No answer. He put his other hand against the door. He gave the wood a firm shove. The door swung inward.

Deputy Portney was on the toilet. His pants were down around his ankles. One end of the shotgun was in his hands, the other end in what was left of his mouth.

Jeremy leapt back, nearly crashing into Robin.

"Christ," Robin gasped.

The top of Portney's head was missing. The wall behind him dripped blood and brains, like modern art without the canvas.

"Back. Go. Now!"

Jeremy grabbed Robin's arm and ran down the hallway, barely in control. He crashed through the inner door and collided knee-first into the desk. She fell against him, then pulled him to his feet. Together they sprinted across the waiting area.

A second later they were out in the parking lot, breathing hard, staring at each other with wide eyes.

"This is out of control," he whispered. "These people are *beyond* vicious."

Robin ran her hands through her wet hair. "What do we do now?"

Jeremy looked at his watch. *Three hours.* He glanced at the two police cruisers sitting in the center of the parking lot. He had a sudden thought: Portney was dead, but he could still help. He set his jaw.

"I'm going back inside."

"What for?"

"You'll see. Wait here."

This time, she didn't argue. He was gone for close to two minutes. When he returned, he was lugging a pair of portable stretchers and a heavy plastic flashlight. The stretchers had shiny chrome frames and sturdy steel wheels, folded into quarters and held tight by plastic clasps. He dropped the stretchers on the pavement, shoved the flashlight into his doctor's bag, and turned back toward the sheriff's office.

"One more trip," he said. "This might take a little longer. There's enough stuff back there to build a miniature city."

Four minutes later, he returned. He had his arms around a thick black wet suit. Robin raised her eyebrows. He smiled at her, dropping the wet suit next to the stretchers. Then he headed straight for the closest cruiser. He pulled a set of keys out of his pocket and attacked the front door. The door clicked open on the third try. She watched as he slid into the driver's seat.

"So we're going to just drive right in?" she asked.

The cruiser's engine came to life with a sputter. He left the headlights off and stepped back out into the rain.

"In a matter of speaking. First, I have to get dressed."

"What do you mean?"

He crossed toward the rubber wet suit. "Come on. Show me how to put this on."

She threw him a look of exasperation, but somehow restrained her curiosity. He suited up quickly, Robin giving directions while he struggled with the thick black rubber. When he was ready, he stood with his hands on his hips, looking himself over; only his face and hands were still exposed to the rain.

"What about an oxygen tank and a regulator?" she asked.

He retrieved his doctor's bag and the portable stretchers, and led her toward the police cruiser.

"Where we're going, I won't need them. Just the wet suit."

"Jeremy—"

"I'll explain when we get there."

He pulled open the passenger door and beckoned her inside. She sighed, sliding into the seat. He slammed the door shut and smiled at her through the window.

"In case you're wondering, yes, I *am* crazy."

He crossed to the driver's side and slid in next to her. Then he kicked the cruiser into reverse and spun out of the parking lot.

The ventilation tower rose in front of them like a tear in an oil painting. The rain had abated, but black rain clouds still swirled around it, threatening to burst open again. Jeremy skidded to a stop twenty feet in front of the electric fence. He put the cruiser into park but left the engine running. Then he turned to face Robin.

"The tower is connected to Tucsome by about two miles of underground ventilation corridors. We should be able to glide right past their security. The only real obstacle is that fence."

Her eyes slid up the high chain links, pausing when she reached the swirls of barbed wire. "And we're going to drive through it?"

"Not we. *Me*. You see, there's a little hitch. The fence is electrified. Seriously electrified. Fifty thousand volts."

"That sounds like a lot."

"It's enough to melt the windows off this car."

Her face was incredulous. "And you expect that wet suit to protect you?"

"It should. When I started out at Dartmouth, I minored in electrical engineering. If I've got it figured right, when I hit the fence, the metal shell of the cruiser will create something called a Faraday cage. Most of the electricity will run around the car and down into the cruiser's tires. I'm hoping that the rubber in the wet suit protects me from whatever's left over."

"You're *hoping*?"

"I'm wearing a wet suit while driving a police cruiser through an electric fence. It's not an exact science."

She wrung her hands nervously. "Jeremy, this sounds too risky. There must be some other—"

"No, there's no other way," he said, shaking his head. His eyes welled up with emotion. "Listen, I sure as hell don't want to die . . . not now, when I have you back in my life. But this is a gamble I *have* to take. You understand that, don't you?"

"I suppose," she said quietly.

"You can come through afterward," he said, smiling. "I'm going to punch one hell of a hole in the fence; after that, you should be able to jump right through."

She pressed her lips together, silent. Finally, she nodded. Then she reached for the door handle and slowly pushed the cruiser door open.

"What about an alarm system?" she asked, still in her seat. "Won't crashing the fence alert the Tucsome security force?"

He rolled his shoulders. "Honestly, I don't know. They

might have assumed that the fifty thousand volts was deterrent enough. Either way, we'll have to move fast once we burst through. We want to get inside as quickly as possible. Especially if we set off an alarm."

"And what happens once we're inside?"

He settled his hands against the steering wheel. "We have two goals. First, we need to find evidence that links Tucsome to the killer gene I found in Mike's body. We need to find the DNA sequence—"

"And do what with it? Who do you plan to show it to?"

He paused, touching his fingers together. "I've given that a lot of thought. From what you've told me, we can't trust anyone in the political arena. Not the CIA, certainly nobody in the Pentagon. But this isn't simply a political issue. It's scientific. The Human Genome Project involves thousands of scientists across the globe. If we can get our hands on the killer gene sequence, we can cause a hell of a storm in the scientific community. The pressure will come at the government from all directions—global directions—and they'll have to shut Tucsome down."

She paused, digesting what he'd said. Finally, she nodded. "Makes sense. And our second goal?"

He took a deep breath. "We have to sabotage stage three. My guess is, it will be unveiled in Lester Auditorium in approximately two hours. The security there is sure to be tight; which means we have to get inside Waters's private laboratory—before he transports whatever hardware is involved to the auditorium. Once there, we have to find out what stage three is—and destroy it."

She sighed and shook her head. "Why do I feel like we're kidding ourselves? The odds of our getting past security and discovering—"

"Hey," he interrupted, his face determined. "Who was it who said 'Self-delusion is a precondition for every act of consequence'?"

"I don't know," she replied, "but remind me to give him a piece of my mind after this is all over."

"Will do," Jeremy said, smiling. The moment of irresolution had passed.

"One last question," she said, bracing herself in her seat. "Once we achieve our two goals, how do we get back out? The same way we went in?"

He shrugged his shoulders. In truth, he wasn't sure. He had a few escape routes in mind—including a backward trek through the ventilation tunnel—but he assumed that the situation would dictate its own plausible resolution.

"Hopefully, we'll be able to cause some sort of a distraction to cover our escape. The exact route will depend on what happens once we're inside. I know, it's not a great answer—but it's the best I can do."

She squeezed his arm through the rubber of the wet suit, then stepped out of the cruiser.

Alone in the vehicle, Jeremy took a deep breath. *This is going to work*, he told himself. *This has to work*. He pulled the cruiser out of park and positioned his foot above the gas pedal. Then he threw Robin one last glance.

"Get ready for some fireworks," he said, trying to make his voice confident. She smiled, but he could see that there was real fear in her eyes. He turned back toward the fence.

"Ready or not," he whispered, "here I come."

He slammed his foot against the pedal.

The cruiser rocketed forward. It hit the fence dead center and there was an enormous flash of white light, rising straight up into the sky. The front windshield buckled and caught fire, bursting upward in a sheet of bright red flame. Jeremy kept his foot pinned to the accelerator as he covered his face with his rubber sleeves. He felt a searing heat—and then the heat dissipated. He uncovered his eyes and grasped for the steering wheel, fighting to regain control. The cruiser skidded in the sand and came to an abrupt stop at the base of the tower.

He let go of the steering wheel and collapsed back in his seat. His ears were ringing and there was a strange, smoky taste in his mouth. But otherwise, he felt fine. He turned in his seat, looking back toward the fence.

Just as he'd predicted, the cruiser had punched a ten-foot-wide hole in the fence.

Satisfied, he quickly retrieved his doctor's bag and the two portable stretchers from under the dashboard and shifted toward the cruiser door. The side window had melted right out of its frame, and a thin veil of smoke was rising up from the vinyl interior. Careful not to touch anything metal, he braced himself and kicked at the plastic handle. The door swung open and Jeremy leapt out onto the sand.

"Jeremy!"

Robin was standing a few feet beyond the hole created by the cruiser. Her face glowed with relief.

"I'm fine," he said. "How was it from your angle?"

"Like the Fourth of July," she answered. "Only closer. Can I come through?"

"Just be careful not to touch anything metal."

He watched as she followed the cruiser's tire tracks. In a few seconds she had her arms around him, her lips against his cheek. Then she helped him struggle free from the wet suit, and together they backed away from the destroyed cruiser. From outside, it was quite a sight; the front hood of the car was bent almost in half, and the windshield was completely gone. The rear bumper was on fire, flames sending sparks swirling upward into the sky. A large section of the fence curled over the top of the cruiser, melted almost beyond recognition.

"Hell of a barbecue," Jeremy said. "Come on."

He led her to the base of the steel tower. Up close it looked much larger, its surface still slick and shiny from the rain.

"How do we get inside?"

"There's got to be an access panel. Probably near the top."

"The top?"

He pointed at the metal rungs that started at waist level.

The rungs reached skyward, slithering up the side of the steel tower and vanishing nearly thirty feet above.

"This wasn't in the brochure," Robin commented, trying some bravado.

"Extras included, no charge," Jeremy said as he put his foot on the bottom rung. It felt sturdy. He hefted his weight against it, reaching for the rung by his head. "Doesn't look too rough," he called down to her. "You take one of the stretchers."

He slung his doctor's bag under one elbow, a portable stretcher under the other, and carefully pulled himself up to the first rung. The wind whipped against his back, and he pressed as close to the tower as he could. Slowly, he worked upward, rung by rung. When he got past the tenth rung he looked down. Robin was a few feet below, hanging tight to the tower.

"You okay?"

"I'm managing."

He continued upward. A few feet closer to the top he paused. There was a hinged metal panel to his right, about three feet across. The panel was bolted shut.

"Here we are."

"Is it locked?"

Jeremy hooked his arm around a rung and leaned out toward the panel. He gave the bolt a good shove with the heel of his hand. It didn't move. He ran his fingers above and below the bolt. Then he shook his head, surprised. "Not locked. Soldered shut."

"How do they make repairs?"

"It's a recent job. Very recent."

"How can you tell?"

"The texture of the solder. Someone came up here within the last few weeks and sealed the panel shut."

"Why?"

"I don't know."

"What are we going to do? Don't tell me we climbed all the way up here for nothing."

Jeremy smiled, reaching for his doctor's bag. "Give me a little credit. I didn't think this was going to be easy."

He rummaged through the bag and found a small vial of clear liquid. Carefully, he broke the safety seal on the vial and unscrewed the cap. A strong chemical scent hit him in the face. He coughed, turning his head to the side.

"What's that awful smell?"

"Fluoric acid. I borrowed it from a lab in the hospital. Thought it might come in handy."

He steadied himself against the rung, the stretcher balanced between his body and the tower, and leaned out over the access panel. Carefully, he dripped the fluoric acid over the soldered bolt. A dull hissing erupted, and the metal began to bubble.

"That stuff is serious," Robin murmured.

"One of the most powerful acids. It can eat through solid steel in seconds."

"And you've been carrying it around in that doctor's bag?"

"The vial is made of special glass, coated with chemical bases that neutralize the acid's strength."

"But what if the vial had broken?"

He shrugged. "Then we'd have had a real mess on our hands." He screwed the vial shut and returned it to his bag. "Okay, let's see if it worked."

He made his hand into a fist and slammed it into the panel. There was a loud crack, and the entire bolt snapped out. The access panel swung open, slapping against the side of the tower. A rush of warm air erupted into the night.

He leaned his head through the open hole in the side of the tower. His ears throbbed with the sound of the huge fan, and he immediately glanced up. The convex blades were a spinning blur barely ten feet above, creating an incredible vacuum. He braced his hands on the side of the opening, shifting his eyes downward. Metal rungs disappeared into the darkness.

"Looks wide enough," he shouted. "I'm going in—"

And then he paused. There was something wrong, something missing. He glanced back upward, toward the fan. He saw seven metal ridges chiseled into the tower walls, beginning just a few inches below the fan. The ridges were lined with tiny holes.

"Rivets," he whispered. "Someone ripped out the rivets."

"The what?" Robin shouted from below.

"The filters are missing," Jeremy explained, half to himself. "There should be seven separate filters up near the fan. Someone tore them out."

"What were the filters for?"

"To purify Tucsome's exhaust—get rid of viruses, bacteria, anything dangerous in the air."

"Maybe they're being serviced."

He nodded. It was possible. But something nagged at him, something he couldn't quite figure out.

"I'm missing something."

"Sorry?"

"Never mind," he said, turning back to face her. "Take a last look at the sky. We've got a long dark road ahead of us."

"Hurry up already. This wind is cold."

Jeremy heaved himself through the open access panel. His feet found the rungs on the other side, and he worked his way down into the darkness. A strong wind pulled at him from above, and he fought the urge to stare at the enormous, dizzying fan. He stopped a yard below the open panel and watched as Robin's body hooked over the edge. She was struggling with the portable stretcher, and it took her a good minute to steady herself on the inside rung. When she looked secure, he reached up and touched her ankle.

"This might get kind of tight. But we should have room to move."

"How do you know?"

"Basic physics. Have you ever tried to suck air through one of those little red swizzle sticks? Much harder than sucking air through a straw. The principle is the same here. The wider the tunnels, the less vacuum needed to pull the air through."

"Anyone ever tell you that you give good brain? No wonder I'm in love with you."

"So you *are* in love with me?"

"Or maybe it's just the flu. All this rain and wind is getting to me."

"Or the electricity," Jeremy said, starting down into the darkness. "Don't forget the electricity."

"How much did you say it was? Fifty thousand volts? You're right, it might be the electricity."

The conversation continued as they worked their way downward, rung by rung.

Approximately twenty feet below the base of the tower, Jeremy's feet hit solid ground. He touched Robin's leg, stopping her, and bent toward the floor. It was pitch black; the moonlight dribbling in through the open access panel had long since been swallowed by the sheer tower walls. He could barely see his own fingers as he touched the cold metal beneath his feet.

"Feels like steel."

He reached into the doctor's bag and pulled out the heavy flashlight. He flicked it on, glancing into the cone of light. The ventilation tunnel seemed to go on forever, four walls of smooth, bluish metal running into eternity.

"Can you tell which way to go?"

He nodded. A stiff wind was coming from his right.

"There isn't much of a choice."

He aimed the flashlight toward the wind. There was an opening a few yards away. It looked to be about three feet across and four feet high. He dropped to his knees and crawled toward it, inspecting it with his hands.

"We'll have to go one after another. It'll be tight, but we'll make it."

Robin crouched next to him in the darkness. He could feel the warmth of her breath, the rise and fall of her chest.

"It's going to be a long two miles," she said.

He took a step back and began unfolding his portable stretcher.

"That's what these are for. They'll make the trip considerably easier."

She nodded, unfolding her own. When they were both ready, he touched her arm.

"I'll go in first, you stay as close as possible. We'll make it in an hour. Maybe faster."

"How much time will that leave us?"

Jeremy aimed the flashlight at his watch. "This is going to come right down to the wire."

He reached back and ran a finger over her cheek. Then he pushed his stretcher through the opening and crawled on top of it. He balanced the flashlight and the doctor's bag under his chin, and reached out for the walls. He found that he could push himself along with his palms, keeping a fairly steady pace with little effort. The flashlight illuminated a tiny section of the tunnel ahead of him, an orange comfort zone carved out of the almost liquid darkness. He rolled a few feet forward, then waited for the sound of Robin's stretcher rolling in behind him.

"If you need to rest," he whispered over his shoulder, "give me a whack."

"Lead on," she whispered back.

He pushed off, concentrating on the squeak of the stretcher's wheels and the shimmering cone of light. The steel walls were cold against his palms, and there was a steady breeze in his face. Soon he fell into a gentle rhythm, embraced by the darkness on either side and succored by the thought of Robin a few feet away.

Time passed like melting glass. They stopped once after what seemed like forty minutes to stretch their arms, lying face-to-face in the darkness, whispering comforting inanities, trying not to think about where they were going, where they were coming from, how far they still had to go. Then they were moving forward again, wrists and elbows aching, stretchers squeaking against the steel tunnel floor.

Jeremy's mind wandered as he pushed himself along, cycling through the mysteries that still inhabited his thoughts. What was stage three? Wasn't $60 billion too much money for the sequencing of a few killer genes? Why had the filters been removed from the ventilation tunnel?

Was Jason Waters behind it all? Could he have betrayed the science that had made him an idol?

"I just don't believe it," Jeremy finally mumbled, sliding along in the darkness. "Jason Waters was there with Watson and Crick. He was there at the dawn of genetics. How could he allow his science to be so utterly abused?"

"Technology is always getting used for violent purposes," Robin responded, her voice echoing down the tunnel. "Why not genetics? And why not Waters? He's just a man, with the same vanities and frustrations as everyone else."

Jeremy shook his head, his hands slapping against the steel walls.

"He's also a scientist. And the science he's helped discover is more than just a new technology. A thousand years from now, the names of Watson, Crick—and Waters—will overshadow Einstein, Galileo, even Newton. Genetics has redefined humanity. I can't believe that he'd betray everything he's worked for just to make a weapon."

"You make genetics sound like a religion."

He paused, his stretcher coasting forward. The cone of light quivered in front of him, the blue-steel walls flashing by on either side.

"In many ways it *is* a religion. For the first time in history, science is handing us objective answers to questions of life and mortality. And Waters understands this better than anyone. This is *his* revolution; I just don't believe that he'd let the Human Genome Project become another Manhattan Project. There has to be something else—"

Suddenly, Jeremy's stretcher lurched forward. He gasped, his hands splaying outward. His palms slammed against the steel walls and his body contorted as he fought to keep his balance. His stretcher twisted underneath him—and then it was gone, chasing the cone of light straight down into the blackness. He made a grab for his doctor's bag, barely catching it with his fingers. Then his knees crashed against the steel floor, his head hanging out over nothingness. He could hear his stretcher clanging against the walls as it fell.

Then there was another sound, the squeal of wheels behind him. Robin's stretcher hit him square in the back, and he teetered forward, his body crying out from the impact. Somehow, his grip on the walls held. He felt Robin clutching at his shoulders as she rolled off of her stretcher, gasping.

"What happened?" she gasped. "Are you okay? I tried to stop but I couldn't—"

"I'm okay," he coughed, steadying himself. "We ran into a shaft of some sort. A hell of a drop."

He straightened his back, carefully. He could feel a dark bruise growing where her stretcher had hit him—but thankfully, nothing was broken. He took a deep breath and leaned forward, squinting his eyes against the darkness.

There was no telling how deep the shaft extended. He felt around the edge of the drop-off and quickly found descending metal rungs.

"We don't want to go down, do we?" she asked.

"No, we don't. Maybe the shaft extends in both directions."

He extended his arms upwards. His fingers found more rungs. He paused, his head out over the shaft. He could see cracks of yellow light far above.

"I think we're directly beneath the Project. This shaft must run up through the wall, branching out between each floor."

"We're going to be climbing up the inside of a wall?"

"Rats do it all the time."

"Great. That makes me feel a whole lot better."

"Come on." Jeremy swung his legs out into the shaft and found a metal rung with his heel. Then he pushed himself upward, twisting his body against the sheer wall. His back cried out at the motion, but he ignored the pain. It took him a minute to regain his equilibrium; then he was sliding up the wall, his hands finding the rungs in the darkness with surprising ease. He paused after a few feet, glancing downward. He could barely make out Robin's shape as she slowly eased herself vertical.

"Take your time," he whispered. "Be careful. We don't know how far down the shaft extends. There could be multiple basements."

She glided toward him, her lithe movements smooth and confident. "Okay, I'm here. Just keep the rats out of my hair."

He moved upward, his body filling with tension. They were close, getting closer. The wind in his face carried with it familiar smells and sounds. In a fashion, they were already inside Tucsome. Deep inside.

A few minutes later Jeremy paused. Flickering fluorescent light dribbled out of a horizontal shaft a few feet above his head. He cautioned Robin to remain where she was, then pulled himself up to the next rung. He stuck his head into the shaft, carefully pulling his body after him.

He crawled a few feet down the horizontal shaft, his hands trembling against the steel beneath him. He could see the source of the light—a square metal grate on the floor of the shaft, a yard beyond his fingers. He crawled to the edge and peered down through the tiny holes.

Blue walls. Red carpet. Empty kiosk. Jeremy nodded to himself, doubling back. He exited into the vertical tunnel, leaning close to Robin's ear:

"We're above the reception atrium. First floor."

Then he continued upward. The excitement was building in his chest. He felt a new rush of confidence. They were going to be able to climb all the way to Waters's lab. Unseen, unnoticed, scaling the ventilation tunnel like a backwards draft of air. There was a chance they would even be able to get out the way they had come—although without his stretcher, it would be a hell of a crawl.

They passed another flicker of yellow light and a similar horizontal shaft. Second floor. He moved by the opening without pausing, his hands firm against the metal rungs.

A third flash of light caught his eyes, and he quickened his pace. He was coming up on the third floor of the Project— the place where he'd spent most of his time in Tucsome. His mind wandered from Lyle's lab to Jason Waters's elevator as he tried to position himself mentally. If he was right, Lyle's lab should have been directly in front of him, Waters's elevator twenty feet to his left. He guessed that he had two more floors to go, and then he'd have to work horizontally, feeling his way toward Waters's lab.

He was about to pass the opening to the third-floor shaft when he stopped, suddenly. A familiar sound echoed off the walls around him. The clink of test tubes, mixed with the squeak of sneakers against a cement floor.

"Lyle," Jeremy whispered.

He raised his eyebrows. What was Lyle doing on the third floor? It was almost midnight; Lyle was supposed to be waiting with the rest of the staff in the Lester Auditorium. Why was he in his lab?

Jeremy bit his lip, his hands a few inches from the horizontal opening. Was Lyle somehow involved? Was he assisting Waters with his experiment?

"Why are we stopping?" Robin whispered. "Are we there?"

He shook his head. Whatever Lyle was up to, they didn't have time for a confrontation. He had to get to Waters's lab. He was certain that the lab contained the information he needed. And he had to get there before the unveiling. He owed that to Callahan, to Warren T. Walker, to Matthew Aronson, to everyone who'd died en route to stage three.

He started upward again, rung by rung. He was moving quickly now, his muscles stretching beyond their capacity, faster, faster, faster. . . .

Suddenly, his fingers scraped against something hard. He looked up—and gasped.

There was a thick metal grill three feet above him. It spanned the entire length of the ventilation tunnel, sealing the shaft halfway between the third and fourth floors.

Jeremy cursed and pushed upward, putting his hands against the grill. He pushed as hard as he could—but the grill was sealed in place. It was at least four inches thick, too strong for the fluoric acid in his doctor's bag. He checked the edges of the thick metal and saw traces of fresh solder; the job had been done recently, perhaps within the last few hours. That could only mean—

"Jeremy, look!"

He spun around. Robin's face was a frozen mask, and she was pointing over his shoulder, at a spot a few feet beyond the metal grill.

He followed her finger with his eyes. Then his stomach dropped.

A video camera was mounted on the shaft wall, staring downward with its single gray eye. It was held in place by twists of thick black electrical tape. Another recent job.

"Back down!" Jeremy hissed. "Fast!"

Christ, he screamed at himself as he followed Robin down the rungs, they'd outguessed him. No doubt they were already on their way into the shaft. The camera had Robin and him directly in its sights, tracking them as they moved through the shaft. They were trapped.

"Wait," Jeremy said, stopping Robin with his voice.

The horizontal shaft that lead to Lyle's lab was just a few rungs away. Jeremy made a quick decision. He slid past Robin, taking the lead. If they couldn't go all the way to Waters's lab, they'd get as close as they could. If Lyle was innocent, he'd have to help them. If he was a part of whatever was going on—Jeremy didn't want to finish the thought.

He crawled into the horizontal shaft, Robin a few lengths behind him. He approached the glowing grate that looked out over the lab, his heart thumping in his chest. He knew he had to move fast; the video camera had assuredly caught their progress back to the third floor. He hurried to the edge of the grate and pressed his face close to the metal.

Lyle's back was to him, his thin shoulders rising and falling under his white lab coat. The top of his head shined, his white-blond hair marred by the straps of his dark safety lenses. He was holding the fluorescing tube in both hands as he scanned a row of petri dishes. The ideal scientist, intent on his experiment, completely oblivious to the time, they day, the world around him.

Jeremy took a deep breath and reached forward with his fingers, feeling the edges of the grate for anything resembling a latch, a hook, a fastening. As far as he could tell, the grate was simply resting on its frame, held tight by its own weight.

He grasped the grate with his fingers and pulled, using his body for leverage. The grate came free, and he carefully handed it over his head to Robin. Then he swung his legs over the edge

He gently lowered himself through the opening. When he was within range of the floor he let go, dropping into the center of the lab.

Lyle didn't look up; he was still completely focused on his petri dishes. Jeremy slid forward, his hands clasped behind his back. When he was close enough he leaned over Lyle's shoulder.

"Hello, Lyle. Are we having fun yet?"

34

LYLE DROPPED THE FLUORESCING TUBE AND WHIRLED ON HIS heels. An initial look of fright changed to puzzlement. "Ross? Where the hell did you come from?"

Just then Robin dropped down from the ceiling, landing in a catlike crouch. Lyle took a step back, ripping off his safety goggles.

"What the hell is going on?"

Jeremy shifted his eyes toward the petri dishes. "Working late? Aren't you supposed to be at the unveiling, along with the rest of the staff?"

Lyle swallowed, his brow furrowing deeper with confusion.

"Yes, well, I was going to head over there as soon as I finished some last-minute work. After the refrigerator mishap set me so far behind—why am I explaining myself to you? You're supposed to be in New York. Victor told me about your friend."

Jeremy's lips became a straight line. "Victor told you?"

"Yes, Victor. About your friend's sudden death. Why you had to leave so abruptly."

Jeremy stared directly into Lyle's eyes. "Yes," he said, "another 'tragedy.' Like Matthew. And his wife. And Warren T. Walker."

Lyle blinked. "Warren T. Walker?"

"You really don't know what I'm talking about?"

Lyle shook his head. Jeremy's chest filled with relief. Lyle was telling the truth. He wasn't involved. Jeremy quickly grabbed his arm.

"Victor killed him. And Matthew. And my friend. He killed all of them. We've got to move fast. They'll be here soon. There was a video camera in the shaft—"

"What are you talking about?"

"They've sequenced a killer gene—"

"Jeremy!" Robin shouted.

Jeremy spun on his heels.

Christina Guarrez was standing in the doorway. A nine-millimeter automatic pistol dangled from her fingers.

"It's okay," Jeremy said as Robin moved next to him. "Guarrez is on our side."

Guarrez nodded, lowering the gun a fraction of an inch. "That's right, Jeremy. We're a team. But you've been keeping secrets from me. I want to know everything—now. What did you hope to find in Waters's lab?"

Jeremy swallowed. A sudden question entered his mind. "How do you know where I was going? How did you find me?"

She reached into her pocket and pulled out a tiny metallic device. A red diode blinked in the center of the device, underneath which a digital readout gave distance and direction. She pointed the device at him, and the red diode blinked faster.

"Technology is wonderful, isn't it? I can follow you anywhere. I let you lead me here; now I want answers."

Jeremy had a sudden memory and reached up and touched the back of his neck. His eyes widened. A tracking device implanted under his skin? He knew immediately that it was possible. "Christ," he whispered, staring at the blinking red diode.

Then Lyle tapped him on the shoulder. "Will someone please tell me what the fuck is going on here?"

"Jeremy," Guarrez angrily interrupted, still standing in the doorway. "Tell me what you know—"

Suddenly, there was a flash of motion behind her. An arm whipped around her throat, pulling her back. A hand pressed against the side of her head, and there was a vicious snap. Her head twisted ninety degrees to the right.

Her entire body went limp, and she slid to the floor. Victor Alexander stepped through the doorway, a bandage on his head and a thin smile on his lips.

"Wonderful, the gang's all here. Very thoughtful of you, Jeremy. This makes it so much easier for me."

His left hand moved toward his jacket pocket.

Jeremy didn't stop to think. He leapt past Lyle and grabbed the fluorescing tube off the counter. He hit the switch and aimed the tube at Victor's face.

Victor screamed, reaching for his eyes. His face glowed in the blue light as he stumbled backward, blinded. Jeremy threw the tube at him, hitting him in the shoulder.

"Quick! Lyle, we've got to get to Waters's lab!"

"How? I told you, the elevator has a palm-plate lock!"

"We have to find some other way."

Suddenly, there were footsteps in the doorway. A man in a blue suit crashed into the room, stopping next to Victor's crouched form. He had a submachine gun slung over his shoulder.

Jeremy caught Robin around her waist and shoved her into the first aisle, throwing himself on top of her. The submachine gun erupted, spraying the lab. Test tubes exploded around Jeremy as he lay on top of Robin, shielded by the row of sinks. He had no idea where Lyle was, whether or not he was still alive. He covered his face as the rain of glass continued.

Then he felt Robin struggling beneath him. He rolled to one side and she came up on one knee, the partially open doctor's bag clutched between her hands. On the floor, directly in front of her, was the vial of fluoric acid. She quickly snatched it up.

Instantly, Jeremy knew what she was thinking. He watched as she hurled the vial at the doorway.

There was a loud pop and suddenly, the submachine gun went silent. The sound was replaced by a high-pitched scream.

Jeremy leapt to his feet. The man had dropped his gun and was slapping at his face, spinning like a possessed top. Victor was off to one side, watching him through swollen red eyes. The Englishman was about to say something when a figure sprung toward him, catching him from behind. There was a flash of white lab coat as they hit the ground, and Jeremy called out:

"Lyle!"

The two bodies rolled across the lab, Lyle's thin fists churning against Victor's injured body. Jeremy grabbed Robin's hand and pulled her toward the door.

"We have to help him," she said.

Then there was a loud crack and Lyle's body went limp. Jeremy screamed to himself, then hastily pulled Robin through the open doorway.

The hallway was empty. Jeremy threw a glance in the direction of the private elevator, then shook his head. There was no way past the palm plate. He led Robin in the opposite direction, his mind whirling.

Without warning, something slammed into his shoulder, sending him spinning away from Robin. He hit the wall, one knee dropping to the ground, pain shooting down his arm. He reached for the source of the pain and felt blood.

Terrified, he realized he'd just been shot. He looked back toward the lab.

Victor was halfway through the open doorway, his .38 hanging from his fingers. He was fighting to focus his eyes.

"Jeremy," he whispered. "I can almost see you. Better run, run fast, run away."

Jeremy reached for Robin's hand and scrambled to his feet.

"Jeremy," Victor rasped, "better run . . ."

Jeremy and Robin sprinted around the corner.

From the skywalk, Jeremy could see that it had begun raining again, and this time the storm appeared even more frightening and violent. Raindrops clattered against the Plexiglas walls, and the entire complex seemed to sway, battered by the powerful gusts of wind.

Jeremy plodded through the skywalk, his hand pressed tightly against his shoulder. Dark blood dribbled out between his fingers.

Robin touched the back of his neck. He could feel the damp sweat on her palm.

"Jeremy," she whispered. "Are you all right?"

He didn't answer. The pain was horrible, ripping up and down his shoulder. But worse than the pain was the frustration. They'd come so close. Now they had no choice but to run.

"Have to go out through the hospital," he said through clenched teeth. "Get outside, away from here."

But he knew that the thought was absurd. There were sure to be men with guns waiting in the emergency room. And there was no way to double back—Victor was behind them, somewhere. They were trapped. They couldn't go back through the ventilation tunnel—and the only escape routes he knew of were behind him, blocked by Victor.

Jeremy groaned, coming to a halt. The pain was filling him up, weighing him down.

"Jeremy," Robin pleaded. "Stay in control. Please . . ."

He squeezed his eyes shut. She was right, he had to fight through the pain. He took a deep breath and removed his hand from the wound. Thankfully, it didn't look as bad as it felt.

"The bullet didn't go too deep," he murmured. "It just tore through the skin."

With Robin's help, he ripped off a section of his sleeve and tied it around the wound, a makeshift bandage. It wasn't great, but it was enough to stop the bleeding. Then he had another thought. He turned his head, showing Robin the scratch on the back of his neck.

"There's something just under the skin. Can you see it?"

She ran her fingers over the ridged scratch. Then she nodded. "A tiny bump."

"Get it out." Guarrez was dead, but there was no telling who else was tracking him.

She carefully dragged her fingernails across the scratch. He felt a tiny sting, then Robin held out her hand. The tracking device was half the size of a tick, with infinitesimal leads. He took it from her and tossed it to the floor. He crushed it with two twists of his foot. Meanwhile, his mind went to work.

Only four minutes had passed since they'd left Victor, but it seemed like hours. Their situation was desperate. They had no choice but to keep moving. Maybe someone in the hospital would be able to help—a doctor, or a nurse. Maybe they'd find another way out.

They pushed forward, not speaking—there was little left to say and no time to say it. At the western end of the skywalk, he glanced back over his shoulder. No sign of Victor. But there was no doubt in Jeremy's mind—the man was coming. Sooner or later, he'd find them.

Jeremy grimaced at the thought. Then he reached up with his good hand and found the button next to the steel door. There was a tiny whirring, and the door to West slid open.

He and Robin stumbled forward into the hospital.

35

THE HALLWAYS WERE FULL OF THE SOUND OF SLEEPING PA-
tients and gentle monitoring devices, but there were no signs
of any doctors—in itself, an unsettling thought. A hospital
without doctors wasn't a hospital; it was a place where people gathered to die.

Jeremy coughed, shivering. His mind was blurry, and he
wondered how much blood he'd lost. Enough to send him
into shock? He glanced at Robin, moving beside him. Her
face was a grim mask. He had to stay alert, in control. She
was counting on him.

They continued down the dark hallways. With each step,
his frustration multiplied. Waters's lab was in the other direction. And every second brought them closer to the final
moment—stage three. By now, all of Tucsome's staff
would be gathered at Lester Auditorium. Perhaps Waters
was already on his way, ready to unveil his experiment.
Could it already be too late? Was Waters behind the killer
genes? Was stage three the highlight of his unveiling?

"Must be *some* way to stop them," Jeremy said out loud.

Robin looked at him, read his mind. "We have to stay *alive*. That's what matters now."

They turned another corner, and Jeremy saw something that made him pause. A door with silver lettering on it: MRI CENTER.

He suddenly realized where they were. He led Robin forward, taking the last few steps in a daze. The sound of a baseball game swam in his ears.

Stephen was strapped to his bed, his head resting against a firm pillow. His eyes were wide open, his jaw grinding. A Mets-Cubs game was on the television screen, flashing colors echoing off the room's white walls.

Jeremy stood next to Robin in the doorway, watching the Lesch-Nyhan child. What a horrible hand fate had dealt him.

"Fate," Jeremy whispered. "Or perhaps Jason Waters."

"Jeremy," Robin said. "Come on. We have to keep moving."

As if to reinforce what she'd just said, they heard muffled footsteps coming from the hallway. Suddenly, Victor's voice echoed through the hospital.

"Jeremy. Come out, come out, wherever you are."

Jeremy stared grimly at Robin. Then he shifted his eyes to the little boy strapped to the bed. Stephen began to thrash against his bonds. Jeremy paused as a memory surfaced.

"Jeremy," Victor's voice continued. "We have unfinished business, you and I."

Jeremy searched the hospital room with his eyes.

"Come on," Robin whispered. "He's going to find us—"

"Wait. I have an idea."

He found the Little Slugger baseball bat where he'd seen it before, leaning beneath the television. He hefted it in front of his face. It weighed about six pounds, carved from a thick wood that might have been ash.

"What are you going to do with that?"

He turned toward her. "Follow my lead."

"I hope you know what you're doing."

He set his jaw, balancing the bat between his hands, then tried a little mock bravado: "At the least we'll go down swinging."

The hallway was empty, but the sound of Victor's footsteps reverberated off the walls. He was right around the corner, moving closer.

Jeremy led Robin across the hall and through the door with silver lettering. The MRI center was set up the same as at New York City Hospital, the computer room and the MRI machine separated by a thick glass wall. To Jeremy's right, a bank of 3-D visualization computers glowed, screens churning through colors as some preprogrammed screen saver pitched pixels against one another, a war of rainbows.

Robin raised her eyebrows, staring at the machine on the other side of the glass wall. "I recognize that thing. They put you inside it, after your attack."

He nodded, leading her into the center of the room. He shifted his weight from foot to foot, his hands tight against the baseball bat. This was going to be tricky. Very tricky.

He peered through the glass wall. The huge MRI machine hummed in untroubled loneliness, its purring magnified by the thick glass.

"I think the cat-and-mouse game is over, Jeremy."

Jeremy whirled around, hiding the baseball bat behind his back. Robin rushed to his side.

Victor was standing in the doorway. His eyes were red slits, his face a collage of welts, burns, and bruises. But the .38 automatic was still there, delicately balanced between the fingers of his right hand.

"I've really enjoyed working with you," he said, his voice more air than sound. "You impress me to no end. And you—Ms. Kelly, isn't it? I should have put two and two together. Still, it doesn't matter. The game ends here. I won't underestimate either of you again."

Jeremy swallowed and took a step back. Robin followed.

He forced a visible shudder through his shoulders, bending slightly forward.

Victor smiled. "Ah, there it is. The fear. The panic. I know all about the panic."

Jeremy took another step back. His chest quivered, and his breath became short. Robin stared at him, but remained silent, moving with him. Victor took another small step forward.

"Panic-anxiety syndrome. Did I get it right? A nervous condition. You and I are really more similar than you could imagine."

Jeremy felt the glass door behind him. He pushed back, and it swung open. He took a tiny step into the glass room. Robin stopped where she was, but Victor moved with him, coming forward, the gun rising.

"Ironic, isn't it? You'd think we'd have nothing in common. But there it is—a certain sensitivity. Perhaps that's what has made us such an even match. Up until now, that is."

Jeremy coughed, as if choking. He stumbled, moving back three steps at once. Victor swept after him, his gun extended in front of him. Robin was on the other side of the glass, watching.

"I'm going to enjoy killing you," Victor said carefully. "I want you to know that. You, and then Ms. Kelly here." He gave a nod of the head. "I'm going to enjoy every moment."

Jeremy bowed his head and took one last step back.

Victor moved a few inches forward, aiming the gun at the center of Jeremy's bowed head. "Even though it's just a job—"

The gun began to tremble. At first, the motion was imperceptible. Then the trembling grew stronger, the gun jumping up and down as if buffeted by a strong wind.

Victor stared at the gun, confused. His eyes widened. The trembling grew even stronger. Vicious. The gun jagged back and forth.

Suddenly, the gun ripped out of his hand. It flew through the air and crashed into the MRI machine.

Victor's jaw dropped open. "How?"

Jeremy swung the baseball bat with all of his strength, and the bat crashed into the side of Victor's head. There was a sickening crunch, and Victor collapsed to the ground.

Jeremy stood over him, the bat gripped tightly in his hands.

"That one was for Mike."

Robin rushed into the room, her face a mixture of relief and nausea. She looked down at Victor's crumpled form, blood spewing from his head. "Is he dead?"

Jeremy bent to one knee. Tucsome's "director of Human Resources" no longer had a pulse, and his chest was flat, not moving. "He's not going to bother us anymore," Jeremy murmured.

As he raised himself to his feet, he had a sudden realization. His throat wasn't constricted. His breathing was fine. There was no sign of the panic, not even the slightest tinge of fear. He'd delivered a fatal blow—and had remained in control.

What for the past few days had been a merely an intuition was now a conviction. He'd pulled the monkey off his back. He'd put panic-anxiety syndrome behind him—permanently.

"Can we double back now?" Robin asked. "Find our way out through the labs?"

Jeremy paused. "I have a better idea."

He reached into the doctor's bag and drew out the scalpel. Then he crossed back to the crumpled body.

"What are you going to do?"

"Save us some time. We need to get inside Waters's lab—and good old Victor's going to give us a hand."

Jeremy unrolled Victor's sleeve. He paused, steeling himself for what he was about to do. He thought of the call informing him Mike Callahan had died . . . and of how many times he himself had almost died this night . . . and of how close he'd come to losing Robin—and a flush of red anger swept away any squeamishness. He carefully pressed the scalpel against Victor's flesh, just below the wrist. Then, with one steady twist, he sliced off a three-inch section of Victor's palm.

36

THE TWIN STEEL DOORS WAITED PATIENTLY AT THE END OF THE hall. Jeremy and Robin approached the elevator cautiously, their feet silent against the thick carpet. Robin had the Little Slugger baseball bat clenched tight in her hands. Jeremy held the three-inch slice of skin.

They paused a few feet in front of the steel doors.

"This is it?" she asked.

He nodded. He turned toward the palm plate and raised the slab of skin. Victor's disembodied palm fit across the center of the metal imprint. There was a mechanical whir, and the steel doors slid open.

Jeremy let the skin fall to the floor. He followed Robin into the elevator and watched as the doors slid shut behind them.

"Why am I so frightened?" she whispered as the elevator rumbled upward.

He felt a sweat break out on his own back. There was a good chance they were already too late. Waters could already be on his way to Lester Auditorium, stage three in hand. And even if they weren't too late, they still had no idea what they were going to face. Was stage three some sort of terrible weapon, a step past the killer gene that had killed Mike Callahan and Warren Walker? Or was it something else entirely? Something that would explain the $60 billion of government money? Something that could explain Jason Waters's involvement, how one of the greatest scientists in history came to be involved with a man like Victor Alexander?

"Robin," Jeremy said, holding out his good hand. "Maybe I better take the bat."

A current of electricity ran up his spine as he wrapped his hands around the stiff wood. He repeated to himself his two goals: He had to find the killer-gene sequences. Then he had to stop stage three. Even if that meant going head-to-head with Waters himself.

As the elevator rushed upward, Robin touched his arm. "You said we had to find the gene sequences. What are they, exactly? How will I know if I see them?"

"They'll be stored somewhere in the lab—perhaps in a computer, or on CD-ROMs, or even on floppies. With the sequences, we can prove that your father was murdered. And Mike Callahan."

She nodded, and he could read the determination in her eyes. He touched her hand and was amazed at the warm surge that swept through his body. His other hand tightened against the baseball bat.

Suddenly, the elevator doors whiffed open.

"Bright enough in here," Robin whispered, shielding her eyes as she stepped forward into the lab.

Jeremy followed after her, his gaze shifting back and forth. The lab was as he'd remembered it, an awesome sight.

"This stuff looks expensive."

"More expensive than you can imagine," he whispered back.

She took another step forward and paused.

"What the hell is that?"

She was pointing at an enormous pressurized cylinder full of clear liquid. On top of the cylinder was a galvanized rubber nozzle, attached by a long wire to a foot pedal on the floor.

"A supercooled liquid nitrogen dispenser," he responded. "It's used to freeze things. The container is specially designed to keep the nitrogen at less than negative thirty degrees Celsius."

"That's pretty cold."

"And state-of-the-art. Everything in here is years ahead of the market. This is what a genetics laboratory will look like in ten years."

"Including the wolves?" Robin said, her eyes wide.

Jeremy followed her toward the corner of the lab. The two adult wolves in the larger cage were standing stock-still, their red eyes narrow, their teeth bared.

"Be careful," he warned. "They don't look friendly."

"What are they staring at?"

He followed the animals' eyes. The smaller cage was empty. On top of the cage was a glass cubicle, barely three feet high. The small wolf cub was inside, its snout pressed against the glass. The cub looked unhappy, and Jeremy could understand why. Instead of airholes, there was a strange valve contraption on the lid of the cubicle. One shift of the valve and the poor animal would suffocate.

"Should we set it free?" Robin whispered.

Jeremy shook his head. "We don't have time."

"Then let's get moving. Spread out. We're looking for computer disks?"

"Right."

She took the left half of the lab; he shifted toward the right. He passed a counter with a row of Bunsen burners, a glass cabinet full of flammables, a test-tube rack, a shelf cluttered with beakers—and then he paused. He was a few feet from the back wall. The row of steel canisters stood in front of him. He counted them with his eyes.

This time there were only fifty-nine. He shifted his eyes to the black valves that connected the canisters to the rubber shaft that led toward the ceiling. He moved up the shaft, pausing at the black sign with the bright red digital display.

INTEGRITY: NINETY PERCENT.

He tried to remember what it had said the last time he was in Waters's lab. Something lower, he thought. The integrity was rising. What the hell did that mean? Was it significant? He shifted his eyes back to the canisters—

"Jeremy! Over here. I think I found something."

He turned toward Robin's voice. She was standing beneath an open cabinet. She smiled, holding something up.

CD-ROMs. At least a dozen disks.

"There's a computer over here. Come on, let's see what we've got."

He hurried across the lab. She had the computer warmed up by the time he got to her, and shoved one of the CD-ROMs into the proper slot.

The screen blinked, and then a long list filled the screen. Jeremy leaned forward, confused.

"What the hell?"

The screen began to scroll. The list continued growing, the green letters doubling and tripling.

"Hold on. Make it slow down."

"How?"

"I don't know. Do something."

She hit the keyboard. The screen froze. He stared at the list, shock spreading through his body.

"MUSCULATURE POTENTIAL: CHROMOSOME 9: LOCI-D18S232."

"MARROW CONSISTENCY: CHROMOSOME 13: LOCI-D78G452."

"COGNITIVE FACILITIES: CHROMOSOME 15: LOCI . . ."

"EPIDERMAL TEXTURE: CHROMOSOME 9 . . ."

"ANGER RESPONSE . . ."

"AGILITY QUOTIENT . . ."

He continued down the list. Trembling, he touched the keyboard. The list began to scroll, hundreds of lines passing across the screen. He hit the keyboard again:

"HAIR COLOR. JAW STRUCTURE. SKULL SIZE. VIOLENCE POTENTIAL . . ."

"Jeremy, what is this?"

He didn't answer. He found the arrow keys and moved the cursor so that it was blinking in front of the entry marked "HAIR COLOR." Then he hit the space bar.

"ATAGTCTCTAGCATCCTAGCAAGT . . ."

"It's a sequence, right? The DNA code you were talking about?"

He nodded, his eyes wide. "Yes, it's a sequence. It codes for the color of human hair."

"Human hair? What does that have to do with the killer genes?"

He turned away from the screen. He looked at the CD-ROMs in her hands. Twelve, including the one in the computer. How many sequences could be stored on twelve CD-ROMs? A thousand? Ten thousand? He wiped the sweat from his forehead.

"Jeremy, what is it? What does this mean?"

"I'm not sure . . . I—" Suddenly, he turned back toward the canisters by the far wall. His eyes slid up the rubber shaft, to where it disappeared into the ceiling. Then he shifted his gaze to the digital scoreboard.

INTEGRITY: NINETY-ONE PERCENT.

"Oh, my God."

Suddenly, it all clicked into place. Sixty billion dollars. The difference between stage one and stage two, the method of infection. The missing filters in the ventilation tunnel. And something else, something he'd seen the last time he was in Waters's lab.

He turned toward the back wall, a few yards to the right of the canisters. His eyes found the sealed steel door with the rounded edges—the low-pressure room, kept extremely close to an artificial vacuum. The perfect place to develop a virus.

An airborne virus.

"Robin," he said loudly, grabbing one of the CD-ROMs out of her hand. "Stage three! It's not a weapon at all! It's something worse. Much worse."

"What are you talking about? The funding came from the Defense Department—"

"The people behind the money might think it's a weapon. But the killer genes were just a ruse. Waters is planning something else entirely."

She stared at him. "What do you mean?"

He leaned over the computer. He found a menu of options and chose a command: "TIME-CODED VISUALIZATION." The screen went blank, then was replaced by a crude graphic representation of a man and a woman, standing side by side. Underneath the picture was a time bar, beginning at year zero. As the time bar moved across the bottom of the screen, the pictures began to change.

"What's happening?" Robin whispered, enthralled by the pictures on the screen.

Jeremy didn't answer. He was similarly captivated by the display.

The first changes ensued almost immediately. The figures on the screen shifted in form, representing modifications in musculature and bone structure. The male grew wider in the shoulders, longer in the legs, taller, his spine adding vertebrae, his rib cage doubling in capacity. The woman also grew in height, her body conforming to a new feminine ideal; hips wide and long, skeleton lithe and perfectly symmetrical, cranium three-quarters the size of the male, shoulders pulled back in a classic arch.

Next came the surface changes, color, physical attributes. Both figures were given white-blond hair, startlingly blue eyes, strong white teeth, skin like oiled caramel. Then came the more striking changes: As Jeremy watched in awe, the figures' hands became longer, almost fluid. A sixth finger sprouted between the thumb and pointer, and the wrist became completely tensile, allowing 360 degrees of rotation. Other joints followed the same model: the knees, ankles, elbows, shoulders. The two figures began to move across the screen, turning at impossible angles, mimicking immense speeds.

"My God," Robin whispered. "They're beautiful."

Jeremy couldn't help but agree. The creatures on the screen *were* beautiful; still human in form, but something more, something smoother and faster and exquisitely graceful. They returned to the center of the screen, shoulders wide, arms spread, legs firmly stationed. Then the screen started to shimmer.

"What's happening now?" Robin asked. Jeremy shifted his eyes to the time bar. It swept across the bottom of the screen, marking the passage of years: ten, twenty, thirty—then generations, centuries. He moved his eyes back to the two figures in the center of the screen.

Again they began to change; but this time the changes were more subtle, many of them difficult to comprehend. As he watched, the male figure's brain magnified to fill half the screen, and sections changed colors, some growing, others dwindling away.

"I think I understand," he said, pointing. "Over here is the cerebrum, the center of the brain dedicated to logical thought. It's almost doubled in size. And over here is the limbic system, which is associated with emotions and violence. It's shrunk down—almost a quarter of its original capacity. Over here is the cerebral cortex; it's the center of motor control. There are some changes here in shape and density—"

"Jeremy," Robin interrupted, staring at the screen, "what does this mean?"

"Look at the time bar. These changes are generational. The earlier changes ensued almost immediately. Others, I'm sure, will take even longer. But it's clear what's happening." He turned toward her. "Eugenics."

"Eugenics?" she whispered. "You mean, the 'master race' stuff the Nazis used to talk about?"

"Sort of," Jeremy said. "We're talking genetic engineering on a massive scale." He looked back at the computer screen. "Linking genes to specific characteristics, then deciding which characteristics should be enhanced, which eliminated. Controlled evolution. Using genes to change our muscles, our brains, our personalities."

Robin pointed at the two figures in the center of the screen. "You mean this is what we'll become? How is that possible?"

Jeremy turned back toward the canisters on the other side of the lab. He ran his eyes up the rubber shaft that led to the grate in the ceiling.

"First," he said, "there were the autopsy reports. The retroviruses were inserted into the victims' bloodstreams in a controlled environment—stage one. Then, your father was infected with the retroviruses in an uncontrolled environment—stage two. And now—"

"The human species crosses a new threshold."

Jeremy spun on his heels. Jason Waters was standing in the doorway to the laboratory, a canister in his hands.

"The power of the genome," Waters continued, "is without limitation. Man perfects himself by perfecting his genome. Do you know what we call a man with a perfect genome?"

Jeremy stared at the scientist. Waters smiled back.

"We call that man God."

Waters moved forward, the steel canister steady in his hands. It was identical to the fifty-nine lined up against the laboratory wall.

"All this so that you can dictate the next phase of evolution," Jeremy whispered, gesturing around the lab. "You've gone insane."

Waters shook his head, still moving forward. He crossed a few feet away from Jeremy and Robin and paused in front of the glass cubicle containing the wolf cub. Before Jeremy could do anything, he leaned forward and screwed the canister into the valve on the lid of the cubicle.

"Actually, my sanity is quite intact. As much as you'd like to believe otherwise, I'm not mad, cackling away in my private lab. I'm a geneticist who's managed to take our science to an entirely new level."

Jeremy took a step toward him, the bat tight in his fist. "This plan of yours—what gives you the right?"

Waters laughed. "It isn't my right—it's my responsibility. Isn't it the scientist's duty to create a better future? Isn't that the point of technology? I'm doing what any responsible man in my position would do. I'm giving humanity a precious gift. Perfection."

He leaned forward and pressed something on the glass cubicle containing the wolf cub. Then he took a step back.

There was a soft hissing sound. Suddenly, the wolf cub began to tremble. A low whimper rose from its chest. The two adult wolves crashed against the side of their cage, howling in anger.

Jeremy had the sudden urge to break the glass, to free the poor animal. Waters held up his hands.

"The cubicle is made out of high-tensile Plexiglas. It's completely airtight, and can withstand three thousand pounds of pressure."

Jeremy stared at the cub. Robin moved beside him.

"What's happening to it?"

The animal had begun to twitch. Suddenly, it lurched into the air, pawing at its own face. Then it collapsed to the ground. The adult wolves screamed in rage, tearing at the cage door. But the steel padlock held them back.

"Governments are only interested in one thing," Waters said. "Weapons." He gestured to the cage. "This is a part of the demonstration my 'financiers,' so to speak, believed would take place in Lester Auditorium. My speech was to have read: 'Genetics has produced a weapon powerful enough to protect our way of life'—so on and so forth.

"Of course, I intend to stage a far more dramatic unveiling. No doubt, the people who've funded me these many years will be livid, but, I feel sure that history will acknowledge my accomplishment."

Jeremy turned toward the fifty-nine steel canisters that lined the back wall. The digital display gaped at him.

INTEGRITY: NINETY-TWO PERCENT.

He turned back toward Waters. "You've made the retrovirus airborne. You're going to release it into the ventilation system. It will be carried outside, where it will multiply, infecting everyone. Everywhere. And the human race will change. Some of the changes will be immediate. Others will take place over generations."

Waters looked Jeremy straight in the eyes. "This is the power that genetics has given us—the power to re-create ourselves. Don't you see—this is what we've worked so hard to achieve! Here it is, right in front of you! Can't you understand, this is a time for celebration!"

Jeremy's cheeks whitened. In truth, a tiny part of him felt a rush of excitement at Waters's bold words. But a larger part saw the arrogance—the sweeping arrogance—that had spurred Waters to do what he'd done. Who was Waters to decide what the human race should look like? Or how it should behave? Or what it should think about? Who was *he* to decide the future?

"This is wrong," Jeremy said finally. "You've abused your genius. You've violated science. You have no right to tamper with the genetic evolution of an entire species. Damn it, you have to stop this—"

"There is no stopping the inevitable," said Waters. He pointed toward the digital display hanging above the steel canisters:

INTEGRITY: NINETY-THREE PERCENT.

"That display represents the viral integrity inside the canisters. When the integrity reaches a hundred percent, the valves will automatically open."

He gestured toward the rubber shaft that disappeared into

the ceiling. "By the time the retroviruses reach the outside world, they will number in the trillions. They'll enter the airstream, traveling around the world in a matter of days. There's nothing you or I can do—except breathe deep the future."

Deep inside of him, Jeremy knew that he didn't want to live in a society where everyone was modeled on Jason Waters's vision of perfection. Waters's vision was skewed. If Jeremy hadn't known it before, he knew it now.

"There's got to be a way. I'll destroy them, incinerate them—"

"You'll do nothing of the sort."

Waters's white lab coat fluttered as he extended his right arm. In his hand was a tiny revolver. Jeremy's eyes focused on the centimeter-wide barrel.

"Drop the bat and take a step back," Waters ordered.

Jeremy felt his stomach tighten. Waters was six feet away, the revolver hanging in the air, his grip loose but steady. He'd get off one shot before Jeremy reached him. At that range, it was doubtful he'd miss.

"You heard me," Waters repeated. "I'm not a killer, but if I have to shoot you to ensure the successful completion of this project, I will. Drop the bat and step back."

Behind him, the digital display clicked: INTEGRITY: NINETY-FOUR PERCENT. Jeremy brought his eyes back to the tiny gun. An absurd thought danced through his head: He'd taken a bullet before. . . .

But not at such close range. He needed a distraction, something to put Waters off guard. He flicked his eyes back and forth, feverishly searching for something, anything.

And then he saw it, a few feet from his right foot. A plastic pedal. His eyes followed the twist of wire that ran from the pedal up the side of the enormous container of liquid nitrogen. The nozzle was roughly pointing in Waters's direction.

Jeremy loosened his fingers, letting the baseball bat fall to the floor. It hit with a clatter, and Waters relaxed. The tiny revolver dipped a fraction of an inch.

"I'm glad you've come to your senses," Waters started. "Now, if you and your lady friend here will just move—"

Suddenly, Jeremy slammed his foot against the plastic pedal. A spray of thick white steam erupted out of the nozzle, instantly cutting off Waters's line of vision. Waters recoiled backward, cursing. Jeremy lunged forward, hurling himself through the steam. The steam bit at his skin, singeing him, but in a second he was through to the other side, rage and pain spurring him on.

Waters saw him and his eyes went wide. The revolver bucked upward, but too late. There was a high-pitched cough and Jeremy felt something whiz by his right ear. Then there was a loud pop, followed by a fearful, tremendous gushing. Jeremy looked back over his shoulder and gasped. The projectile had ruptured the liquid nitrogen dispenser. The clear liquid was streaming out onto the floor, skidding unnaturally across the porcelain tiles, freezing everything it touched.

"Robin!" Jeremy screamed, still careening forward. "Stay away from the—"

His warning was interrupted as he collided with Waters. The two men hit a low counter and test tubes crashed to the floor. Waters screamed, trying to reaim the revolver, while Jeremy grabbed at him with both hands. Jeremy's fingers found Waters's wrist and the gun froze in the air, inches from Jeremy's head. Jeremy's hurt shoulder cried out but he focused his strength, pinning Waters back against the counter.

Waters howled, twisting with amazing strength. Jeremy almost lost his grip but somehow held on, the revolver still hanging in the air, the barrel pointing straight toward the ceiling. Waters shoved off the counter, sending them spinning toward the center of the lab. Jeremy's feet touched something slippery and he gasped, fighting to keep his balance. The floor beneath him had frozen solid. Out of the corner of his eyes, he saw that the liquid nitrogen dispenser had fallen over and was now leaning up against the back wall, spraying clear liquid in an upward arc. The liquid had completely coated a section of the wall and was dribbling down the steel door that led to the low-pressure room. He felt a new burst of fear; tiny cracks had begun to form in the steel.

Jeremy knew he had to end this, quickly. But Waters was much stronger than he'd assumed—and Jeremy was weakened by exhaustion and the wound in his shoulder. Slowly, the revolver inched downward.

Then there was a flash of motion and something hit Waters from behind, pitching both of them forward. Jeremy caught a glimpse of Robin, the baseball bat in her hands, before the breath was knocked out of him as he crashed back into the wolf cage. He lost his grip for an instant and the gun swung toward him. At the last second, he caught Waters's wrist, turning the barrel away; there was another loud cough, and Jeremy's eyes went wide.

He watched as the projectile hit the direct center of the steel door to the low-pressure room. A three-foot section of the steel—frozen to brittleness—shattered like glass. Suddenly, there was a sound like nothing he'd ever heard before. The entire lab seemed to buckle inward; then everything was flying toward the gaping hole in the steel door. He felt the air rip out of his lungs as his eardrums popped, and he grasped at the wolf cage. A rack of test tubes flew by his shoulder. A beaker ripped past his head, colliding midair with a portable fire extinguisher. Glass shards swirled toward the back wall, propelled by the vacuum, deadly sharp rockets crisscrossing the lab at unbelievable speeds.

Jeremy felt his feet slipping off of the floor, and he tightened his grip against the wolf cage. Waters was still next to him, also desperately hanging on to the cage, the gun pinned against the metal links. Jeremy could see Robin on the other side of the lab, her hands wrapped around the leg of the computer table. As he watched, the computer table skidded a few inches toward the back wall, and she screamed, scrambling to hold on.

With immense effort, he filled his lungs with air.

"Keep your head down!" he shouted in her direction.

A test tube missed her by a fraction of an inch, shattering against the tabletop. The table skidded another foot, then jammed against a cabinet, finally anchored. Jeremy gasped in relief. She'd be okay. The table would hold.

He shifted his eyes toward the center of the lab and watched as the half-empty liquid nitrogen dispenser lifted off the ground and disappeared into the low-pressure room. Then his eyes moved to the fifty-nine steel canisters. They hadn't moved; obviously, they were welded tightly together, moored to the rubber shaft that led to the ceiling. Above them, the digital display clicked again, oblivious to the discord: INTEGRITY: NINETY-FIVE PERCENT.

He felt the breath run out of him. He had to do something quick.

Suddenly, there was a flicker of motion to his right. Waters had turned toward him and was struggling to aim the gun. Jeremy cursed and dove at him. He caught Waters's wrist, pinning it back against the top of the cage. The wolves howled, crashing upward, maddened by the chaos. Jeremy's feet skidded against the floor as he fought the vacuum, his eyes focused on a sealed circular vent directly above the wolves, about twelve inches in diameter; next to the vent was a DNA palm plate, similar to the one outside Waters's private elevator.

Waters was grunting now, struggling to lift his arm, trying to regain control of the gun. Jeremy let up for a second, then slammed Waters's hand against the top of the cage. Waters's grip held, but his arm weakened, and Jeremy repeated the motion.

This time, Waters's hand hit the palm plate dead center, and there was a sudden whirring. The feeding vent opened up, and Jeremy could see the snapping jaws of the wolves, the vicious triangular fangs. Reflex took over and he fell back, his hands involuntarily loosening. Waters snarled in victory, and suddenly the gun was racing toward Jeremy's face.

Without thinking, Jeremy gathered all his strength and dove at Waters's arm, catching him a few inches below the wrist. Both men toppled backward onto the cage, Jeremy's eyes wildly searching for the gun. Somehow, the gun had disappeared. Jeremy realized with a start that Waters's hand was gone too, shoved directly through the circular vent in the top of the wolf cage.

Suddenly, an immense scream erupted across the lab. Waters's entire body jerked upward, his right arm disappearing through the feeding vent. Jeremy's hands opened and he toppled away, skidding across the floor, picked up by the vacuum. He could hear the wolves thrashing, their feet scraping against the cage floor. Waters was halfway on top of the cage, his right arm pulled deep inside, his body twitching as the wolves tore at him, his face a mask of agony.

Then Jeremy's back slammed into something hard and he groaned, his hands flailing. He whipped his head to the side and was suddenly staring at a dead wolf cub. The Plexiglas cubicle was against his back, also sliding toward the low-pressure room. As the gaping opening came closer and closer, Jeremy's eyes measured the width of the Plexiglas cube and the width of the shattered steel door—and he realized instantly that it was going to be close. Extremely close. But if the angle was right . . .

At the last second, he shoved his weight against the cube and turned it sideways. It jammed against the opening and stopped dead, pinned by the differences in pressure. There was still a hiss of vacuum around the edges of the cube, but barely enough to lift a test tube.

Jeremy collapsed back from the cube and pushed himself to his knees. The floor beneath him was frozen solid, and he slid forward, his eyes wide, taking in the ruined laboratory. He focused on Waters, still hunched over the wolf cage, his body motionless. *I should free him,* he thought. *Even if he's dead.* Grasping the edge of a console, he raised himself up and stagger-stepped in Waters's direction.

"Jeremy, hurry! The canisters!"

Hearing Robin's voice, all thoughts of Waters vanished.

Jeremy's eyes were immediately caught by the digital display:

INTEGRITY: NINETY-SIX PERCENT.

He scrambled past Robin and skidded to a stop next to the nearest canister, reaching for its black valve. The valve was sealed tight, immovable. He cursed, his fingers scraping helplessly against the rubber.

"Damn it. These things aren't going to come loose."

He glanced up at the digital display. INTEGRITY: NINETY-SEVEN PERCENT. Shit, he screamed at himself, think of *something*.

Robin ran to his side, offering him the bat. He shook his head.

"That won't do any good. If we rupture the canisters, the virus will come pouring out—"

He thought furiously. There was no way of stopping the virus from being released. But if it could be contained . . .

He took the bat from Robin and centered his eyes on the rubber duct. He swung with all of his strength, hitting the duct high, close to the ceiling. There was a sharp tearing and the duct came loose. He dropped the bat and grabbed the duct, using his weight to pull it down. In a few seconds he had it against his chest, aiming toward the back wall. The length looked about right; pulled tight, the duct would just barely reach.

"What are you doing?" she asked, staring at him.

"We've got to send the virus into a vacuum. Come on, help me pull this over to the opening."

She added her weight to his, and together they dragged the duct toward the back wall. When they reached the Plexiglas cubicle they stopped, sweating from the effort. Above them, the digital display clicked on:

INTEGRITY: NINETY-EIGHT PERCENT.

Jeremy spun toward Robin. "We don't have much time. Brace yourself as best you can. And whatever else happens, we have to keep the duct aimed toward the vacuum. We can't risk any of the retroviruses escaping into the lab."

She nodded, anchoring her body against the back wall, both hands tight around the rubber duct. He turned toward the Plexiglas cube. It was stuck tight—but if he was lucky, the floor underneath was still frozen and slippery. He put his palms against the Plexiglas, gathering his strength. Then he shoved with everything he had left.

Slowly, the Plexiglas cube slid forward. Jeremy grunted, kicking back with his heels—and the vacuum suddenly reopened, ripping him forward. He flailed his hands behind his back, grasping wildly. At the last second, his fingers found the rubber duct, and he managed to steady himself against the wall.

Then he nodded at Robin, and together they carefully worked the end of the duct into the opening. When the duct was firmly in place, Jeremy turned back toward the digital display.

INTEGRITY: NINETY-NINE PERCENT.

"Here we go," he whispered to Robin, bracing himself.

The digital display clicked again, and there was a loud hissing sound. He felt the duct shiver beneath his fingers, and he grasped it tightly, making sure it was aimed directly into the vacuum. The hissing lasted a good thirty seconds, then stopped abruptly.

"Was that it?" Robin asked, her voice meek against the sound of the vacuum.

"I think so," he responded. "But I think we should leave the duct where it is. Just in case."

She nodded. He carefully reached around the duct and grabbed the edge of the Plexiglas cube. With Robin's help, he managed to slide the cube back over part of the hole, pinning the duct in place. The vacuum decreased to a manageable breeze.

"Will the vacuum kill the virus?" Robin asked as they backed away from the mostly plugged opening.

Jeremy shrugged. His entire body was trembling, a mixture of blood loss, exhaustion, and raw emotion. Was it really over?

"There's no way to be certain. We have to get out of here and find help—somebody who can make sure this low-pressure room is bombarded with high-intensity radiation."

He put his arm on her shoulder and together they turned toward the private elevator. As Jeremy hit the button, he threw one last look at Waters's ruined lab—and froze. The CD-ROMs. In the rush to stop the virus from being released, he'd forgotten about them.

"Damn it, we forgot the disks," he cursed, his eyes searching through the wreckage. No doubt the vacuum had gotten them. They were gone for good. His shoulders sagged. All that science, gone. The genetic revolution, won and lost in a single day.

Robin looked up at him, her eyes sparkling. "Two goals, right? Isn't that what you said?" She held up a CD-ROM. Jeremy stared at it, shocked. "How?" was all he could manage.

She smiled. "I grabbed it while you were wrestling with Waters. Now we have all the proof we need."

He grabbed Robin around the waist and pulled her toward him. "I love you. You know that?"

"I love you, too," she said, squeezing back, but then her features darkened. "Jeremy, what if there are more men with guns out there?"

He was about to respond when the elevator doors suddenly slid open.

There were four men inside, three with submachine guns strapped over their shoulders. The fourth was tall, with strawberry blond hair. Jeremy's cheeks went pale and he stepped back, pulling Robin with him. Then he noticed Robin's face. She wasn't scared. In fact, she looked relieved.

"Mr. Leary," she said, smiling broadly. "How did you—?"

"Guarrez got a message to our relay station an hour ago," he said. "Unfortunately, we didn't make it here in time to prevent the worst from happening." He looked around at the devastated lab. "Or did we?"

"The worst?" Jeremy responded. He glanced at Robin and smiled. "No, *that* didn't happen. Not by a long shot."

Standing there, in the middle of nearly a billion dollars' worth of destroyed equipment, with the director of the CIA in front of him and the ravaged body of Jason Waters—the greatest geneticist the world had ever known—a few feet away, Jeremy suddenly had a series of incongruous thoughts.

He wondered if Elron Finney had gotten that transplant he needed. . . .

He wondered if Franklin "Frankie" Gordon was still as prickly as ever. . . .

And he wondered if Robin would consent to marry him.

Somehow, he vowed, he'd coax her to New York. Nothing was ever going to separate them again.

EPILOGUE

THE LX90 SCAVENGER-CLASS MILITARY HELICOPTER CUT LOW over the treetops, its thin black body twisting effortlessly at a speed close to three hundred miles per hour. At that velocity, the air seemed to shimmer around the Scavenger's ebony curves—what the engineers at McDonnell Douglas called a kinetic blanket, a phenomenon that served to block out the roar of the copter's long steel rotors. The Scavenger's cockpit was said to be as quiet as a tomb—and if the Scavenger ever graduated from the Pentagon's list of "experimental technologies," its tranquil interior would top its list of selling points.

But strapped into the Scavenger's leather copilot seat, Arthur Dice felt anything but tranquil. He pressed his face against a cold Plexiglas window, his thick lips opening and closing. His eyes were tilted upward, trained on the blur of the helicopter's rotors. The sweat was pouring freely down his back, staining his shirt and moistening the thick leather seat beneath him.

"Can't you make this thing go any faster?" he asked.

The SSO pilot in the seat next to him glanced up from the controls. "Sir, we're traveling at two hundred and ninety-six—"

"Just make it go faster. Now!"

The pilot swallowed, moving his hands over various buttons and levers. The interior of the cockpit was filled with computerized control panels, a sort of high-tech cocoon whose inner workings Dice was ignorant of. He didn't care. All that mattered was that the technology was the best and that it was his. *His,* damn it. His hands clenched into fists and he slammed them together.

"How could it have happened?" he said. "How?"

The pilot looked at him. "Sir, I'm not sure I understand—"

"Just shut up and fly."

The pilot quickly looked away. The helicopter burst forward, and Dice was pushed back into his seat. He clamped his jaw shut, his body seething with anger.

It had been a grim sixteen hours. THRESHOLD, which had cost the U.S. government more than $60 billion over the course of forty years, had been destroyed in less than twenty minutes. Jason Waters's private laboratory had been overrun, and both the scientist himself and Victor Alexander were missing, presumed dead. Dice's grandest plans, his greatest accomplishment—the project that would have immortalized the SSO—had been reduced to nothing. And all because of a kid. A fucking kid.

Although the people at headquarters were still trying to piece together what had happened in those last few hours, Dice had a hunch of his own. The kid had been a professional, probably CIA. He'd infiltrated the lab and had somehow aborted stage three. And now Steven Leary would have the last laugh.

The anger rose inside him. He'd come so close. So close! Now THRESHOLD was finished. He threw his hands in the air, sighing. What could he do but accept it? Accept it and start again. There was no real evidence to link the SSO with the debacle in Tucsome. There'd be no legal reprisals. There *was* a slim chance that a record of the breakthroughs that had occurred on the project could be recovered and used to launch a second attempt.

Dice found some comfort in the thought. Sooner or later, he'd find another scientist to take over. After all, there were thousands of disgruntled scientists in search of funding. One day, he swore to himself, THRESHOLD would reach completion. He'd have his genetic weapon yet.

And until that day, he was still the head of the most powerful organization in the country. In a few hours, he'd arrive at his private headquarters, where he'd lay low until the situation was more fully understood.

Life went on. He still had his health. And Ella; he'd always have Ella. . . .

A high-pitched beep echoed through the helicopter's cockpit. The pilot glanced at a bank of lights above his head.

"Posterior radar, sir. Bogey closing fast."

Dice's eyes widened. "At three hundred miles per hour?"

The pilot hunched forward, reading numbers off of a digital display.

"From the engine sounds and the wingspan, I'd say it's a P-7 patrol plane. U.S. Air Force. Two miles and still closing."

Dice cursed to himself. A P-7? Chasing him down? That was absurd. He wasn't on the run. He was the director of the SSO, traveling from his office in Washington to his private headquarters deep in the interior of West Virginia. Who the hell was bearing down on him in a P-7?

"Sir," the pilot interrupted. "The aircraft has matched speed, approximately one mile back. We're being hailed. Security frequency, precoded, authorization level one. Should I respond?"

Dice bit his lip. Level one was reserved for the highest government officials. "Out of curiosity," he asked, "could we outmaneuver him?"

The pilot looked at him. "You mean a dogfight, sir?"

Dice nodded, and the pilot's cheeks went white. "I don't know, sir. The Scavenger has never been proved in a combat situation."

Dice clasped his fingers. Then he shrugged—he had nothing to worry about. There was nothing to link him with the catastrophe at Tucsome. He was above reproach.

"Then I guess we'll stick to conversation," he said. "Answer the hailing, same frequency."

The pilot hit a sequence of buttons, sending out a scrambled packet of information. Flight plan, authorization level, and Dice's security clearance. There was a brief pause, then a new series of high-pitched beeps.

"The P-7 wants to chat, sir. Shall I open an airwave?"

Dice grimaced. He could refuse, but he had a hunch that the air force jet wasn't going to just go away. "Go ahead," he grunted, "still security coded. Level one."

The pilot complied, then gave Dice a thumbs-up.

"This is Arthur Dice in the Scavenger," Dice said, speaking stiffly toward a speaker embedded in the console in front of him. "I'm on official Pentagon business. Please identify yourself."

There was a brief pause. Dice felt the sweat dripping down the sides of his face. He was about to repeat his request when a familiar voice echoed through the helicopter cockpit.

"Arthur. You seem to be in quite a hurry. Even grabbed yourself a Scavenger. I wonder where you're off to, on such a lovely afternoon."

Dice frozen in his seat. He stared at the console, his heart pounding against his rib cage. "Leary. What the hell are you doing here?"

Leary's laughter bounced through the helicopter. "How did *you* put it? Official Pentagon business. Actually, Arthur, I'm here to talk to you."

Dice's stomach filled with venom. "We don't have anything to talk about."

"Oh, I don't agree. I think we have a lot to talk about. For instance, how about Tucsome, South Carolina? Or a dead secretary of defense? Either of those ring a bell?"

Dice's fingernails bit into his palms. "I don't know what you're talking about."

"Come now, Arthur, surely you've heard of something called THRESHOLD. Cost a pretty penny, that one. Well, you'll be happy to know that I've thoroughly cleaned up the little mess you left behind. As we speak, Waters's laboratory is being bombarded with enough radiation to melt a small city. You, it seems, are the only loose end left."

Dice's body went weak. He gripped the leather copilot seat, glancing at the pilot next to him. The man was busy with the Scavenger's controls.

"You have no proof," Dice said indignantly.

"I have all the proof I need," Leary answered from the P-7. "You're finished, Arthur."

There was a moment of dead air. Dice's throat went completely dry. He couldn't believe what was happening.

"You have no authority," he whispered. "The SSO is autonomous—"

"There is no such thing as the SSO," Leary interrupted harshly. "It no longer exists. In fact, officially, it never did."

Dice felt his chest constrict. He looked to his right and saw that the pilot was staring at him. He closed his eyes, trying to calm himself. Leary had no right. Leary had no authority. It couldn't be happening.

"The President won't stand for this," Dice finally blustered.

"I assure you, the President will be fully briefed on the situation—in good time. But right now, the President has nothing to do with this. This is just between us."

Dice felt the air run out of his body. "What are you going to do? Shoot me down?"

The pilot looked startled at the words, but Leary just

laughed. "And leave evidence of air combat? I'm not a fool, Arthur."

Dice's jaw clenched. Maybe he still had a chance.

"Then what *are* you going to do?"

Leary paused for a full second while Arthur stewed in a pool of his own sweat. Finally, Leary's voice returned. "I'm sure you've heard the news about North Korea. Backed off at the last second. So there won't be any invasion."

"What does that have to do with anything?"

Leary's voice changed, became cold, dangerous. "We never had the chance to try out those wonderful new gadgets Melissa told us about. You remember, don't you? The electromagnetic pulse weapons?"

Dice's body began to tremble. "Look, Leary—"

"It's too late to beg, Arthur."

Dice longed to close his fingers around Leary's throat. That big-eared bastard! Who the hell did he think he was? The SSO couldn't be finished. It was too important. It was bigger than the CIA, bigger than the President, bigger than the fucking Constitution! Who did that bastard think he was—?

"Good-bye, Arthur. And good riddance."

"Leary!" Arthur howled. "God damn you—"

Suddenly, there was a loud click. All the lights in the Scavenger's cockpit went out. A few of the computer consoles began to smoke. The pilot cursed, his eyes wild, his hands savagely punching buttons.

"Shit! What the hell?"

"What is it?" Arthur demanded.

"The controls, gone. Hydraulics, radar—everything!"

Dice stared at him. Then he noticed something. The cockpit wasn't quiet anymore; instead of silence, there was a fierce rushing of air. He felt his stomach drop and quickly looked up through the cockpit window.

"Christ," he whispered, staring.

The steel rotors had stopped spinning.

*   *   *

Arthur Dice was still cursing God, man, and anything else he could think of when his dead helicopter cut a vicious swath through the canopy of trees, cartwheeled across a glacial boulder field, and exploded in a towering cone of fire.